A 'BELT TO MAINTAIN CHASTITY'

Iliana donned her wedding gown and watched as her sister-in-law turned to the door. "Get ye into bed. I'll go see what is takin' the men so long."

Iliana nibbled at her lip as she watched the woman go, then whirled to face her maid. "Fetch me that belt Francesco gave Papa. 'Tis in the chest this gown was in."

Ebba's eyes widened in horror. "Oh no, my lady. You cannot wear that contraption."

Iliana's expression darkened. "I can and I will. Fetch it."

The maid hesitated briefly, then did as she was told. Finding the item, she grimaced with distaste as she held it out to her.

Iliana took the leather belt sadly. Her father had obtained it on his last trip to Italy. A 'belt to maintain chastity,' he had called it. It was a belt made of thick leather, but with a wide center strap that attached to it at the back, then slid between the thighs and was fastened to the belt in the front by a metal lock. It looked most uncomfortable.

Undoing the lock, Iliana let the center strap drop and worried her lip as she examined the ridiculous thing. Then, stiffening her resolve, she grimaced and yanked her gown up to fasten it on. It was an awkward trick to manage. She had to grab at the strap hanging behind her and draw it up between her legs. Locking it into place, she nodded her satisfaction, then looked at the key. What to do with that?

She peered around the room briefly, then glanced up at the bed drapes. Giving a shrug, she tossed it atop them, checked to be sure it was not obvious through the heavy cloth, then scampered into bed as the boisterous sound of approaching voices warned of her husband's imminent arrival.

Other *Leisure* books by Lynsay Sands:
THE DEED

The Key

Lynsay Sands

LEISURE BOOKS NEW YORK CITY

For Lawrence S. Currie:
my lover,
life partner,
and best friend.

A LEISURE BOOK®

February 1999

Published by

Dorchester Publishing Co., Inc.
276 Fifth Avenue
New York, NY 10001

ISBN 0-8439-4482-X

The name "Leisure Books" and the stylized "L" with design are trademarks of Dorchester Publishing Co., Inc.

Printed in the United States of America.

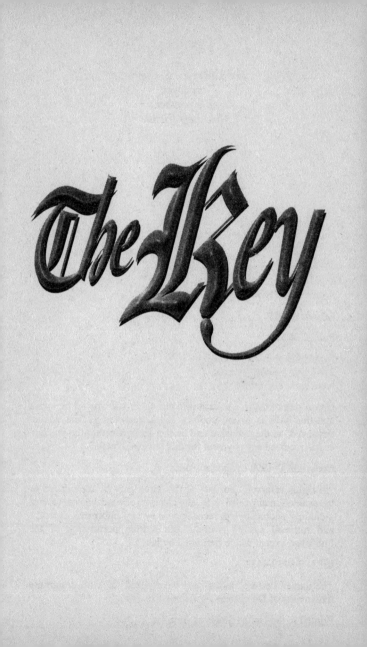

Prologue

Dunbar Keep, Scotland—June 1395

"Marry what?"

"Not a what! A *who*. And as I have already said, the king would consider it a great favor if you would marry Lady Iliana Wildwood." Lord Rolfe Kenwick glared at the Scot before him, silently cursing King Richard II for sending him on this quest. This was the second wedding he had arranged in as many months, the first being that of his own cousin Emmalene to Amaury de Aneford. He supposed he should be grateful that that wedding had been easy. This one was proving next to impossible.

"An English." Duncan Dunbar grimaced in distaste at the idea. "Aye. 'Tis sure I am that he would consider it a favor fer me to take one o' his pasty-faced cows off his hands. What is she, one o' his by-blows?"

"You—" His temper finally snapping, Rolfe grabbed for the hilt of his sword.

"Nay."

His sword half out of its sheath, Rolfe paused and glanced at the man who had spoken. Bishop Wykeham. King Richard had pressed the retired prelate back into service to marry Emmalene and Amaury. That chore done, however, he had not been allowed to return quietly to retirement. Nay. On their arrival at court to report the success of their mission, they had learned of another marriage that must take place in haste, one to protect Lady Wildwood. Oddly enough, to afford that protection to Lady Wildwood, her daughter must marry as soon as possible, and to someone who lived as far from Wildwood manor in southern England as they could manage on such short notice.

Scotland had seemed the best bet. The problem was that they needed a nobleman who was not already betrothed and who could be bribed into marriage. There were few men like that around. Most of the nobility saw their children betrothed ere they were walking. The only man who came close to fitting their needs had been Angus Dunbar, the aging widower and clan chief of the Dunbars.

Unfortunately, Angus had made it more than clear that he had no interest in remarrying, no matter what was offered as an incentive. Just when Rolfe had thought he would have to return to his king in failure, the old man had suggested they make the offer to his son, Duncan. Nearly thirty though he was, he was still unmarried. His betrothed had died young, and rather than arrange another match for his son, the Dunbar had left it for Duncan to tend to in his own time.

"Nay," Bishop Wykeham repeated now in answer to the Scot. "Lady Wildwood is the daughter of a wealthy baron who died while in service to the king in Ireland."

Sighing, Rolfe let his sword slide back into its sheath, adding, "She has a most generous dowry."

"Hmm." Duncan's lips pursed in obvious disappointment. "How generous?"

Rolfe repeated the amount King Richard had quoted to him, frowning slightly when the Scot showed no reaction.

Shifting, he added reluctantly, "If that is not enough, the king has agreed to add to it."

Duncan continued to stare, apparently unimpressed.

"How much is the king willing to add?" Angus asked, speaking for the first time since leading them to his son.

"He would go so far as to double it," Rolfe admitted reluctantly, worried that by the lack of response of the Dunbars even that would not be enough. Much to his amazement, the younger Dunbar cursed at that, drew his sword, whirled away with a roar, and charged off across the courtyard, his plaid slapping against his legs as he ran.

Everyone in the bailey paused to watch him race madly toward a small group of men practicing at battle. Reaching the nearest of them, he released a second roar and raised his sword high. That warrior immediately brought his own sword up and the clang of metal meeting metal rang through the bailey. As if it were some sort of cue, all who had stopped went about their business again, wholly unconcerned by the man's daft behavior.

Turning slowly to Angus Dunbar, Rolfe raised one eyebrow in question.

"He be thinkin' on it," the old Scot explained with a toothy grin. "We'll go in an' have a mug o' ale while he decides." Turning away, he started up the steps to the keep.

Shaking his head, Rolfe glanced at the bishop. "What think you?"

"I think we should have a mug o' ale and await his decision," the bishop murmured with amusement; then seeing the younger man's bewilderment, clapped a hand on his back, urging him toward the stairs. "You have not had much experience of Scots, have you, my boy?"

"Nay," Rolfe admitted with a slight frown.

"Well, I have had some small opportunity to deal with them and I should tell you, they are not like the English."

"Aye." Rolfe grimaced. "I had come to that conclusion myself."

*   *   *

"Ho! And what is it has me brother so afire?"

Recognizing his sister's voice, Duncan plowed his free fist into the jaw of the man whose sword was locked with his own. Without waiting to see him fall to the ground, he turned, drove the tip of his sword into the ground, grabbed Seonaid up in a bear hug, and whirled her around. "Congratulate me, sweetling. 'Tis a happy man I be."

"I can see that, brother." She laughed breathlessly as he dropped her lightly back to her feet. She stepped back, grinning broadly, and Duncan saw that she was accompanied by their two cousins, Allistair and Aelfread. "Now tell me why," his sister said.

"What is it I have dreamed o' doin' since I turned eighteen? What is it I have worked the men near to death fer? What would I ask fer were I given a wish?"

Hands propped on her hips, Seonaid Dunbar tipped her head to the side. "Enlarge the castle and replace the crumbling old wall that surrounds it?"

"Aye." Duncan could barely contain his glee. "We shall do that now. That an' more. We shall dig a new well. Purchase fine horses. We shall e'en increase the size o' our flock o' sheep!"

"And how would ye be plannin' to manage all that?" Seonaid asked skeptically.

"With coins from the English king."

"Oh, aye," Seonaid shared a disbelieving glance with the men around them. "And why exactly would the king o' England be givin' ye so much wealth?"

"He wants me to marry an Englishman's whelp."

"Marry?" The word was a bare whisper. Seonaid looked stunned, even a little hurt, and Duncan's amusement faded, replaced with the beginnings of guilt.

Seonaid was his only sibling. She had been his only playmate as a child until their uncle had died and his children, Allistair and Aelfread, had come to live with them. Then it had been the four of them rolling and romping in the muck, tromping through the woods, and hunting or playing at games of war. When it had come time for the two boys to train in battle, Aelfread and Seonaid had joined in the practice sessions as if it were their right, and no one had said them nay. Both women now handled the sword with a skill equal to any man's.

"She must be a cow for the king to pay so handsomely," Allistair said with disdain as he moved to stand beside Seonaid.

"Aye, the veriest cow," Aelfread agreed, taking up position on Seonaid's other side.

Ignoring his cousins, Duncan peered silently at his sister, taking in her pale face and pinched lips. Like him, she had inherited the Dunbar height, almost matching his own six feet. But where Duncan was thick through the shoulders and chest, she was svelte, and where Duncan had their father's wavy red-brown tresses, Seonaid had inherited their mother's coloring. Her hair was black as night, flowing straight down her back like water out of a pail. She was strong, beautiful, twenty-four years old, and still not wed.

Cursing, Duncan turned away.

"Where be ye going?" Seonaid grasped at his arm.

Covering her hand with his own, he flashed her a reassuring smile. "I've some hagglin' to do," he murmured, then gently pulled free and headed for the keep.

He would marry the English. He would marry her for the money. But he would also marry her for Seonaid, for he would ask a favor of the king in return. Duncan would see Seonaid married. He would have the king force Lord Sherwell, his sister's betrothed, to either fulfill their betrothal contract or set her free to marry another. Either way, she would no longer be left in the limbo that made her so unhappy.

Duncan had decided.

Chapter One

"The English be comin'!"

"What?" Angus Dunbar shook his gray head and roused himself from the semi-stupor he had been enjoying to peer around. The stablemaster's young son was slipping back through the open door of the keep. "Ho! Lad! What was that?"

"The English be acomin' over the bridge!" the boy cried, his faced wreathed in excitement as he turned away and slammed the keep door.

"Damn!" Staggering to his feet, Angus gave the man who lay slumped at the table beside him a shake. "Duncan! Wake up, lad. She be here. Wake up, damn ye!"

Grabbing a pitcher of ale off the table, he turned his son's head by the hair and splashed it in his face, then stepped quickly out of the way as Duncan came to sputtering life. "Rouse yerself, man! Yer bride be here."

"Me what?" Duncan tried to frown and squint at the same time, but found the effort to accomplish either task made the pulsing in his head increase to a horrid pound-

12

ing. Groaning miserably, he lowered it to the table again.

He had definitely overindulged; in fact, Duncan could not recall the last time he had imbibed like that. He and his father had been on a binge since the English had left two weeks earlier. At least he thought it had been two weeks ago. They had been celebrating ever since. Well, mayhap they had been holding more of a wake. He, Duncan Dunbar, heir to the title of laird of the Dunbars, had agreed to be married. At the age of twenty-nine, he was finally giving up his freedom and taking on the responsibility of a wife and, eventually, children.

Damn. Now he'd done it. He'd gotten himself into a fix that made him fair froth to even consider. Even the fortune he had been offered no longer seemed worth losing his freedom. Mayhap 'twas not too late to back out of the deal, he thought hopefully.

"Where the devil did your sister get to? Seonaid should be here to greet the lass."

Duncan sighed, his hopes for escape vanishing. Were he to back out now, the king would not be under any obligation to see to Seonaid's long-neglected betrothal. It had been his one demand before agreeing to the wedding, rather than asking for a doubling of the dowry. His sister's reluctant groom was to be brought to heel and either forced to fulfill the contract that had been arranged when they were children, or to set Seonaid free. The latter option was what Duncan hoped for. He was sure his father would never forgive him should Sherwell arrive prepared to fulfill his part of the contract.

"Damn ye, Duncan, they are here I tell ye! Rouse yerself, man!"

That bellow near his ear drove all thought out of Duncan's head. Eyes popping open, he was about to force himself to sit up when a second pitcher, this one full of whiskey, splashed into his face. That brought him upright at once, cursing and spluttering as the liquid burned his eyes. "Dammit father, I be awake! Jist give me a minute to—"

"There be no minute to give ye. Git up, man!" Grabbing his arm, the Dunbar tugged Duncan to his feet, then sighed at the sight he made.

"Ye've blinded me! Damn ye!"

"It'll pass. But ye've ale and whiskey all over ye, lad," his father chastised gruffly, taking up a corner of his own plaid to wipe roughly at his face.

"Aye, well, *ye* put it there, didn't ye?" Duncan muttered, grabbing at the cloth moving across his face and trying to use it to wipe at his burning eyes.

"Never mind that." Angus tugged the plaid away and straightened it about himself, then turned toward the door. "Come along."

"I cannot see!" Duncan protested, still rubbing at his eyes.

"Then I shall lead ye! I want to see the mother o' me grandbabies."

"We are no even wed yet, Father. 'Twill be awhile ere there is fruit from it," Duncan muttered, allowing himself to be dragged across the great hall.

"Nine months. 'Tis all the time I'll be givin' ye. Then I expect the squall o' bairns to echo off these old walls. It has been too long since that sound has filled these hollow chambers."

Pushing the keep doors open, his father dragged him out onto the steps and paused as he saw the riders crossing the bailey toward them.

"Damn," Angus murmured suddenly. "Damn me all to hell."

"What?" Duncan scowled into the bleary distance. All he could make out was the blur of a large party crossing the bailey toward them on horseback.

"She's bonnie."

"Bonnie?"

"Aye. No beauty, but bonnie. She looks fair delicate, though," he added, worry obvious in his tones. "A real lady. Sits her mount like a queen, she does. Her wee back straight as a sword. . . . Aye, a real lady."

14

Duncan watched the blurred figures draw nearer suspiciously. "What exactly do ya mean by a *real lady?*"

"I mean the kind that'll no approve o' yer sister's shenanigans," he said dryly, then shook his head. "Mark me words, lad. Yon wee Sassenach lass'll set this place to rights straight off."

Duncan frowned over that. To his mind, there was nothing that needed setting to rights at Dunbar.

"Ah well." The older man sighed resignedly. "We couldna expect to live the grand bachelor's life forever."

"Which one do you think he is, my lady?"

Iliana Wildwood gave a start at that question and drew her eyes from the two men standing on the keep steps to glance worriedly down at her maid.

Seated in the wagon that held all of their belongings, Ebba's plain face was aglow with excitement. An excitement most likely born of the fact that they would no longer be sleeping in the open, Iliana thought with a sigh, but she could not blame the other woman. They had been riding from dawn to well into the evenings, and camping in two inches of mud, for over a week.

"Of course, you do not know either," the maid murmured apologetically when her mistress remained silent.

"Nay," Iliana admitted faintly, her now troubled gaze returning to the men in question. She had assumed that the younger of the two was to be her husband, but now realized that she could be wrong. Young women were married off to old men all the time, but she had not even considered that. Not once during the long, dreary trip here had she thought to ask what her betrothed was like. If he was cruel or kind. Strong in battle or not. If he had all his teeth and was healthy.

Sighing, she shook her head in self-disgust at her own oversight. And oversight it had surely been. Though to be fair, she *had* been slightly distracted of late, what with her father's death and her mother's predicament. Between one worry and another, she had quite neglected to consider the possibility that her husband might be much older than herself. Considering that possibility now, she began to nibble at her lip anxiously.

Both men were attractive in their own way. 'Twas obvious they were father and son. The son appeared to be in his late twenties, while the father was at least fifty. The son's hair was a reddish brown and long and wavy. The father's hair was a mass of wiry white strings that shot in every direction from his head. The son's face was hard and strong, all planes and edges like the land they had crossed to reach him. The father's, just so, but with lines of character to soften it. Both men had generous mouths, strong noses, and eyes she suspected could be both hard and gentle. They were also both tall and hard and lean of body.

" 'Tis the younger one," Bishop Wykeham murmured from where he rode at her other side, drawing a grateful smile from Iliana that lingered until they reached the base of the steps. Then she got her first really good look at the two men. Her smile was immediately replaced with a frown of dismay as she took in their tattered garments and filthy faces.

Iliana had paid little attention to the people in the bailey as she had crossed it. Now she shifted, craning her neck to peer about, and immediately began to worry at her lip as she saw that they appeared in need of a good cleaning and some attention. Their clothes were worn and stained, their hair shaggy and unkempt, and most of their faces dirty. As for the bailey and the keep itself, both were in sore need of repair.

"Lady Wildwood."

Iliana turned at that bluff greeting, unaware that she was still frowning as she met the gaze of her future father-in-law.

Startled by her expression, the older man reached back to grab his son's shoulder. "Help 'er down, Duncan," he ordered, giving his son a shove forward that sent him stumbling into the side of her mare.

Iliana peered wide-eyed at the grimy hands that were now raised in her general direction, then glanced to their owner's dirt-streaked face and red-eyed, squinting state. Swallowing unhappily, she reluctantly released her reins and slid off her mount. He caught her easily and set her gently on the ground, and Iliana swiftly stepped away from him, unable to keep her nose from wrinkling at the heavy, stale scent of ale, spirits, and sweat that wafted from him.

Despite his squinting, Duncan evidently caught her action, for he raised an arm to sniff at himself, then shrugged. He smelled fine to himself, though she smelled finer. There was the scent of wildflowers about her.

"My lords." Iliana dropped a curtsy, then hesitated and peered toward the bishop for help. She felt quite out of her depth in this situation, and she had no idea what to say or do. *This* was the man she was to marry. A veritable stranger . . . who stank.

"Mayhap we should move indoors, Angus," the bishop suggested gently. "It has been a long journey and refreshments would not go amiss."

"Oh, aye. This way, lass." Suddenly remembering his somewhat rusty manners, Angus Dunbar took Iliana's arm and turned to lead her up the stairs to the keep, leaving the others to follow.

The older man's legs were a fair sight longer than hers. She had to grab up the hem of her skirt and nearly run to keep up with him. By the time they reached the top step, she was panting slightly from the effort.

Taking in her breathless state, Angus frowned at her worriedly. "Frail," he muttered to himself with a sad shake of the head.

Iliana caught the word but had little time to worry over it as he opened the door of Dunbar keep and her attention was turned to what was to be her new home. If she had hoped that the inside would show more promise than the outside, she had been sorely mistaken. 'Twas an old building. A set of stairs to her right led up to a second floor where a narrow walkway had three doors leading off of it. Bed chambers, she guessed, turning to survey the great hall. It took up most of the main floor and was a large, dark cave with arrow slits for windows that were too high up for the feeble beams of light they allowed inside to penetrate the gloom in the room. If not for the fire roaring in a large fireplace against the far wall, she doubted she would have been able to see anything.

Which might not have been a bad thing, she thought with dismay, taking it all in. The floor was covered with filthy rushes, the walls were marked and smoke stained, the tapestries that graced them showed the effects of age and neglect, and the trestle tables and benches looked as if they were quite ready to give up the ghost. Iliana was almost afraid to sit on them, and not just because they appeared about to shatter under the least weight, but because they were also stained and splattered with grease and bits of food.

She was appalled. Wildwood, her childhood home, had been run efficiently and well. One could almost eat off the tabletop there. The floors no longer sported rushes, but several rugs that were warmer in winter and softer underfoot. Iliana had never seen the likes of this place and did not know whether to burst into tears or turn and flee. She simply could not live like this, could not manage amid such filth.

"Some ale?" Oblivious of her thoughts, the laird of Dunbar ushered her to the table and pushed her down onto one of those frightful benches. He then reached for a pitcher, straightened, saw that she had risen to her feet again, and frowned slightly as he pushed her back onto the seat with his free hand. "Rest, lass. Ye've had a long trip."

She watched, horrified, as he grabbed a nearby tankard, emptied the dregs of ale that still remained in it out onto

18

the floor, then grabbed up a pitcher, only to scowl. " 'Tis empty. Oh, aye, I er . . ."

The man's gaze slid enigmatically to his son, who scowled; then Angus started to turn toward the kitchen, only to pause and frown as he saw that Iliana had stood once again. Grunting, he pushed her back down onto the bench before bellowing toward the kitchen door, "Giorsal! Bring me more ale, wench!"

Turning back, he saw that Iliana had risen once more and his scowl deepened. "Yer rather like a rabbit, are ye no, lass? I press ye down and ye pop right back up. Settle yerself," he instructed not unkindly and pressed her back onto the bench before his gaze slid over her head.

He began a storm of twitching and nodding then. Iliana began to think the poor man was suffering a fit, until she glanced over her shoulder and saw his son standing behind her, squinting at the signals his father was giving him.

Growing impatient, the elder Dunbar finally snapped, "Set yerself beside her, lad. Woo her a bit."

"Woo her?" Duncan was taken aback. "We are getting wed, Da. Not acourtin'."

Angus Dunbar rolled his eyes at that, then peered at Bishop Wykeham as if for commiseration. "The young today, eh, Bishop?" He shook his head, then his attention was caught by a gray-haired woman who entered the room from what Iliana suspected were the kitchens. "Ah, good. Refreshments." Taking the pitcher from her, he handed the empty one over, then turned to pour the liquid into the tankard he had decided would be Iliana's. Filling it to the brim, he set it before her, then moved on to first empty, then fill, tankards for the bishop and Lord Rolfe.

Iliana lifted the tankard she had been given toward her mouth, only to pause and stare down into the murky drink doubtfully. There appeared to be something foreign floating on the top of the liquid. It was a bug of some sort.

"What be bothering ye? Do ye no care fer ale?"

Iliana glanced at her betrothed. He was still squinting,

but it seemed he could make out enough to know that she was not drinking the ale his father had poured her.

"Nay, there is—I am not thirsty just now," she lied faintly, unwilling to offend.

"Ah well." Taking the tankard, he lifted it to his mouth.

"Oh! But—" Iliana began in dismay, but it was too late. He downed almost the entire tankard in one swallow. . . . And the bug with it, she saw as he rested the now empty tankard back upon the table between them.

" 'Tis no sense it agoin' to waste," he murmured cheerfully, flashing her a brief smile before wiping his mouth on his sleeve.

Iliana stared at him wide-eyed. For one brief moment when he had smiled, his emerald eyes sparkling with good humor, her husband-to-be had taken on the look of an entirely different man. He had looked quite handsome for a moment, despite the grime and soot on his face and whatever else was staining it just now. Of course, he had ruined that at once by wiping his mouth on his sleeve and bringing her attention to the fact that the fine, white fabric was hopelessly stained from such repeated actions. Among others.

"My lady?"

Sighing, Iliana tore her eyes away from Duncan to peer questioningly at her maid.

"Your skirt." The woman gestured and Iliana stood again, twisting her head to peer over one shoulder at the skirt of her gown. There were stains, smudges, and crumbs of food on it just from sitting. There was also a great wet spot on it. Apparently, the bench had not been wholly dry when she had been forced to sit there. From the scent wafting up to her she guessed she had sat in a puddle of ale.

Frowning, she began brushing at it fretfully. Care for clothing had been hammered into her from a very early age. Clothing was often expensive and difficult to replace so far from the city tailors and dressmakers. That being the case, she had never been allowed to run or roll about on the ground with the other children at Wildwood. She had ever been expected to be a little lady and always act with decorum. Her mother would have been appalled at the state of her gown just now.

Ebba knelt to try to aid in removing the marks on her skirt, but it quickly became obvious that it was an impossible task. The skirt was ruined, Iliana realized with dismay.

"Aye. There's no time like the present."

Angus Dunbar's words caught Iliana's attention, dragging it away from her skirt and to the conversation Lord Rolfe and the bishop were holding with him.

" 'Tis true," Rolfe murmured now. "The sooner we get this business finished, the sooner we can move on to tending to Lady Seonaid's problem."

Turning sharply toward his son, Laird Angus glared at him meaningfully until Duncan sighed and murmured, "Me father does not agree that ye go to Sherwell and force 'is hand. He fears the man may agree to the marriage takin' place."

Rolfe's eyebrows rose. "But I thought marriage was what you were hoping to achieve for Lady Seonaid?"

"Not to that stinkin' sack o' manure English whelp!" Angus snapped furiously.

"I see." Rolfe frowned over that, then shook his head helplessly. "I—" he began, only to pause when the bishop leaned forward to murmur something in his ear. Nodding his head with relief, the younger man then turned back to his host and forced a smile. "Mayhap we should leave this worry for now. Once we've tended to Lady Iliana and your son, we can discuss what to do about Lady Seonaid and Lord Sherwell."

There was a moment of tense silence, then Angus nodded grimly. "Aye. I'll inform the men and send one out to fetch Seonaid."

"Fetch her? Is she not here?"

"Nay. She's gone ahuntin'. She'll not have gone far.

21

'Twill take no time at all to find her. We can begin the ceremony when she returns.''

Brushing her maid's efforts away, Iliana hurried anxiously to Lord Rolfe's side as Angus Dunbar headed for the doors of the keep.

''My lords!'' Her gaze slid toward her would-be husband. He sat where she had left him, but was turned toward them, obviously listening to the conversation. Beseeching the king's emissaries, she hissed, ''I do not think I can go through with this.''

''Praise the Lord,'' Ebba murmured behind her.

Lord Rolfe was a little less moved. Expression blank, he shook his head. ''Go through—?''

''Have you not looked about you?'' she asked with bewilderment. ''How could you expect me to live here? How could you expect me to marry *him?*'' She gestured toward the man seated at the table. ''He *smells.* This whole place smells. They are drunken louts. They reek of spirits. It fair *oozes* from their very flesh.''

Rolfe took a look about, appearing to notice for the first time the frayed edges that seemed to grace every strip of material in the place, from Duncan's less-than-pristine clothes to the stained tapestries on the walls. A glance down showed him bones and gristle mixed in with the rushes on the floor, along with several other things she did not care to identify. ''Well . . . aye, 'tis a bit messy,'' he agreed slowly.

''*Messy?* 'Tis a pigsty, and these people are pigs!''

''Mayhap it just needs a woman's touch, Lady Iliana,'' the bishop began, but Iliana was not in a mood to be soothed.

''My dear lord bishop, the touch of ten thousand women could not set this keep to rights. These people are barbarians and I will not stay here. Look at my gown from simply sitting on that bench. 'Tis *ruined!* 'Tis simply impossible. I will not marry him.''

There was silence for a moment as Lord Rolfe and the

bishop exchanged helpless glances, then the younger man sighed. "What of your mother?"

Iliana stiffened. A vivid image of her mother's bruised and tear-streaked face filled her mind and she sagged unhappily, beaten. She had no choice. She was in dire straits. She needed a strong husband, far from Wildwood, who could keep her safe from her stepfather. 'Twas the only way to free her mother from the troubles that had descended on them with her father's death.

"Is there no one else?" she asked dismally.

The bishop's expression was sympathetic. "I fear not, my lady. No one so far north. Besides, the claim has already been made to Greenweld that this contract was arranged by your father ere his death. 'Twas in the letter bearing the king's seal. We could not claim another betrothal now."

"No, of course not," she agreed miserably, then sighed. "I suppose I really have no choice then?"

"I fear not," Lord Rolfe agreed gently. "The contract was signed by both Lord Dunbar and the king. 'Tis done."

Chapter Two

"You look lovely."

Iliana peered unhappily at her maid as the woman continued fussing over her veil and gown. Lord Rolfe and the bishop had suggested she go upstairs and prepare for the wedding. She supposed it was their way of giving her time alone to face her fate.

It was a stunning blow. . . . And just one in a seemingly neverending series of late. The first had come a little more than two months ago with the news that her beloved father, Abod Wildwood, was dead. The second had been the form in which the news reached them. Those sad tidings had come in the person of Lord Greenweld, an ambitious baron who shared a border with their property. He had delivered the news with little more sympathy than he had shown while beating Iliana's mother. The beating had been to force her to sign her name to the marriage decree he had brought with him. The effort had succeeded, though Iliana had since learned that it wasn't the beating itself that had worked, but Greenweld's threats against Iliana if her mother did not comply.

Out riding at the time, Iliana had returned just as the mock ceremony had ended. Before she had even really grasped the fact that they had guests, her mother had flown into her arms, nearly knocking her over as she blurted out the news. Iliana had still been trying to unravel the meaning of the words pouring from her mother's swollen lips when Greenweld had torn the women apart and had Iliana removed from her childhood home.

Her mother's cries had rung in her ears as Iliana had been bound, tossed unceremoniously into the back of a cart, and taken away like a common thief. Confused and in shock, she had found herself transported to Greenweld castle, two long hours ride from Wildwood. For three days she had lain in a guarded room and grieved the loss of her father. Refusing food or drink, she had simply lain upon the bed, sobbing. On the fourth day, however, she had awoken angry, her eyes filled with the image of her mother's battered beauty and tear-filled eyes. Then she had begun to plan.

Escape was the only answer. To escape her guards at Greenweld, sneak back to collect her mother from Wildwood, and flee to their nearest relatives.

How naive she had been. How greatly she had underestimated her enemy, she realized now. He had removed her to Greenweld castle, far and away from everyone and everything she had ever known, to ensure Lady Wildwood's cooperation while he'd seen to exerting his power over the people of Wildwood. And he'd been determined to keep her there.

Time after time, Iliana had tried to escape and time after time she had been caught, restrained, and finally beaten and locked in the tower. Then the baron himself had arrived, announcing that she was to be married.

A bath had been brought to her, the first she had been allowed since her imprisonment, and he had sent her a fresh gown. Then Ebba had led her below and she had been introduced to Lord Rolfe and Bishop Wykeham, who were purportedly to escort her to Scotland and see her married. Iliana had been skeptical. She'd left Greenweld castle determined to make her escape the first chance she got . . . until they had made camp that night and Lord Rolfe and the bishop had spoken with her.

Iliana's mother had been a friend and favorite of Queen Anne's. Depending upon that friendship and the king's affection for his deceased wife, Lady Wildwood had written a letter and slipped it out with a servant to be carried to court. The letter had informed him of the dire straits in which she'd found herself, as well as the news that Greenweld was also attempting to arrange a marriage between Iliana and one of several powerful nobles known to be less than supportive of Richard's reign.

The king had dispatched Rolfe and the bishop at once, sending them first to Scotland to make the deal with Dunbar, then to Wildwood. They had been told to appear surprised at Lady Wildwood's remarriage, since Greenweld had not yet informed the king of it. They were also to tell Greenweld that a marriage contract had already been drawn up for Iliana by her father; that Lord Wildwood and the laird of Dunbar had arranged it during the expedition in Ireland just before his death, and the king himself had witnessed it. Upon realizing that her father could no longer see to the completion of the contract himself, the king had sent Lord Rolfe and the bishop to tend to it. He had supplied them with a letter to that effect, addressed to Lady Wildwood.

Faced with this claim, Greenweld had had little choice but to give Iliana up.

When she had asked why the king had arranged the marriage to a Scot, and not someone closer to home, Rolfe had explained that Richard wished her to be as far away as possible for now. He intended on aiding her mother, but could not do so as long as Iliana was within Greenweld's reach. The baron had separated her from her mother for the express purpose of insuring Lady Wildwood would cooperate with him and not attempt to annul the marriage. The older woman had been informed that, should she do anything of the sort, Iliana would pay the

price. Married and living in Scotland, she would be safe
from that possibility and Greenweld would have less lev-
erge against her mother. She would be free to seek an
annulment with the king's assistance.

Iliana had relaxed at that news, sure that all would be
well. Soon after she was safely married in Scotland, her
mother would be removed from her contemptible marriage, and Greenweld would be dealt with.

Now Iliana realized what a fool she had been. She had
never once considered what sort of man the king had chosen to husband her, merely trusting him to see to her best
interests. But if Duncan Dunbar was his idea of a suitable
husband, then the king had very poor taste. She moved to
sit on the edge of the bed dispiritedly. 'Twas a shame she
had not realized that ere giving up her chance at escape.
But she had not. She had been more than satisfied to allow
the king to see to everything. She had actually been *relieved* to place her future, her happiness, her very life—
and her mother's as well—in the hands of these men.
More the fool, she. It was obvious that by doing so, she
had lost any chance at happiness. She could only hope
her mother would be able to gain her freedom through
this sacrifice.

Worrying her lower lip, she tugged fretfully at the skirt
of the pale cream dress Ebba had chosen for her to wear.
'Twas the best she had. No doubt it would be ruined by
day's end as well. Grimacing, she dropped back to lie
upon the bed with a sigh. What could be more foolish
than worrying over a gown when she was expected to
marry and perform intimacies with that creature below?

Her gaze caught on the drapes above the bed and she
frowned. They were a lovely shade of cream with em-
broidered dark red and blue flowers underneath, though
she could have sworn . . .

Sitting up, she stood and turned to stare at the bed. Aye,
'twas more a brown with burgundy and muddy blue flowers on the outside. No doubt the effect of smoke from the
fire. Were she to hazard a guess, Iliana would say that the

bed drapes had not been cleaned in at least ten years. Perhaps more. She would not hazard a guess as to the state of the bed linens themselves.

" 'Tis a shame we have no flowers for you to hold."

Iliana whirled to gape at her maid as she brushed fretfully at the stains on the yellow gown Iliana had worn earlier.

"Flowers?" she exclaimed, bringing Ebba's startled gaze to her own. "Flowers! What for? So that I might look *pretty* while marrying into this family? I suppose you think we should put bows on sheep on the way to the slaughter as well?"

Ebba merely stared at her mistress blankly. She had never seen the young woman lose her temper so before. Her gaze became incredulous when in the next moment, her mistress tore off her veil and launched herself at the bed, ripping at the linens that covered it.

"I shall not sleep on these despicable, disgusting—Where are my bed linens?"

Ebba blinked. "Your what?"

"My bed linens!" Iliana snapped. "My mother and I have been preparing for years for the day when I marry. We prepared bed linens, Ebba. Where are they? Surely she sent them with you?"

"Oh, aye." Setting the yellow gown down, the maid began sorting through the dozen or so chests Lady Wildwood had insisted must go with her daughter to Scotland, despite Lord Greenweld's protestations. He had not been able to protest overmuch with Lord Rolfe and the bishop there.

"Here they are!" Straightening, she held up a set of soft, pure white linens, their edges hand-embroidered with flowers and peacocks. "Will these do?"

"Aye." Iliana reached for them, her expression tender as she recalled the many hours she had sat with her mother by the fire working upon them. Sighing, she lifted the material, rubbing it across her cheeks and enjoying its clean softness. Then she closed her eyes, her mind immediately drawing forth a picture of her mother's face. A knock at the door drove the image away.

"Who is it?" Ebba asked, a nervous shake to her voice.

"Lord Rolfe. 'Tis time."

Opening her eyes, Iliana met Ebba's uncertain expression, then sighed and nodded.

"Just a moment!" Ebba called.

Handing her maid the linens, Iliana picked up her veil and covered her face. "Strip the bed and remake it. I will not sleep in filth. Then find some servants to assist you in moving the trunks against the walls."

"Shall I unpack them?"

"Nay. Not 'til we've cleaned this sty up some," Iliana said grimly, moving to the door. Pausing, she glanced back. "Have a bath brought up. My husband bathes tonight or he does not sleep on those linens."

She may have no choice regarding marrying the barbarian below, but she could choose how that marriage went, Iliana decided grimly. She would not live like this. He could beat her, throttle her, even kill her, but she would not live like this. She would rather be dead, she thought bleakly, opening the door and moving out to take the arm of a worried-looking Lord Rolfe. He had obviously heard her last words to her maid.

Duncan laughed along with the others at his sister's jest and tipped his tankard to his mouth, swilling down half its contents before lowering the mug to peer at his bride. She sat at the main table next to his father, the same grim expression gracing her face that had tightened it since coming downstairs on Lord Rolfe's arm. She had held it throughout the wedding, saying her vows in a dead voice, making it more than to one and all that she was not overjoyed by her fortune.

Duncan had slowly moved from irritated to furious during the ceremony. He was aware of the circumstances behind this wedding, he was saving her from her stepfather. He was her Sir Galahad. And how did she thank him? By making it obvious that she would wish herself anywhere but here and humiliating him in front of his own people. Hell! The worst of it was, by the time his wife had arrived for the wedding, he had been able to fully see again . . . and he found her oddly appealing.

Grimacing, Duncan glared at her. He did not have a clue what appealed to him so. Her hair was brown. 'Twas a lovely shade of brown, a mixture of the color of walnuts and cherry wood, but brown all the same. He had always been partial to blondes before now. Her eyes were large and gray, rather like a rainy day. He'd always preferred green eyes. Her nose was small and straight. That was fine, but her lips were heart-shaped, sweet and full. Duncan had never seen lips quite like hers. They were enough to give a man ideas, and had been giving him many diverse and erotic ones for the past several hours.

His friends and clansmen were not helping much. What with their jests and good-natured teasing about the night ahead, they were only managing to fan the fire that had already been growing in his nether regions at an alarming rate. It seemed no amount of ale was going to drown it either, for he had been pouring that liquid down his throat steadily all night and still it had not dampened his ardor any. He was becoming fair impatient to bed her, and that fact was infuriating when she was making it so obvious that she did not feel the same way.

"Does yer gaze fer yer wee wife become any hotter, it'll set the rushes ablaze. Mayhap ye should take a dip in the loch."

Tearing his eyes from his bride, Duncan glanced at the man who had spoken. Flame-haired, as tall as he himself was, and near as wide, Allistair was as much a friend as a cousin. Or at least he used to be, Duncan realized with regret. That closeness had dissipated somewhat over the last few years as he had begun to take over some of the responsibilities of clan chief from his father. As more and more of his time was taken up with the task, Duncan had less and less time to spare for hunting trips with Allistair, Aelfread, and Seonaid. Not that those three had drifted apart. If anything, his absence had seemed to push them closer together.

"No night swim'll be helping what ails him, Allie," Aelfread murmured with amusement, sharing a look with Seonaid that made Duncan's sister grin widely.

"Aelfread's right. I'm thinkin' there be only one thing that'll quench the fire that's burning him up and that's he and his bride finally gettin' down to the business o' *houghmagandie.*"

Duncan stiffened at her use of the Gaelic word for fornication. She may fight like a man and be able to drink them all under the table, but there were just some things a woman shouldn't do. Brows drawing down in disapproval, he slammed his tankard onto the filthy tabletop and snapped, "Ye'll no be acursin' like that, Seonaid! Do ye do so again I'll wash yer mouth out with soap meself."

Unimpressed, she rolled her eyes at this threat and laughed. " 'Tis no good usin' such threats with me, me true-sworn brother. 'Tis far too late to be atryin' to change me ways and amakin' me into a lady like yer wife." She glanced toward Iliana with distaste. "She's a puny lass. Prissy as the day is long, too. I doona ken how ye'll be aputtin' up with 'er."

"Well, 'tis good 'tis not yer problem then, isna it?" Duncan muttered, following her gaze.

"Aye. 'Tis well and good. Howbeit, as I said, I be thinkin' 'tis well past time the beddin' began. C'mon, Aelfread."

Grinning widely, the smaller woman nodded and hurried after Seonaid as she crossed the room toward the head table. Duncan had eaten his meal at that table, seated next to his bride, but once that chore was finished he had abandoned it in favor of getting rip-roaring drunk with his men, something he now concluded was impossible—since he still felt as sober as an English virgin. Now he watched blankly as his sister moved toward the space he had abandoned, his mind slow to grasp her intentions. That was his first hint that the ale had been affecting him after all. His second hint came when he lunged to his feet to catch her back and found himself sprawled upon the floor, having tripped over the bench he sat on.

By the time Allistair and the other men had raised him back to his feet, razzing him all the while, 'twas too late. Seonaid and Aelfread were dragging his wife to the stairs. She looked a little less than willing, but his sister and cousin looked quite unconcerned by this lack as they hauled her along by the arms.

"I can dress myself, thank you very much," Iliana offered the protest again, but Lady Seonaid had been ignoring her since dragging her up to the room. Since before that even, she thought with exasperation, her gaze sliding to the much smaller redhead who was now rifling through her once neatly packed chests.

When the two women had appeared at her side at the table announcing 'twas time for the bedding, Iliana had stilled, panic rising up in her. In an attempt to delay, she had claimed that she was still thirsty, but Duncan's sister and her tiny cousin had not even seemed to hear the excuse. Grabbing her arms, they had tugged her from her seat and headed for the stairs, dragging her protesting form behind.

Once in the room, the door had been slammed shut and the little one had started to ransack her chests, while Seonaid had concentrated her attention on "helping" Iliana out of her gown. . . . Completely uncaring of the fact that Iliana did not wish her "help!"

A gasp drew her exasperated struggles to a halt and Iliana glanced toward the smaller woman as Aelfread slowly raised a sheer white tunic from one of the chests. Something squeezed tight around Iliana's heart as she peered at that gown. Her mother had had it made special for her and presented it to Iliana to put in her chest for

her wedding night. At the time, they had both thought it
perfect for a first night for husband and bride. But then,
they had thought she would at least *like* the man she
would marry. They had never imagined circumstances like
this.

Her teeth clamping together with a snap, Iliana glanced
furiously toward Ebba, who had been cowering uselessly
in the corner of the room since their arrival. "That will
not do. Ebba, fetch my cream gown."

The maid hesitated, then moved cautiously forward,
sorting through the clothes Aelfread had strewn on the
floor until she came across the thick, warm gown in question. One that left everything to the imagination.

Lady Seonaid, of course, ignored her wishes in this as
well. "Nay, ye'll wear the white gown," she announced,
continuing to tug Iliana's clothes from her body. "Bring
it here, Aelfread."

"I said I would wear the cream-colored one," Iliana
snapped sharply as the shorter of her tormentors moved
forward.

"The white one is nicer."

"I like the cream one better."

"My brother will like the white one."

"I do not care what your brother—" Iliana cut her own
words off as Lady Seonaid went still. Had she offended
her? Angering the Amazon who towered over her was
something Iliana was not quite brave enough to do. Iliana
was a little above average height at five-foot-six, but Lady
Seonaid was a good five inches taller and quite a bit
stronger. She also seemed the rough-and-tumble type. A
barbarian—like the rest of these people—Iliana thought
irritably, then frowned when Seonaid continued to simply
stare at her.

"What is it?" she asked stiltedly when the silence became unbearable.

"You . . ." Seonaid gestured helplessly unable to say
that 'twas the other woman's figure that had her attention.

33

'Twas the type of figure she herself had longed for as a teen, all soft curves and plains.

"Oh, give me the blasted gown," Iliana snapped in exasperation, reaching out to rip the sheer gown from Aelfread's hands. 'Twas a drafty old castle and she'd had enough of this ridiculousness.

She donned the gown as Seonaid watched, and then the woman turned to the door. "Get ye into bed. Aelfread and I'll go see what is takin' the men so long."

Iliana nibbled at her lip as she watched the women go, then whirled to face Ebba. "Fetch me that belt Francesco gave Papa. 'Tis in the chest this gown was in."

Ebba's eyes widened in horror. "Oh no, my lady. You can not wear that contraption."

Iliana's expression darkened. "I can and I will. Fetch it."

The maid hesitated briefly, then did as she was told. Finding the item, she grimaced with distaste as she held it out to her.

Iliana took the leather belt sadly. Lord Wildwood had always endeavored to bring back odd and exotic gifts from his travels. This was one of the oddest. He had gained two of the belts on his last trip to Italy. Her father had laughed heartily as he had produced one for both his wife and daughter, explaining it to them as he did. They were an invention of his friend, Francesco Carraro. He'd called them "belts to maintain chastity."

Iliana shook her head as she thought of the man. She had no idea what would make him create the silly thing. 'Twas a belt made of thick leather, but with a wide center strap that attached to it at the back, then slid between the thighs and was fastened to the belt in the front by a metal lock. It looked most uncomfortable.

Undoing the lock, Iliana let the center strap drop to hang and worried her lip as she examined the ridiculous thing. Then, stiffening her resolve, she grimaced and yanked her gown up to fasten it on. 'Twas an awkward trick to manage. She had to grab at the strap hanging behind her and draw it up between her legs. Locking it into place, she nodded her satisfaction, then peered at the key. What to do with that?

She peered around the room briefly, then glanced up at the bed drapes. Giving a shrug, she tossed it atop them, checked to be sure 'twas not obvious through the heavy cloth, then scampered into bed as the boisterous sound of approaching voices warned of her husband's imminent arrival.

Chapter Three

Blushing brightly, Iliana watched as her husband was carried into the room by a bunch of men, laughing loudly and jesting in Gaelic. She was momentarily glad she couldn't understand them. Angus Dunbar was at the head of the group. Winking at her, he ordered the men to set Duncan on the ground; then they all began removing his clothes.

Iliana's eyes became great, round holes in her head as they removed his plaid and then the long shirt he had worn beneath it. Her mother had prepared Iliana well for her wedding night and had even given her an idea of what to expect a naked man to look like, but the body exposed to her now was a bit more than she had ever imagined.

Truth to tell, it was a lot more, she thought faintly, her gaze finding and fixing on his manhood. There was no way in heaven that that thing was going to fit inside her, she thought with dismay. By God! 'Twould rip her to shreds. 'Twould—

Iliana reined her thoughts in viciously, reminding herself that 'twas not a worry. She wore the belt of chastity. The key was hidden and would remain so until her husband bathed. But what if he did bathe?

She was forced from that worry to more immediate ones as the men hurried her husband to the bed and drew the linens back to put him in beside her.

For a moment, her scanty gown was revealed to one and all, then Iliana tugged the linens back over herself, fearing they might see the leather of the belt through the thin material of her gown.

Iliana waited as Ebba followed the men out, catching the worried glance the woman threw over her shoulder. Then the door closed, leaving her alone with her husband. It was not until she turned to peer at him solemnly that she realized why the men had had to carry him. Her husband was thoroughly sotted and now that the men who had supported him were gone, he could hardly sit upright.

"Get out of this bed."

Duncan blinked, the meaning of her words slow to weave their way through the ale pickling his brain. "Get out?"

"Aye. You will not sleep in this bed until you have taken a bath."

"Bath?" He appeared to catch on to the last word and shook his head as she shifted until she sat facing him. Her knees drawn up under the linens, she rested her feet beside his body, and contemplated him grimly.

"Nay," Duncan said finally. "I do no bathe 'til July."

"Then you do not sleep here until July," she announced primly.

He was still trying to absorb her words when she suddenly slid her feet forward, rested them on the hip facing her, and gave him a push that sent him toppling off the bed.

Iliana fully expected him to rise up from the floor, furious and ready for a fight. Taking a deep breath, she tried to prepare herself for the battle ahead, but after several moments of silence, she began to worry her lip nervously. After several more moments, she managed to gather the courage necessary to move hesitantly to the edge of the bed and peer cautiously down at him.

He lay silent and still on his back upon the floor. Iliana had the brief, mad fear that she had killed him, but then she saw that his chest was rising and falling slowly and she relaxed. It seemed he was just unconscious. Iliana was not sure if that was due to the drink he had consumed or from hitting his head on the floor, but she was too relieved to care overmuch either way. For tonight at least, she need not fear his displeasure.

Feeling it was safe to allow her curiosity free rein now that he was unconscious, she let her gaze slide to his manhood. Her eyebrows rose as she stared at it. Iliana had seen chests and arms and legs before, but this was something new. 'Twas a most curious appendage. The only description she could think of was to say that it looked like a large, angry pink mushroom was growing out of his groin. Most interesting, she decided, and wondered how it might feel.

After glancing nervously at his face to be sure that he was still unconscious, she reached out tentatively to run one finger lightly over it, only to pull quickly away in surprise. The skin was soft and smooth. Not what she had expected. But that was not what had made her react as if she had been bitten. At her mere touch, her husband's manhood had reared up, seeming to grow an inch or so out of his body like a tree seeking the sun.

Fascinated, Iliana turned her attention to the rest of him. Her husband was a fine figure of a man. His arms and shoulders were at least twice the width of her own, as was his chest. It tapered down into a narrow waist and hips, and finished off with truly magnificent thighs and calves. His feet were a bit odd, however, she decided, taking in the way his second largest toes poked up a bit higher than the big toes.

Duncan suddenly snorted and snuffled in his drunken sleep, and Iliana glanced toward his face warily, but he settled and began to snore lightly. Releasing her breath in a slow sigh, she returned to her side of the bed, blew out the candle, and eased onto her back, worrying over her husband's reaction when he awoke in the morning and remembered her tossing him out of their bed. No doubt he would be furious. But she would not live in such filth, and she would not allow so filthy a man to touch her. Her mother had taught her too well for that. *Begin as you mean to go on,* Lady Wildwood had always said. And she was following that advice, Iliana reassured herself as her husband's snores lulled her into a deep sleep of her own.

Duncan shivered and started to turn onto his side, then grunted as he collided with something hard. Opening his eyes, he stared at the white linens hanging before him, bewilderment briefly gnawing at his brain. Then he realized that the bone-chilling cold beneath his back and buttocks was the drafty castle floor, and that the white cloth before his eyes was a bedsheet. He'd fallen out of bed.

Grimacing, Duncan eased into a sitting position, groaning as his back protested the shabby treatment it had received. He was getting too old to be subjecting his body to cold, hard stone for a bed. There had been a time when he would have simply bounded from the floor after a night spent there and gone cheerfully about his day. This was no longer that time. His back was aching, his head throbbing, and he'd be damned if the early morning light pouring through the chamber window was not blinding him as well.

Sighing, Duncan rubbed the back of his neck to ease its aching and glanced toward the bed, his movements stilling as his gaze fell upon the young woman sleeping there. Who? Oh, aye. He'd been married the day before, he remembered and smiled to himself. She looked fair worn out, his little bride. He could not recall, but was sure that he had worked her hard through the night. Duncan had never let too much drink stop him before.

Moving to sit on the side of the bed, he eyed her silently. He had found her appealing when she was awake, but while sleeping, with no sign of the stiff disapproval on her face that he had borne since meeting her, she looked even more so. Reaching down, he scratched his nether regions and smiled to himself. No doubt he had loved the disapproval right out of her.

'Twas a shame he could not recall it, however, Duncan thought with a sudden frown. Just the thought of bedding her made him stiff as a dead cornish hen. 'Twas sore irritating that he could not remember the act. Scratching his scalp above one ear, he peered at her a bit irritably. No doubt she would recall. She had not drunk overmuch at sup. Come to that, she had not eaten overmuch either, mostly picking at the food presented. In truth, she had looked more repulsed than anything by the fare. There seemed very little here that pleased her. What if his loving was one of those things?

The thought was a bit dismaying. If he had been too drunk to even recall now what he had done, mayhap he had been too drunk to offer her the tenderness and care bedding a virgin required.

Damn! Duncan thought with sudden alarm. If that was the case, she would no doubt awake to spear him with one of those cold looks she had given everything since arriving. Except his father, he thought. Angus Dunbar had not garnered one of her despising looks yet. It seemed she did not find him as despicable as she did Duncan, his home, and the rest of his people. He was almost jealous.

Well, he decided, he would not have it. If he had treated her roughly last night, he would correct that now, before she could wake up and give him one of those looks. On that thought, Duncan eased the bed linens down to her waist and gazed at what he had revealed. The women had dressed her in a gown of purest white, but the material was so thin and diaphanous it looked pink where her skin showed through.

For a moment, Duncan simply stared. His father had

called her "bonnie but no beauty" when she had first arrived and mayhap he was right, but at that moment, she looked as good to him as a platter of haggis to a starving man.

Iliana was seated in a small clearing on the edge of a river. The sun was warm and soothing. Sighing as the breeze caressed her flesh, she closed her eyes and lay back on the soft grass, allowing the sun to warm her body. She had not lain there long when a hand began to smooth its way along her cheek.

Opening her eyes, she peered at the man-at-arms kneeling over her. He looked vaguely familiar and it seemed perfectly natural that he should be there. His hand ran along her neck, then slid between her breasts, and Iliana purred. Stretching where she lay, she reached her hands above her head, her body arching upward. A moan slipped from between her lips when the hand finally moved to cover one breast, kneading and plucking at her nipple through the material of her gown. When Iliana moaned again, his lips lowered to cover hers and somehow, in her dream, that seemed natural, too. Her mouth opened beneath his when his tongue sought entrance, her own lips and tongue mimicking his and setting about a love play that had her curving into the body that now moved to cover hers.

When his lips left hers and began nibbling a path down her throat, she took a deep breath and opened her mouth to protest at the loss, then froze as the rank smell of sweat mixed with ale began to tug her out of her sweet dream.

Frowning, Iliana waved a hand vaguely in front of her nose, trying to dispel the smell and return her attention to the sweet caresses moving along her throat, but it would not go away. Murmuring aloud, she brought herself fully to wakefulness and forced her eyes open.

Even then it took a moment for her to realize what was happening. She was not on the bank of a river. She was lying abed. And the familiar-looking man now nibbling away so industriously at her flesh was her great, reeking oaf of a husband . . . and on her mother's clean linens, no less!

Duncan smiled against her skin appreciatively. His little wife was like a red-hot fire, the flames twisting and flickering this way and that in his hands. Murmuring appreciatively at the sweet smell and taste of her, he moved his lips along her skin.

When he reached the neckline of her gown, he began pushing at the flimsy material, fretting over it until her left breast popped free, presenting itself for his attention. Releasing a victorious exclamation, he dropped his mouth on the rosy aureole at once, then stiffened as his little wife let loose a scream loud enough to deafen him. 'Twas a scream a woman loosed only when in horrible peril. Thinking there must be some danger in the room, Duncan released her at once and whirled about. Only there was no danger.

Frowning as he saw that the room was empty but for her chests and a full tub of water, he turned back to his wife. His eyebrows rose when he saw that she was no longer staked out on the bed, but had scooted up into the top corner of it and now knelt there, eyeing him as if he was a madman bent on dismembering her.

"What?" he asked in bewilderment. Then, thinking he understood, Duncan slumped. "I feared I may have been less than gentle with ye yester eve, lass. 'Tis sorry I am, I was fair *fou*. I promise I'll not be so rough this time."

Iliana's eyes widened.

"You did naught last night," she said curtly. Shocked, his eyes widened when she continued, "You passed out drunk on the floor."

"Nay!" he protested proudly. He had never *ever* been too drunk to bed a woman and could not believe that he would be so last night of all nights.

"Aye."

Duncan tugged the blankets aside and peered at the pristine white bed linen. He had just realized that what she said was true when a knock sounded at the door. Cursing under his breath, he leapt to his feet and grabbed his sword from where the men had left it lying in the middle of the floor the night before.

For a moment, as he turned toward her, sword in hand, Iliana had the mad thought that he meant to run her through; then he slid the blade along his own hand, producing a thin sliver of a cut that immediately gave up blood. While she watched, amazed, he set the blade back on the floor, leapt into bed beside her, and quickly wiped his hand on the bottom linen of the bed as the knock sounded again. Her mother's fine linen!

Iliana opened her mouth to blast him for staining it but did not get the chance. In the next instant, he had whipped her gown up over her head, thrown it across the room, and tugged her down to lie beside him. "Come in!"

Iliana ducked beneath the linens with a squeal of dismay as the door opened.

"Good morn," Duncan murmured as his father, Seonaid, Lord Rolfe, and the bishop crowded into the room.

"Good morn, son." Angus beamed at his progeny as Iliana peeked out from under the bed linen. "Ye . . . er . . . slept well, I hope?" He turned his head away as he asked that, embarrassment painting a blush on his rugged skin.

"Well. But not long," was Duncan's answer, and Iliana reddened at his suggestive tone, wishing herself dead.

"We are here for the bed linens," the bishop explained gently when Angus Dunbar could not seem to do so.

"The bed linens?" Ignoring the way his wife had suddenly stiffened beside him, Duncan peered at them in feigned confusion. "Why would ye be needin' the bed linens?"

There was complete silence as the men peered help-lessly at each other while Seonaid watched in confusion; then Angus suddenly turned on him irritably. "Just give us the bleedin'—I mean the bloody—I mean—Just give me the damn things!"

"All right, all right. No need to sic a splore. Seonaid, turn yer head." He waited until she had done so, then rose, gathered Iliana in the top linen, and carried her to the side.

All four visitors peered at the bed then, taking in the splotch of blood with differing reactions. Lord Rolfe appeared relieved. Lord Angus looked satisfied. Lady Seonaid seemed stunned, and the bishop simply smiled in approval. Then Lord Rolfe turned to gesture to someone in the hall and Ebba rushed in. Stripping the linen off the bed, she hurried out of the room with it, barely sparing a glance for Duncan, who stood naked as the day he was born, a bundled Iliana his only cover.

"Well." The laird of Dunbar nodded, his face brilliant red as he shifted toward the door, dragging Seonaid with him. "Well done . . . we'll . . . Will ye be down to break-fast . . . ?" His voice faded away, the red of his face deepening at his son's grin as he shook his head. "Well, then . . . We'll . . . er . . . leave ye to it. Shall we? Gentle-men?" He glanced about for Lord Rolfe and the bishop, only to find that they had already exited. "Good night, then—I mean . . . er . . ." Nodding with relief as he reached the door, he pushed his daughter through, fol-lowed, and slammed it closed.

When the arms holding her suddenly started to shake, Iliana peered at Duncan, stunned to see that he was shak-ing with silent mirth. She took a moment to wonder what he thought was so funny, then kicked her feet unhappily. "Set me down."

When he did so, Iliana clasped the bed linens closer about her and turned to glare accusingly, "You ruined by mother's bed linens." That only seemed to make him laugh harder. Iliana stamped her foot furiously. " 'Tis not funny, my lord. My mother and I spent many hours embroidering those linens. They were very special to me. I would have an explanation as to why you ruined them.''

Duncan's laughter slowed at that and he did manage a slightly repentant look, then he sighed and shook his head. '' 'Tis sorry I be, madame wife. Me amusement is not at ye. I have jest never seen me da so overset. He was a picture, he was.'' His laughter ended on a sigh as he took in her solemn face. She obviously did not see the humor. Tilting his head, he eyed her curiously. ''Didna yer mother explain the facts o' life to ye, lass?''

''Of course she did.'' Iliana glared at him for thinking it might be otherwise.

''Well, I didna mean to insult ye with the question,'' he soothed. '' 'Tis just that ye appeared a muckle muddled about the blood. 'Tis no shame in that,'' he added hastily when she started to stiffen up again. ''Me sister, too, was a mite confused by it, ye noticed?''

''Aye, I did notice,'' Iliana said warily.

''Well, Da and I have never explained the facts o' life to her. There seemed no need when her betrothed could not be bothered to collect her.''

He fell silent for a moment, taking in her expression, then sighed. It seemed obvious to him that while she might have been given *some* of the facts of life, she had not been *fully* educated; She had started worrying her lower lip the moment he mentioned Seonaid's ignorance.

Shifting, he explained delicately, ''The blood is caused by the maiden's veil.''

Iliana's eyes narrowed at that. Her mother had not mentioned anything about a maiden's veil. Mayhap he meant the bridal veil, she thought pensively. He quickly disillusioned her of that.

''Ye see, a lass is born with a wee bit o' . . . er . . . flesh. Skin . . . in there.'' He gestured vaguely toward the apex of her thighs. ''The first time she and her mate . . . join . . . the veil be torn and there be blood. The blood proves she came to her man a virgin.'' He watched her expression closely, satisfied that she understood when she began to look horrified.

"So ye see, they wished fer the sheets to prove ye were untried ere yester eve."

For a moment, Iliana was too busy considering the blood to think of anything else. To her, blood meant a wound, and a wound meant pain. Her mother had said there was a little bit of discomfort the first time but had not mentioned anything about pain or blood. Then the other part of his explanation caught at her attention and her wide eyes raised to his. "What did they want with the sheet? Why did they take it?"

Duncan grimaced at the question, knowing before he spoke that she would not like the answer. " 'Twas taken to hang over the rail at the top o' the stairs. To prove to one and all that ye came to me pure, and that the marriage was consummated yester eve."

She did not look pleased by the news, but merely sighed and moved around the bed to her chests. She had begun rifling through the nearest one in search of a gown when she was suddenly grabbed from behind and picked up in a pair of strong arms. Gasping, she grabbed at the arms holding her and opened her mouth to ask her husband what he thought he was doing, then cried out in surprise as she was dropped upon the bed.

Duncan fell upon her before she had even bounced once upon its soft surface. His mouth muffled her startled cry and his hands moved hungrily here and there, seemingly touching every part of her body almost at once.

Gasping for breath as soon as his lips left hers, Iliana pushed at his chest in an attempt to remove him, but it was impossible. He did not even seem to notice her efforts as he tugged at the bed linens to bare her body to his view. Iliana immediately gave up pushing at him and caught at those instead, trying to retain the small covering, but she lost that battle as well. The cloth slipped through her clutching fingers until her breasts were bared.

Much to her combined relief and dismay, the moment

he spied those, Duncan left off tugging at the linens, leaving them tangled and bunched about her waist and hips. Eyes lighting up like a child's at Christmas, he released an exclamation and lunged for the two orbs he had revealed, pouncing on them like a miser on money. Testing their weight, he kneaded their softness, then fastened his mouth on one and suckled like a starving child briefly before turning to the other.

For a moment, Iliana was so stunned she forgot to fight. 'Twas just long enough for a betraying heat to steal through her body, the same heat that had assailed her during her erotic dream. Then her nose wrinkled as it was assaulted by the foul odor of him and she renewed her struggles.

Duncan was so caught up in the scent, feel, and taste of his bride, it took him a moment to notice her efforts at escape. Once he did, he ignored them. To his mind, she was just a bit frightened by the knowledge he had imparted regarding the first time between a man and a woman. She most likely feared the bedding now. 'Twas to be expected, but 'twas better to get such things over and done with quickly. 'Twas a good thing, too, for he feared the feel of her wiggling beneath him was going to make it fair difficult to go slow and tender. Damn! She was like a flame and he dry tinder, he thought, then felt something hard press against his groin as she arched and twisted beneath him.

Stilling, he frowned against the pink flesh of one breast and pressed himself against her again. When he felt the hardness once more, then felt it shift, he released her at once and pulled away in horror, tales of odd men who liked to dress as women flashing through his head. "What have ye got down there?"

Iliana was so caught up in the struggle, it took a moment for her to realize she had nothing to fight anymore. Once it registered, however, and she saw the stunned, horrified look on her husband's face as he awaited her answer, she frowned in confusion. "What?"

Duncan reached for the linens tangled around her hips, then paused. Fear flashing across his face, he raised his eyes to her breasts. Aye, they were breasts all right. Rather than remove the linens, he reached down suddenly and pressed his hand to her crotch, barely catching a feel of the hardness there before she scooted away and tried to flee the bed. He let her escape, leaping from the bed himself as she did.

"What the devil be ye?" he asked hoarsely, facing her across the bed as she struggled to cover herself with the linens without revealing what lay between her legs.

His eyes devoured her breasts with a sort of desperation now, all fire gone from his face and all color with it. Iliana frowned at this turn of events. "What the devil do you think I am?"

"I donna ken. Ye've the face and breasts of a woman, but . . ." Misery twisted his brow as his gaze dropped below her waist. "Ye've something hard where a woman has no business havin' something hard."

Iliana's eyes widened in amazement as she realized he had felt the lock hanging from the front of the chastity belt and seemed at a loss as to what to make of it. She could not, for the life of her, think what conclusions he was coming to, but was fair sure from his reaction that they were not complimentary. What did he think she had between her legs?

She was so busy pondering that, that it took her a second to realize that he was moving again, heading around the bed toward her. Giving a squeal, she whirled and started across the bed. A glance over her shoulder showed her husband reaching the side of the bed and lunging for her. She felt a tug on the linens, tried to hold on to the cloth and keep moving, but felt it slip from her fingers as she lurched off the bed and stumbled into the wall beside the door. With nothing left to do, Iliana covered her breasts with her hands and turned warily to face her husband.

Chapter Four

Duncan gaped at the contraption she wore, but had barely taken in the leather straps with the gleaming lock in front before she turned to flee toward her chests. Nothing on earth could have stopped him from leaping the bed to reach her side.

Catching her about the waist, he tugged her backward, twisting so that they landed side by side on the bed. He then threw a leg over both of hers and leaned up slightly so that he could peer once more at the contraption she wore.

"Damn." The word came out in a hiss of air as he examined the apparatus. Catching her hands easily in one of his own when she started to struggle, he held them above her head, his eyes never leaving the belt. "What be it?" he asked with awe.

" 'Tis a belt of chastity," Iliana admitted grimly, then caught at her lower lip and began to worry it between her teeth.

"I have never seen the like."

49

" 'Twas invented by Francesco Carrarro. A . . . a friend of my father's."

"How did ye come by it?"

"Father brought it back from his last visit," Iliana answered reluctantly. "He gave my mother and myself both one."

"And yer mother had ye wear it to ensure yer chastity 'til ye reached me," he guessed, giving the front strap an experimental tug. " 'Tis leather."

"Aye," Iliana gasped, her head turned to the side to avoid the stink of his armpits as she tried to tug her hands loose. Damn, he smelled foul.

Shifting, he turned her abruptly onto her stomach so that he could look at the back of it, taking in the way the center strap was sturdily fastened to the belt there.

"Let me up," Iliana snapped over her shoulder, embarrassment flushing her face.

Duncan ignored her, his gaze wandering to the cheeks of her bottom on either side of the leather. 'Twas a fascinating sight. The round, smooth pink flesh, separated by the dark brown leather. Reaching out, he caressed one cheek lightly and smiled. The belt was a great relief to him. For a moment, he had thought he had gotten more than he had bargained for in a wife. Pinching one perfect cheek for the scare he'd had, Duncan smiled over her startled squeal, then flipped her onto her back again, his gaze turning to the lock that held the contraption closed.

"How do ye undo this?" Slipping a finger beneath the center strip, he ran it along her skin until it rested against her womanhood, where he gave the leather a gentle tug.

"A key," Iliana answered thickly, then swallowed.

"Where be the key?" His finger slid back up along the belt, setting off a clamoring within Iliana that occupied her briefly. She was damn relieved when his hand stilled and his head raised toward her in question.

Clearing her throat, she met his gaze. "I . . ." Pausing, she swallowed and tried again. "I will give you the key if you take a bath."

Duncan stilled, confusion his only expression. "A bath? 'Tis not July yet. Why the devil should I take a bath?"

"July?" Iliana frowned. "What has that to do with it?"

"I bathe twice a year," he told her proudly. "The last day o' every January and every July. Why would ye wish me to change that and bathe in the middle o' June?"

"Because . . . because I find your odor offensive?" she offered timidly.

"What?"

"I said—"

"I heard what ye said, woman! I am not deaf. What the devil do ye *mean?*"

Arms stretched above her head and lower body trapped beneath his, Iliana was beginning to feel like a sacrificial virgin. Temper flaring, she snapped, "You smell like a chamber pot! I do not care to be near you and I will not give you the key unless you take a bath!"

Duncan pulled back to stare at her in dismay, completely flummoxed by her audacity. "Ye are denyin' me rights as yer lawful wedded husband?"

"Nay! I deny you nothing," Iliana contradicted at once, trying to sound reasonable as she added, "But if you will not do me the courtesy of taking a bath, I will not—"

"Ye *are* denyin' me!" he accused, storm clouds gathering on his forehead.

"Nay, I—" Her words died as he suddenly released her and threw himself from the bed.

"Well! We shall just see about that!" he snarled, collecting his discarded clothes.

Sitting up slowly, Iliana anxiously watched him dress. "What will you do?" Her mouth tightened when an angry look was her only answer. He was nearly fully dressed ere she gave in and asked, "Will you have the wedding annulled?"

Iliana cringed even as she asked the question. The consequences of such an action were horrendous even to consider. She would be returned to Wildwood in shame and her mother would likely be well and truly trapped with Greenweld. That could not happen. Her gaze rose instinctively to the drapes above the bed where the key rested.

"Annulled?" Duncan turned on her, drawing her gaze back to his face. "Now that would be a trick, would it not? The bloody linens are probably already ahangin' from the railin'. Ye recall them, do ye not? Yer mother's linens with *my* blood on them?"

Iliana nodded her head slowly, relief rushing through her. He could not have the marriage annulled. Everyone thought it consummated. "What will you do then?" she asked now, but got no answer as he finished dressing and stormed out of the room.

Duncan pulled the door closed with an angry bang. Pausing, he lifted one arm to sniff at it and scowled. He smelled just as he should in June. That did not seem good enough for his wife, however. It seemed she would have him bathed and powdered like one of her English dandies. Well, he would not have it. Should he give in on this, next she would have him wearing braies and hose. An indecent outfit as far as he was concerned, what with the way they clung to the body, emphasizing the lumps and bumps of a man's personal apparatus.

Nay. He bathed every July and January and had done so for a long time now . . . and he would continue to do so. If his wee wife thought to change him, she could think again. And should she continue to refuse him his rights . . . well, he would just have to see to it that she did not refuse, Duncan decided, recalling the brief image he had been given of her in naught but the small scraps of leather and the lock at her groin.

'Twas a damn exciting contraption no matter its name. And his wife had a luscious figure. He would not mind seeing her in that belt again. Hell, he would rather see her without it.

So much for the wedding night, he thought gloomily, leaving the door to stride down the hall. He should set her aside. Have the wedding annulled no matter the fact that everyone would then know that it had not been consummated. But damned if she did not now have the same attraction as a gift all wrapped up and left on his bed Christmas morn. Duncan dearly wanted to unwrap her.

Mayhap he could, he thought suddenly, as he reached the top of the stairs leading down to the great hall. Aye, mayhap he could. He would have a talk with the smithy.

Iliana sighed dismally and forced herself to get up and dress. She ran into some small difficulty right away. The belt of chastity was good for keeping unwanted intimacies at bay but was quite inconvenient when it came to certain personal needs. It would have to be removed.

Still clad in only the belt, she stepped onto the foot of the bed, grasped an end post to maintain her balance, and stretched a hand up to feel around in the drapes that were gathered over the bed. It did not take long to realize that this was not a good hiding spot. It seemed she had thrown the key farther than she had meant to. She could not feel it.

A knock at the door made her stiffen. "Who is it?"

Ebba's voice answered and Iliana relaxed with a sigh. Calling out to her to enter, she immediately turned back to the bed drapes, this time poking at the underside of them, trying to pop the key out.

"My lady!" Ebba gaped at her briefly, then hurriedly closed the door and rushed to her side. "What are you doing, my lady?"

"Trying to get the blasted key out of the drapes. Find me something long to fetch it out with. I fear I have an urgent need to relieve myself."

The maid's eyes widened at that, and she made a brief search of the room, coming up with a poker from beside the fire. "Will this do?"

"Aye, it should." Taking the poker, Iliana began jabbing at the material again.

"Did you . . . He . . . You did not wear that thing all the night long, did you?"

"Aye."

After a brief silence, the woman asked, "Was his lordship very put out?"

"My husband passed out on the floor last night. He did not awake 'til morn."

"But the sheets were—"

"He cut his hand and spread the blood on the linens. My best linens," she added grimly.

"He knows not about the belt, then?" Ebba ventured hopefully as she eyed with distaste the single item of clothing her mistress was wearing.

"He knows. He found out this morn after everyone left."

"How did he react?"

"How do you think?" she asked dryly, then cried out with relief as the key finally slid off of the drapes. Dropping the poker on the bed, she jumped to the floor to retrieve the small item, sighing with mingled relief and pleasure as she finally clasped it in her hand.

"What will you do?"

Iliana looked surprised. "Why, take it off, of course." Just as Ebba began to look relieved, she added, " 'Twill be nice to be without it for a few minutes at least."

The woman gaped at her. "Surely you do not intend to put it back on?"

"Of course." She frowned over her maid's disapproving expression. "I told you last night, Ebba. I shall not live like this. I will have a clean home, a clean bed, and a clean man in it. If it kills us both," she added on a mutter as she unlocked the belt.

"Gilley." Duncan caught the smithy's arm as he drew abreast of him and urged him to a halt, forcing a stiff smile to his own lips as he did. He had meant to have a word with the man directly on leaving the bedchamber that morn. Howbeit, he had been caught up by one concern or another all morning. Now, when it was nearing midday, he had finally managed to get away long enough to seek out the locksmith. "I would have a word with ye."

Gilley hesitated, then nodded. "Aye, but yer da is awaitin' me inside. He wishes another set o' keys made. Fer yer bride," he explained when Duncan looked perplexed.

"Why would she be needin' a set o' keys?"

"She is chatelaine now," the man pointed out with surprise.

Duncan grunted over that, then shrugged it aside. "I shall be quick. 'Tis about locks and keys I wished to speak with ye as well. Ye see, I have this lock I need to unlock, but I have no key and kenned mayhap ye could tell me how to do it?"

He blinked. "Well, if ye bring it to me, I can surely do it fer ye."

Duncan imagined carting Iliana to the locksmith's hut, setting her on his table, and throwing her skirts over her head to reveal the lock. Nay, 'twas not an option. The tale would reach every corner of the keep ere the nooning meal. Besides, he did not like the idea of having another man's eyes on his wife's belt of chastity. Or what it hid.

"Nay. I canna be doin' that. 'Tis not possible." He shook his head firmly. "Ye'll have to be tellin' me how to do it on me own."

The locksmith frowned. "I canna be tellin' ye how, less I be seein' the lock in question. If ye canna bring it to me, then surely I can be goin' to it?"

"Nay. Ye canna." He scowled irritably. "Just tell me how to open locks."

"If 'twas that easy, everyone would be a locksmith. I canna help ye less I see it."

"Well . . . Damn!" Reaching for the sword at his belt, he tugged it from his sheath and used it to draw a rough sketch of the lock in the dirt at their feet. "There," he said with satisfaction as he finished the picture. "Does that not help ye?"

The locksmith's eyebrows rose slightly. "What be it?"

"What do ye think 'tis, ye bloody fool! 'Tis the lock."

Gilley shrugged, unconcerned by the insult. "Looks more like a mouse to me."

"Aye. A mouse." Angus's voice sounded by his left shoulder.

Slumping in defeat, Duncan turned to peer at his father. "What do *ye* want?"

Angus raised his eyebrows but smiled slightly despite his son's irritation. "I was lookin' fer Gilley here."

"Well, I'll leave ye to him then."

"Nay, I'd ha'e a word with ye as well."

When Duncan turned back questioningly, Angus gestured toward the men in the bailey. "Have ye a man or two to spare this afternoon?"

"There may be one or two I could do without," he admitted slowly. Ever since he had turned nineteen his father had been giving him responsibility over Dunbar keep and its people. It had started with a little here and a little there, adding more and more with each passing year until now, he was pretty much in charge of all who served them. Unofficially. Officially, his father was laird and had veto power over any decision Duncan made until he died. In reality, they worked serious decisions out between them, benefiting from Angus's wisdom and Duncan's vigor and passion.

"Good, good. Send 'em up to the keep when ye be gettin' the chance then, hmm?" He smiled at him cheerfully, then turned to Gilley. "Now, about those keys—"

"What be ye needin' the men in the keep fer?" Duncan interrupted suspiciously. He very rarely saw his father so cheerful. The man had been solemn and grim most of Duncan's life. At least since his wife, Lady Muireall, had died. In Duncan's faint memories his mother had been a bolt of sunshine that had made everyone around her happy . . . including her irascible husband.

" 'Tis not me. 'Tis yer wife," his father told him easily. "She's made a start on cleanin' up the great hall. She had the women throw out all the old rushes, then set 'em to ascrubbin' the stone floor, and she'll need new rushes to—''

"What the devil was wrong with the old rushes?"

Angus Dunbar raised his eyebrows in slight surprise at his son's show of temper. "Well, lad, they have been there fer nigh on a year."

"And would have lasted another year just fine. We always leave the rushes about fer a year or two ere changin' 'em."

"Aye, 'tis true that we have let things go a bit—"

"Let things go!" Duncan stared at him in disbelief, feeling suddenly betrayed at the mere suggestion that his wife might actually have something to complain about.

"Aye." Angus sighed. "The truth is, son, yer mother wid never have put up with the keep being in the state it has been in since 'er death. I fear I let it get so. I fair fell apart when she died. Sank deep into sadness and never pulled meself back out. I neglected the state o' the keep and even me people—"

"Now, me laird," Gilley interrupted, but Angus waved him to silence.

"Say what ye will, Gilley, but 'tis true and well I ken it. I am no sayin' I did not keep ye all safe. 'S truth, anger was about the only thing likely to get a rise from me. I worked out much anger on many an enemy's neck and chest with me sword. But when it came to the softer needs, I have not been here. Even fer me own children. Howbeit," he went on, when both men opened their mouths to argue. "Iliana is here now and wishes to set the place to rights . . . as yer mother did ere her, and it fair warms me heart a bit. We are lucky to have her."

Duncan would have had a great deal of difficulty agreeing with that right then but kept his opinion to himself as he turned away. "I'll send two men fer rushes, but no more."

"Giorsal."

"Aye, me lady?" Other than glancing over from where

57

she stood, hands on hips, supervising the women, who were on their hands and knees scrubbing the floor, the servant did not move except to arch an eyebrow in question. Servant or no, there was little doubt that she thought herself the queen bee at Dunbar.

Forcing herself to maintain her patience, Iliana set down the edge of the tapestry she had been helping Ebba with and moved to the woman's side so that she would not have to yell across the room. Her mother had taught her that there was little authority, let alone dignity, in shrieking from a distance like a fishwife selling her wares. Pausing at the woman's side, Iliana graced her with a somewhat cool smile, then announced, "Lord Angus is seeing to fresh rushes for the floor, but I thought mayhap something pleasant smelling would be nice to add to them. Mayhap you could take a couple of women and go collect some—"

"Heather."

Iliana blinked at the interruption. "Heather?"

Pursing her lips, the woman nodded her head with firm certainty. "Aye. 'Tis what 'er ladyship put among the rushes."

Trying not to grit her teeth, Iliana forced a smile that was even chillier than the first. "That may be so, but I prefer lavender."

Giorsal shook her head at once. "Lady Muireall always put heather—"

"I am not Lady Muireall," Iliana snapped coldly, "and I prefer lavender."

"There is no lavender this far north," the servant announced.

Iliana sighed in defeat, not needing to see the satisfaction on the other woman's face to know when she had lost. "I see."

"There be a muckle o' heather, though."

"I am sure there is," she commented dryly.

"I'll take the women and go find some." Barking a word in Gaelic that immediately drew the other women

to her side, she led them away without even pretending
to await permission.

Watching them go, Iliana moved dispiritedly to the trestle table and dropped onto its bench with a sigh. She was
definitely not having a good day.

The great hall had been empty when she had made her
way down that morning. Determined to begin work on
setting the castle to rights, Iliana had not bothered with
breaking her fast, but had sent Ebba in search of servants.
The maid had returned with Giorsal and three other
women older than her own grandmother would have been
were she still alive. Despite their elevated ages, they had
gotten a great deal done that morning, but Iliana began to
think that setting Dunbar keep to rights might very well
kill her. 'Twas not the work so much. While she could
not say she was used to the hard labor she had been performing that morning, she had certainly worked before.
The real problem was the women, or at least their atti-
tudes.

Iliana thought if she had to hear Lady Muireall's name
and how she used to run this keep one more time, she
might very well kill herself. She had heard a great deal
on Lady Agnes as well. Lady Muireall was apparently
Lord Angus's deceased wife. Lady Agnes was his mother.
It seemed both women had been paragons of perfection.
All she had heard the morning through was Lady Muireall
this and Lady Agnes; or Black Agnes, as they tended to
call her, that.

Lady Muireall had insisted the rushes be changed reg-
ularly in the future. Lady Muireall had whitewashed the
walls every spring. Lady Muireall had thrown herself before her husband, taking an arrow and saving Laird Dunbar's life by sacrificing her own. Black Agnes had kept
the keep arights, raised seven children, and held off the
English for six months while her husband was away.

It was pretty obvious to Iliana that her new people
did not think she lived up to her predecessors' standards.
Not that anyone had refused any orders she had given.

Not openly, at least. They had simply listened to what she had to say, then told her how Lady Muireall had done it and set about doing it that way. A couple of times she had nearly spat that if they were so versed on how the manor should be kept, why had they let it go to such ruin? But she had managed to restrain herself. So far.

'' 'Tis starting to shape up.''

Iliana glanced around at her maid's attempt to cheer her. The old rushes had been removed and the floor swept; then the women had set to work scrubbing the stone slabs clean of the years of filth they bore, while she and Ebba saw to the removal of the tapestries and wall hangings so that the walls could be washed. She was almost sorry now that she had set her sights on whitewashing. 'Twas not that the walls did not need it, but one glance at the family shield and all the tapestries on the walls was enough to tell her that every single item in the room needed a good scrubbing.

Including the trestle tables and benches, she thought with a grimace as she shifted on her seat and her skirt showed some reluctance to move with her. No doubt she'd sat in a puddle of something or other, she thought with disgust and was grateful she had worn a plain, old, and frayed gown today. Still, she made a mental note to herself that, no matter whether the floor was finished today or not, she must attend to scrubbing the benches at least. She was unwilling to see another of her fine gowns ruined here.

Sighing and glancing around the room again, she considered all that must still be done. By the looks of it, the floor beneath the rushes had not been cleaned since Lady Muireall's death, some twenty years ago. Once the rushes had been cleared away it was to reveal a multitude of clumps of various descriptions on the floor. Iliana did not even wish to guess at the source of the majority of them, but they were hard—almost petrified. They were also difficult to remove. That much had been obvious as she had watched the women work. There had been three of them scrubbing the floor for the better part of the morning. There would have been four had Giorsal seen her way clear to lending her own effort, but apparently her position here was merely to direct others. Not wishing to start a row on her first day at Dunbar, Iliana had said nothing about the woman's lack of labor. But she intended to talk to Lord Angus and find out the woman's exact position. She would also ask if it was possible to attain some more help. With only the three women working, even after the better part of the morning, not even a quarter of the floor had managed to get scrubbed. And the nooning meal was fast approaching.

"Come," Ebba murmured, when her mistress sighed yet again. " 'Tis not so bad. This room is starting to smell better at least."

That was true enough, but 'twas due only to the removal of the rushes. There was still a great deal to do. She had to see to finishing the floor, whitewashing the walls, cleaning the wall hangings. By her estimate, 'twould take them at least three days to finish this room alone. Only then would she feel she could turn her attention to the bedchambers. That thought did not please her much. She was not used to living in such squalor and the bedchamber was full of just as much filth as the great hall.

Moving to the nearest of the buckets the women had left behind, Iliana knelt on the floor and retrieved a cloth. She dunked it in the bucket, wrung it out, then began to scrub.

"Nay, my lady!" Ebba gasped, hurrying to her side. "I shall do that. Why do you not take a walk and get a breath of fresh air?"

Iliana shook her head. "There is too much to do. Fetch a cloth and help me."

Chapter Five

"Gor!"

Quitting her prolonged perusal of the petrified cheese and stale bread that the cook had produced for lunch, Iliana raised her head slowly at that exclamation.

Duncan's sister, Seonaid, was standing just inside the keep doors, her eyes, and those of her constant companions, Allistair and Aelfread, wide as they gaped at the changes made in the great hall. They were late, the last to enter for the nooning meal, yet oddly, the first to even seem to notice what Iliana and her crew had accomplished over the last three days. At least they were the first to bother to comment on it, aside from Angus.

Iliana had not seen her sister-in-law since she had left the bedchamber with the others on the morning after the wedding. Three days ago. Seonaid and her two cohorts had disappeared the morning after the wedding and not returned since. Off hunting had been Laird Angus's guess when Iliana had commented on it.

"What goes on here?" Seonaid asked in a hushed murmur as she and her cousins made room for themselves at the table.

"They be acleanin' the hall."

Iliana stiffened at the derision her husband put into those words.

"Cleanin'?" Seonaid said the word as if she had never heard it afore. Iliana was not impressed. Neither was Angus, she realized when he turned to scowl at her.

"Aye, *acleanin'*. Iliana and the women have been workin' themselves to the bone for nigh on three days now. The same amount o' time ye've been lollygaggin' about the woods." He paused to let that sink in, then added, " 'Twould not hurt fer ye to stick about to learn a thing or two on the matter. Yer betrothed'll not be pleased to have a wife so ignorant o' such an' the like."

"Wife!" Seonaid snorted as she reached for some ale. "Ye ken well enough I shall never be that, Da."

"I ken no such thing."

There was a sudden silence down the length of the main table, everyone turning to peer at the drama taking place.

"What mean ye by that?" she asked suspiciously.

Laird Angus chewed grimly at the stale cheese in his mouth, then swallowed before answering. "It is arranged. Laird Rolfe has persuaded me. We hashed it out the morning after the wedding. He left ere noon on that day to fetch the reluctant groom back."

"What? But I thought—" Her voice failed her. She had obviously expected a different outcome to her father's talk with Lord Rolfe. Seonaid looked as if she had been punched.

Oddly enough, so did Duncan, Iliana noted curiously. Her husband was as aware as the rest of them as to when Lord Rolfe and the bishop had departed. All she could think was that he had not spoken with his father since his leaving to learn the outcome of their discussions. But then, how could he have? she thought dryly. He was never here long enough to talk to anyone. He was out of the keep first thing in the morning and returned only long enough to eat his meals during the day. At night he crept in late enough that most people were asleep when he entered.

"Ye heard me," was the old man's calm response. "Yer wastin' away here and I've a mind to see that that stops. Ye were born to have bairns. 'Tis time we saw some from ye."

"Ye would have me marry that—that . . . *Englishman?*" She said the word as if it was the worst of insults.

"I would see ye *married.*"

Iliana held her breath in the hush that followed but was still unprepared for her sudden lunge to her feet. Seonaid deliberately tipped the trestle table over as she rose, sending pewter tankards and pitchers clanging loudly to the stone floor. "Well I'll not marry the bastard!" she yelled furiously over the din, then whirled on her heel and raced from the room.

Silence descended on the hall again, then Duncan got slowly to his feet, giving Iliana an accusing glare as he did. As if Seonaid's upset were somehow her fault, she thought with dismay as he turned and took the path the woman had taken.

Heaving a long sigh as Aelfread and Allistair rose and followed their cousins, Angus stood to straighten the table. After collecting the fallen mugs with the help of the other men, he sank back onto his seat beside Iliana, waiting patiently for Giorsal to hurry to the kitchen and back with a fresh pitcher of ale.

"I apologize fer me daughter," he sighed as he refreshed first her tankard, then his own. "She believed herself likely to remain a maid forever. No without reason, mind ye."

Iliana nodded silently, unsure what to say.

"I allowed 'er much freedom as she grew up," he continued. "In truth, 'twas not that I gave 'er freedom so much as I neglected to bother to take 'er in hand. I fear I have neglected much over the years. At any rate, she is poorly prepared for this marriage and would benefit greatly from any wee help ye could give her in learning to be a real lady.''

Iliana stilled as she realized that he was asking her to tutor his daughter in womanly pursuits. The idea was more than daunting. She had seen enough of the girl to know that Seonaid was not simply lacking such skills but completely bereft of them.

"When is the wedding to be?" she asked worriedly.

"Soon as the man can be fetched back here. A month, mayhap."

"A month?" The words came out on a squeak and Iliana raised her tankard abruptly to her lips for a sip that turned into a gulp that downed half the liquid in her tankard. When she lowered the mug it was to find Angus Dunbar eyeing her with one brow cocked.

"Ye've a fair thirst there, lass. 'Tis said our alewife makes the finest ale in Scotland. I daresay ye'd be agreein' with that?"

"Aye, 'tis fine ale," she murmured, forcing a smile. Then her gaze fell to the floor and she added under her breath, " 'Tis a shame the same cannot be said for the cook's fare."

Angus followed her gaze and nodded wryly. " 'Tis true the cook has let things slip a might over the years. His da was cook here when Lady Muireall, me late wife, was alive. She kept him on his toes, she did. But after her passing . . ." He shrugged. "We all let things slide." He was silent for a moment, his thoughts far away, presumably with his dead wife, then jerked himself out of it and glanced at her. "Mayhap ye could do something to encourage him to improve his offerings?"

"Aye, mayhap I can," Iliana said firmly, rising to her feet. "In fact, if you will excuse me, I think I will have a word with him right now." Turning, she marched determinedly toward the kitchens.

"I have never had complaints afore. The laird seems well pleased with me work."

"He is the one who asked me to speak with you," Iliana told the man solemnly.

The cook's only response was to glare at her from beneath his bushy brows and spit on the floor at her feet, barely missing the hem of her gown.

Iliana forced herself to count to ten, an effort to control her temper as she considered how to deal with the man. She had known as she had suffered through the stale bread and watery stews that he had served for meals over the last three days that she would have to do something about him eventually but had put him on her list of priorities between cleaning the great hall and whitewashing it. Well, other than a few of the wall hangings, which she could clean on nights in front of the fire, the great hall was done. The floors had been scrubbed clean, and the trestle table and benches were pristine. She had even seen to scrubbing away the smoke and soot on the wall around the fireplace. Now 'twas well past time she dealt with the cook.

He was short, with hair as black as soot, and a body that resembled a barrel. The man was round everywhere. Even his cheeks were chubby and florid. Iliana could only think that he either ate better fare than he served everyone else, or his palate was less discerning. He certainly lacked in respect and courtesy when it came to his new English lady. He had been uncooperative as the devil since she had entered the kitchen to speak with him. First, he would not even do her the courtesy of stopping what he was doing to hear her out, and second, he kept spitting on the floor by her skirts as she spoke. 'Twas a most disgusting habit. Especially in the kitchen while preparing food, she decided, staring down at the foamy gobs on the floor.

"Fine," she said at last. "If 'tis too much trouble for you to discuss your duties, I shall find someone else to perform them." She had a bare glimpse of the dismay on his face, then turned to leave the room.

" 'Ere now! Ye canna be doin' that! I've done this job all me life, and me father afore me. Ye canna be replacin' me!"

She had his attention at last, it seemed. Pausing at the door, Iliana turned back, feigned surprise on her face. "Certainly I can, Mr. Dunbar."

"Cummin," he muttered resentfully. "Elgin Cummin. Me mother was a Dunbar. Me da married her after he came here to cook."

"Well, Elgin Cummin, yer laird has given me a free hand in putting my new home to rights." Not exactly true, but this was no time to quibble, she thought, her gaze moving grimly over the others in the room now as well, in warning. The kitchen help and a handful of servants, including Giorsal, all stilled under her look. "That means I may release or retain whomever I wish." Her gaze slid back to the cook. "Including you. I had not intended to do so when I entered, but if you will not even discuss the matter with me, I see no alternative but to replace you."

"I'll discuss it with ye. Discussin' is good." There was a desperate look about the man now. Iliana was not terribly surprised. Being head cook carried a certain amount of prestige and a lot of benefits with it. Besides, the man would have been trained in it and little else. Iliana's only concern now was how rigorous that training might or might not have been.

"Can you cook?" The question was blunt and to the point, puffing up the cook's chest with ruffled pride.

"Aye. Me da was the best cook in all Scotland. Lady Muireall said so, and he trained me in all he kenned."

"Did he teach you to serve stale bread and dry, hard cheese to your laird?"

His chest deflated somewhat, shame upon his face now. "Nay."

"Hmm." Iliana eyed him solemnly. "Then I will not expect it again. What did you plan for sup tonight?" She had already spied the contents of the cauldron simmering over the fire. It looked to be a repeat of the stew that had been served every night since her arrival: a rather thin and tasteless gruel.

The cook's gaze moved to the cauldron, worry puckering his brow, then he peered at her helplessly. "We have no spices."

Her brows rose at that. "None at all?"

"Nay. Laird Angus did not replace his wife as chatelaine on her death."

Iliana was not surprised at this news; she had come to that conclusion herself by the state of things. "Is there not even an herb garden?"

"Lady Muireall used to have one, but it went to rot and ruin when she died."

"I see." Iliana shifted where she stood, her mind working over a solution to the problem. She would have to have a look at the garden at once. 'Twas June. Spices would have to be planted soon if she would gain anything from them. Spices were too expensive for her to purchase those that they could grow themselves. Still, some would have to be purchased. "When does the spiceman come around?"

"He doesn't. He stopped acomin' years ago. Laird Angus was never around to purchase from him."

She was frowning over that when Giorsal piped up, "He passed by here this morn. I heard one of the men reportin' it to the laird. He crossed our land on the way to Innes."

"Innes?"

"The McInnes holdins. They be our neighbors," the cook explained, worry on his face. "He will not be around fer months again after this trip. He has a wide circuit to make and only passes this way four times a year. I canna make tasty fare if I have no spices."

Her eyebrows rose slightly at his anxiety. It seemed he had taken her at her word and now feared losing his position unless he could supply tasty fare at mealtime. Iliana could not blame him for bland food when he had no spices, but she would not accept stale or leftover meals. She was about to tell him that, then changed her mind. Let him think her a tough taskmaster. Fear was a great inducement. After she had seen what he was capable of,

she would tell him he would never be taken to task for
such things.

Turning, she headed for the door. "I shall ask Laird
Angus to send someone after the man. Mayhap we can
lure him back here for some commerce."

Unfortunately, Angus was not around when she went
out to the bailey to search for him. Her gaze moved reluctantly to her husband, who stood talking to the stablemaster. They had been fighting a war of wills for the last
three days. It consisted mostly of ignoring each other. She
did not look forward to approaching him now, but they
desperately needed spices.

Sighing resolutely, she moved toward him. "Husband?" She saw him stiffen; then he turned slowly to peer
at her, his face expressionless. Iliana shifted uncomfortably but forced herself to continue. "I . . . is your father
about?"

Duncan had seen his wife come out into the bailey and
feared she might approach him. A problem, that. He had
no idea how to deal with the wench. She was refusing
him his rights as husband, had told him he stank, and was
now running willy-nilly over his home, changing and
cleaning everything. What was a man to do with a wife
like that?

If this was a normal problem, he would most likely
have taken it to his father for a pearl or two of wisdom,
but in this case he could not. He would be damned if he
would let anyone, even his father, know the humiliating
fact that he had yet to bed his wife.

As for explaining the contraption she wore, that was a
nightmare he wished not even to consider. Besides, his
father seemed quite taken with the wench. He certainly
seemed pleased that she was setting her hand to running
the keep. That outcome was bewildering to Duncan, who
had been a mere five years old when his mother had died.
Too young to recall what Dunbar had been like in her

day. All he knew was that the way it had been the day his bride had arrived was the way it had been for as long as he could recall. It had been good enough for everyone else but was not good enough for his wife, and quite suddenly appeared not good enough for his father either. It was as if his wife had bewitched the man. She had made him smile. And somehow, her very presence had made him decide that Seonaid should marry her Englishman, the same man he had spent both of their lives villifying and calling "Sassenach scum!"

"Husband?"

Duncan grimaced. She should not be allowed to call him that. The marriage was not consummated. But he could hardly take her to task for it in front of the stablemaster. "Nay, he went to talk to a crofter. What be ye wantin'?"

Duncan heard Iliana sigh unhappily. What was she so put out about? He was the one being denied his rights.

"I don't have all day, wench," he snapped, then paused and forced a smile for the stablemaster's benefit. "What be ye needin'?"

"I was told that the spice merchant crossed our land this morn?"

"Aye."

"Well, we have no spices and I wondered if 'twould be possible to send a messenger after the merchant, requesting that he stop here ere he moves on," Iliana blurted.

Duncan shook his head. So, here was another change she wished to instigate. A fine and expensive change that would be. He had not known the spice man to stop here in all his memory. Now she thought he should. He would not have it. "We need no spices. And I'll not be wastin' a man on sendin' him on such a fool errand."

Iliana opened her mouth on a protest, but he turned abruptly and headed away.

An hour later, Duncan was crossing the bailey toward the keep when the stablemaster came charging up, calling after him urgently. "Me laird! Thank the saints! I been lookin' fer ye all this past hour and could find ye no-where."

"What is it, Rabbie?" Duncan frowned at the man's obvious distress.

"Yer wife, me laird. She rode out right after ye left us."

"Rode out? What mean ye, she *rode out?* Rode out where?"

"After the spice merchant. Alone."

Cursing, Duncan turned toward the stables. "Fool woman. She kens nothing about this land or its dangers. I doubt she even kens in which direction McInnes land is."

"I pointed out the direction," Rabbie admitted reluc-tantly. When his laird turned a furious expression on him, he shrugged helplessly. "She ordered me to tell her. She is chatelaine here now, me laird. I tried to convince her not to go, but she is fair stubborn."

Duncan grimaced over that and strode into the stables to fetch his mount. Moments later, he was heading out of the bailey.

Scotland was a wild and lovely land. Unfortunately, it was also damned confusing. Determined to have the spices the keep needed, Iliana had started out very con-fident as she had left Dunbar. The stablemaster had pointed out the direction toward Innes land and she had thought she would have no problem finding it when she left. She had thought wrong. It had been close to an hour since she had left the keep and she was no longer even sure she was still heading in the direction in which he had pointed. Nor was she sure in which direction she should go to return home.

Bringing her mount to a halt, Iliana peered about. All there was to see were trees, rolling green hills, and craggy cliffs. They all looked the same. Nothing looked the least familiar, but then why should it? She was a stranger here.

Deciding she would get nowhere by sitting about, Iliana urged her horse forward again, but after another hour of riding, she decided she'd best stop and take the lay of the land again.

She was just slowing her mount to do so when men began dropping from the trees around her. A startled scream slipped from her throat, but then her attention was forced to her mount as the mare began to rear beneath her. Before Iliana could regain control of the animal, one of the men did so for her, grabbing the reins and tugging her back to all fours, then murmuring soothingly to the beast as he eyed her.

Nibbling viciously at her lower lip, Iliana peered at the men surrounding her. There were six of them altogether. Tall, grim-looking men who were eyeing her in a most unfriendly manner. Were they from Innes? She hoped so.

The man holding her reins said something in Gaelic and Iliana frowned as the gobbledygook of words hit her ears. She forced a polite smile. " 'Tis sorry I am to admit it, but I fear I have not learned your language yet."

There was silence as he absorbed her accent, then he murmured, "A Sassenach?"

"Aye." Iliana managed a smile. "I am Iliana of Wild-wood, the new wife of Duncan Dunbar, and you, I hope, are of the McInnes clan?"

There was a moment as the men all shared surprised glances, then the speaker nodded slowly. "If ye be o' Dunbar, what be ye doin' ridin' about on yer own? And why're ye on Innes land?"

So they *were* Innes men. She had gone the right way after all. "I apologize for coming without an invitation, but 'twas quite important. You see, I have only been at Dunbar for a few days and the cook told me that we had no spices; then Giorsal said that the spice merchant had crossed our land this morn on his way to Innes. It seems he gave up coming by Dunbar because Laird Angus was never home to make a purchase when he called."

Realizing that she was babbling, Iliana paused and

forced a pained smile. "At any rate, I feared he might not be by again for months, and we are in dire need of his goods, so I thought to ride over and see if I could persuade him to stop by ere he moves on. After finishing his business with you, of course," she added on a winsome smile.

"And Dunbar agreed to this?" The man looked quite doubtful at the idea.

Iliana phrased her answer carefully. "Well, now . . . You see, my new father-in-law was away from the keep at the time, visiting crofters or some such thing. And my husband claimed to be too busy for such a task . . . If you see what I mean?"

"Aye." His lips quirked upward. "Ye mean ye dinna tell him ye were acomin'."

Iliana colored slightly but only gave a wry grimace and a shrug as response.

His amusement apparent, the man murmured something in Gaelic, then led her horse forward. The other men followed at once. "We'll take ye to the keep."

"Thank you," Iliana murmured as they moved into a clearing where six horses waited. Still holding on to her reins, the man mounted his horse and set out in the direction in which she had been heading.

Worrying her lip, Iliana held on to her mare's mane and peered at the silent, solemn men about her. They had not actually *said* they were McInnes men. Actually, whether they were or not might not be a good thing anyway. She had never thought to ask if the Dunbars got along with their neighbors. What if the Dunbars were at war with the McInneses?

Now was a brilliant time to think of that, she scolded herself, then supposed she would know soon enough. If they were McInneses they would take her to the McInnes keep. Otherwise, they would take her to another keep. And, if they were feuding with the Dunbars, she would most likely be shackled up and ransomed off to her husband. If he paid for her. If they even did things like that here. Mayhap they just kept you.

'Twas not long after running into the men that a keep
came into view. Iliana relaxed then, for it could be none
other than the McInnes keep. They had not traveled long
enough to have reached another clan's keep, she hoped.
She was distracted from that thought when one of the men
broke away from the group and rode ahead. Probably with
the news of her arrival, she realized, and began to fret
anew over whether the Dunbars were presently feuding
with the McInneses.

Before she could work herself up over that worry too
much, they had reached the castle walls. She found herself
being led into the bailey and directly up to the steps where
what appeared to be the lord and lady of the manor waited
to greet her.

Judging by their welcoming smiles, the McInneses were
not presently feuding with the Dunbars. Iliana relaxed
again and smiled as her horse was brought to a halt.

Lord and Lady McInnes were somewhere in their fif-
ties. The man's hair was salt and pepper, but surely once
had been a mantle of pure ebony. Of average height, but
well-formed, he was quite attractive. Iliana returned his
smile briefly, then turned to his wife. Her hair was fairer,
a medium brown with a mere fleck of blue-gray here and
there. She was also quite lovely. Iliana stared in bemuse-
ment at the smiling woman, then glanced down as one
of the men moved to her side to help her dismount.

"Me lady, 'tis a pleasure to meet ye!"

Once again on her feet, Iliana whirled to meet the
owner of that bluff, cheerful voice. "Lord McInnes." She
gave a slight curtsy. "Lady McInnes."

"When was the weddin'?" Lord McInnes asked curiously.

"Three days ago."

"I am sorry we missed it." There was a miffed quality
to Lady MacInnes's voice as she said that, and Iliana offered an apologetic smile.

" 'Tis most likely my fault. I suspect we arrived earlier

than expected. And the wedding was held a mere hour after our arrival.''

Lady McInnes blinked. ''But we did not even ken Duncan planned on amarryin'.''

Iliana shifted uncomfortably. ''Well, that would be my fault as well. You see, he married me to save me from my stepfather, and to help save my mother from him as well. 'Twas arranged quickly.''

Lady McInnes's eyebrows had risen with every word she spoke. The woman eyed Iliana with fascination. ''Oh, my dear. We definitely must discuss this. Come along inside and I shall offer ye a beverage.''

Chapter Six

"So ye dinna have time to be aseein' to the task yersel' and let yer wee wife come out on her own!"

Duncan drew his mount to a halt, his gaze darting around the trees until he spied Ian McInnes perched in the lowest branch of one on his left. "Ye found 'er?"

"Aye." Dropping out of the tree, Ian walked toward him and Duncan sank back in his saddle with relief.

"Ye should keep a closer eye on 'er, Duncan," Ian chastised mildly, sweeping his long black hair back from his face as he paused and peered up at where his friend sat his horse. "She's fair bonnie. Anything could have happened to her out here."

"I dinna ken she'd left 'til Rabbie found me."

"I thought it might be something like that," his friend murmured, holding out his hand.

Leaning forward, Duncan grabbed the offered hand, then sat back, pulling at the same time as the other man leapt. Between the two, they managed to bring him up onto the saddle behind him. "Where be yer mount?"

"Ahead."

Nodding, he urged his horse forward. Within moments they came across Ian's gray beast. Reining in beside the animal, he waited until his friend had slung himself off his mount and onto his own before asking, "She was a'right?"

"Right as rain. She's at the keep now, chattin' with Ma and Da," he announced, gathering his reins before straightening to eye him. "Ye dinna mention ye were aplannin' to get wed."

Duncan shrugged. " 'Twas no a plan 'til just afore it happened."

"Hmm." Ian urged his horse forward, waiting until Duncan brought his mount into step with his own before saying, "She mentioned as much. How'd it come about?"

Duncan shrugged. "The English king sent a fellow up to ask me would I do it and I said I would if he would see to rectifying the situation fer Seonaid."

"That's all he needed to persuade ye?" Ian looked a bit surprised.

"That an' a dowry only a wee bit smaller than a king's ransom."

Ian grinned. "I kenned there'd be more to it. How much?"

"Not nearly enough," Duncan muttered grimly.

"Nay! Ye've only been wed a few days! Doona tell me ye be complainin' already?"

"Aye."

"Why? Wha' has she done?"

Duncan glared ahead briefly, then grumbled, "She be acleanin' the keep."

Ian burst out laughing.

"And she expects me to bathe, too."

His friend's amusement only deepened at that and Duncan glared at him irritably.

" 'Tis sorry I am, friend. But ye must admit ye smell a fair bit rank right now. Should ye try huntin', the beasties'd smell ye comin' and flee fer their lives."

" 'Tis June," Duncan muttered. "I always smell this way in June."

"Aye, and well I ken it, but it may have been a surprise to yer bride." He was silent for a moment, then glanced at him curiously. "I also heard yer wife atellin' me ma that the marriage was to save her from her stepda?"

"Aye. 'Tis why they searched fer a groom so far north and paid so generously. The king wished her far and away from her home in England."

"Hmm." Taking in Duncan's irritation, he murmured, "She seems a fair brave wench."

" 'Tis no brave to go riding about a country ye ken nothing about. 'Tis foolish."

"Aye," Ian allowed fairly, then added, "But she showed no fear when we stopped her. The wench simply introduced herself and told us what she was about."

"That just shows she doesna even have the sense to be afraid," Duncan muttered, but had to wonder himself. Iliana was proving herself to be a bit more than he had first thought she was. The cold, prissy image he'd had of her did not fit with a lass who went charging off on her own in a foreign land in search of spices. She seemed to have one or two surprises up her sleeves . . . not to mention under that damn belt of chastity of hers.

"Is there something amiss, Lady Dunbar?" When Iliana merely continued to stare at the servants working across the room, Adina McInnes glanced at her husband questioningly. But he merely shrugged his own uncertainty.

Frowning, Adina turned back to the younger woman. "Lady Dunbar? Lady Dunbar!"

Iliana turned finally at the strident note in her hostess's voice, concern wrinkling her brow. Then, understanding struck and her eyes widened in surprise. "Oh, you mean *me?* Of course! I am sorry. I fear I am not used to being called 'Lady Dunbar'." She paused, flushing brightly, and shrugged helplessly as she admitted, " 'Tis the first time I have been addressed so.''

Lady McInnes relaxed and laughed lightly. "Aye, 'tis fair odd to be addressed by one name all yer life, then suddenly find yersel' with a new one.''

"Aye.''

"Mayhap 'twould help if I addressed ye by yer given name?''

"Oh, aye. That would be fine,'' Iliana agreed at once. "You must call me Iliana.''

"And I am Adina and my husband is Robert,'' Lady McInnes announced, then lifted an eyebrow. "Ye seemed preoccupied by our servants . . . Iliana. Is anything amiss?''

"Oh, nay. 'Tis just . . . Well, truthfully, I was noticing how well dressed they are.'' Her gaze slid around the room again, running over the impeccably clean plaids on every servant present.

"Ahhh.'' There was a depth of understanding in that drawn-out word. "Then no doubt ye are wondering why yer own servants are not so well garbed?''

Biting her lip, Iliana nodded reluctantly.

"Well, me dear, 'tis no from lack o' coins, I can tell ye that,'' Robert McInnes announced, joining the conversation. " 'Tis a well-kept secret, but what with his sheep and the plaids their wool produces, yer husband is rich.''

"Duncan makes plaids?'' Iliana asked with surprise.

"Aye. Well, no hissel'. But his people do. They make a muckle coin from it, too, I can tell ye. They make some o' the finest plaid in Scotland.''

Iliana's eyebrows raised at that. "But then why do they all dress so shabbily?''

There was silence for a minute, then Adina McInnes sighed. "My dear, there are a few myths about the Scots that ye may have heard ere coming?''

Aye, she had heard a thing or two ere coming to this land, Iliana thought wryly, but most of it was so unflattering she dared not repeat it, so merely nodded.

"Well, there is one myth in particular that says Scots are . . . er . . . cheap." Forcing a pained smile, she cleared her throat. " 'Tis not true."

"Except in Duncan's case," Lord McInnis inserted with amusement.

Adina whirled on her husband in horror. "Nay, husband. He is simply very frugal."

"Hah!" Robert laughed. "Don't fret, wife. He be friend to me and would not mind me sayin' he is cheap . . . and cheap he is," he announced firmly with some pride. "He also be muckle rich from it. There's no doubt in me mind that he has a mountain o' coins hid somewhere. He must. Dunbar plaids sell like cow chips during a cold winter. We even buy some from him."

"Then there is his trade in protection," Adina murmured.

Iliana blinked at that. "Protection?"

Robert nodded solemnly. "Dunbar has some o' the finest warriors around. And the women are damned prolific. They breed 'em by the bushel. Duncan sorta rents them out to those in need when they can afford to hire 'em. He makes a muckle o' coins that way as well."

Iliana digested this silently. She was less interested in the fact that Duncan hired himself and his men out to those in need of a strong arm than the knowledge that he actually had a plaid-making enterprise right there at Dunbar. "But if his people make the finest plaids around, then why do they all wear—" Iliana began, stopping when Lord McInnes waved the question away.

"Because he sells them all, lass. He gives his own people only one a year. At the New Year. He sells the rest."

"I see," Iliana murmured with a frown.

Adina cleared her throat. "I would like to give ye a proper welcome, lass. Mayhap ye and Duncan will honor us by staying to take sup with us?"

Iliana's eyebrows rose at that. "Oh, Duncan is not coming."

Adina arched one eyebrow, her mouth tilting in slight

amusement at that. "Oh, I've no doubt he'll be along. He's hardly likely to leave his wee bride runnin' about on her own."

"Aye, well . . . He does not even know I am here," she confessed with a sigh.

This only seemed to amuse the older woman more. Leaning forward in her seat, she smiled gently. "My dear child, there is little, if anything, that a laird—and his son—don't ken, or learn about, here in Scotland." She paused and sat back then, a smile of satisfaction gracing her lips as the front doors burst open.

Turning, Iliana glanced toward the door and felt her heart sink. It was Duncan entering and he looked angry. Very angry. Almost rabid. Aye, he looked as if he could not wait to get her alone. Oddly enough, that simply stimulated an urge in Iliana to avoid such an occurrence.

Turning abruptly to Lady McInnes, she forced a smile and babbled, "Well, surely then if the invitation is still open, my lord husband and I would be pleased to stay for sup."

She knew she'd made a mistake the moment the words left her mouth. She could actually feel her husband's fury as he moved up behind her.

As he and Ian joined them at the table his expression promised that she would regret accepting the invitation. Sighing inwardly, Iliana listened as Ian repeated what he had learned from Duncan regarding their marriage. The news that it had been arranged to protect Iliana and her mother was not new to them, of course, but what she had not told them—quite simply because she had not known— was the exact amount of the dowry that the king had provided to ensure that the wedding took place.

There was silence for a moment after the young man revealed the amount. His parents were obviously staggered by the size of it. Iliana was shocked herself and was not sure whether to be flattered that the king would offer so much to keep her and her mother safe, or insulted that so much had to be offered for Duncan to marry her.

She got little chance to ponder that, however, as Laird McInnis snapped out of his surprise to ask, "And what will ye be doin' with the coins?"

Iliana turned curiously toward her husband, amazed at the sudden change that overcame him. All the stiffness and anger slid from him like water off a duck's back and his eyes, his face, his very person seemed suddenly aglow with excitement.

"I'm plowing most o' it back into Dunbar. Between that and the coins I've stored away over the years, there is much I can finally get done. I plan to start by reinforcing the wall. 'Tis in rough shape and constantly threatens to crumble about our very ears. Then there is the moat; I would have it deeper, I think, and wider. Then I thought I might enlarge the castle itself, and I also wish to increase our flock o' sheep . . ."

Iliana stared at her husband's animated expression. 'Twas like seeing an entirely different person, someone completely foreign from the sullen, grim-faced man she had married. She rather liked this character. He was ambitious and enthusiastic. Energy seemed almost to be pouring off his body as he spoke. Iliana could actually feel the heat of him warming her side as she sat beside him. It was a pleasant feeling. Almost a tingling that danced along her left side, energizing her.

Duncan smiled suddenly at a comment from Laird McInnes, and Iliana found her breath catching in her throat. She had seen that smile once before. On the day she had arrived at Dunbar. It had taken her by surprise then and managed to do so again now as she realized that her husband was truly an attractive man beneath all that grime. Very attractive.

"McInnes ends here. Ye're now on Dunbar land."

Iliana took in her husband's grim expression, then turned to peer at their surroundings.

They had dined with the McInneses, enjoying far better

fare than had yet been served at Dunbar, then sat on for
a while, the women chatting about various things as the
men continued discussing Duncan's plans for his home.
Iliana had learned a thing or two about her husband while
listening to the conversation flow back and forth. First,
beneath all of that dirt and gruff behavior, was a very
intelligent man. It had become obvious as he spoke that
a lot of the plans he had outlined had been well thought
out. It had also become obvious that he was not simply
cheap. At least not when it came to updating and reinforcing Dunbar keep. His miserly manner when it came
to dressing and feeding his people was merely a matter
of necessity to save the coins he needed to ensure their
future. Something she found herself admiring deeply. He
was very disciplined. Far more so than she herself.

Iliana had also concluded that evening that her husband
was very ambitious. She actually found herself in awe of
the grand plans he had for Dunbar. Plans he had already
set in motion, she had realized at one point as Duncan
had explained the renovations already underway. He'd
been accomplishing it bit by bit over the years, and now
the large dowry had made it possible for him to do much
at once. It seemed that while she had been busy scrubbing
the great hall, Duncan and his men had been working
diligently on the moat and wall. Deepening, expanding,
reinforcing . . .

'Twas a large undertaking, involving heavy work and
long hours. This had been something of a relief to her. It
explained the air of weary satisfaction that had hung over
him these last three days, and why he had not pestered
her unduly over his husbandly rights. Iliana had fully expected there to be a nightly battle over the matter, so she
had been surprised, mayhap even a bit insulted, that he
had seemed so indifferent to her. He had not even bothered to come to their room since their wedding night. That
had truly annoyed her at first, for she'd feared that he had
turned his attention to one of the village women.

Iliana was not sure why she was bothered by the idea

of Duncan's taking a mistress. 'Twas common for husbands to do; besides, she did not want the great, smelly oaf in her own bed. Still, she had not been pleased at the possibility. In fact, the thought of it had plagued her, making her most irritable the first morning after he had not joined her in their chamber. But Ebba had informed her that her husband had spent the night sleeping in his sister's empty room. Alone. He had done so every night since then, much to her relief.

"Are ye even listening to me?"

Iliana pulled herself from her thoughts and met her husband's annoyed glare. He had held his temper through dinner and during the first part of their ride home, waiting until they'd reached this spot. Then he had suddenly grabbed the reins of her mount and drawn their horses to a halt to make his announcement.

"Aye, husband," Iliana murmured now. "This is where Dunbar land begins."

He nodded grimly. "Ye would do well to remember that in future, wife. For if ye ever leave Dunbar land again without me permission, I shall beat ye."

Her back stiffening, Iliana eyed him warily.

"And once I've finished beatin' ye, I'll most like lock ye up fer a goodly time as well." The grim expression that accompanied his words seemed to indicate the conviction behind them, and Iliana shifted uncomfortably as he continued. "I do not make such a threat idly. Yer actions were beyond foolish today. They could have got ye killed. I don't ken who yer enemies were at Wildwood, but as a member o' the Dunbar clan, ye now have a whole new set o' 'em to add to it. Anyone o' them could have taken ye today and done with ye as they willed; whether that be rapin', or killin', or both, and I would've been able to do naught about it except to avenge the wrong done ye after the fact."

Iliana blanched, only now beginning to realize just how foolish she had been.

Duncan nodded solemnly. "I can see ye understand

how thoughtless and emptyheaded yer actions were. That bein' the case, I'll say no more about yer foolishness in chasing after the spice merchant so. Howbeit, know this. It was a waste o' time. Ye'll no be wastin' me coins on spices. I've plans for them already as ye heard this night, and I'll not have ye wastin' me newfound wealth on spices and cloth and the like.''

"Aye, husband," Iliana murmured, eager to soothe him.

Iliana was silent and subdued for the rest of the journey, weariness creeping over her so that it was a relief when they finally arrived home. Not wishing to anger Duncan and bring more censure upon herself, she did her best not to shrink from him as he helped her to dismount. But once he had set her upon the ground and released her, she hurried up the steps to the keep, not waiting to see whether he followed.

As late as it was, Laird Angus was still up. Seated in one of the two chairs by the fire, he was staring sadly into its depths but glanced up when she entered. Spying her, he smiled and offered a word of welcome.

Managing a weak smile in response, Iliana murmured a greeting as she crossed to the stairway, then trudged silently up the steps to the second floor. The door of the bed chamber she had come to think of as her own had never looked so welcoming as it did at that moment. Pushing it open, Iliana stepped inside and started to close the door, only to find it resist her push. Turning back in surprise, her eyes widened as she saw that Duncan had followed her and was now entering the room. She had not even considered that he might expect to sleep here tonight. A foolish oversight, she supposed wearily. After all, her husband had been sleeping in Seonaid's room, but that young woman had returned from her hunting trip today. That being the case, Iliana supposed she should have expected Duncan to join her in their room that night, but the thought had not occurred to her, and she now eyed him warily as he entered.

*   *   *

Closing the door, Duncan walked to the bed, thoroughly ignoring his wife's glare. Her expression made him feel something of an interloper as he began to unbuckle his sword, and that annoyed him. It was his bloody room. And she was his wife. Though one could be forgiven for not believing that since she seemed to have no concept of how a wife should behave. A wife was her husband's possession as surely as his castle, his cattle, and his sword. She was to subject herself to her husband's will, not stomp about in a belt of chastity, insulting his odor and demanding that he bathe.

His gaze slid to his wife as an image of her standing in naught but that damn belt came to mind. Her flesh had been nearly as white as those precious linens of hers, with just a blush of pink, he remembered, licking his lips.

Aware that his body was growing excited at the memory, Duncan sighed and turned his back to her. 'Twas a form of torture to do otherwise and he had suffered enough such torment of late. Duncan had found it impossible to forget the way she had trembled and shuddered in his arms on the morning after the wedding. In fact, he seemed to think of little else but that and how to get her out of her bloody belt so that he could finish what had been started that morning. He had considered the matter carefully these last three days. He had considered simply cutting the belt from her body, for other than the metal locking device itself, the rest of the contraption was merely leather. But it was thick leather that pressed tight to her flesh. He could do her great damage trying such a trick. That morning, while she had been busy below, he had ransacked her chests in search of the key but hadn't found it. He had even considered beating her until she gave him the key, but Duncan had always despised men who were violent to those weaker than themselves, and could not justify such behavior to himself. His threat to beat her should she leave Dunbar unattended again had been an empty one, made out of fear for her safety. He had not overstated the peril she faced by such foolish behavior.

It was foolish of him to feel the way he did, he supposed, but he could not seem to help himself. Once the worst of his anger over her refusal had passed, Duncan had found he actually admired her spirit in doing so. Few women would have dared to say nay to their husbands, especially since husbands had every legal right—and were even encouraged by the church—to beat their wives for lesser crimes. But despite her fear—and he had seen it plain on her face as she had stated her decisions on the matter—she had stuck to her guns.

Aye, she had spirit. Her refusal of him, as well as her activities today, were evidence of that. Unfortunately, they also demonstrated her complete ignorance in the matter of how a wife should behave. She had many lessons to learn. He only hoped he could find the patience to teach her properly, for he had found himself unusually short-tempered since his unsuccessful wedding night. So far he had taken the worst of it out on the men, driving them, as well as himself, to work to the point of exhaustion on the wall they were constructing. Even so, when he dragged his exhausted body to bed at night, he could only sleep fitfully.

Successfully bedding his wife would no doubt go a long way toward curing this sudden bout of insomnia he was suffering, and he had even considered bathing a bit early to gain the pleasure that would be his once the belt was gone. But Duncan felt sure that if he gave way in this matter it would begin a dangerous pattern. Nay. Unless he came up with another way to remove the belt, he very much feared he would have a long wait ere finally managing to bed his wife. That realization was not one that pleased a man used to getting his own way.

Iliana winced as her husband's sword crashed noisily to the floor. She scowled at his back, then blinked as his plaid suddenly dropped to the floor as well. Now he stood with his back to her, the shirt he wore beneath his plaid hanging just to the top of his behind, and Iliana found her eyes drawn involuntarily to those chiseled curves, and following the lines of his buttocks to the hard muscled length of his legs. Oddly enough, she found herself having a bit of difficulty breathing as she examined him so.

Disturbed by her body's reaction to her husband's physique, Iliana started to turn away, only to pause, her eyes instinctively rising to his wide, strong back and arms as he jerked his shirt upward and tugged it off over his head. She drank in the sight of his muscles shifting and rippling as he moved, reminded that, for all his odor and irritating manner, her husband was a very fine figure of a man. Every muscle in his body seemed to swell and undulate as he bent to tug back the rumpled bed linens, then crawl between them.

That was when Iliana snapped out of her almost mesmerized state. Moved to action, she hurried forward and snatched at the top linen, trying to whip it off as her husband crawled beneath it. Duncan was quicker than she had expected. Catching the tail end, he tugged back, nearly toppling her onto him. But Iliana caught herself in time, and glared at him.

"I told you, you shall not sleep on my mother's linens until you take a bath. You will not stink them up with your filth."

Duncan went still, then released the linen abruptly, nearly sending Iliana tumbling to the floor.

Catching herself, she stared in amazement as he suddenly stood, gloriously naked, before her. Reaching down, he grabbed the bottom linen that Ebba had used to replace the original and ripped it from the bed. Tossing it at her, he bent to sweep up his plaid from the floor and tumbled back onto the bare mattress, pulling the dirty tartan over himself like a blanket.

Clutching the linens to her chest, Iliana stared at him blankly, not quite sure what to do. She could hardly order him from his own bed but would be deviled if she intended on joining the great smelly oaf in it. After briefly hesitating where she stood, she spun away and trudged to the corner of the room near the door. It was the only spot that was clear of her chests. Her expression grim and shoulders stiff, she made a nest of the linens on the floor, then crawled into her makeshift bed and closed her eyes.

Chapter Seven

"Ah, there ye be, lassie!" Smiling benignly, Laird Angus crossed the great hall to meet Iliana as she descended the stairs. "I've somethin' fer ye. Gilley finished makin' them up yesterday. I would've given 'em to ye when ye returned from McInnes last eve, but 'twas so late and ye looked so tired, I thought to leave it fer today."

Iliana paused at the base of the stairs and forced a smile as she reached for the keys he held out. "Thank you, my lord."

"No need for thanks, lass. They be yours by right," he assured her with a pat on the shoulder, then turned toward the door. "I'm off then. I'll be out and about if ye need me."

Closing her fingers around the keys in her hand, Iliana watched him go, then turned to peer toward the trestle tables at the other end of the room. Relief rippled through her on gentle waves when she saw that, but for herself, the great hall now appeared all but empty. Actually, it was not the fact that the room was empty that made her relax suddenly, but that it was empty of her husband. It meant she could put off thanking him for his thoughtfulness of the night before.

'Twas a cold, hard bed she had chosen for herself last eve. Castles were invariably drafty, and while the unyielding stone floor of the bedchamber was covered with rushes, they had done little to cushion her body. Iliana had shifted and twisted stubbornly about on her makeshift bed for hours in an effort to get comfortable before finally dozing off. However, when she had awoken this morn, it was to find herself curled up on the bed, her gown wrinkled beyond redemption and caught up in the linens she was bundled in. It did not take a genius to realize that her husband must have moved her to the bed at some point during the night. Or this morning. He had not been in the room when she had awoken.

Duncan's kindness in moving her to the bed had been unexpected. It was also appreciated. Iliana was aware that she would most likely have been stiff and sore on awaking had he not moved her, and could only be grateful for his kindness. She supposed it was only right that she thank him for the deed and had been prepared to do so on coming below. Now that she knew he was not available to thank, however, she was more than happy to avoid the necessity for a few hours. It would give her time to sort out her feelings. They seemed to be in a bit of a muddle at the moment. Much to her distress, while Iliana was grateful for his thoughtfulness, it somehow made her feel guilty for refusing him his husbandly rights.

Sighing, she started toward the trestle tables, pausing halfway there as she finally noticed the walls. As per her orders, the servants had apparently whitewashed them while she was gone—and done a miserable job of it. They looked almost worse now than they had before the whitewashing. Something she had not thought possible.

"Ebba!" Turning, she peered about the empty great hall with a frown. It seemed everyone had been to breakfast and gone. She was a late riser this morning, thanks to her maid. Where the devil was that woman anyway? Ebba always presented herself at Iliana's door first thing in the morning to aid her in dressing. Had she done so this morn, Iliana would not have slept so long. Why, half the morning was already gone and there was much to do.

"Ebb—Oh, there you are," she cut herself off as the woman hurried through the keep doors and rushed toward her. "Where have you been?"

"His lordship said to let you rest. He said you had not slept well last night." There was a question in her eyes that Iliana waved away. She was not in the mood to explain that she had slept on the floor for part of the night.

"What is this?" She gestured toward the walls, and Ebba sighed.

"Aye. 'Tis awful, is it not? I tried to tell them they were doing it all wrong, but Giorsal just keep saying 'twas the way Lady Muireall had done it, and kept on about the business."

Iliana grimaced unhappily. She was sick unto death of hearing that woman's name quoted at her. "I somehow doubt Lady Muireall liked streaked walls."

The maid nodded in agreement. "Shall I fetch Giorsal?"

"Aye. Tell her Lady Iliana does it differently and wishes it done again . . . And again, if necessary, until it is right. If they will not follow your instructions, fetch me and I shall tend to it."

Her maid nodded determinedly. "Where will you be, my lady?"

"Down in the village. Send someone to fetch me when the spice merchant gets here."

"Aye, my lady."

Turning away, Iliana headed out of the keep. Despite what her husband had said the night before, she fully intended on purchasing the spices. She had no intention of disobeying him. He had said only that she was not to use *his* coins to purchase them. Iliana had her own to work with. She had found them in a bag in one of her trunks

when she had first rifled through the chests on her arrival.
There had also been a letter from her mother and father,
telling her that the coins were a wedding gift.

Iliana supposed the money had been placed there long
ago, when she and her mother had first started the chests.
Finding the gift and letter had brought tears to her eyes.
The thought that her father and mother had done such a
thing while her father still lived had made her unbearably
sad. Now her thoughts when she pictured the sack in her
mind were far more practical. If her husband refused to
pay for the spices, she would do so herself. She would
have her spices.

She also intended to use some of those coins to pay for
a couple of women from the village to come up to the
keep and help her start work on the garden. The extra
help was needed. There was much to get done and Iliana
was loath to pull any of the other women away from
cleaning the keep itself. Hiring some extra help seemed
the best option. Once she had those two necessities taken
care of, she would turn her attention to clothing for her
people. They would not look like paupers for any longer
than necessary, but just now, due to the time of year,
spices and a garden were the more important issues.

Half an hour later Iliana returned, well pleased with
herself and the four women she had in tow. All of them
were strong, able, and more than willing to work for a
few coins. Entering the keep, she cast a glance and an
approving nod at the women reworking the whitewashing.
It seemed this time they were willing to listen to Ebba's
instructions. Though, judging from her maid's expression
of grim satisfaction, it had taken some work to impress
upon them the need to redo the wall properly.

Leading the four new women, Iliana continued on into
the kitchens. "Elgin?"

"Aye? Oh! Good morn, me lady." Wiping the sweat
from his brow, the cook smiled at her anxiously and gave
a nod and a bow. "Did ye wish to break fast, me lady?"

The difference in his attitude from when she had first

approached him was both noticeable and appreciated and Iliana showed it by beaming at him. "Nay. Thank you. Actually, I hoped you might show me where Lady Muireall had her garden?"

"Her garden?" He blinked.

"Aye. Yester morn ye said she had had a garden that had gone to rot and ruin—"

"Oh, aye. Well . . ." He glanced toward the pot he'd been working over, then nodded. "Aye, me lady. I'll show ye." Setting down the cloth he'd been holding, he started to lead the way, then paused to glance back at her. "Ebba said the spice man was acomin' today."

"Aye."

"I was a wonderin' what ye planned to purchase?"

Iliana smiled reassuringly at him. "Actually, I thought to discuss it with you after you showed me where the gardens were, so that I could get these ladies working on it. In fact, I thought you might have a thought or two on what to plant as well."

"Oh." The worry disappeared from his face at once, a smile replacing it. "Oh, that'd be fine, me lady. Just fine." Hurrying now, he turned and ushered them out of the kitchen.

Iliana had thought that if they placed the garden where Lady Muireall had hers, there would be less work involved in renewing it. One look at the spot where the garden used to be told her how wrong she had been. Twenty years was more than enough time for the garden to be reclaimed by nature.

" 'Tis a muckle mess."

"Aye." Iliana sighed, her gaze moving over the women looking dubiously at the "garden." "I fear we shall be needing a man or two to help with the heavy work."

"Aye." Elgin nodded his balding head.

"I have a brother, me lady. He's fair braugh." It was the youngest of the women who spoke, a girl of perhaps fourteen.

Iliana peered at her uncertainly. "Braugh?"

94

"Strong," the cook explained from behind her, saying the word under his breath so that none of the women heard.

Touched by his attempt to help her save face, Iliana smiled at him slightly, then nodded. "Is there anyone else who knows of a strong man in need of a few extra coins?"

The oldest of the women stepped forward. "My boy's sixteen and strong, me lady."

Nodding again, Iliana glanced at the younger girl. "Go fetch both boys, please." She waited until the girl hurried off, then turned to the older woman again. "I shall leave you in charge while I see to the spices we need. I wish the garden to be from that tree"—she gestured toward a gnarled old tree on the far side of the garden, then turned to point to another on the other side—"to that one. We shall have to clear the space first and turn the dirt." She paused to frown as she peered at the would-be garden. "You shall need tools. Some spades."

"I can fetch those, me lady. The laird will have what we need."

Iliana glanced at the dark-haired woman now and inclined her head. "Ask Laird Angus then. My husband would be annoyed to be bothered with such a trifling issue."

The woman nodded and hurried off.

"All right, then. You know what to do. Should you have a question, I shall be inside with the cook." Iliana waited for their nods, then turned and led the cook back inside to discuss what spices he would need.

As it turned out there was very little discussion necessary. Elgin had been thinking hard on the subject. He knew exactly what he wanted. Iliana considered the amount and variety he requested, then gave her approval. He asked for nothing that was too generous or unusual. If anything, she wondered whether he would have enough spices until the merchant returned again and decided to purchase a little more than he asked for. Leaving him to his work, she returned to the garden once more.

The spades and the two boys had been fetched and everyone was hard at work when she reached the garden. Picking up one of the spades herself, Iliana bent to the task of digging out weeds and old herbs and turning the earth, ignoring the surprised glances of the other women as she did. Her mother had taught her to respect clothing, but she had also taught her the importance of hard work. How could you expect servants to perform a chore were you not willing to join them in it? Digging a garden had never hurt anyone.

"Son!"

Duncan turned at his father's shout, the irritation on his face sending the older man's eyebrows up in surprise.

"Well, donna ye look a mite unhappy. What be the matter, lad?"

Duncan grimaced at the term *lad*, his irritation deepening. His father did not usually refer to him in such a manner in front of the men. But then, it had been one of those days so far. Duncan had awoken that morning to find his wife wrapped around him like English ivy clinging to a castle wall. He'd had trouble sleeping the night before and had still been awake when Iliana had started snoring from her spot in the corner. Slipping from the bed, he'd lifted her carefully into his arms and shifted her to the bed. Not that she didn't deserve to sleep on the floor, but the stone floors in the old keep were fair cold, and she would most like have caught a chill sleeping there.

'Twas the only reason he'd done it, he'd assured himself then and did so again now. At any rate, it had been a sublime experience, awakening this morning to find her cuddled against him. Until she had shifted and that damn contraption she wore had rammed him in the side. It was then, when so close and yet so impossibly far from all her body had to offer, that he had determined to find a lock just like hers and take it to Gilley to learn how to pick it.

But there was not a damn lock anywhere within the keep walls or the village with a similar design. All he could think was that the Italians—for he was sure 'twas an Italian name she had mentioned as the maker of the thing—used some odd Italian sort of lock. At this point, he was beginning to think he would have to take her to Italy to get it off her . . . or take a bath, some part of his brain whispered, and he grimaced at the thought. Damned if he was going to do that! A man had to start out as he intended to go on. He would not bow to her whims.

"Nothing be the matter," he muttered. " 'Tis just that I slept little last night."

Angus grinned. "All this *houghmagandie* is catchin' up to ye. Ye need more stamina."

Duncan's only answer was a grunt. He was damned if he was going to correct his father's beliefs regarding his lack of sleep. But taking in his father's teasing expression, he wished wistfully that he deserved it. "What do ye be needin', Da?"

"Oh, aye." Face sobering, Angus sighed. " 'Tis yer sister I actually be lookin' fer. I would have her learn the duties o' a wife ere she marries the Englishman. Sweet wee Iliana has agreed to do the trainin', but I canna find the chit. Have ye seen her?"

Duncan grimaced over the virago that was tormenting his sleep being called "sweet wee Iliana" but shrugged. "I have not seen her." He turned to walk away then, but paused and turned back as his upset the day before came to mind. "When did ye decide she should marry the Englishman?" he asked accusingly. Had it been his wife had changed his father's mind? It certainly seemed so.

All sorts of things had been changing since Iliana's arrival. For instance, his father had seemed to smile more in the past few days than he had in all the time Duncan had known him. He was not sure that was a good thing. It made him nervous. If his father had been sullen and quiet up to now, at least everyone had known what to expect. Now he could not tell from one moment to the next whether the old man would be silent or smiling. He had even caught him humming under his breath earlier that morning.

"Well, lad," Angus murmured now, "I would see your sister married and bearing ere I die. 'Sides, the contract *was* made."

"Aye, but not fulfilled yet. Mayhap he will break it and Seonaid can marry another."

Angus Dunbar shook his head mournfully. "Nay. If Sherwell is anything like his father, he'll not be breaking the contract. He'll have too much honor fer that."

His father turned and strode away, leaving Duncan staring after him in amazement. All his life he had heard about the cheating, lying, sneaky Sherwells. Now his father seemed to be saying the exact opposite. Damn! Everything in his life seemed to have turned topsy-turvy just now. Since Iliana's arrival.

"There ye be."

"Aye. Here I be," Duncan said dryly as Gilley approached. "And what problem would *ye* be havin' fer me?"

Gilley raised his eyebrows slightly at Duncan's irritation but merely waved toward the stables. " 'Tis not my problem exactly," he murmured as Duncan followed his gesture to Gavin, one of his youngest guards, chatting up the stablemaster's daughter. The young man had the pretty young lass trapped between his arms and the stable wall as he murmured to her.

"Ye'd best be havin' a talk with the lad ere her father catches them."

"Aye." Duncan sighed as the girl giggled and turned her head away when Gavin tried to kiss her. "He's been workin' pretty hard at talkin' his way under her skirts."

"He's been doing a lot more than talkin'," Gilley said dryly. "And if her father catches him at his tricks, he'll be havin' his head."

"Hmm," Duncan murmured as Gavin ducked in for another try and this time, softened by his wooing, the girl allowed the kiss. Given the chance, Duncan had no doubt that young Gavin would woo his way under her skirt. While that meant he should have a chat with the lad and remind him of responsibilities, bairns, and not seducing nice young girls, it also started him to thinking about his wife, and the fact that there was more than one way to filet a fish.

Mayhap he could seduce her out of her belt, he thought. Recalling her heated response to him the morning after their wedding gave him hope, and Duncan was just beginning to grin over the prospect when Gilley suddenly shifted beside him.

"And there be her da now."

Putting his thoughts briefly aside, Duncan glanced up as Rabbie came charging around the side of the stable, toward the young couple. Sighing, Duncan pushed his plans aside and moved toward the stables. He had things to attend to now. He would consider how to seduce his wife later.

Iliana stared blearily down at the food before her and tried to open her eyes fully. They were not following instructions. All they seemed to want to do was close and stay that way. But she knew she really should eat. She had missed breaking fast that day as well as lunch, then had worked the day through. She really should have taken the time to eat lunch, she thought now. Mayhap she would not be so weary now if she had.

She had intended on eating, had even sat down with the others to eat. But then Cook had approached to murmur that the spice merchant had arrived. Nodding, Iliana had ignored her husband's curious expression and quickly left the table, headed for the kitchens, where the man was waiting. He was a wiry little man with a wide, cheerful smile and a pleasant demeanor. Iliana had quite enjoyed dealing with him, despite the speed with which she had felt forced to do so.

In the twenty short minutes that they had haggled, he

had managed to spit out more gossip than Iliana would have believed possible. From what he had said, nearly everyone in Scotland was feuding with everyone else. She was interested to learn that the Dunbars were currently feuding with the Lindsays, Campbells, MacGregors, and Colquhouns. She now knew her enemies. But that was all she had been able to keep straight. There were so many clans feuding with each other, and often for such silly reasons, she hardly believed it. It seemed that refusing a second serving while dining at another keep could cause a feud. Hearing that, Iliana had immediately rerun the evening before in her mind, wondering if she had said or done anything while dining at the McInnes keep that might have been taken as an insult. She did not think she had, but supposed she would find out if the clan came charging across the land. Other than that, there was nothing she could do about it now.

Iliana had also learned the cloth merchant's schedule from the man, and elicited a promise that he would mention to the other fellow that there was commerce to be done at Dunbar.

Cook had been happy as a pig in mud by the time they were done with the man. It was obvious that he was now excited at the idea of preparing more interesting fare. He had chatted away excitedly as he set out some food for the merchant to eat as she had returned to the great hall. Unfortunately, she had been gone long enough that everyone was rising to make their way back to work when she returned. Iliana had hesitated, considered finishing her meal, then shrugged and went back through the kitchen to the gardens. She had not been all that hungry anyway.

She had worked in the gardens throughout the afternoon, dividing her attention between what she had been doing and watching the other women as they labored. She had known by the end of the morning's work that she had hired good workers, and was considering keeping two or three of them on to work in the castle once the garden was finished. Pondering which ones she should keep had distracted her throughout the afternoon as she bent to the backbreaking work of clearing the way for a garden. Distracted as she had been by such thoughts, and her own anticipation of the first really good meal she had yet been served in her new home, time had passed swiftly.

Iliana had looked forward to supper all afternoon. With the spices now purchased and available, she expected it to be quite good. Lunch, as little of it as she had managed, had already shown a noticeable improvement. Elgin had once again offered a simple fare of bread and cheese, but this time there had been no sign of mold on the cheese and the bread had been so fresh it had still retained some heat from the baking. He had also offered some fresh fruit to add variety.

Her eyelids began to droop again and Iliana concentrated on forcing them open, sighing wearily at the effort. As much as she had looked forward to it, she had nearly worked her temporary gang right through the meal. It had taken the cook arriving at her side to announce that sup was ready for her to realize that the afternoon had flown past. Calling a halt, she had straightened slowly and frowned over the light-headedness that had assailed her, then grimaced to herself as various aches and pains followed. Then the weariness had set in with a vengeance and she had recognized that she might have overdone it.

Now she sat slumped at the table, a lovely meal of mutton before her, and she too weary to even raise the food to her mouth. 'Twas an upsetting turn of events, for she knew Cook was watching her with distress, eager for a word of praise and fearful of complaint.

Sighing, she tried to push her eyes open again and lifted her dirk to stab at a piece of meat, grimacing over the aching of her arm. Every muscle in her body seemed sore, tired, and eager to let her know it, she thought with dismay, tightening her lips and raising the food to her mouth. She already knew the food was lovely. It smelled so wonderful that it made her dizzy. Besides, every single person at the three trestle tables were commenting on its quality.

Angus had taken one bite, closed his eyes, sighed, then turned to Elgin and shouted, "Damn me, man! Ye've been aholdin' back all this time! Ye cook like an angel! I'd swear ye had wings beneath yer plaid had I no witnessed ye swimmin' naked in the loch last month and seen fer mesel' that ye don't!"

Everyone had backed up the compliment. Even Duncan had grunted and managed a reluctant " 'S good," for the man. Now Elgin stood waiting only for her remark.

Iliana managed to lift her dirk all the way to her mouth, closed her lips around the food, then dropped her hand with relief and sank back on the bench, releasing an "Mmmm" of pleasure, aware that Elgin was sagging with relief as she did.

Turning, she forced a smile to her tired lips and murmured, " 'Tis finer fare than even my mother's cook has ever supplied, Monsieur Cummin, and that is no small compliment. My mother is very particular about what is served and went all the way to France to bring back a cook she thought good enough to serve my father."

The man beamed at that. Grinning and nodding, he finally took his seat at the table and began to eat. Iliana turned back to her plate with a sigh. Truly, it *was* wonderful. She only wished she could manage to eat, but she very much feared . . .

A shout of warning from one of the men made Duncan turn to glance at his wife. He was just in time to see her drop backward off the bench to land upon the now clean rushes on the floor.

Chapter Eight

"Ye've killed her!" Angus Dunbar roared.

Duncan glanced up from examining his unconscious wife to see that his father had risen to his feet and now stood glaring accusingly at the dismayed cook. "Nay, Da. She lives," he said quietly. " 'Sides, we are all eating what she did."

The old man's gaze moved to Iliana and worry plucked at his brow. "Well then, what the devil has happened? Is she ill?"

Kneeling at her mistress's other side, Ebba pulled a pinch of some herb from the bag at her waist. Waving it beneath the unconscious woman's nose, she sighed as Iliana stirred enough to turn her head away from the annoying smell.

"She's fainted," the servant announced grimly, lips tightening as she noted that Iliana's face was flushed. Reaching out, she touched her lady's heated skin.

"Why? What be the matter with the poor lass?" Angus asked gruffly, moving to stand behind the woman and peer over her shoulder at Iliana's face.

"Work."

The older man stiffened at that, eyebrows rising. "Work?"

"Aye. Too much work and most like too much sun," she said accusingly, then turned to glare at Laird Dunbar. "Lady Iliana has worked herself like a serf since arriving here. First she was scrubbing, then today she was working in the garden all day, digging and dragging heavy plants. 'Twas a fair bit sunnier than she is used to just now. And more work than she is presently used to as well. Add that to the upset of her father's death, her worry over her mother since then, as well as the added worry of the trip here and—" She shrugged on a sigh. "I should have warned her to take it easier."

"I noticed she seemed a mite pale when she arrived here. Scrawny, too."

"Aye, well, let us lock you up in a windowless tower for near a month, and most oft without food, and we shall see how hale and hearty you look," Ebba muttered bitterly, resenting what she considered to be a criticism.

"Locked up?" Duncan finally spoke, shocked.

Ebba glanced at him then. "Aye, locked up. 'Tis how Greenweld punished her when he grew tired of her trying to escape to rescue her mother."

"Greenweld?" Seonaid murmured, not having been privy to all the reasons behind the marriage. All she had been told was that the king wished the wedding, not the reasons why.

"Her stepda," Duncan told the girl now, bringing a sneer to Ebba's lips.

"Nay," she nearly spit the word. " 'Tis true Greenweld forced Lady Wildwood to marry him, but the king will soon have it annulled. 'Tis why he sent Iliana to you. To get her away from the man so that he would no longer be able to use her safety against her mother. Now that she is safe, they have no doubt already petitioned for an annulment."

Sighing, Ebba felt Iliana's face again and frowned. "I

am worried that she has had too much sun. She was ill with it once as a child and has been kept from the sun since. She got a fair bit of it today. She knows better.''

''She most like did not realize how much she was getting,'' Cook murmured, moving to join them now that Angus no longer blamed him for her condition. ''While 'tis true 'twas sunny, 'twas also chill. She would not have noticed the sun so much.''

Angus frowned. ''Aye. She is not used to the ways here. We must remember that. Keep an eye out fer her. Make sure she gets less sun and plenty o' rest.'' He glanced at his son meaningfully as he added that last bit.

Duncan rolled his eyes. While he was glad no one knew that the marriage was not yet consummated, it was a bit galling to be blamed for her exhaustion when he had not enjoyed the benefits of it. And it looked as if he would not be enjoying them again tonight. So much for the seduction he had planned.

''Did she really get locked in the tower fer tryin' to escape?'' Elgin asked curiously, and everyone went silent as they awaited the maid's answer.

''Aye. Greenweld is a devil. After forcing Lady Wildwood to marry him, he sent Iliana away to Greenweld keep to use her safety against her mother. Iliana tried to escape almost right away. She sneaked from her bed, crept to the stables, took a horse, and tried to get away, but was heard and caught.''

''What happened then?'' Angus asked.

''His man, Chisholm, sent word to Lord Greenweld who sent the message back that he had his permission to beat her should she try it again.''

''And still she tried to escape again?'' Seonaid sounded impressed.

''Three times,'' Ebba announced with pride. ''Each attempt was better planned than the one before. The last time she made it as far as Wildwood and nearly reached her mother. That scared Greenweld into having her locked up.''

"Did he harm her?" The question was asked in unison by Duncan, Angus, and Seonaid. Ebba met their narrowed gazes briefly, then peered down at her mistress. Iliana would not want her to speak of the beatings she had received. She had too much pride to want anyone's pity, as much as Ebba felt she deserved it.

"We should put her to bed," Ebba murmured instead of answering the question.

Duncan grabbed the servant's arm and stared into her face, reading the answer there for himself. His expression tightening, he released her and bent to pick up his wife, then carried her toward the stairs. His father followed, fretting like an old woman as he ordered that she must get more sleep, and take things much more easily.

Iliana opened her eyes, stared at the draperies overhead, then glanced to the side, eyebrows rising slightly as her gaze fell on her husband's sleeping form. She was in bed.

Frowning, she peered down at herself, eyes widening as she saw that she no longer wore her gown. Raising the bed linens, she peered down the length of her body and sighed with relief as she saw that she still wore Francesco's belt, then frowned once more. She did not recall coming to bed. In truth, she did not much recall the day before at all.

Letting the linen drop back to rest against her skin, she briefly searched her mind for the memory of how she had gotten there. It was the stiffness in her arm as she raised her hand to rest it above her head that brought back the memories she sought.

Oh, aye, she had worked in the garden all day. Then at dinner she had sat down to take sup but had been so stiff and sore that she had barely managed one mouthful of food. Exhausted and light-headed, she had feared fainting. She must have done so, for the next thing she recalled was waking up as Ebba undressed her. The woman had shushed her questions and urged her to sleep as she had gone about the chore, and Iliana had given in to the instructions.

The next time she had opened them 'twas to find her husband crawling into bed beside her. Iliana had muttered a complaint at him for disturbing her but managed little more before dropping off again, only to awake in the wee hours of the morning to the sound of his cursing. Unable to sleep, he had risen to quit the room, had tripped over one of her chests, lost his bearings, and was having difficulty finding the door. She had listened to him curse and stumble out of the room, then dropped off again, only to later be awoken by his return as he muttered and cursed his way out of his clothes and back into bed.

The distinct odor of ale had reached her as he had shifted restlessly about. It was not surprising really; Duncan ever seemed to reek of the stuff. His plaid carried the scent like the clouds carried rain. Still, the smell had been fresh on him last night, and she was sure he had slipped below for a tankard or two. Probably to help him sleep, she had decided, and pretended to be asleep, ignoring the way he had tossed and turned beside her.

She had nearly drifted off again when he was suddenly out of bed once more, dressing himself and making his way from the room. And so the night had passed for her with her husband up and down, in bed and out. He could not have slept long.

That thought in mind, Iliana eased carefully out of bed now, not wishing to disturb him. Grimacing at her aching body, she was as quick as she could manage about her ablutions in the early morning chill of the room.

She tended to her more personal needs first, careful to be sure Duncan was sleeping before seeking out the key to Francesco's belt. After the difficulty she'd had fetching it from the bed drapes the first morning, Iliana had taken to hiding the key between the upper mattress of feathers and the lower one of straw. Now she sought it out and undid the belt, sighing in relief as the cool air hit her skin.

It was with some regret that she replaced it moments

later and returned the key to its hiding place. Iliana had started to straighten from the foot of the bed when she suddenly paused to take it back out. 'Twas not really a very good place to hide it, she thought suddenly. She had always found that the best place to hide something was in plain sight. That being the case, she cast a swift glance at her husband, then quickly and quietly slid the key onto the ring of keys Laird Angus had given her the day before.

Smiling in satisfaction, she moved silently to the door and eased it open, grimacing over the squeaking it immediately set up. A glance at her husband showed him stirring and starting to roll onto his back. Iliana crept quickly out into the hall and tugged the door closed once more. His exclamation as he realized that the bed was empty beside him brought a grimace to her face.

Sighing, she shrugged and started down the hall. She had done her best not to wake him, she reassured herself, then pasted a smile on her face as she spotted Laird Angus stepping from his room near the top of the stairs.

"Good morn, my lord."

Angus whirled, eyes widening when he spotted her. "Yer awake!"

"Aye." She raised an eyebrow at his surprise.

"Ye should be resting, lass," he told her, frowning now. "We would not have ye ill."

Smiling slightly at his concerns, Iliana slid her hand through his arm as they moved to the stairs and started down them. "Thank you, my lord. But I feel quite well now. A bit stiff perhaps, but much better than yester eve."

"Ye slept well?" he asked, still looking worried, and Iliana nodded.

"Aye . . . Well, for the most part," she added wryly as she recalled Duncan's restlessness. "I fear my husband had an excess of energy last night."

His eyes narrowed at once. "He woke ye up last eve?"

"Aye," she murmured, then seeing the anger begin to cloud his face added quickly, "I do not think 'twas deliberate. In fact, I know 'twas not. As exhausted as I was, 'tis sure I am I would not have awoken at all but for the fact that he could not find the entrance in the dark.''

''Could not find . . . ?''

''Aye. But then there was all that in and out, in and out. . . .'' She shook her head as they reached the bottom of the stairs. ''It fair made me dizzy. Oh, my! There is Elgin. I must apologize for dinner last eve and assure him 'twas good. Excuse me.''

Angus was gaping after her when he heard a footstep behind him.

''Morning, Da.''

Whirling, he took in the exhaustion on his son's face with disgust. ''A wee bit tired this morn, are ye?''

Duncan's eyebrows rose at the sarcasm behind the question, but nodded. ''I was up most o' the night.''

''Aye. Iliana told me, ye randy bastard,'' he snapped sharply. ''As exhausted as she was, could ye not let her be for one wee night?'' On that note, he whirled away and stomped across the great hall to the trestle tables, leaving Duncan staring after him in bewilderment.

''Me lady!'' Elgin eyed her with some concern as Iliana approached. ''Are ye feeling a'right this morn? Mayhap ye shouldna be up.''

''Thank you for your concern, Elgin, but I am fine. 'Twas just exhausted I was yester eve. I feel much better now,'' she assured him, then offered an apologetic smile. ''Actually, I am more concerned now with you and your feelings.''

''My feelings?'' He appeared surprised.

''Aye. You made one of the finest meals it has been my pleasure to sit down to and I fear I made a poor show of appreciating it.''

''Oh.'' He flushed with pleasure but shook his head. ''There is no need to worry, me lady. I understood.''

''Nay. You worked very hard on the meal, Elgin, and

it was lovely. In fact, I am now quite looking forward to this evening's efforts. If they are half as good, 'twill be a great success.''

"Thank ye, me lady. 'Tis kind o' ye to say so.'' He hesitated briefly, then added, "Me lady, I did wonder if . . .''

Iliana raised her eyebrows at his hesitation, then prompted. "Aye?''

"Well . . .'' He glanced down at his plaid, scratching absently at one of the many stains on it, then sighed. "Ebba was a'talkin' yesterday about yer mother's cook, and she was sayin' that he had a . . . er . . . fine hat and an apron that helped to keep his clothes clean, and I was awonderin'—''

"You need not say another word,'' Iliana assured him, noting for the first time that his plaid was so speckled with food that 'twas difficult to tell what colors had originally been used in the pattern. "We will purchase material to make a proper apron from the merchant as soon as he arrives. In the meantime, mayhap we can find something suitable.'' Her gaze slid to the bloodstained bed linen hanging from the railing at the top of the stairs as she spoke and she grimaced. It had hung there since the wedding and she would be more than happy to have an excuse to remove it. Cutting out the stain, cutting up the rest, and making an apron out of it for the cook was as good an excuse as any.

"Aye,'' she said determinedly. "We shall find something suitable this very day.''

"Thank ye, me lady.'' Elgin grinned widely, then began backing toward the kitchen door. "Now ye best be settin' yerself down an' I'll bring ye some nice pasties. Ye need to be keepin' yer strength up.''

Smiling, Iliana moved to take her place at the table, her mind distracted by a new worry. The state of Elgin's plaid had reminded her of her plan to see to new plaids for everyone. She had spent very few of the coins her parents had put in her chests on the spices and now had every intention of using what was left on ensuring that her people were garbed in a fitting manner.

Distracted by such thoughts, Iliana did not notice the way Angus was glaring at Duncan. Neither did she notice the half-accusing, half-suspicious glances her husband sent her way, as if suspecting she was to blame for his father's animosity. In fact, she was so distracted that when she finished her meal and stood to leave the table and Duncan said he would have a word with her, she merely smiled absently, nodded, and walked away, leaving him glaring furiously after her.

"How many what?"

Drawing on her patience, Iliana forced a smile for Cailean Cummins's benefit, doing her best to ignore the rather unpleasant smoke wafting from the pipe between his teeth. It had taken nearly half an hour for her to find out where the plaids were made, then another fifteen minutes to track down who was in charge of the operation. She had been sorely disappointed upon meeting that man.

Cailean Cummins. He was Elgin's cousin. He was also testy, cantankerous, and not prone to liking to deal with females. He made that more than obvious by the way he managed to answer every question with a question of his own. She would also swear he was deliberately blowing the smoke from his pipe directly into her face. He was making what should have been a brief and simple conversation into a torturous trial. And quite frankly, she'd had enough.

" 'Tis not that difficult a question to understand, Cailean Cummins. If you do not know the answer, you need simply say so."

"I ken the answer," he snapped, affronted enough to take the pipe out of his mouth.

Having started to turn as if to walk away, Iliana swung back now, eyebrows rising in doubt to hide her satisfaction. "Aye? Well then, how many people are there at Dunbar?"

"About four hundred."

"Fine. Then I should like that many plaids."

His eyes goggled at that, his jaw dropping open to allow his pipe to tumble out. Regaining himself, he quickly tried to catch the well-used item, cursed as he burned himself in the effort, then flushed as he realized just how foul a curse he had used and exactly in front of whom. "Sorry," he muttered. But what did ye say?"

"I should like four hundred plaids, please," Iliana said patiently. "I shall, of course, pay for them."

"I . . . Ye . . . What . . ."

Iliana rolled her eyes as the man continued to stammer at her, then patted his arm soothingly. "You need only tell me if you can supply that many plaids. If you cannot," she added with a pleasant smile, "I shall, of course, purchase them elsewhere."

His expression now shifted from dismayed to offended. Drawing himself up to his full height, which was still a good inch shorter than Iliana, he asked, "Would I be correct in thinkin' ye be buyin' the plaids fer the people here?"

"Aye, ye would. 'Tis well past time each had a new plaid, do you not think?"

"Nay, I do not. His lairdship gives them one every year in January. 'Tis only June now. These plaids will last another seven months."

"They'll last a lot longer with two of them available," Iliana responded at once. " 'Sides, with only one, they have nothing to wear while cleaning it."

"Ye don't clean a plaid, me lady!" He seemed truly taken aback at the suggestion. "They canna keep ye warm should ye clean them."

Iliana rolled her eyes at that. "Can you or can you not supply me the plaids?"

He frowned over that, worry plucking at his brows. "My lady, 'tis not that I can *not* supply them, but his laird—"

"Has given me a free hand in tending to the keep and

its people," Iliana finished. The lie had served her well so far; there seemed little reason to give it up. "As I said, if you cannot supply them, I will purchase them elsewhere." It was an unfair threat to use. She knew he would not wish his people wearing any but their own plaids.

"He can supply the plaids."

Iliana glanced toward the door of the hut they stood in front of, eyebrows rising slightly as a tall, robust redhead moved toward them. Mr. Cummins's wife was a good six inches taller than her husband. She also appeared to have a forceful personality. "Tell 'er ye can, Cailie."

The man grimaced at the order but nodded. "Aye. It would slow me down on filling another order, but aye, I could sell ye the plaids."

"When might I expect them?"

"Ere the nooning meal," his wife answered for him.

"Ere the nooning! Eda, 'tis almost noon now," Cailean protested heatedly.

"Ye must have that many made, Cailean. All ye needs must do is count them out."

"Aye, but—"

"That would be perfect," Iliana enthused. "I can make the announcement at table. I will expect you at noon, then."

"Aye, me lady," he answered resignedly, then turned to glare at his wife.

Iliana headed back toward the keep, smiling slightly as she heard Mr. Cummins berate his wife for her interference, and she in turn put him in his place, adding 'twould be nice to have more than one plaid at hand. Her smile faded abruptly, however, as the squabbling suddenly stopped and Mr. Cummins called out a greeting that drew her head up in surprise to see her husband striding toward her.

"Me laird."

The older man rushed past her then, eager to tattle, and for a moment, Iliana feared that her attempt to gain new plaids for her people was about to be nixed, for she feared

113

her husband would not be thrilled by the idea. But whether he would allow her to buy them or not never became a concern, since he had no time for Mr. Cummins.

Ignoring the man's attempts to draw him aside, Duncan strode right past him to his wife. Grabbing her arm, he whirled back the way he had come. "I would have a word with ye, wife."

"A word, my lord?" Iliana asked worriedly, glancing over her shoulder at the consternation on Mr. Cummins's face and the amusement on his wife's face as she took it all in.

"Aye."

"What about, my lord?" Iliana panted, hurrying to keep up with his stride.

"Did I not say at table this morn that I would have a word with ye?"

"I . . . Did you, my lord? I am sorry, I do not recall."

"Well, I did."

"I see. Well, I am sorry. I may have been distracted."

"Duncan!"

Having just reached the steps to the keep, they both slid to a halt at that roar from Angus Dunbar as he crossed the bailey toward them.

"What the devil are ye doin', boy? Ye ken she's suppose to rest, yet yer joggin' her about like a—"

"Ye're absolutely right, Da," Duncan interrupted. " 'Tis wrong o' me to hurry her about so." Scooping Iliana up into his arms, he arched an eyebrow. "Better?" Without waiting for a response, he whirled and jogged up the steps, bouncing her about in his arms as he went.

Chapter Nine

Iliana held on for dear life as Duncan charged up the steps to the keep doors, wincing when he paused to kick one of them open. A glance behind them, as he then started directly up the stairs to the second floor with her, showed his father in hot pursuit. Angus had just started determinedly up the steps after them when Seonaid appeared from the kitchen, hailing her father. Iliana saw the Dunbar hesitate, then he turned reluctantly to meet her.

"Open the door." Glancing around, Iliana saw that they had reached the bedchamber and reached out to do as her husband ordered, her gaze narrowing with suspicion as it fell on the bed. But in the next moment, Duncan had carried her inside, kicked the door closed and turned toward the opposite end of the room. When he set her down before the fireplace, she took a quick step away from him, and cleared her throat nervously. "You wished to speak to me, husband?"

Duncan nodded. He intended on wooing his way into her belt, but knew he would have to go about it with stealth and cunning. It was not unlike stealing a herd of cows from an enemy. He had to catch her unawares. Sneak up on her, so to speak. Which was why he had not taken her directly to the bed. She would have realized what he was about and built fences to keep him out.

"I've a wound ye must see to," he announced, noting her sudden concern with surprise pleasure.

"You do not appear wounded," she murmured, eyeing him.

" 'Tis a trifling injury. Little more than a sliver, but 'tis festering and I have some worry over it." Slipping the top of his plaid off of his shoulder to hang around his waist, he quickly removed his shirt.

Iliana stood still, eyes wide as he half-disrobed before her. 'Twas not the first time she had seen her husband's naked chest, yet still it was an impressive sight. Her eyes slid over the skin he was baring as he shrugged off the shirt, watching the muscles in his arms and chest ripple beneath the velvet of his tanned skin as he dropped the shirt to the floor.

"I . . . I see no wound—" she began, her gaze devouring his chest, then paused as he held out his arm toward her, revealing that he did indeed have an injury, but she would hardly call it trifling. It was a two-inch cut in his upper arm, and it was indeed festering.

Frowning, she moved to the trunk nearest the bed and dug out some herbs and a small swath of clean linen. Then she moved to the basin of water at the head of the bed. "Come. Sit."

Duncan sat upon the edge of the bed, waiting patiently as she mixed some water with her herbs, then dipped a strip of linen in the mixture.

"Hold out your arm," she instructed, turning back to him.

Duncan lifted his arm, watching with interest as she cleaned the injury. He wasn't sure how he had gained it. Probably when he had taken that tumble over the bench while trying to stop Seonaid from starting the bedding ceremony. Whatever the case, he had first noticed it the morning after the wedding, but it had seemed insignificant then. He had only realized this morning that it was beginning to fester. He had thought to take a hot poker to it to burn off the poison tonight after sup. Infection was dangerous. It could take a limb, or worse, a life. Now he watched his wife minister to it and decided to give her herbs a day or so to work, then tend to it himself if they did not.

His gaze slid to Iliana's face and a slow smile tugged at his lips. She was nibbling away fiercely at her lower lip as she worked, her forehead drawn into a frown of concentration. He would not mind smoothing that frown away and nibbling at her lip himself. And he would. Her wariness was gone now.

"There." Straightening, Iliana discarded the soiled linen and retrieved a clean one. "I shall bandage it for now, but it shall have to be cleaned again this eve before we retire," she told him, beginning to wrap the strip of cloth around his arm as she spoke.

"Aye," he murmured, beginning to tense on the bed.

"You should have shown it to me earlier. 'Tis dangerous to allow infection to grow," she lectured, tying off the bandage. Then she straightened to look over her handiwork. Satisfied, she nodded, then turned toward the table again, intent on putting her herbs away and returning belowstairs. But before she even grabbed up her pouch, she felt Duncan take her hand. Turning, she was surprised to find him now standing.

"I would thank ye fer yer efforts on me behalf," he rumbled, then tipped up her chin with one finger and dropped his mouth to cover hers.

Iliana went as still as death in his arms. Even her heart seemed startled into stopping. She simply stood there, eyes wide and mouth still beneath his as he rubbed his own lips across them.

One benefit of such a surprise was that she had been startled into holding her breath. At least she'd stopped breathing, which meant she wasn't breathing in the scent of him as he kissed her. It allowed her the opportunity to simply enjoy the sensations his touch awoke inside her, without suffering his scent. And oddly enough, he *was* stirring things to life in her with that soft caress.

Alarmed by the odd sensations, Iliana brought her hands up to push at his chest, her lips opening on a protest. Her mouth was invaded at once by his seeking tongue. Gasping in surprise, she found that the hands that had started out pushing at him began tugging at his bare shoulders instead as her legs suddenly grew weak beneath her.

Sensing her response, Duncan smiled against her mouth, the tension leaving his body. He was sure he had found the way to her key. In a few minutes she would be begging him to unlock her secrets. Placing his hands at either side of her waist, he slid them up to cup her breasts through the material of her gown. When she jumped slightly in his arms in surprise, then moaned, he squeezed gently, then continued to massage a breast with one hand as the other slid down to cup her behind and draw her against him. This time he was not startled by the hardness that pressed against his own. He savored it as the temporary obstruction he was now sure it was, then set about removing her gown, distracting her from the fact that he was doing so by deepening his kisses and caresses.

As soon as he had her gown undone, he urged it down her shoulders, then rolled it off her hips. It slid to the floor with a rustle as he quickly stepped backward to the edge of the bed. Catching Iliana up in his arms, he dropped to sit upon it, settling her on his lap and continuing to kiss her as he set to work unlacing her undertunic. Pushing that off her shoulders a moment later, he left it to gather in a pool at her waist as his hands slid to caress the soft flesh he had revealed. He enjoyed the weight of her generous breasts in his palms briefly, finding their hard centers with his thumbs and teasing them to excited life, then found it wasn't enough and tugged his lips from hers.

In that brief moment after he abandoned her lips, Iliana blinked her eyes open, amazed to find herself seated on his lap, naked but for the undertunic gathered around her waist. Alarm bells began ringing inside her head at once. Then her husband closed his lips around one of the ripe nipples he had bared to the afternoon air, and she cried out in surprise and need, all protests forgotten as new sensations, more powerful even than those he had roused before, clamored to life.

Gasping and shuddering as he set to suckling at her breast, Iliana caught his head in her hands and pressed him closer. She arched against the arm around her back and wiggled in his lap as he slid one hand up her leg beneath the undertunic until it rested against the thick leather of her belt. But when he slid one finger beneath to explore her more intimately, Iliana stiffened in his lap, her head snapping up.

Catching her mouth quickly, he silenced any protest she might have given and continued to slide his finger between the leather and her skin. Grunting at the telltale damp heat he found, he did his best to increase her excitement with his touch as he kissed her.

Iliana's entire body clenched. Her legs tightened on either side of his hand. Her fingers knotted in his hair. Even her nipples seemed to clench in an agony of wanting. Part of her wanted to make him stop. The other part thought she would die if he did. Moaning, she twisted her face into his neck, then quickly away as the scent of him began to intrude on the excitement she was experiencing.

"Sweetling," he groaned as she twisted, rubbing against him, pressing the belt tightly against herself.

Barely hearing him, Iliana moaned and gasped as he nipped gently at her ear.

"Sweetling."

"Mmm?" she breathed.

"I want to pleasure ye, sweetling," he told her in a pained gasp.

"Pleasure me?" she whimpered, catching those two words only.

"Aye. Pleasure ye proper."

"Proper?"

"Hmmm. I need the key, sweetling," he whispered by her ear. Then he leaned back slightly to take in her expression, frowning as some of the dazed passion in her eyes faded away like mist under the heat of the sun.

"I do not—" she began, her body stilling, and Duncan covered her mouth with his, kissing her with desperate passion. He had moved too soon. He should have been more patient, he berated himself, working feverishly to rekindle the fire he had seen dying in her eyes. When she lay still in his arms, neither responding nor pushing him away, he knew she was teetering dangerously on the brink.

Taking the risk of breaking the kiss briefly again, he turned to lay her across the bottom of the bed. He quickly lowered himself atop her, his mouth taking possession of her lips again as he slid one of his legs between hers and urged them apart.

Iliana tried to hang on to the brief clearing of her thoughts, but his kisses, coupled with the feel of his bare chest moving against her own, was hard to ignore. The small, wiry hairs of his chest were bringing her skin to startling life. Then he tore his lips from hers and kissed a trail down her neck until he found and suckled at one ripe breast. But it was just a teasing he offered this time; at the first moan she gave, he pressed on, his lips sliding over her ribs to her stomach.

When her undertunic got in the way, he raised his head and flipped it up to lie against her stomach. Then he dropped his head to nibble at the sensitive flesh of her hip just above the belt, his hands sliding beneath her to cup her buttocks as he did.

"No . . . Oh," Iliana gasped, writhing in his hands under the caress, then groaned in disappointment despite her words when his lips left the area. In the next instant, Iliana was twisting her head on the bed and moaning aloud as he set to work nibbling at the flesh of her inner thigh. Her heart was beating so fast, she feared she'd die. When he slid one hand out from beneath her and slid his finger back beneath the leather of her belt again to caress her, she was sure she had.

Drawing her legs up on either side of his head, Iliana dug her heels into the bed and arched her pelvis upward instinctively, unsure of what she sought, but some inner voice was telling her this was how to gain it. Her focus was so intent on his caresses, she hardly even noticed when he stopped his nibbling kisses, though she noticed when he slid back along her body to kiss her lips.

Turning her face into the kiss, her own tongue came out to duel with his this time, and she continued to arch into his touch. She was disappointed when he broke the kiss again to speak but could not avoid the words he murmured as he nibbled away at her ear.

"Do ye like this, sweetling?" he murmured silkily.

She nodded her head a bit frantically.

"Me, too." He followed that with a sigh. "Would that I could help ye to find satisfaction."

"Satisfaction?" Iliana murmured dazedly.

" 'Tis what yer body is straining fer. Do ye feel it? Straining toward something like a flower toward the sun?"

"Aye," she gasped, arching again as he slid a second finger beneath the belt, adding to the pressure as he massaged her woman's parts. "Aye, I'd like that. Please."

"I cannot."

"You cannot?" she gasped, disappointment obvious in her tone.

"Nay, my sweet. Not without the key."

"But—"

" 'Tis sorry I am, sweetling, but I cannot," he breathed. "Unless ye'd be giving me the key."

121

"The key?" she panted, too distracted to pay attention to the alarms this time. The fire in her was building to an almost frightening level.

"Where be it?"

"What?" she gasped.

"The key."

"It's—oooh," she breathed. Her entire body was shaking with passion. It was difficult to concentrate on anything but what she was feeling, yet Duncan kept pestering her about something. What was it? she wondered, trying to shut out the low hum that was dancing along her nerves.

"Where is the key, sweetling?"

"Oh, aye," she breathed. "The key. It's—"

"My lady?" Ebba's voice was accompanied by a tap on the door, and Iliana stiffened at the sounds. They were as effective as a pail of cold water being thrown over her.

"Go away!" Duncan bellowed even as Iliana asked, "What is it?"

There was a hesitation, then, " 'Tis nooning time. And there is a Mr. Cummins below asking for you. He says he has some goods for you."

"Go away!" Duncan roared again, cursing as Iliana struggled out from under him and hurried to the door, tugging her tunic back on as she went. She had the thin gown on and done up before reaching it. Careless of his own nudity, Duncan muttered a string of curses and dropped back on the bed in despair.

"I—" Ebba's words came to a halt as Iliana tugged the door open.

Iliana blushed under her gaze, suddenly wishing she had put on her gown. In the next second, as she whirled away to do just that, she saw Lord Angus approaching. While her maid had seemed surprised and speculative upon seeing Iliana's rumpled state, the Dunbar looked positively grim. Flying back to the bed, she scooped her gown off the floor, but had barely managed to straighten with it when Duncan grabbed her about the waist and tugged her back into his lap.

"I told ye to go away an' I meant it," he bellowed toward the door, trying to remove the gown from his wife's clutching fingers. It would be difficult to get her back to the place he'd had her a moment ago. But having been so close to success, he was damned if he was going to give up now. She had been a hairsbreadth away from revealing where the key was. So close he could almost feel her hot flesh closing around his.

"Would ye keep her from eatin' as well as sleepin'?"

Sighing in defeat as he recognized that voice, Duncan released his wife. Iliana immediately slid from his lap and set to tugging on her gown as Angus stepped into the room to glare at his son.

"Did we not agree the lass was needin' her rest, boy?" he demanded as Iliana rushed to do up her lacings, her eyes wide as she heard this bit of news. "Can ye not keep yer randy hands off her fer one blessed day? The poor child fainted from exhaustion yester eve, or have ye forgotten? Are ye trying to work her into the grave with yer blasted demands both night and day? Damn me, I'm almost ashamed to call ye son." On that note, he turned to eye Iliana as she finished dressing and peered at him anxiously.

"Come, child. 'Tis obvious me son cannot be trusted around ye. He'll not give ye the care and concern ye be needin' just now. 'Tis a chaperone ye need, and 'tis a chaperone ye'll have 'til yer better."

With that, he drew Iliana's arm through his and led her toward the door, leaving her to glance worriedly over her shoulder at her husband. He sat watching them leave with resigned misery.

Iliana stared nervously at the horde of faces turned toward her and swallowed the anxiety at the back of her throat. She had told Lord Angus her intentions as they had descended the stairs to the great hall. He had thought it a fine idea and had been good enough to gather everyone's attention once they had all filed into the great hall for the noon meal. Everyone but Duncan. He had not put in an appearance yet. In fact, he had not come down at all yet. She supposed he was still in their room, sulking.

She realized now that he had set out to deliberately seduce her. She could only be grateful that his plans had been thwarted. Else she would never get him to bathe. That was becoming a necessity in her mind. 'Twas not so much the sounds he had made as he had got into and risen from their bed that had awoken her all through the last night, she thought. It had been the scent of him. She could not bear to share a bed with such an odiferous man.

Sighing, she peered once more at the people awaiting her words, grateful that, for whatever reason, her husband was not there.

On that thought, Iliana took a deep breath and forced a smile. "I wish to show my appreciation for all your kindness in welcoming me to Dunbar with a small gift to you in return. I understand that you are each granted one plaid in January, and I thought it would be nice if you each had two, so I commissioned a plaid for each of you from Mr. Cummins. But," she added as the inhabitants of the room showed surprised pleasure at this announcement, "I do have a . . . condition you each must fulfill to gain it."

She paused then to lick her lips nervously before continuing. "At Wildwood, my childhood home, my mother insisted that everyone bathe at least once a month. Some even bathed as often as once a week." She sighed at the gasps her words elicited but pushed on. "While I do not insist that you bathe that often, I would see you bathe before accepting the gift of a plaid. I see little sense in putting a lovely clean plaid on a filthy body."

Iliana waited for their murmurs to die down before continuing, "I will make my tub available to anyone who wishes to use it." Smiling uncertainly, she gave a faint nod, then sank into her seat and silence enveloped the room. She did not think that was a good sign, and very much feared she had purchased four hundred plaids that would sit collecting dust until their next communal bath time.

Iliana peered down at the cheese and bread before her and sighed unhappily. It did seem nothing was going to come easy here. Not the garden. Not the cleaning. Not even the gathering of herbs had been easy.

"Me lady?"

Iliana glanced up with a start, a smile on her lips as she recognized Janna, one of the women who had been aiding her in the gardens.

A tentative smile on her face, the woman murmured, "I should like a plaid and would be pleased to use yer tub, if I might?"

"Really?" Iliana's smile stretched clear across her face; then she glanced toward the kitchen anxiously and stood. "You may be first then," she assured her. "I'll just go make sure there is some water over the fire." She moved toward the kitchen as she spoke, aware that Elgin was rising and hurrying to follow her. He had become very proprietary of his kitchen since rediscovering his cooking abilities.

Iliana was stopped by six more women before reaching the kitchen. Three of them were the women from the garden and two were servants from the keep itself. The last was Eda, the plaid man's wife. Iliana assured them all of an opportunity to get at her tub, then burst into the kitchen to find that Elgin already had the water on to heat. He also requested an opportunity in her tub, and Iliana assured him she was pleased to offer him its use.

She was smiling widely when she returned to the great hall. That smile disappeared, her mouth dropping open in surprise as she saw the women all lined up to have a word with her about her tub.

The men were conspicuously absent, but Iliana could

only think it a good thing. 'Twould most like take two or three days to put everyone through the tub as it was.

"What think you?" Iliana held up the hat she had been working on for the other women to inspect. She had tried to fashion the item in the manner of her mother's cook's hat, one he had brought from Paris with him. But this one did not seem to stand up as his did, merely flopping about the wide band that sat on the head.

"Mayhap some starch would do the trick," Ebba suggested from her seat a few feet away, the makings of the apron in her lap.

Iliana perked up at once. "Aye. That may do it," she agreed, then paused as Janna walked into the room, her hair still damp from its washing and a lovely new plaid fastened around her body. Janna had decided to wait till the end of the day to take her turn in the tub, thinking it made more sense to bathe after work than to bathe and return to the gardens in her new plaid. Iliana'd had to agree with her, but promised she would place her at the start of a fresh batch of bathwater. They had been changing the water after every third bather.

The bathers had been waiting in line patiently as one person after another rushed through the tub, then donned their new plaids. Now, almost all were through. Iliana's original fear that it would take days to bathe everyone had been quite wrong. It had helped that Elgin had suggested they set up the tub in a corner of the kitchen, with dirty linens used as curtains to partition off the section. That had sped up the changing of the water somewhat, speeding up the whole process altogether. Now there were two or three dozen children chasing each other about in fresh plaids, their hair shiny and clean and their cheeks pink. Their mothers, meantime, were assisting in the cleaning of the hall tapestries as they chatted by the fire, their hair drying as they worked.

That had been a pleasant surprise for Iliana. Her morning had been taken up with arranging for the plaids and tending to her husband's injury, but she had intended on returning to her work in the gardens that afternoon. In fact, after the nooning meal, she had checked with Elgin to see that all went well with arranging the baths, then headed for the door that led from the kitchens out into the garden. Elgin had immediately hurtled past her, throwing his round little body in front of the door, his arms and legs spread wide to bar the way as he shook his head frantically. He would not see her return to her labor of the day before. She was to rest.

Iliana might have argued with the little man over his obstinate behavior, but his stance had quickly been backed up by Ebba, the women she had hired to work the garden, and even Giorsal and the other servants from the castle itself. Under such unanimous insistence, Iliana had been forced to give in gracefully and retire to the great hall.

Ebba had then suggested she relax by the fire and start work upon the apron she had promised Elgin. The idea of sitting about, plying her needle, had not truly appealed to her. She was eager to finish with the great hall and move her cleaning efforts on to the bedchambers. For that reason, Iliana had decided that finishing cleaning the wall tapestries was a more attractive endeavor.

Unfortunately, the moment she had started to work on the tapestries, several women hurried over. Taking over the task from her, they had claimed they would be "well pleased" to fill their time while waiting for their turn in the tub by helping her with "sech and the like." And why did she not go fix up that apron for Elgin?

Iliana had seemed to have little choice but to turn to that task, but had been less than pleased with the knowledge. It was not that she minded needlework, and she truly wished to see Elgin with an apron to protect his plaid, but she was feeling oddly restless and would have preferred to do something a bit more physical. While she had collapsed from exhaustion the day before, and had still been a bit tired that morning, she found herself oddly energized now. She suspected that it had something to do with the episode in the bedroom but did not wish to ponder the idea too closely.

"All done?" she asked Janna, and the other woman nodded.

"Cook said sup would be ready as soon as he finishes his bath."

"Which should not be long; he was in the tub almost ere ye were out o' it," Giorsal commented dryly.

"Aye." Janna laughed. "I have never seen a man so eager to bathe."

" 'Tis not the bath he is eager fer," one of the women said with amusement.

"Aye," another agreed. "He's gone on all afternoon about his new apron and hat."

Biting her lip, Iliana glanced anxiously at Ebba. Once she and the other women had finished whitewashing the walls, Ebba had offered to assist with the making of the apron. Iliana had handed over the nearly done item, leaving her maid to merely finish the hem, as she herself turned her attention to making the hat. Unfortunately, Ebba had a tendency to chat as she worked and she did seem to find it difficult to concentrate on the two things at the same time. Her work on the apron had gone much slower than it should have. "How much more is there for you to do, Ebba? Mayhap I could help."

"No need, my lady. This is the very . . . last . . . stitch. There. 'Tis done." Breaking the thread, she set it aside and stood, holding up the apron for inspection. "What think you?"

"Perfect."

"He shall love it."

"Cook will be so happy."

Iliana smiled at the excited murmurings of the others and nodded her agreement.

"Oh!"

They all turned toward the kitchen at that excited exclamation. Elgin had finished his bath—surely the fastest in history—and now stood in the doorway of the kitchen in his new plaid, his gaze fixed on the apron Ebba was still holding up.

" 'Tis magnificent!" Charging across the great hall, he ripped the apron from Ebba's hands and held it up as if it was a priceless golden necklace.

"Put it on," Janna suggested when he merely stood staring at it.

"Oh." His smile faded under uncertainty. "But it might get dirty."

Iliana laughed at that. " 'Tis what 'tis for, Elgin. To keep your lovely plaid lovely."

"Oh. Aye." Smiling crookedly, he donned the apron, quickly tying the straps around his waist. Once he was done, Iliana stepped forward and set his hat on his head, fussing with it until it lay in a way she thought suitable. Then the women crowded close, inspecting and complimenting him until he was red in the face.

"What the devil is going on here!"

Everyone in the room turned to stare at Duncan when he bellowed that question. Except Iliana. She took a moment to compose herself first, then started to turn toward him, her expression calm. That calm fled when she found her arm caught up in her husband's hand and herself being dragged toward the stairs. Again.

Chapter Ten

"What do you mean, you *bought* them?"

Iliana shook her head helplessly. She had explained twice now about the coins in her trunk, and how she had used some to purchase the plaids. Twice now Duncan had demanded she repeat herself. She doubted whether explaining again would help.

"Ye bought those spices!" he accused suddenly. "When the food got better, I jest thought that ye had come across a few in the garden. But 'tis not what happened. Ye expressly went against me orders and bought some spices, too, didn't ye?"

"Aye," she admitted on a sigh. "But I did not go against your orders."

"I told ye—"

"Not to purchase them with *your* money," she said triumphantly. "I used the money my mother and father put in *my* trunks."

Rather than become angrier at her words, Duncan seemed to grow suddenly calm, and that made Iliana extremely wary.

"Being an uneducated woman, ye could be forgiven yer lack when it comes to the law, wife—"

"I am not uneducated," Iliana snapped indignantly.

"Ye must be," he snapped back. "Else ye would ken that from the minute we were married, everything ye own became mine. *Everything.*"

"I—" Flushing, Iliana looked away. She *had* known of that rather annoying little law. "You said yourself that the food is better," she said in self-defense.

"Aye." He nodded solemnly. "Elgin's fare is much improved."

"And your people were wearing rags. 'Tis shameful."

"Shameful to who? They have never said 'twas so."

"Mayhap not, but just look how eagerly they bathed to get to wear the plaids."

"You made them *bathe* ere ye would give them these '*gifts*'?" he sneered, and Iliana found herself blushing again, then frowned at her own reaction and lifted her chin. It had been the proper thing to do. It made no sense to put a clean plaid on a dirty body.

"The only ones who bathed to gain their plaids were the women," he said quietly, as if to himself. "And women like to look pretty."

"What is wrong with that?" she asked.

"Nothing. So long as they dinna forget 'tis what's inside that is most important. I would stand next to any one o' me 'filthy' men, ere I would a clean but shallow coward."

Iliana's gaze narrowed. She got the distinct impression he was referring to her. She was no coward. Had she not tried to escape Greenweld three times? Had she not risked a brutal beating, perhaps even death, repeatedly to save her mother? But when she said as much to her husband, he seemed unimpressed.

"Mayhap ye should consider what ye were really risking so much fer," was all he said.

"What do you mean by that?" Iliana asked warily.

"I mean I suspect ye did all that fer yerself as much

as yer mother. Ye don't appear to take well to change.''

"That is the biggest load of cow chips I have ever heard!" Iliana snapped, incensed.

"Is it?" he asked quietly. "Every time ye've done something here, ye've used Wildwood as the excuse. Ye want Dunbar and its people as clean as Wildwood. Ye want spices and herbs like at Wildwood. Ye even have Elgin all got up like yer mother's chef.''

Iliana frowned at his words, uncertainty plucking at her; then she smiled triumphantly. "What of you? I did not—"

"Have anyone in yer bed at Wildwood either, much as it is now. Yer nearly as pure now as when ye came to me.'' Walking to the door, he paused to glance back. "When ye've decided to grow up and accept change as a part o' life, ye can come ask me why a clean plaid is not healthy, or why we bathe so little, mayhap even why we have had few spices in our food. There are reasons. Just as there is a reason ye willna share me bed as a proper wife. There are always reasons, and most often they have little to do with the obvious.''

Iliana watched the door close behind him, then dropped onto the bed with a sigh.

Iliana peered at the sewing in her hands and sighed. Often the activity soothed her. Not tonight. Nothing seemed to be able to settle her tonight. She kept hearing Duncan's words in her head. Was he right? Did she fear change? It was true that she had been trying to make this place and its people more like Wildwood, but it was because . . . Well, because it was better to be clean. And better to wear clean clothes . . . wasn't it? And surely there was nothing wrong with tasty food?

She glanced at the woman seated in the chair across from her. Seonaid. Angus had announced at dinner that the girl was to stay after the meal so that Iliana could teach her some wifery . . . or else. She'd spent the past hour trying to teach the girl how to make a simple stitch, but Seonaid seemed to have no concept of what a small stitch was, no matter how many times Iliana showed her. She suspected the girl was being deliberately obtuse.

Her gaze slid to the tattered old plaid her sister-in-law wore and she sighed. Iliana had offered her a bath and a new plaid, but Seonaid had refused, claiming hers would do quite nicely for a while longer. Now Iliana couldn't help recalling her husband's words. "Why is a clean plaid unhealthy?"

Seonaid glanced up from her sewing blankly. "What?"

"Duncan said clean plaids are not healthy. Why is that?"

"Why do ye not ask Duncan?"

Iliana's lips tightened at that. "Because I am asking you."

Seonaid shrugged and glanced back at the needle in her hand; then, seeming to decide that this was a good way to get out of the fussy task, set it on her lap and turned her attention to Iliana. " 'Tis not that they are unhealthy, 'tis just that a dirty plaid can be *more* healthy. Ye see, while a plaid is muckle warm, 'tis not waterproof. 'Less it's dirty enough."

Iliana blinked at that. "Dirty plaids are waterproof?"

"Sometimes. It depends on what they're dirty with or how dirty they are. Some men grease their plaids soon as they get 'em, to make 'em waterproof."

"I see." Iliana nodded her head at that, then just as quickly shook it. "But why would one need a waterproof plaid? Why not simply stay indoors when 'tis raining?"

Seonaid laughed. "That is fine if ye've nothing to do, but if ye've to watch the sheep, or stand guard, or if yer marching to a war, or on a hunting trip . . ." She shook her head. "There is not always shelter. Sometimes yer plaid is yer only shelter. We even sleep in them at times."

A memory of Duncan wrapping himself in his plaid the

night she had taken the bed linens from the bed suddenly filled Iliana's mind.

"O' course, that is only true fer the men. The women rarely need their plaids to shelter them from the wind and rain. Most oft they're at home warm and dry."

Iliana considered that, then said, "But the McInnes men wear clean plaids. Surely—?"

"The McInnes are'na warriors."

Iliana blinked at that. "They aren't?"

"Nay. They have muckle money, but few men trained fer battle. They hire Duncan and his men if they have need o' warriors."

Iliana accepted that, then asked, "Why do the men hate to bathe?"

" 'Tis cold."

Iliana frowned at the simple explanation. "It may be cold in the loch and out of doors, but 'tis warm inside, and water can be heated for a bath—"

"And then ye'd have to get back into yer dirty plaid," Seonaid pointed out.

Iliana grimaced, then asked, "Why does yer brother not wish the food spiced? It tastes better."

"Aye, and makes oat cakes rather bland in comparison."

When Iliana stared at her blankly, Seonaid sighed. "Duncan has always planned to build an addition onto the keep, and to make the walls extend farther to offer protection to more o' our people. The only way fer him to gain those ends was to earn and save a lot o' coin. To do that, he sold every stitch o' plaid the women weave here, and he and the men hired out fer other people's wars, or to stand guard over other people's flocks. 'Tis hard work. It gets cold at night and the men must put up with bugs, foul weather, and naught but oatcakes fer food. 'Tis not so bad when the alternative is a drafty old keep, with bland food. But next to a warm great hall with clean rushes and tasty food the outdoors seem unbearable."

"He's afraid they'll go soft," Iliana realized, and Seonaid nodded. "But, now that he has my dowry, he can afford all that. There is no need to hire out the men or—"

"The dowry will be enough to pay for the renovations he wishes, 'tis true. But we must continue to make money somehow to feed our people. No doubt he will still have to hire out the men and sell plaid. Just not as often." Shrugging, she turned grimly back to her sewing.

Iliana sat back with a sigh, her gaze far off as she considered what she had just learned. After what Seonaid had said, she could well understand her husband's annoyance with her over the changes she had made, but had no idea what to do about it. She could hardly tell Elgin to stop spicing the food. He would pitch a fit at the suggestion, as would everyone else now that they had sampled the tastier fare. She supposed she could stop insisting that the men must take a bath to gain their plaids.

A frustrated mutter drew her gaze back to her sister-in-law. The girl had her thread in a terrible knot. Before she could comment or offer help, Seonaid slapped it down onto her lap and peered at her solemnly. "Ye ken that I'm useless at this stuff."

"Nay," Iliana protested at once. "You are simply unpracticed at it."

She rolled her eyes, then sighed. "Is it very important for a wife to ken how to do this?"

Iliana hesitated briefly. "I do not know. 'Tis expected, but . . ." She paused and bit her lip, and Seonaid gave a growl of frustration.

"*Expected.* I am no good at any of the things *expected.* 'Tis the truth I remember nothing ye told me about herbs this morning, and I have no clue what needs to be doin' in a keep. I shall make a terrible wife. 'Tis no wonder Sherwell never came for me."

Iliana felt her heart clench at those pained words and immediately sought to cheer the other woman. "Nay. You shall make a wonderful wife, Seonaid, and there is much for a husband to admire in you. Why, just look at your skill in . . . with the sword." She nodded her head firmly.

"Well, goodness, any man would be grateful to have a wife capable with the sword."

Seeing doubt in the other woman's eyes, Iliana forced herself to go on. "And then there is your skill at . . . er . . . hunting. Aye, hunting is a most valuable skill. You shall never go hungry." She nodded vigorously again to back that up. "And, why, I have never seen a woman ride as well as you do. Never. 'Tis a most valuable skill."

"Yer a very poor liar." When Iliana deflated at the gentle accusation, Seonaid smiled slightly. "But 'twas kind of you to do so, me sister."

Iliana blinked at the title in surprise, then brightened. "We *are* sisters now, are we not? My goodness, I have ever wanted a sister to play with. I often thought that. . . ." Sighing, she smiled wryly at the wistful sound to her own voice and shook her head as she sank back in her seat.

"Who *did* you play with?" Seonaid asked curiously.

Iliana blinked at the question. "Well, I played with . . . well, I did not really play much. I was busy you see, with classes and—" Seeing the pity on the other woman's face, Iliana frowned and shook her head. "I really had a fine childhood. I had the best dresses, the best tutors . . . I had everything."

"Everything but friends. Ye were lonely."

Iliana shook her head at once. "I had my parents. They loved me very much and I spent most of my time with them."

"Mayhap, but they had each other. Ye must have felt like the third wheel on a hand cart."

"I . . . do not . . ."

"'Tis all right. I am sorry if I upset ye, 'twas just thinkin aloud I was doing. But, ye see, it explains a lot about ye to me."

"What does it explain?" Iliana asked warily, and Seonaid shrugged.

"Yer very quiet. Ye hardly speak at all sometimes except to give orders and such. It makes ye seem standoffish, but I think now 'tis just shyness. Ye've no experience at socializing except with your parents.''

When Iliana's eyes widened in surprised acknowledgment of the truth of those words, Seonaid seemed encouraged to go on. "And then there is the way ye take charge.''

"Take charge?'' Iliana said, dismayed.

"Aye. The mornin' after ye arrived here, ye took over running the place. Not that there is anything wrong with that,'' she added quickly at Iliana's alarm. "The place needed taking charge of, but ye didn't e'en think to ask was anyone else in charge. Ye just set to. Ye must not have had to share yer toys as a child.''

When Iliana opened her mouth, then closed it again helplessly, Seonaid peered down at her failed attempt at mending, then sighed. "I shall never master this,'' she muttered, tossing it aside and getting to her feet. "Thank ye fer tryin' to teach me, though. I am to bed.''

Iliana watched her go, then sank back in her seat to consider all the woman had said. She hardly noticed when her eyes began to slip wearily closed.

"Elgin, do you have any idea what is going on?'' Iliana asked in exasperation as she slammed into the kitchen late the next morning.

Elgin straightened from the pastry dough he was rolling out and raised his eyebrows at her question, nearly making Iliana laugh aloud. The man's apron and hat were impeccably clean, both items as pristine as they had been when he had donned them the night before. However, his face was smudged with at least three different cooking ingredients.

Smiling slightly, she sank onto a stool beside his work table. She had awoken alone in bed again that morning. Apparently, Duncan had again carried her up to bed and undressed her. Embarrassed by that fact, she had dressed herself quickly and hurried below to join the household as they sat down to breakfast.

It had taken Iliana several minutes to notice the tension in the room. Angus had been in a foul mood and surly to both Seonaid and Duncan, though he had managed a weak smile and "Good morn" for Iliana. But both Seonaid and Duncan had been in foul tempers and surly with everyone, including herself. Iliana had merely sighed over that. It had not been difficult for her to realize what was wrong with them.

Angus had again insisted that Seonaid would learn lessons in proper behavior. She was to accompany Iliana throughout the day. Seonaid, understandably, was not happy about that.

Duncan, on the other hand, was just plain surly. Iliana was becoming used to that. What had her thoroughly flummoxed was what was wrong with everyone else, for the Dunbar chief and his children were not the only ones whose moods were suffering today. It seemed as if everyone in the keep was angry. Even the women who worked in the garden with her . . .

Iliana grimaced at the memory of her morning. She had planned on helping the women again today. Seonaid had quickly put paid to that. It seemed Angus had lectured everyone on his concern with her health, so Iliana had spent the morning overseeing the work in the garden and instructing Seonaid in the uses of herbs. Not a very satisfying task, since she had few samples to show her, and could only give her names of herbs and what they were useful for.

Judging by the way the women had been hacking at the ground and snarling at each other, Iliana had decided that everyone was very definitely angry about something. She simply had no idea what it could be, so when Seonaid had excused herself to find the privy, Iliana had decided to take the opportunity to question Elgin.

"I do not ken what ye mean, me lady."

Shrugging, Iliana began to write her initials in the excess flour on the tabletop. "Everyone seems so unhappy

138

today. The women are sniping and snarling at each other and . . ." She shrugged again helplessly.

"Aaaah. Well, me lady, that would be because o' the plaids."

Her head shot up at that. "What?"

He nodded apologetically. "Ye see, the plaids usually come in January, the same day as the men usually bathe. Everyone bathes that day, and everyone dons their new plaid that day. But this time only the women have them. And meself. And only the women and meself bathed."

When Iliana stared at him, Elgin shrugged. "The men stink."

"The men—"

"Stink," he repeated succinctly. "They also refuse to bathe and stop stinking. And last night when everyone went to their beds, most o' the husbands, impressed no doubt by how fine their wives looked and smelled, thought to . . . er . . . indulge themselves," he said meaningfully. "But the wives, impressed with how unfine the husbands looked and smelled down to the very last one, told their husbands to . . . er . . . go take a bath."

"I see," Iliana said faintly, taken aback at the trouble she had started, despite the support the women had unknowingly given to her own silent protest.

"Aye. There was fighting all over the keep last night."

"I heard not a word."

"Aye, well, most o' it was not fit fer a lady to hear anyway."

"Mayhap I should just give the men their plaids?" Iliana murmured uncertainly.

" 'Tis not the plaids themselves that are the problem, me lady," he pointed out gently. " 'Tis not as if they wear them when they—" Pausing, he flushed and shrugged.

"Aye, you are right, of course." Sighing, she underlined her initials in the flour and stood, pausing when Elgin suddenly leaned forward to change the W she had written to a D.

139

"Yer a Dunbar now, me lady," he reminded gently as she stared blankly at the letters on the tabletop—somewhat surprised that he could even read.

" 'Tis something me wife has difficulty recalling. I thank ye fer remindin' her, Elgin."

Groaning inwardly, Iliana raised her head slowly to meet Duncan's furious gaze.

"I'd be having a word with ye, *wife*." His emphasis of the title was added with biting sarcasm.

Avoiding Elgin's eyes, Iliana got reluctantly to her feet, mumbled her excuses, then moved to stand in front of Duncan. The minute she came to a halt, he grabbed her arm and turned to drag her out of the kitchen.

Seonaid was crossing the great hall toward the kitchen door when they came through it. She looked once at Duncan's furious face, then raised an eyebrow in Iliana's direction.

"Duncan wishes to talk to me. I won't be a minute," Iliana assured Seonaid as Duncan dragged her past the other woman.

"She'll be quite a while," her husband corrected. "So ye might as well go about yer business."

After a hesitation, Seonaid started to follow them, muttering, "She's supposed to be teaching me wifery. How long do ye plan to keep her?"

"Long enough to teach *her* some wifery," was his grim response.

"Nay, Duncan!" Seonaid cried in alarm. "Yer not to wear her out. Da said—"

"Da can get his own wife," Duncan snarled, charging up the stairs, pulling Iliana behind him. She had time only to throw a vaguely reassuring smile at Seonaid before the great hall was out of sight and Duncan was opening the door to their room.

"In." It was a silly order; he was already propelling her through the door and toward the bed as he spoke. But Iliana kept her thoughts to herself as she bounced onto the bed to the sound of the door being slammed shut.

"Ye've done naught since arriving here but make a nuisance o' yersel'!" he shouted, crossing the room to loom over her. "Ye've disobeyed every order I've given ye. Wasted money on luxuries better done without! And refused me me rights as husband." He glared at her bitterly as he said that, then added, "If that were not bad enough, now ye have every wench in the clan pitted against her own man. What have ye to say fer yersel'?"

Iliana sat up slowly on the bed, frantically searching her mind for the correct response. "I am sorry," she offered helplessly at last, and Duncan gaped at her.

"Yer sorry?"

"I'll give the men their plaids. They need not bathe."

"*That* is yer answer? That will not put the women back in their beds."

"Well . . ." She stared at him helplessly for a moment, then allowed her frustration to rouse her own temper. "Nay, you are right. It will not. No woman wishes to sleep with a stinking, filthy oaf of a man unless she herself stinks so bad she does not notice his stench." She glared at him, chin up. " 'Tis understandable. It seems I am not so different from everyone else."

"Are ye not? Well, I would be reminding ye we did not have this problem ere ye arrived."

"That's because the women stunk then, too."

He glared at her. "The men are all comin' to me, looking fer the answer. They wish to ken if I have the same problem with *ye,* and wha' I do about it."

Iliana shrugged. "What did you tell them?"

"I told them ye caused this problem and ye would fix it. Now . . ." He propped his hands on his hips and raised his eyebrows. "What are ye going to do about it?"

Iliana glared back, then shook her head in bewilderment. "I do not understand why you all do not simply take a bath. If you and the men would simply bathe—"

" 'Tis only the middle of June."

"Aye, I know it is, but surely—"

"We have a certain order here, wife. There is a certain

time o' year that the sheep are sheared, a certain time o' year that the fields are reaped, and a certain time o' year that we take a bath.''

"Bathing is not a seasonal activity, husband. You could bathe anytime and not suffer for it. You could not harvest the fields at any time. They are two entirely different things.''

"Ye don't ken what I am saying—''

"Aye, I do!'' Iliana snapped, then sighed. "Seonaid explained to me about the plaids and how grease and dirt keep out the rain. She explained about oatcakes on marches. I understand that you fear the men going soft, but what of the women?''

He blinked at that. "What?''

"Are you not lord over all who reside here?''

"My father—'' he began, but Iliana cut him off with irritation.

"Do not quote semantics at me, husband. Legally and technically 'tis true your father is laird here, but in reality you are the one to give the orders. I have seen it. Do you not rule over the women as well as the men?''

"Aye.''

"Then why do you not concern yourself with the welfare of the women as well? 'Tis all well and fine that the men must brave the weather and make do with oatcakes while on marches, but what of the women?''

When he merely frowned at her, Iliana sighed.

"Could there not be a compromise? Could the men not have two plaids? One that is clean and pleasant to look upon while they are here at the keep with their wives, and one that is greased and dirty to protect them from the elements when away?''

Duncan glared at her for the suggestion. "Things have worked well enough the way they have been for years, wife. There is no need fer—''

"Who is the coward afraid of change now?'' Iliana interrupted dryly. Then she rolled to the side of the bed, gained her feet and headed for the door, only to be caught up by Duncan as she moved past him.

"I am not finished with ye yet."

"But *I* am finished with *you!*" Iliana said coldly. Tugging her arm out of his hold when it slackened in surprise, she hurried to the door. She had it open and was rushing down the hall before he regained himself.

"Wife!" he roared, starting after her.

Muttering under her breath, Iliana grabbed up her skirt and raced down the stairs to the great hall, nearly colliding with her father-in-law in the process. Iliana paused long enough to give him a nervous smile and quick curtsy, then skirted around the man and hurried to the kitchen.

"Duncan!"

"Not now, Da!" Duncan snapped, maneuvering around the older man and sparing barely a moment to spear his sister with an accusatory glare before chasing after his wife.

Iliana cast Elgin a nervous smile as she charged through the kitchen, intent on escaping to the gardens. Her steps didn't slow until she pushed through the door and came upon the women, chattering away in the garden as they worked. It seemed her absence had loosened their tongues. While they had been silent and grim all morning, now they were chattering away like magpies.

"And then the smelly fool just stood there naked, bellowing like a sick cow."

"What did ye do?" Janna gasped, seeming totally enthralled by the older woman's story.

"I yelled right back. *'Ye'll not be touchin' me, Willie Dunbar!'* I says to 'im. *'Not til ye take a bath!'* "

"What did he say?"

" *'Yer me wife, Mavis Dunbar, and ye'll be seeing to me needs or else. 'Tis yer duty.'* "

"Nay!" Janna clucked with disgust. "Sean said the very same thing to me! I'd like to have brained 'im."

"I *did* brain Willie."

Janna gaped at the older woman in disbelief. "Nay! Ye dinna! What did he do then?"

"Slept the night through with nary another peep out o' him."

Her jaw dropped at that. "What did he do when he woke this morn?"

"Naught. I told him he'd too much to drink last night and passed out drunk on the floor."

"Ye didna! Oh, Mavis, yer awful." She shook with laughter. "I could never brain Sean."

"Aye, well, yer Sean's a different kettle o' fish than me Willie. He'd never raise a fist to ye."

"Nay, he wouldn't," Janna agreed solemnly, sadness on her face as she peered at the older woman. "Why do ye not tell Duncan about Willie, Mavis? He'd tend to him fer ye."

"I told ye, Janna, Duncan cares little if we women are happy, so long as the men have no complaint and will follow him off to battle."

Janna opened her mouth to respond, then froze, catching sight of Iliana. Fear crossed the woman's features, and Iliana opened her mouth to quickly reassure her that all would be well. But before she could, the scuff of a footfall drew her gaze around to see Duncan standing behind her. The shock on his face told Iliana that he had heard the whole conversation. She actually managed to feel sorry for him. Then his face closed up and he whirled away, rage oozing from every pore of his body as he headed back the way he had come.

"Oh, lord."

Biting her lip, Iliana glanced back at a worried-looking Mavis and tried to offer a reassuring smile. "He is not mad at you, Mavis. There is nothing to fear."

"Aye," Janna agreed, sighing. " 'Tis my guess it's Willie who should be worrying."

Iliana's eyes widened at that; then she muttered under her breath and hurried after her husband, aware that the women were dropping their hoes to follow.

Chapter Eleven

Duncan had already exited the kitchen by the time she reached it. Rushing past a startled Elgin, Iliana hurried to the door that still swung slightly from her husband's exit and pushed through into the great hall. She was just in time to catch a glimpse of his stiff form as, ignoring his father's startled questions, he slammed out of the keep.

"What the devil?" Angus stared after his son with astonishment, then glanced toward Seonaid, who only shrugged in bewilderment. Duncan had looked furious. The swish of the kitchen door opening caught his ear and brought him around in time to step out of the way as Iliana charged by in pursuit of her husband.

"Lass! What—" he began, but she was already charging out of the keep.

"What the devil," Angus repeated and took a step after her, only to pause when several women crashed through the kitchen door and raced across the room with Elgin hard on their heels. Catching the roly-poly little man, Angus drew him to an abrupt halt, demanding, "What goes on here?"

Elgin shook his head in bewilderment. "I don't ken, me laird. First they rushed one way, now they rush another. But judging from everyone's expressions, 'tis not something to be missed." With that, he hurried on.

Muttering under his breath, Angus took up the tail end of this odd parade, gesturing for Seonaid to follow.

Grabbing up her skirts, Iliana sped after her husband as he charged toward the men working on the wall. Her steps slowed, and dismay made an O of her mouth a moment later when Duncan reached them, grabbed a tall burly fellow by the scruff of his neck, and tossed him to the ground.

The man was up at once, ready to defend himself. But he lowered his fists in confusion when he saw through his rage that his assailant was Duncan.

"Me laird?" was all he managed to ask before Duncan plowed his fist into the fellow's face.

Muttering under her breath, Iliana gathered her skirts closer and hurried forward again. By the time she had reached the practice area, the men had formed a circle around the two combatants, their expressions a combination of curiosity and excitement as Duncan yelled at Willie Dunbar.

Iliana had to push her way between and around the larger bodies to reach the inner fringe. She paused there, worrying her lip anxiously as she saw Willie rise again, only to be knocked down once more. It was the gasp behind her that made her look to see that Janna, Mavis, and the other women had followed her through the crowd and were even now being joined by Elgin, Lord Angus, and Seonaid.

"Get up! Get up and fight like a man, ye coward!"

Duncan's bellow drew Iliana's gaze back around.

"What be the matter, me laird?" Willie was asking as he got warily back to his feet. "I don't ken—" His words broke off when Duncan snatched him by the collar and drew him close.

146

"Ye've been raisin' yer fists to Mavis. A woman half yer size and less than that in strength." Willie speared his wife with accusing eyes and Duncan gave him a shake. "She didn't tell me. I overheard it."

His words had little effect on Willie's venomous glare, so Duncan shook him again. "And ye'll not be punishing her fer me kenning. Fer every blow ye dare to give her, I'll be giving ye ten o' these." With that, he released the man's collar and smashed a fist into his face again. This time, Willie was prepared for the blow. He stumbled backward but did not fall. He even managed to bring his fists up and get in a retaliatory blow before Duncan backhanded him, then punched him in the stomach.

Iliana winced at the whoosh of air Willie expelled as he stumbled backward, then grimaced as Duncan slammed his fist into his jaw with enough force to knock the man senseless. He stood there for a moment, panting over the unconscious man, then turned to glare at the others gathered around.

"Any one o' ye who raises a fist to a woman'll receive the same and well ye'll deserve it, fer only a coward beats on someone so much weaker than himself." His gaze landed on Iliana then, and his mouth tightened briefly before he turned away and pushed through the crowd, headed for the stables.

Iliana started after him, only to be held back by Angus.

"Leave him go. He needs time to himsel' to calm down." His gaze slid to the unconscious Willie Dunbar and he shook his head on a sigh. "Duncan never could stomach bullies."

"May I go to him, me lady?"

Iliana glanced at Mavis in surprise when she asked the question, but nodded. "Aye. If you have a wish to."

The woman gazed at her unconscious husband with pity. "Fer good or bad, he's me husband. 'Sides, I don't think he'll be eager to raise his fists to me again."

"Nay," Iliana agreed quietly, and the other woman moved to her husband's side.

147

Angus glanced at Iliana's worried face as she peered toward the stables into which Duncan had disappeared, then urged her toward the keep. "Rabbie has a muckle o' manure he was wonderin' if ye would like fer yer garden."

Iliana frowned at him, distracted. "Rabbie?"

"The stablemaster," Janna reminded, falling into step on her other side.

"Aye. He cleans the stables every other day or so and has been collecting the manure at the back o' it," Angus told her. "He wondered if ye would like some o' it."

"Oh. Aye," she murmured. " 'Twould be helpful."

"I'll have a couple o' men bring some up to the garden after lunch then. That way it'll be handy when yer ready fer it."

"Thank you," Iliana murmured.

Nodding, Angus glanced toward Seonaid, who was sidling toward the stables. "Daughter!"

Duncan's sister froze in her tracks, then turned reluctantly toward her father.

"I believe the gardens are this way," he said pointedly.

Grimacing, Seonaid slumped and moved back toward them.

"Ye're not suppose to be workin' hard."

Iliana sighed at those words from her sister-in-law. Straightening, she brushed the hair back from her face and peered at the sun overhead. It had been more than twenty-four hours since the incident in the bailey that had sent Duncan charging off on his horse. Iliana still did not know where he had gone, only that he had left the castle and ridden off alone into the woods.

She had not been surprised when he did not appear for lunch, but had begun to fret when he was not at sup either. Angus, Seonaid, and Janna had all assured her that he would be fine, but she had found herself oddly worried about him. Iliana was sure he could take care of himself, but he had appeared oddly vulnerable to her when she had first seen him standing on the path to the garden. The conversation he had overheard had appeared to truly stun him. Iliana suspected it had to do with Mavis declaring that he cared little for the well-being of the women of his clan. She supposed the comment had hit too close to what she herself had accused him of only moments earlier.

Oddly enough, rather than being pleased that her own opinion had been supported, however unintentionally, Iliana wished it were not so. She did not truly believe Duncan did not concern himself with the welfare of the women. Instead, she suspected that, having been raised with very little female company after the age of five, he had simply never realized the lack of comfort and warmth of his home. He simply was not aware of what he had been missing.

Worried as she had been, Iliana had found it hard to sleep last night and had been disappointed and anxious when she went down to breakfast and there was still no sign of him. When Duncan had finally shown up for the nooning meal, she had been terribly relieved to see him hale and healthy, but even more worried by his silent and sullen air. It had been obvious that he had not yet gotten over yesterday's incident. Iliana had not known what to say to ease his anger. Perhaps there was nothing she could say.

"Ye should sit in the shade an' rest."

Rolling her eyes, Iliana turned on the other woman. "I am not working hard," she argued for the tenth time since announcing that she would help to plant the garden that day. "I am planting seeds. 'Tis not hard work."

Seonaid glowered at her briefly, then turned back to the seeds she herself was burying in the newly turned soil, muttering under her breath as she did.

Iliana caught Janna's anxious expression.

"Me lady, the job is sore hard on the back. Mayhap ye should rest a bit and—" She paused as Iliana shook her head in disgust.

"You all behave as though I were made of feathers and might blow away in the first wind. I am young, healthy, and strong. I will be fine."

"But ye fainted," the servant pointed out.

"Aye, ye did," Seonaid agreed. "Ye aren't as well as ye like to think."

"I am not ill," Iliana said firmly.

"Mayhap she's with child," Mavis suggested, bringing a scowl to Iliana's face. The older woman had returned to the gardens that morning, announcing that Willie was too ornery to deserve her care. The man had risen at dawn this morning with a splitting headache and complained about it incessantly. Other than that, Mavis had said little about the incident that had seen her husband carried to his bed and sent Duncan riding off into the woods on his own.

"I am not with child," Iliana muttered impatiently, then grimaced and glanced toward the small hill of manure beside her as its putrid smell wafted to her nose. As promised, Angus'd had two men cart the manure the stablemaster had offered her to the garden yesterday afternoon. They'd dumped it at the base of the garden, putting it within easy reach for spreading once they were ready for it. Unfortunately, Iliana kept forgetting about the blessed thing and had stepped it every time she had reached the end of a row of seeds. As she had this time, she saw with a sigh.

She was about to step to the side, away from the pile, when a buzzing by her ear brought her head up warily. A bee was buzzing ominously about her.

Frowning, she waved a hand in front of her face and stepped instinctively backward as the bee swooped at her.

"Me lady!"

Iliana had a glimpse of Janna's dismayed face and realized at once her mistake, but 'twas too late. The manure beneath her feet was slick and wet, and her slippers immediately skidded on the sloppy ground. She twisted frantically, trying to save herself, and instead managed to send

150

herself sideways into the mire of the oozing, smelly muck.

Janna, Mavis, and Seonaid rushed forward at once, gasping and gagging as they grabbed at her hands to pull her free of the mire, but the ground was slippery with the stuff. Janna and Mavis both had her by the hands and were dragging her back to her feet when those feet skidded out from beneath her again. This time when she fell she took both women with her. They landed in the manure beside her with dismayed squeals. Seonaid joined them a split-second later as Janna's flailing legs caught her at the ankles and swept them out from beneath her.

The smell was putrid, the feel disgusting. Iliana was nearly in tears as she struggled to her knees in the goo and crawled to the edge of the pile. Reaching the good clean dirt, she regained her feet, and turned back toward the hill. Janna and Mavis, too, had struggled to their feet and were slip-sliding together out of the manure, while Seonaid was simply lying where she had landed, laughing so hard she could not seem to move.

Iliana shook her head at the other woman in exasperation but could not contain a small smile herself as she peered at her companions. Janna's red hair was red no more. 'Twas a muddy brown, with great clumps of horse dung hanging from it. Her lovely new plaid was in a similar state. As was Mavis, who also had a great smear of the stuff down one side of her face. Both women stood, arms akimbo, heads bent as they peered with disgust at themselves. 'Twas not a picture Iliana would soon forget, she decided, shaking her head with amusement and turning back toward the pile and a still laughing Seonaid.

Stepping to the edge of the pile again, she braced herself and reached out a hand to her sister-in-law. Sobering slightly, Seonaid took the offered hand and tugged even as Iliana lurched backwards. Between the two of them, they got her to her feet and managed to lurch several feet away from the manure.

"Ugh!" Janna muttered, shaking her arms and watching the dung fly.

"Gor!"

" 'Tis disgusting!"

"Putrid."

"I smell like a—"

"Privy?" Iliana supplied dryly.

Janna paused and glanced up at Iliana, then suddenly burst out laughing. "Oh, me lady!" She tried to stem her laughter and replace it with an apologetic expression, but failed. " 'Tis sorry I am, me lady. But yer hair, yer lovely hair looks—"

"Like yours?" Iliana suggested wryly, a small smile tugging at her lips.

"No doubt," came the self-deprecating laugh, then she groaned as she caught a good whiff of herself. "I smell worse than Sean now."

"And I worse than Willie." Mavis muttered. They shared a wry glance; then Janna suddenly perked up, mischief playing on her face.

"I think I'll find him an' plant a nice big kiss on his lips . . . if he doesna fight me off first."

"Do not let him," Iliana suggested lightly. "Mayhap he'll be willing to take his bath early."

"Aye, mayhap." Janna grimaced as she peered down at herself. "If ye'll excuse me, me lady?"

"And me?"

"Aye, of course." Iliana watched the two women go, then glanced toward Seonaid, who was scraping dung from her legs and feet with her sword. "Would you like first crack at my bath?"

"Nay. The loch is good enough fer me."

"As you wish." Iliana turned toward the keep, only to pause. She could not, would not, go through the kitchen like this. Sighing, she headed around the building. Much to her amusement, no one seemed to notice the state she was in as she hurried to the front door of the keep and rushed inside. It was not until she came across Ebba on her way upstairs that she got any reaction at all.

"My lady!"

Iliana smiled at the servant's dismayed expression as she passed her on the stairs. "Aye, Ebba. I shall need a bath."

"At once, my lady."

Iliana was in her room before her own words struck her. "Mayhap he would be willing to take a bath early." Pausing by the bed, she began to worry her lip. Every night she had watched her husband remove his clothes, piece by piece, and every night she had felt a stirring within her. That stirring had become a constant slow burn within the pit of her belly ever since the morning when he had tried to seduce her. She had alternately suffered regret and relief ever since; grateful for the interruption that had saved her from her own body's wants, yet wondering how it would have felt to experience that satisfaction he had spoken of.

Well, now she smelled at least as bad as he did. His scent would not even be noticeable to her, she was sure. Her smell, on the other hand, might affect him. If it did, mayhap she could persuade him to share a bath with her.

The opening of the door drew her attention as Ebba entered, followed by servants carrying a tub and buckets of water. Iliana waited impatiently until the water was poured and all but Ebba gone, then ordered the woman urgently: "Go fetch my husband, Ebba."

"Fetch . . . ?"

"Aye, at once."

"Aye, my lady." She started for the door, only to pause when Iliana called her back.

"My dress; I will need help removing it."

Wrinkling her nose, she set to the chore until Iliana was naked but for the belt of chastity, then departed.

Iliana immediately rushed to the discarded gown and searched through it for the ring of keys her father-in-law had made up for her. With the dress in a tangled bundle, it took her longer than she had expected to retrieve the blasted keys, but once she had them, she quickly unlocked and removed the belt.

She was just trying to decide what to do with it when she recognized the sound of her husband stomping down the hall. Giving a slight squeal, she rushed to the bed and dove under the linens, uncaring at that moment that they would have to be cleaned ere the night, for while most of the manure had been removed with the dress, there was still some clinging to her hair, arms, and lower legs.

She had just arranged herself in what she hoped was a seductive pose when the door burst open and her husband strode in, obviously irritated.

"What the devil be the matter? Ebba said 'twas urgent. That ye—" The words dried up in his mouth as he spied her clothes lying near the bed and realized she must be nude. His eyes widened incredulously, then his gaze slid to the tub and he stiffened, anger returning. "I see. Yer hopin' to lure me to the tub with the promise o' a tumble. Well, it willna work—" The tirade died when she suddenly held up the chastity belt she still held in her hand. "Gor!"

Duncan was across the room in three strides. With the first, he unfastened and removed the belt holding his sword at his waist. With the second, he gave a yank to his plaid that sent it slithering to the floor. With the third, he was tugging his shirt over his head and tossing it away. Then he was upon her, his mouth on hers before he had even landed fully. His left hand tangled in her hair, holding her head still beneath his as his right hand whipped the linen covering her aside and planted itself firmly at the apex of her thighs. Whether he was checking for the equipment a woman should have Iliana wasn't sure, but the summary action startled her into opening her mouth. He immediately took advantage of that, his tongue sliding easily between her lips and ravishing her.

If this was not quite the reaction she had expected, it certainly had her attention. Her body was not exactly yawning either. Gasping as he took full advantage of his sudden freedom to explore her woman's parts, she sucked frantically at the tongue invading her mouth and arched into the touch examining her so thoroughly, writhing as the investigation became a caress that rubbed her flesh in ways she had never imagined.

When his mouth suddenly left hers to kiss a trail down her neck, she moaned in despair and almost missed his garbled gasp of dismay as he caught a whiff of her.

"Gor!" He pulled away in horror, his nose wrinkled beyond distaste. "What the bloody hell!"

"I fell in manure," Iliana explained quickly, catching his hand when he started to pull away. "But 'tis all right. Now I hardly notice *your* odor." She tried to pull his head down to recapture his lips with hers then, but he was having none of that.

"Ye reek, woman!"

"No worse than you!" Iliana cried defensively, rubbing against him. "Kiss me."

Duncan stared at his wife in dismay for a moment. Then his gaze dropped down over her body, taking in her breasts—nipples painfully erect—before shifting to the spot that had been hidden from him for so long. Part of him wanted to get as far away as possible. The other part, a much lower but louder part, was screaming at him to take advantage of this opportunity. His hand slid of its own accord to one of her breasts and he groaned briefly, then lowered his lips to hers again. Unfortunately, even holding his breath did not keep the scent of her from sneaking through and dragging at his passion.

Cursing, he pulled his lips away, picked her up, and carried her across the room to drop her in the tub, splashing water everywhere. Only she did not let go of him as she fell, as he had expected. Instead, she clung to him like moss to a tree. He nearly fell into the tub with her, but at the last moment caught the edges and saved himself.

Ignoring the betrayed look she wore, he straightened, ordering tersely, "Hurry and bathe."

Iliana glared at him from the tub, then leaned back, crossed her arms, and stared straight ahead, making it obvious she was not going to cooperate.

Scowling, he peered at her body in the clear liquid, then glanced at her face and finally her hair. He could see great chunks of manure in the shiny mass of waves. Shifting, he snapped. ''Hurry up or I'll wash ye meself.''

Her only response was an uncaring shrug.

Cursing once more, Duncan moved to kneel beside the tub and started with her hair. Placing a hand flat on the top of her head, he shoved her downward.

Caught by surprise, Iliana went down like a drunken sailor. The water rushed over her face and hair, flowing into her mouth and nose. She burst from under the water seconds later, spluttering, and splashing water everywhere. Before she had even managed to push the wet tresses out of her eyes, Duncan had taken the soap to her hair and started cleaning the long wet masses. Ignoring her shouts and curses when he got soap in her eyes, he worked away, then pushed her beneath the water again and gave her head a shake to help rinse her of the soap he had applied. Then he released her and straightened.

''There. Now clean the rest o' yerself if ye don't like the way I do it.''

''I cannot see,'' Iliana informed him succinctly, brushing at her burning eyes fretfully.

Sighing, Duncan knelt beside the tub again and took up the soap. Grabbing one arm, he began applying the soap to that. His movements were quick and economical as he cleaned first one arm then the other, and they remained that way until he turned the bar of soap to her chest. Somehow, the swift strokes across her flesh slowed, gentling as the soap disappeared altogether and only his soapy hands moved across her breasts, kneading, caressing, palming.

Eyes still sealed shut against the sting of the soap, Iliana concentrated entirely on his touch, her breathing becoming quick and shallow, her body awakening beneath his caresses. When one hand slid between her legs, Iliana groaned, shuddered, and reached instinctively for him. Bumping her hand into his shoulder, she followed the length of it, wrapping her hand around his neck and whimpering slightly as she begged, "Kiss me. Please, Duncan."

His lips met hers at once, his own breathing shallow as his tongue delved inside. Then he pulled his head away and gasped, "The bed."

Iliana went stiff in his arms, then just as quickly relaxed. "Help me," she breathed against his lips.

Grunting, Duncan half-stood and bent to pick her up. Iliana went easily at first, but after the first three inches or so, suddenly grabbed at the side of the tub, bringing him to an abrupt halt. He had saved himself from falling into the tub the first time because his hands had been free. This time they were not. With Iliana in his arms, there was no way to regain or keep his balance, and he stumbled forward hard.

Iliana immediately twisted in his arms, crying out triumphantly as he landed half atop and half beside her. More prepared for this eventuality than he had been, she quickly shifted atop him, forcing him to sit in the water beneath her.

Smiling, she forced her eyes open somewhat, ignoring the burning sensation that elicited, and reached for the soap. She had just managed to grab it up when he regained himself enough to begin to shift beneath her in preparation of leaping from the tub. Desperate, Iliana immediately reached for and grabbed ahold of his manhood. He stilled at once, shock on his face. She stared back, rather shocked herself, then suddenly released him and threw her arms around his chest, hugging him close.

Duncan started to struggle at once, then paused as the feel of her soapy chest sliding across his own caught his attention. Damn, but it was erotic. Stilling, he let her squish herself against him, becoming aware of the fact that she was sitting on his lap facing him, her lower body pressed intimately to his beneath the water . . . and it felt damn good.

Realizing that he was no longer struggling, Iliana pulled back uncertainly.

"If ye stop, I'll take ye to bed," he warned quietly, and she immediately began searching about in the water for the soap with one hand, while massaging the soap she had spread on his chest with her own body with the other. Finding the soap, she went to work on him at once, cleaning and caressing him all at the same time.

Duncan lay still for quite a while, hardly paying attention to the hands working gently over his shoulders, under his arms, and across his chest. Instead, his attention was focused on the way her lower body shifted constantly against his as she worked, rubbing against him in a rhythmic manner. At first, he thought his innocent wife was unaware of the contact. But when she reached to work on his hair, her face moving closer to his, he noticed that she was nearly panting as she massaged the soap into his scalp. That had an even more interesting effect on him, making his manhood throb where it pressed flat against his belly, held there by her body as she rubbed it over him. Reaching out, he grabbed her breasts, his hands slipping against the sudsy skin as he caressed and kneaded them.

Iliana stilled at once, a groan slipping from her lips before she lowered them to seek out his, sighing happily when he began to kiss her wildly. Fingers knotting in his soapy hair, she pressed closer, the movement of her lower body becoming a bit frantic with the need surging in her. She was completely taken by surprise when he suddenly reached to the side, grabbed a bucket full of water, raised, then tipped it

Gasping into his mouth, she shivered as the cold water cascaded over them. Then she clutched at his shoulders as he shifted abruptly in the tub and lifted her from him, raising her as he got to his feet.

Carrying her dripping wet across the room, Duncan dropped her upon the bed and came down on her, their bodies sliding across each other as he kissed her again.

When he suddenly clasped her hand in his and drew it down to press it against his manhood, Iliana stilled, then tentatively closed her fingers, squeezing gently. His kisses immediately became slightly frantic, suggesting that she might be doing the right thing, so she moved her hand along his flesh still closed, like a sheath sliding off a sword.

Duncan froze at that, gasped into her mouth, then reached abruptly for her hand and tugged it above her head. Holding it there with one hand, he reached down and began to caress her. His fingers worked frantically, manipulating her into a fevered need until she arched against him, crying out against his lips. When she did that, he shifted suddenly and plunged inside her.

Iliana cried out in shock as a sharp, abrupt pain forced her eyes open. She stared into her husband's eyes, confusion, shock, and pain flitting across her face, and Duncan groaned.

" 'Tis the breachin'," he gasped apologetically. " 'Tis best done quick."

Iliana nodded uncertainly and he sighed, his forehead dropping to rest on hers. "Tell me when the pain has passed."

Iliana cleared her throat. " 'Tis passed," she murmured with a little embarrassment, and he raised his head, peering at her questioningly.

"Truly?"

She nodded, but still he hesitated. Then, reaching between them, he touched her again, his fingers gentle as they slid across her velvet skin.

Biting her lip, Iliana met his gaze, wishing he would kiss her, but he did not. Instead, he watched her as he rekindled the fires he had started earlier, watching her eyes glaze, passion pulling her face taut as she began to shift beneath his touch. His movements became quicker as she bit her lip and moaned, and he shifted his hips as well, intensifying the sensations she was experiencing. It was only moments later that they both cried out and Iliana experienced that satisfaction of which he had spoken.

Chapter Twelve

"My lady!"

"Mmmm?" Opening her eyes, Iliana peered toward the door, frowning when her husband's bulk blocked her view. Then, as memories of how he had come to be there ran through her head, she smiled and pushed herself onto an elbow to peer at the woman who stood in the doorway. To say that Ebba looked shocked as she took in the state of the room and her lord and lady abed together, was an understatement. It was only then that Iliana noticed that there now appeared to be more water on the floor than in the tub. 'Twas a horrible mess. And Iliana didn't particularly care at that moment. She'd had far too much fun putting it there to care.

Pushing the hair out of her eyes, she smiled widely. "What is it, Ebba?"

"What? Oh! Your mother, my lady. She is approaching the keep."

"Mother?" Leaping from the bed, Iliana rushed for the chests containing her clothes. Sliding the last few feet in a puddle of water, she jarred her knee against the wooden chest and cursed, then threw it open and grabbed the first undertunic she came across. Pausing then, she whirled suddenly. "You are sure?"

"Aye, my lady. Johnny-Boy arrived at the keep but a few moments ago with the news of where she is. He's waiting to take you back to her."

"Johnny-Boy?" Iliana murmured the name as she tugged the undertunic on over her head. He was the son of her mother's maid. "Why did she not simply ride up to the keep herself?"

Ebba shrugged as Iliana pulled a gown out of the chest and tugged it on. "Lord Angus sent me to fetch ye soon as Johnny-Boy spit that part out. I didn't hear the rest."

"Tell his lordship I shall be down directly I am finished dressing."

Nodding, Ebba backed out of the room as Iliana searched her chest for hose. Finding a pair of green ones, she carried them quickly to the bed and sat on the end of it to begin putting them on, only to pause and whirl about as her husband suddenly lunged upright. She thought at first he must have suffered a night terror that had startled him awake, but as he continued forward until he could grab her, then started to fall back, taking her with him, she realized that he must have awakened while Ebba was in the room and waited until now to reveal the fact.

Squealing, she grabbed for the bedpost, but he was faster. She ended lying flat on her back as he shifted atop her. Iliana opened her mouth to protest then, but Duncan was not interested in hearing it. His mouth came down atop hers and his hands began roaming so fast and in so many directions it made her dizzy.

"Husband!" she managed at last when he finally freed her mouth, only to bite down on her lower lip when he jerked her unlaced neckline aside and clamped his mouth enthusiastically on one of her nipples. She caught her breath and tried again, but gave it up and squeezed her eyes shut as he rucked up her skirts and snaked one hand down between her legs to set about stoking her fire.

"Oh, my lord," she breathed with a mixture of shock and pleasure as her body immediately burst back to heaving life beneath his ministrations. "Oh my . . . oh dear . . . Oh, Mother," she moaned, then popped her eyes open as she recalled what she was trying to tell him. "M-mother!" she gasped. "Nay! Please, husband. My mother is here. I needs must—"

"Worry not, wife," he muttered, raising himself away from her breasts to kneel between her legs. "We shall make it quick so you can get below and greet her."

"Quick?" Iliana asked, then gasped as he raised her hips and slid into her.

He paused then to frown at her a bit worriedly and ask, "Are ye tender?"

Flushing with embarrassment, she shook her head quickly.

"Not at all?"

"Nay, but—" The word ended on a grunt when he grabbed her legs by each ankle and tugged them up over his shoulders as he drove deeper into her.

"Good," he groaned, holding her tightly to him briefly before withdrawing slightly and pounding back into her again. "Damn me, yer so tight."

Iliana bit her lip uncertainly. "Is that bad?"

"Nay, nay. 'Tis good. Too damn good, and I have waited too damn long. Hook yer ankles, sweetling."

"Hook my—?"

"Aye, help me hold ye up," he muttered, his face a picture of pain. "Hook yer ankles behind me head."

Iliana did as instructed, then moaned herself and arched into him when he released one hand from holding her hips and moved it between them to caress her again.

"That's it, sweetling," he muttered, urging her to move against him with the one hand still at her hip. "That's it. That's . . . Damn!"

Iliana hardly heard his curse as he poured himself into her. She was too taken up with the waves of feeling that were crashing through her own body as she succumbed to his touch and the feel of him inside her. She was still shuddering with it when he slid her legs gently off his shoulders and collapsed atop her, crushing the gown that was bunched up at her waist.

" 'Tis sorry I am, wee Iliana," he groaned as soon as he could catch his breath.

"Do not be," Iliana gasped back. "I liked it. We must try this quick one again."

A knock at the door had them both peering toward it. Duncan sighed, then growled, "Aye?"

The door opened to reveal Angus. Embarrassment flushed his face as he saw what he had walked in on. Then it was replaced by anger, apparently at having his suspicions confirmed. "Damn ye, Duncan! Ye'll work the poor lass unto death do ye not control yer urges once in a while. Is it not bad enough that the lass gets no rest of a night? Must ye be botherin' her all through the day as well?"

Duncan was amused. "Yer the one who said ye were wantin' grandbabies by nine months' end," he reminded him.

"Well, surely to God ye've planted one in her by now!" the old man snapped. "Ye've certainly been plowin' her enough. Now let the poor lass alone, else she'll not have the strength to survive the birthin'."

Thoroughly embarrassed by this point, Iliana shoved her husband away and leapt from the bed, straightening her gown as she did.

"I need only don my hose, my lord. I'll be along directly," she half-whispered, grabbing the stockings and dropping onto the foot of the bed again to begin tugging them up one leg.

Angus turned his gaze to her, his expression softening along with his voice. "Lass, don't rush yersel' so. A few minutes will not matter so much, and with this muckle brain as a husband ye appear to be needin' whatever strength the Good Lord gave ye." His gaze turned back to Duncan, who was lying exhausted on the bed where Iliana had left him, and he scowled darkly. "Get yer sorry arse out o' bed, man, and dress yersel' quick. Yer wee wife'll need ye."

Iliana stiffened and stared at him at that, but Duncan merely frowned. Unlike Iliana, he had not been taken completely by surprise at the arrival of her mother. Word spread faster in Scotland than a horse could travel, and he and his father had known for several days that Lady Wildwood and two servants were heading for Dunbar. But nothing had suggested she was not in the best of health. Until now.

"Need him?" Iliana asked anxiously. "Is Mother ill?"

Angus hesitated, then sighed. "The servant, Johnny-boy, said she's a muckle mess."

"A muckle mess? What is wrong with her?"

"From what the lad said, yer stepda took his temper to her," he admitted reluctantly.

Gasping, Iliana lunged off the bed and hurried to the door, then whirled back to her chests. After tossing half of one's contents on the floor, she came up with her bag of herbs. Leaving the mess as it was, she hurried out of the room, her hose still on only one leg and dragging on the ground behind her.

Staring after her departing figure, Duncan sighed. "Where does she get the energy?"

"Well, not from any carin' or concern from ye, I can tell ye that much," Angus turned to declare grimly. "Now get up!"

"Oh, 'tis good to see you, my lady!" Johnny-Boy's relief was obvious on his large, weathered face as he rushed to the bottom of the stairs to greet Iliana. Despite his name, Johnny, six foot tall and burly as a barrel, was anything but a boy. He was a good ten years older than Iliana, but had been called Johnny-Boy as a child and somehow, despite the passing years, the name had stuck. "All will be well now."

There was such uncertainty on his face as he spoke that Iliana's anxiety increased tenfold. "How bad is she, Johnny-Boy? He did not take the whip to her?"

"Nay, my lady. Though it may have been kinder had he done so."

When Iliana frowned over that, Johnny-Boy shook his head. "Ma says her ribs are broke, and mayhap her leg. She's not well. Weak. Feverish. Ma was afraid to continue on without a cart or something for her to lie in. Lady Wildwood simply could not ride anymore. She collapsed soon as she knew we were on Dunbar land."

Iliana's legs went weak at that announcement, and she was grateful for Duncan's steadying hand on her arm as he reached her side.

"Did ye order a cart?" Duncan asked Angus as he bent to finish putting his wife's hose on for her.

"Aye," Angus murmured, grabbing Iliana's arm to steady her as Duncan raised her bare foot and stuck it in the hose, then tugged the material upward

Nodding, Duncan straightened and ushered Iliana toward the door, glancing worriedly at her pale face as he did.

Angus had ordered more than a cart. There were twenty mounted men, a cart, and three horses waiting when they started down the stairs. Ebba was already seated in the back of the wagon, her own bag of herbs on her lap.

Hurrying Iliana down the steps, Duncan mounted his horse, then bent and tugged her up before him, barely waiting the moment it took for Angus and Johnny-Boy to mount before turning his beast and heading out of the bailey. Once through the gates, Duncan slowed, allowing Johnny-Boy to take the lead.

Johnny had not been exaggerating when he said Lady Wildwood had collapsed as soon as she had reached Dunbar land. The clearing the man led them to was on the edge of the Dunbar border, a good hour's ride from the keep.

Duncan barely managed to draw his mount to a halt

before Iliana slid out from beneath his arms and dropped
to the ground. She rushed across the clearing to the side
of a haggard old woman who was obviously her mother's
maid before Duncan could finish dismounting.

Her gasp of dismay told him more than anything that
her mother was in a frighteningly bad way. Sharing a grim
glance with his father, Duncan moved to stand behind
Iliana, his own face paling as he took in the state of the
woman lying on the ground.

That she was weak and feverish was obvious—they had
been warned of that—but it was the state of her face that
had shocked Iliana and now had the same effect on Duncan. Greenweld had not satisfied himself with breaking
her body; he had taken his fists to her face as well. The
woman's lip was split, her nose swollen and most like
broken, and she bore two black eyes that a raccoon would
have been proud of. He cringed to think how she must
have looked before setting out on the long journey from
Wildwood.

"The bastard," Angus hissed, pausing beside Duncan.

"Oh, mama," Iliana moaned, reaching a hand toward
the battered face, then drawing it back uncertainly for fear
of hurting her.

Lady Wildwood stirred at the words from her daughter
and struggled to open her eyes, but they were too swollen
to see through. When she opened her mouth to speak, only
a dry croak came out.

"Shh," Iliana murmured, taking the nearest hand. It
appeared to be the only place on the woman that was not
bruised, cut, or swollen. " 'Tis Iliana, Mother. I am here.
We are going to take you to Dunbar. You will be safe
there," she assured her, then glanced toward the hag. Gertie had been with the Wildwoods since Iliana's grandmother's day and had always been maid to the mistress
of the castle, and her wisdom and ability to heal were
reknowned. If anyone could repair the damage done to
Iliana's mother, it was this woman.

Spying the question in her face, the old woman patted

her shoulder. "I have given her something for the fever and pain. She needs rest now."

Nodding, Iliana turned to glance over her shoulder at the wagon rolling into the clearing.

Johnny-Boy immediately moved to pick up his mistress, but Duncan stopped him with a hand on his shoulder. Taking his place, he carefully slid his hands beneath her frail body and gently lifted her. Despite his care, Lady Wildwood moaned in pain as Duncan carried her to the cart.

In the few seconds she had before he reached the wagon, Ebba had done her best to arrange a blanket and bag into as comfortable a bed as she could for the woman. Once Lady Wildwood was settled in the wagon, Iliana started to climb aboard, but Duncan caught her back and gestured to the old woman to mount the cart. Iliana frowned unhappily, but resigned herself to not accompanying her mother. There simply wasn't room for the three of them in the cart.

She made no demur when Duncan led her to his horse, but waited patiently for him to mount the beast, then allowed herself to be lifted before him. She was extremely grateful when he immediately urged his animal to the side of the cart, though, and squeezed his arm to let him know that as they started for the keep.

The hour-long ride out to the clearing became a two-hour trip back as they moved at a crawl to avoid unduly jostling Lady Wildwood. When they finally arrived, Duncan again lifted her mother into his arms. He carried her into the keep and upstairs to their bedchamber, waiting patiently as Iliana and the other two women quickly ripped the soiled linens from the bed, replacing them with fresh ones. Once the chore was finished, Duncan set Lady Wildwood gently down, then quickly found himself nudged away from the bed and ordered from his own chamber as the women set to work.

"I be thinkin ye might want to build those extra rooms ye've been planning fer so long."

Duncan glanced at his father in surprise as they descended the stairs to the great hall. "I thought to leave it 'til I got a bit further along on rebuilding the outer wall. 'Tis no sense in the whole place being in an uproar."

"Hmmm. Well . . . I be thinkin' ye'll be changing yer mind on that soon enough."

When his father said no more, Duncan's frown deepened. "Why would ye be thinkin' that?"

"Well, now, it seems to me, what with Iliana's mother so ill, the lass will insist on her stayin' in yer room. And no doubt she'll insist on sleepin' on the floor in there, so she can keep an eye on her mother."

Duncan came to a halt as the ramifications of the situation hit him. His father was right; Lady Wildwood was now firmly ensconced in his chamber and would be for some time. Which left him without a bed. He would have to sack out on the great hall floor. That did not bother him. He had done it before. But he very much feared his father was also right about Iliana wishing to be near her mother for a while at least. And even once she agreed to leave her mother's side and joined him in the great hall, 'twould be nothing but torture for him. With only the three chambers, the servants were forced to sleep on pallets on the great hall floor. Duncan had no doubt his wife would refuse to even consider letting him love her with the servants so close at hand. Good God, he had just managed to consummate his marriage and already he was being denied again. Impossible!

"Aye." Angus slapped him on the back good-naturedly. "It seems God himself has seen to it that wee Iliana gets the rest she is so sore in need of."

"I'll build a room," Duncan decided grimly. "Tomorrow."

"Ye'd best make it two or three, boy," Angus murmured, enjoying himself.

"Two or three?"

"Aye, well, 'tis thinkin' ahead I'm doing. It seems to me that Lord Rolfe and the bishop will be returning soon with that Sherwell bastard. We can hardly make the bishop sleep on the floor. I gave him my bed last time because it was yer wedding night. I won't be doing it this time. . . . And then there are the bairns.''

"Bairns?"

''Aye. Well, ye've been working at it pretty hard, 'tis sure I am there'll be a babe or two to show fer it soon enough, and as I recall, there was only the one room when yer mother and I married and when ye were first born, ye slept in there with us. 'Twas most inconvenient. Yer mother wouldna tend to me wishes fer worry of yer waking.'' Irritation tugged at the old man's face as he peered at Duncan, as if even now he blamed him for those lost nights. ''Aye, 'tis best to be prepared fer such things. Build on two more rooms, boy. Trust me, ye'll not be sorry.''

It was a mixture of shouting and banging that awoke Iliana. Frowning as the cacophony of sound filled her ears and drew her relentlessly from the deep sleep she had finally dropped into, Iliana slowly forced her eyes open and grimaced at the light that flooded into them.

It was daylight.

That was not at all surprising. The sun had been peeking up over the horizon, painting the room in a grayish orange glow before she had finally allowed Ebba and Gertie to persuade her to leave her vigil at her mother's side and seek some rest on the small straw-stuffed mat they had had placed in the corner of the room for her. She had only agreed then because she had twice caught herself dozing off where she had sat on the side of the bed, and had feared she would doze off, fall forward, and add more damage to her poor mother.

A virulent string of curses sounded from the hallway and Iliana forced her eyes open once more, realizing only then that they had somehow closed again. Frowning at the pain the bright light seemed to send stabbing into her head, she glanced toward the bed to see that Gertie had dozed off in the chair at the side of the bed. Ebba was absent.

Pushing herself slowly to a sitting position, Iliana peered at the woman asleep in the bed. Her mother seemed undisturbed by the racket. She was still sleeping peacefully. That merely made Iliana more worried. Such a deep sleep was not a good sign, was it?

A second string of curses drew her eyes toward the door once more. Her mouth set with displeasure at such a racket occurring outside a sick room. Shoving away the blanket she had drawn over herself when she had laid down, Iliana got stiffly to her feet. Wincing at the pain that immediately shot from the base of her spine, she paused a bare second to stretch. Then she moved toward the door, ready to give someone an earful.

The sight that met Iliana's eyes, however, when she stepped out into the hall stole the angry words that had been bubbling up inside her head. All she could do at first was gape at the small army of men milling about. It looked as if every single man who had been working on the wall and moat had been reassigned and crammed into this small hallway and was working industriously, and noisily, away.

Iliana gaped at them briefly, then, spying her husband at the end of the hall, she set her mouth and strode purposefully toward him.

Duncan was removing another post from the railing that guarded the end of the upper floor when a tap on his shoulder made him stop what he was doing to look around. The sight of his wee bride brought an instinctive smile to his face that faded once he took in her expression. She was smiling, but by the saints, it was one of the coldest smiles he had ever looked upon.

"Husband, what is about?"

Noting that her honey-sweet voice was in definite contrast to her frigid smile, Duncan considered her briefly before admitting, "I thought to extend the upper floor."

"Extend the upper floor?" she asked.

"Aye, well, we'll be havin' a bairn or two soon enough, and I thought that an extra two or three rooms would not go amiss."

Her eyebrows rose at that. "Two or three rooms?"

He shifted uncomfortably. "I thought a room fer yer mother would be nice so she might visit as long as she liked. And then, one can never have too many guest rooms."

"A room for my mother?" Her eyebrows rose slightly at the thoughtfulness of the gesture, then dropped just as abruptly in displeasure. "So you *do* recall that my poor, battered, ailing mother is lying just beyond that door, trying to get some much-needed rest while you and all of your men are out here *making the devil's own racket!*"

The hallway fell into dead silence around them, all eyes turning with some surprise to Duncan and Iliana. But Duncan was oblivious to that. His gaze was fastened on his wife as she roared, drinking in her heaving chest, the glorious color of fury in her flushed cheeks, and the fire in her eyes. Lord almighty, he could recall this same flush of passion about her on the afternoon before, but then it had been from desire. He could also recall her softness afterward, the dreamy look she had worn as she lay pressed against him, her body warm and sated. Feeling his own body responding to those memories, he muttered suddenly and caught one of her clenched hands in his own, then headed abruptly for the end of the hall.

"What *are* you doing?" Iliana snapped, trying to tug her hand free.

"Ye are obviously overset, wife. I would take ye somewhere where we can discuss this in private so that yer screamin' doesn't awaken yer poor ailin' mother. To work, men!" he ordered as he moved.

"*My* screaming?" She gaped at the back of his head as he dragged her along, her ears ringing as the men set back to work, and pounding and sawing filled the air around them. Tugging free, she propped both hands on her hips and glared at him as he paused and turned toward her. "Do you not see that that is why I am out here? All this racket is sure to wake my mother. She needs her rest, Duncan. I—"

"Aye. Yer right. She does. And so she'll have it. Work as quietly as ye can, men. No shoutin' or the like," he instructed, then grabbed up her hand and started out again. This time he got as far as the stairs and halfway down them before Iliana managed to free her hand again. "Duncan! They cannot be pounding and hammering in the hallway while my mother tries to rest. She will wake—"

"Nay, my lady."

Ebba's voice drew both Iliana's and Duncan's eyes to the bottom of the stairs where the other woman now stood looking up at them.

"Gertie gave Lady Wildwood a tincture. A war could not awaken her."

"There ye are, then. See?" Duncan smiled at her widely. "Come. We should discuss this." Sweeping her up in his arms, he hurried down the stairs with her, unwilling to give her the opportunity to free herself again.

Taken by surprise, Iliana could do little but grab at his shoulders nervously as he started out of the keep.

"Husband," she said at last as he hurried toward the stables. "Husband?"

"Aye, sweetling?"

"What are you doing?"

"I told ye, I'm takin' ye somewhere where we can talk without disturbin' yer mo—Oh, damn!" He stiffened suddenly, then broke into a jog, jostling Iliana wildly in his arms as he nearly ran the last few feet to the stables.

Glancing sharply around, she tried to spy the source of her husband's agitation. But all she saw was Lord Angus hurrying toward them; then they were inside the stable. "What—" Iliana began, but paused as he shouted to the stablemaster.

Duncan had barely finished the order for his horse to be brought when the stablemaster was leading it to stand before them. Her husband set her down long enough to mount the beast, unsaddled as it was, then reached down to pull her up before him. As soon as he had her situated, he sent it charging out of the stables, right past his father.

"Duncan!"

Iliana caught a glimpse of her father-in-law's tight-lipped face as they flew past him; then he was out of sight beyond Duncan's shoulder. Clutching those shoulders, Iliana held on for dear life as they rode out of the bailey.

"He seemed angry at you," she murmured as the woods closed around them.

"Who? Father?"

"Aye."

"Hmm. Well, and most like he is."

Iliana frowned slightly when he did not explain, but merely asked, "Where are we going?"

"To a clearin' I ken. Yer screams'll not be heard there."

Iliana rolled her eyes with tired exasperation. "There is no need for it. I am no longer yelling."

"Nay, ye aren't are ye?" He grinned at her slightly, then kissed the tip of her nose before murmuring, "I shall have to see to that first thing."

Iliana frowned at him with confusion at that. "See to what, husband?"

"To teachin' ye to scream," was his confusing response.

Chapter Thirteen

They rode a good distance before Duncan began to slow. Despite the jarring ride and her own curiosity, Iliana had nearly dozed off when they finally broke from the trees into a clearing. It was the horse being drawn to an abrupt halt that caught her drifting attention and made her gaze sleepily around as Duncan slipped from the animal. She was yawning indelicately as she took in the beauty of the spot when she felt his hands at her waist. He plucked her from the horse, allowing her body to slide down his until their faces were on a level. Iliana immediately tried to cut off the yawn that had her mouth wide open, but was too slow. Her husband, taking advantage of this sign of exhaustion, covered her mouth with his own, his tongue sliding past her lips, and delving inside.

Weariness dropping away, Iliana quickly joined in the mating of their mouths, only to moan with disappointment when he drew his lips away.

"Da is mad at me because he kens why I brought ye here."

Iliana opened her eyes slowly at his amused words, confusion plain on her face.

"Why *did* you bring me here?"

"To make ye scream. With pleasure."

She blinked at that announcement, her weary mind slow to grasp his meaning until his hands rose from her waist to cup her breasts.

"I've a mind to taste me wife's passion again," he murmured, squeezing the round orbs he held before running his thumbs over the suddenly erect nipples that were pressing against the restraining material of her clothing.

Iliana stared down at the hands gently kneading her and swallowed. "Here, my lord? Out in the open?" she asked thickly.

"Here," he agreed.

"But what if someone should come along and—"

"But nothing," he murmured, pausing to kiss her again when she raised her head. Releasing her lips a moment later, he brushed his mouth along her cheek to her ear. "Nothing on God's green earth could stop me from—"

When he stiffened suddenly, Iliana went still as well, then gasped in surprise when he suddenly dropped one hand to cup her womanhood through her gown.

The ungiving hardness of thick leather and its metal lock that had met his touch repeatedly until the day before were blessedly absent and Duncan relaxed, a wry smile curving his lips as he admitted, "Well, almost nothing."

Iliana did not get a chance to comment before he had captured her lips again in a kiss that sent her head spinning. When his lips finally left hers several moments later and her head cleared slightly, she found that they were now several feet from the middle of the clearing where they had been just moments before. Much to her surprise, they were now at the edge. Duncan had moved her to lean against a tree. She could feel the rough bark pressing into her back. Oddly enough, she could also feel cool air hitting her body seemingly everywhere.

Glancing down as her husband kissed a trail down her

neck toward her chest, she was shocked to see the reason she suddenly felt so cool. Her gown was torn and now gaped wide open to her belly, leaving her breasts covered only with small goose bumps. Added to that, her left leg was bare, raised, and half-hooked about his hip, held in place by one of his hands, which slid up the back of her leg toward her bottom, pushing her gown before it.

Iliana opened her mouth in shock at her own wanton display. But all that came out was a gasp of pleasure as she shuddered under the caress of Duncan's hot mouth, finding and closing over one chilled erect nipple.

Catching his head between her hands, she licked her lips and swallowed as she watched him suckle at her breast, finding the image amazingly erotic. Then she felt his free hand slide down between their bodies and she clenched her fingers in his hair, her head tipping back against the tree, a wild moan slipping from her lips as he opened the folds of her womanhood and found the bud of her pleasure.

"Husband!" she gasped with pleading as the feelings she had begun to explore the day before built within her.

Grunting, Duncan left off caressing her to grab her other leg and draw it around his hips. With her skirt now bunched up around her waist, he pressed her back into the tree and took a moment to shift his plaid out of the way. Then he was sliding into her.

Iliana shuddered and moaned as her body expanded to accommodate him, then moaned again as he drew himself out. Clasping her by the buttocks, he dropped his lips to cover hers as he continued to love her.

Iliana could feel the bark pressing into her back, could feel the soft material of his linen shirt against one naked breast and the rougher material of the tartan that sat over his shoulder against the other. But mostly she could feel him inside and around her as he drove her to the edge of insanity, then finally gave her the release that waited there.

*   *   *

"You were right to bring me here."

Duncan stiffened at those softly panted words by his ear. Letting her legs slip back to the ground, he lifted his head from her shoulder, where he had dropped it after finding his own fulfillment.

Seeing the soft, sated look in her eyes and face, he smiled to himself with satisfaction at the compliment he imagined she gave him, only to pause when she added, "Surely the whole castle would have heard your screams were we not so far away."

Catching the teasing light in her eyes, Duncan's face split in a grin. He had indeed screamed as he had spilled his seed inside her. He had howled like a wolf on a cold winter night. He'd probably scared away all the game for miles. "As I recall, 'twas ye who were supposed to scream," he murmured, sliding his hands up and down her arms.

"That would not be ladylike," she demurred coyly, and Duncan's grin widened further before he lifted her in his arms and moved to a less rocky patch of grass to lay her there.

"I've a mind to see me lady unladylike," he murmured, sprawling out beside her and moving his hand across the sweet flesh revealed by her gaping gown.

"You tore my gown." It was more an observation than an accusation.

"I was eager. Ye did not seem to mind at the time."

"I did not even notice at the time," Iliana admitted wryly.

His eyes filled with interest at that admission, then brightened. "So! I drove ye to distraction?"

"Aye, husband," she admitted gently, deciding he deserved to preen a bit.

"But ye didn't scream," he pointed out, his hand sliding across her belly and lower. "And ye will scream ere we leave here, sweetling. Ye'll scream with pleasure ere we leave here, and that's a solemn oath."

177

Deciding she rather liked the sound of that oath, Iliana smiled widely and drew his head down to hers for a kiss.

"Iliana?" Shaking off the web of sleep that had been drifting gently over her, Iliana sat up in the bedside chair, her gaze immediately alert as she saw that her mother had awakened. It was a week since the older woman had arrived. A week during which Iliana had not left the room but once when Duncan had dragged her off on his horse. Since that sojourn into the woods, she had remained in the room, taking her meals and sleeping there, spending the hours of wakefulness hovering anxiously over her mother.

"Mama?" Reaching for the woman's uninjured hand, she clasped it gently and leaned closer. Lady Wildwood did not look much better than she had upon arriving. The bruises she bore were only just beginning to fade and her eyes were all but sealed shut with the swelling. "Can you see?"

Lady Wildwood started to shake her head but paused at once, wincing in pain. "Nay, but I can smell the scent your father brought you back from his trip to Spain," she explained.

"How do you feel?"

Her mother smiled grimly. "How do I look?" At Iliana's hesitant silence, she grimaced. "That is about how I feel."

Iliana squeezed her hand sympathetically, then reached gently to brush a strand of hair from her mother's damaged face. "Gertie went below to collect some mead to put some of her tonic in. We've been giving that to you to keep you sleeping while you heal. She should return shortly."

The hand in hers shifted impatiently. "I do not wish to sleep. I have no doubt slept for days already."

"A week," Iliana agreed quietly.

"Aye, well, that is long enough."

"Gertie thought you would heal swifter if—"

"Bruises and broken bones take time to heal no matter if the patient sleeps or not. She would just have me sleep through the pain."

"Mayhap," Iliana agreed quietly. "And mayhap that is not such a bad idea. You—"

" 'Tis a bad idea," Lady Wildwood disagreed at once. "The pain my body gives me is naught compared to the pain of losing your father. 'Sides, I seem to have done naught but sleep these last months since his death. 'Tis time I awoke and faced life."

"But you *have* faced life," Iliana argued. "You arranged for my marriage and even managed to escape Greenweld yourself."

"I sent a letter to the king and fled Greenweld as soon as I knew you were safely away," she corrected, then turned her face toward Iliana, seeming to try to see through her swollen eyes as she asked gently, "Have you been all right? All is well with you?"

"Aye," Iliana murmured at once, eager to ease her mother's worry.

"Your husband is kind to you?"

Iliana hesitated over answering that. Saying that Duncan was kind to her was slightly overstating the case. On the other hand, he was not unkind to her. She did not know exactly how to classify their relationship. They had seemed to do little but argue until they had consummated the marriage. Their relationship had recently taken a vast turn in direction, but she was not sure how exactly. Her husband was demanding and passionate, yet at the same time gentle as a lover. But they had not exactly talked since the afternoon that she had fallen in the dung heap and lured him to their bed. The only time they had even seen each other since her mother's arrival was the day she had gone to complain of the noise his men were making. She did not think what they had done in the clearing he had dragged her to would be considered meaningful conversation.

Iliana had not seen him since then. She had awoken later that same day to find herself sleeping on her corner pallet. Ebba had told her that Duncan had brought her back to the keep, carried her there, laid her down, and gently covered her before leaving to rejoin his men working on the new rooms. This time, Iliana had slept through the racket along with her mother. She had not managed to do so in the days between then and now, but neither had she gone out to complain of the noise again. Firstly, the noise had not disturbed her mother's drugged sleep in the least. And secondly, silly as it might seem, she found herself shrinking from facing her husband again. Every time she thought of that morning in the woods, she flushed a brilliant red. The things he had done to her. Dear Lord, the things she had done back. He had said he wished to see his wife unladylike, and gain his wish he had. She had behaved no better than an animal there in the woods. Her own cries and screams still echoed in her ears. If she closed her eyes she could feel the grass cool and damp beneath her back and the chill morning breeze drifting across her sweat-dampened body as her husband's lips had traveled across her aroused skin.

"Child?"

Flushing, Iliana tore her mind away from her thoughts and glanced guiltily at her mother's face. "I am not unhappy, Mother. All is well."

Lady Wildwood did not look convinced but let it go and sighed.

Deciding a change of topic would be expedient, Iliana asked about her imprisonment. "Did he beat you often, Mother?"

"Only every time I disobeyed him," was the dry response. Oddly enough, those words were followed by a satisfied smile as Lady Wildwood told her, "And I disobeyed the bastard every time I saw him."

Iliana stared at her blankly, unsure how to respond to the proud confession. Part of her wanted to berate her mother for putting herself in such danger. The other part—

the part that had urged her to attempt escape repeatedly herself—wanted to congratulate the older woman. If nothing else, Greenweld had learned that Lady Wildwood and her daughter were not sheep to be led blindly by the first shepherd with a stick.

Instead, Iliana said nothing at all, but merely squeezed the hand she held in understanding, then glanced up as the bedchamber door opened and Gertie reentered.

Spying the turning of her mistress's head toward the door at the slight sound she made in entering, the servant hurried toward the bed. "Yer awake."

"Aye."

"Never fear, we'll fix that in a jiffy. I'll just put a bit of powder in the mead and—"

"Nay, Gertie. I have done with sleep. I would stay awake now."

"You'll do naught but suffer by staying awake."

"Then suffer I will, for I shall stay awake."

The old woman glared at her mistress briefly, then sighed with resignation and set the powder aside. "Are you thirsty?"

"Aye."

Nodding, the woman seated herself carefully on the opposite side of the bed and helped Lady Wildwood to drink some of the liquid, her mouth tightening at the other woman's pained grimace as the liquid irritated her cut and bruised lips. "You should rest."

"If I did that, I should not be able to eat. And should I not eat, I shall not heal."

"You are hungry?" Iliana smiled as she asked that, somewhat relieved. If she was hungry, her mother felt better than she looked. That was a good sign.

"Aye."

"Then I shall have the cook make you something." Rising, she hurried toward the door. "I shall return directly."

* * *

Duncan paused in his work to wipe the sweat from his forehead, his gaze moving automatically toward the door that was now off limits to him. His own bloody room. But now it was inhabited by Iliana's mother. Not that he begrudged her the bed. The woman was in a bad way and needed its comfort more than he. Nay, what he begrudged was his wife's absence. Damn, but he had just managed to gain her attentions. He much resented having them withheld so again.

Duncan had not seen his wife since the day he had made love to her in the woods. He had sought her out repeatedly since then, knocking on the chamber door in an effort to lure his bride away for a bit of *houghmagandie*. Both times the door had been opened by that English hag servant of the mother's, and he had been told that Iliana was resting after spending the night watching over her mother. He was feeling sore neglected and was also growing worried. It seemed obvious to him that his wee wife was avoiding him, but he could not understand why. He had thought that their time in the woods would have set a new tone to their relationship. It had been an incredibly enjoyable interlude for him, and he was positive she had enjoyed it as much, if not more.

As unfair as it was, Duncan had discovered long ago that women could find their satisfaction time and again, while a man was held back by the need for rest between the times when passion overcame him. And so it had been that day. His wife had stiffened and twisted and cried out at least half a dozen times in the woods, while he himself had been restricted by his own body to finding satisfaction only three times. Not that he was complaining: Those three times had been more than enough to leave him weak in the knees and standing on shaking legs afterward.

He wanted those weak knees again. Howbeit, his wife was not being the least cooperative.

As he frowned at that thought, the door he had been glaring at suddenly opened and the focus of his thoughts stepped out and hurried toward the stairs. Stiffening, Duncan watched blankly as she hurried out of sight, then he dropped the plank of wood he had been holding and started after her.

Elgin wasn't in the kitchens. Iliana paused in the center of the room and peered at the empty tables and the fire where workers would normally be busy preparing the evening meal, perplexed. The kitchen was rarely empty. There was usually at least one person there, cleaning vegetables or performing some other such chore, but just now that was not the case.

She had just turned back toward the door, intent on seeking out Elgin or someone who could find him for her, when the door swung open and Duncan strode in. Iliana froze where she stood, her eyes widening at the sight of him. It was obvious he had been working. His usual linen shirt was missing, his upper body bare but for various streaks of dirt among the sweat that glistened there, leaving him with only his plaid hanging about his waist.

The sight of him brought vivid memories back to Iliana, coloring her cheeks with a heat that was reflected in her eyes as he moved toward her. His purposeful stride as he closed the distance between them told her that he had followed her here, and not with the intention of asking how her mother was. Then all thought fled Iliana's mind and she stepped forward to meet him as he reached for her.

He kissed her with a passion that left her breathless and wanting. When he released her lips and his mouth began roaming down her cheek, to her neck, she gasped and released a moan that quickly turned into a groan of dismay. Iliana began struggling in his arms.

Her sudden struggling was enough to bring Duncan back to his senses. They were standing in the kitchen, for God's sake, and here he was, intent on ravishing her right there on the floor where anyone might walk in and find them. Cursing, he scooped her up and hurried to the locked storage closet where the spices and more expensive cooking items were kept. Pausing there, he set his wife down and slipped the ring of keys that his father'd had made for her from her waist.

"What do you do?" Iliana asked with bewilderment as he began searching through her keys.

"Shh, sweetling, all will be well," he muttered, pausing in his search for the key as he came across one oddly shaped one. Bewilderment crossed his face briefly; then he shrugged and continued through the ring until he came to the one he sought. Finding it, he quickly unlocked the storage door and pushed it open, then grabbed his wife's wrist and hurried through it.

The scent of several spices assailed Iliana's nose as she was tugged into the small storage space. She could make out marjoram and nutmeg and the earthier smell of stored vegetables. Then Duncan pulled the door closed and they were enclosed in darkness.

"What—" she began uncertainly, only to fall silent as she found herself tugged into his embrace again, her mouth being ravaged as he leaned her back against what she suspected, from the lumps and bumps pressing against her back, was a sack of potatoes.

Duncan was like a starving man faced with a four-course meal, and all four courses presented on one plate. His mouth and hands were everywhere, seeming to try to touch and kiss every part of her at once. His lips were dancing from her mouth to her cheek, to her ears, to her neck, while his one hand was busy tugging at the neckline of her gown and alternately delving inside of it for a quick squeeze and feel before returning to tugging. His other hand was struggling its way up under her skirts, pushing the gown before it as his leg slid between hers, spreading her own farther apart.

"Husband," Iliana muttered, only to have her lips covered by his again. She tried to keep her mouth closed against the invasion, but when he reached and cupped her womanhood, she gasped in surprise and his tongue slid into her mouth. Her discomfort was forgotten as his tongue twined around her own, and he finally succeeded at nudging her gown aside enough to free one breast for his attention. Iliana moaned into his mouth and arched her back as he began plucking at an immediately erect nipple. Then she felt his other hand spread the folds of her womanhood to caress her and she clutched convulsively at his shoulders, gasping in a breath of air as his mouth slipped from hers, dipping down to capture her exposed nipple.

Unfortunately, it was that gasp that reminded her of what she had noticed in the kitchen and what had made her struggle there. There was no delicate way to put it. Quite simply, Duncan stunk. Again.

Her previous excitement slipping away like so much smoke in a breeze, Iliana straightened as much as she could in his embrace and began to push at his chest.

Frowning at the heel of her palm suddenly pressing into his collarbone, Duncan pushed her hand away and suckled at her nipple, noting even as he did so that it was becoming soft in his mouth. Frowning, he applied more attention to the aureole, nibbling at it gently, but then his wife's hand was again pressing into his collarbone.

"What?" Straightening away from her, he tried to peer at her face in the dim light seeping under the door, but it was not enough for him to see her expression. "Why, sweetling, don't fret so. We'll not be found in here."

"Aye, well," Iliana murmured uncomfortably, resisting being pulled back into his embrace when he tried to tug her against him again. " 'Tis not so much that, my lord. But—" She floundered briefly, not wishing to anger him by stating the problem, then latched onto the only real excuse she had to offer. "Mama is awake and hungry, and I actually came below to fetch her some broth or—"

"Well, we'll make it a quick one then, shall we?" he murmured seductively, bending slightly to catch the hem of her skirt and begin sliding it up her legs, his fingers

185

brushing over the suddenly tingling flesh of her calves as he did.

Iliana gasped in surprise at the warmth that suddenly pooled in the pit of her belly as his hands slid the length of her legs, then moaned aloud as she smelled what she had inhaled in that gasp. It had been bad enough in the kitchen, a wide open area with the scent of tonight's supper simmering on the air, but in this enclosed space, his scent seemed to outweigh the smell of even the spices that surrounded them. All she could smell was—

"Horse dung."

Duncan stilled at that, his hands clasping her thighs beneath her skirt. "What?"

"I—You have been working with the horses?" she asked carefully.

"Aye." She heard rather than saw his surprise at her guess. "I was helpin' in the stables early this morn. One of the mare's was havin' difficulty foaling and needed a wee hand gettin' the foal out."

Iliana groaned aloud at that. She knew what he had been doing to help out. He had knelt in the straw in the stable, reached inside the animal, grabbed the foal by the legs, and pulled the poor wee beast out of its mother, getting himself covered in blood and muck while he was at it. Then he had most likely wiped himself off with a rag and moved on to hammering away upstairs without ever even considering bathing. In fact, she would bet her life that he had not thought to bathe at all since the day she had fallen in the dung nearly a week before. Day by day he had worked at building the new rooms he wished to add, becoming coated in sweat, dust, and dirt, and never once thought of cleaning up. 'Twas no wonder he smelled like the stables. Actually, worse than the stables.

"How did ye ken?"

Iliana sighed at his question. "I could smell it."

He went completely stiff at that.

Sensing his anger, she stepped to the right and felt for the door. Light splayed across both of them as she tugged it open. Wincing at the fury on her husband's face, Iliana decided that, in this instance, retreat might be the better part of valor, and hurried out into the kitchen, nearly running right over a startled Elgin.

"My apologies," she muttered, attempting to hurry past him.

"Wife!"

She did not need to turn around to see that her husband was storming after her. She could hear the thud of his footfalls as he crashed after her. Iliana immediately put on a bit of speed, running for the door. Unfortunately, in her hurry, she didn't notice the fact that her father-in-law was in the room until she collided with him, nearly sending them both crashing to the floor.

Gasping as the senior Dunbar caught her to his chest to steady her, Iliana glanced up into his face and flushed brightly. "Oh, my lord. I—er I was just—My mother is awake and hungry," she babbled nervously, taking a step back from his hold. "I thought to fetch her a bowl of broth and—"

"And me randy bull o' a son jumped ye again," Angus finished for her heavily, reaching out to tug at her gown.

Eyes drawn downward, Iliana saw with some embarrassment that her gown was still out of place, leaving the better portion of one breast in plain view. Flushing brightly, she took over the task of straightening her gown.

"Get ye upstairs, lass, and sit with yer mother. Elgin'll bring some broth to ye. I've a word or two to say to me son."

Nodding with relief, Iliana slipped past him and out of the room, ignoring Duncan's shouting of her name even as his father began to speak to him.

Chapter Fourteen

"Do you not think you have hidden up here long enough?"

Iliana glanced up warily from the chessboard between her and her mother. "What do you mean?"

"You know exactly what I mean."

Shifting uncomfortably under the older woman's keen gaze, she turned back to the game. "I have not been hiding."

"Nay." The dryness of Lady Wildwood's tone was known well by her daughter.

"Nay," Iliana insisted impatiently. "Check."

"I suppose you have been here day and night for the last week out of filial devotion?"

"Of course."

"Hmm." Shaking her head, Lady Wildwood took her own turn at the game "Checkmate."

Iliana blinked at the board. Her mother had turned the game with one simple—and almost impossible—move. Sighing, she sat back and peered at her irritably. "You have not been well."

"Nay. I have not."

"I thought you would appreciate the company."

When her mother merely stared at her, Iliana glanced away uncomfortably.

"All is not well with your husband." It was an accusation and Iliana sighed as she shrugged.

"Well enough, Mother. How well would you expect? We are newly married. Still getting to know each other."

"Aye. Well, it seems to me 'tis hard to get to know someone should you not spend any time with him."

When her daughter merely stared stubbornly at the chessboard and did not answer, Lady Wildwood lifted the game from her lap, where it had rested, and set it aside.

"What are you doing?" Iliana asked in dismay, hurrying around the bed to stop her when she folded the blankets back and shifted her legs to the floor. "You cannot get up, Mother, you are still too weak."

"I will not get any stronger lying about on my back," was Lady Wildwood's pragmatic answer. "'Sides, I believe 'tis time I met my son-in-law."

"Nay. If you wish to meet him, I will send Ebba to ask him to come to see you. But under no circumstances are you going to get out of that bed. You have been far too ill and are still weak."

"Ebba?"

"My lady!" The maid's eyes were wide as she hurried across the great hall toward her. "You are out and about."

Iliana grimaced at the words. "Aye. My mother has decided to join the table for sup. She would like a bath and . . ." Her voice trailed away as a burst of laughter drew her gaze to Lord Angus and several other men seated at the trestle table. Duncan was nowhere in sight, nor was there a single female present, yet every place at the tables was filled, and several men were left to stand about, chatting with the others. Iliana had never seen so many men within the keep walls. Not even when the men had been working on the new rooms. "What goes on here?"

"Lady Seonaid's betrothed was here."

"Lord Sherwell?" Iliana's eyebrows rose when her maid nodded. Ebba had told her nearly two weeks ago that the other woman had fled the keep to avoid her marriage. Seonaid had run off the day after Iliana's mother had arrived. Her maid had also informed her that men had been sent to track Seonaid. They had returned with the news that the girl had fled to St. Simmian's, a nunnery to the north. Iliana's only reaction to that information had been to wonder why she herself had not been that clever. Now her eyes moved over the laughing men around the table, pausing and widening slightly at the sight of Lord Angus in a fine gold doublet. "What—"

" 'Tis Lord Sherwell's," Ebba interrupted to inform her, having followed her gaze. "Lord Sherwell wished Lord Dunbar's plaid, so Lord Angus insisted he must trade his own clothes for them."

"Why did Lord Sherwell wish for Lord Dunbar's plaid?"

"To prove he was a friend to the Dunbars. 'Twill see him safely through those lands friendly to the Dunbars does he wear Dunbar colors."

"Really?" she asked with interest, then pushed such thoughts aside as the sight of Elgin coming out of the kitchen reminded her of her purpose in being downstairs. "My mother wishes to come below for sup this evening." She paused to grimace at Ebba's expression and nodded. "I know. I have told her she should rest, but she will not listen. Mayhap if her leg had truly been broken as we first suspected, she would have the sense to stay abed, but as it is she wishes a bath to prepare."

"I shall see to it," Ebba answered.

Murmuring her thanks, Iliana turned to hurry back upstairs. She had been anxious about leaving it in the first place, but on finding the hallway empty of men had warily braved going below to search out Ebba. The hallway had been empty these past two days. The three rooms Duncan had planned on adding were done. The upper floor now boasted six rooms, a hallway twice its original size, and a new railing. Iliana had yet to see these added rooms but was too wary of running into Duncan to explore them, so she hurried back to her mother to assist her with her bath and dressing.

"You are fortunate, daughter; your cook is excellent. I do not believe Jean-Claude could have made this meal better." Lady Wildwood's words were deliberately said loud enough for Elgin to hear. As expected, he puffed up under the verbal petting, pride swelling him so that he fairly beamed at one and all around the trestle tables.

The meal had gone pleasantly enough. Elgin had made the finest meal Iliana had enjoyed at Dunbar to date. Lord Angus, wearing Lord Sherwell's fine new doublet and braies, had been making an effort all evening to make her mother feel comfortable and welcome. He had even gone so far as to flirt shamelessly with her throughout the meal. Iliana supposed she should not be surprised. Even with fading bruises marring her hands, arms, face, and neck, her mother was an attractive woman. Noting the blush his behavior had brought to her mother's cheeks and her shy smiles, Iliana had almost jumped up and kissed Angus's wrinkled old cheek in gratitude. Her mother had been so frighteningly pale ever since her arrival that the ribbons of color on each cheek were a relief, and Iliana had relaxed and listened idly to the conversation her mother shared with Duncan and Angus, both of whom sat on her mother's right. Iliana had organized those seating arrangements.

When she and her mother had come below to sup, it was to find everyone else already at table. Duncan had been seated between his father and his cousin, Allistair, but all of his attention had been focused on his father as the older man spoke to him. Only Allistair had seemed to notice their arrival. The Dunbar warrior had immediately urged the men to slide along the bench, following the action himself, to make room between himself and Duncan.

Not having seen her husband since the incident in the storage room, she had not been eager to face him. Stepping quickly forward, Iliana had dropped onto the bench next to Allistair, forcing her mother to take the space next to Duncan. She had spent the meal seemingly completely absorbed in her food but had really been listening to the conversation around her.

Once again, listening in on conversations between her husband and someone else had shown her another side to the man she tended to think of as a great stinking bear. Duncan's every action and word toward her mother had been gentle and polite. In truth, his behavior was almost chivalrous. He had also talked with her mother more openly than he had ever seemed to do with her, telling of his plans for the keep and listing what was already accomplished. The upstairs rooms were not only finished being built, all but one were furnished as well. She had also learned that the men had immediately turned their efforts back to the wall, and that was nearly done as well. Then, too, she had learned why there suddenly seemed so many more men in the keep. It seemed that several of the men had been off on a mercenary expedition, but were now finished and returned home. With the crowds that now filled the keep, Iliana could well understand her husband's desperation to enlarge Dunbar.

"You shall have your room back tonight."

Iliana stiffened at her mother's words, her own thoughts flying to the four winds. "What?" she asked, grabbing desperately at her arm when the woman turned away to gesture for her maid to approach.

Glancing back, Lady Wildwood frowned slightly at Iliana's obvious dismay, but nodded. "Now that I know that your husband has gone to the trouble of building extra rooms, it seems only right that I use one."

"But—" Iliana paused when her mother reached out to caress her cheek gently.

"Do not fret, child. He seems to be a good man. All will be well." Her mother kissed her gently on the cheek, then turned toward her maid. "I am ready to retire, Gertie."

"Aye, my lady."

Iliana continued to sit where she was as her mother's maid helped her to rise, until she took a step away from the bench, leaving a clear view of her husband. Duncan met her gaze, the expression in his eyes and the smile on his face telling her that he had overheard her mother's words.

Rising abruptly, she stepped over the bench after her mother. "I shall help you," she announced nervously, sliding her hand beneath her elbow to take some of her weight.

Duncan paused outside the door to the bedchamber and took a deep breath. Hard as it was to accept, he was nervous. It had been so long since he had held his wife in his arms. . . . And then there was her reaction to him in the storeroom. Shrugging such thoughts away, he straightened his shoulders and opened the door.

The room was semi-dark, lit only by the glowing embers in the fireplace. By the dim light they cast, Duncan could just make out his wife's form in the bed. Easing the door closed, he moved uncertainly toward the bed.

Iliana was already asleep. Or pretending to be. He supposed he should not have expected anything else. A hearty welcome would have been too much to hope for after the way she had avoided him these many days. Sighing, he shrugged out of his plaid and quickly lifted his shirt off over his head, dropping both items to the floor. He then lifted the linens to crawl into bed, only to freeze and stare at his wife beneath the sheet. She wore her undertunic, which was not unusual—she often wore that to bed—or had when refusing him his rights. It was the bulky outline of the chastity belt that made him stiffen.

"Ye've got it back on."

Iliana sighed at the tone of his voice and gave up all attempts at feigning sleep. Opening her eyes, she peered at him unhappily. "Tis sorry I am, husband, but—"

"Sorry? Nay, yer not sorry." Glaring at her irately, he let the linen drop back to cover her with disgust. "Yer cold. Yer one o' those women I have heard about who don't enjoy the mating and will do anything to avoid it."

"Nay!" Iliana denied at once, grabbing at his hand when he turned to move away. "I *do* enjoy it. Truly," she assured him when he sneered at the claim, then added, "Truly I do, but I find I can not enjoy it when your scent is so foul that it distracts from the pleasure you give me. Could you not just bathe and . . ." Her voice trailed away to silence as he tugged his arm free.

"Aye, ye would like that, would ye not? Do I bathe, surely ye will favor me with yer attentions," he sneered. "Well, I will remind ye once again, wife, that 'tis yer duty to submit to me. Ye are denying me a husband's rights, which gives me every right to put ye aside."

Iliana stilled at that threat, and he gave a harsh laugh.

"What is the matter? Surely ye don't care? Nay, of course not. Did ye care, ye wouldn't refuse me yer favors."

When Iliana merely stared at him silently, he turned away in disgust. "Worry no more. I'll not sully yer precious linens with my foul smell. I'll take mesel' off to a more welcoming bed."

Iliana stared blankly at the door as it closed behind him, his words repeating themselves in her head. *A more welcoming bed.* Did he intend to seek his pleasure elsewhere? Her eyes narrowed at the very thought, anger welling up within her at the idea of his sharing the passion and intimacy they had experienced with someone else. Teeth snapping together, Iliana pushed the linens aside and got to her feet, only to pause.

She *had* refused him. Did she wish him back in her bed as he was? Iliana shifted uncomfortably. She did not care for his stench. Could she put up with it to keep him from straying?

The years ahead rolled out in her mind, Duncan coming to her after a day of hard labor, his body slick with sweat, glistening in the firelight. He would shrug his plaid to the floor, then his shirt. Shadows from the fire would dance across his wide chest and strong legs as he moved toward her, took her in his arms, and . . . she would catch a whiff of him.

Groaning, Iliana crawled unhappily back into bed. While the idea of his seeking his pleasure in another bed was most distressing, the idea of being forced to welcome him into her own when he smelled of the stables was really no better.

"Yer a buxom wench, Kelly." Duncan addressed the enormous breasts that floated before his eyes. They were bulging out of the top of the low-cut gown that bound them. Thinking they meant to attempt escape at any moment, he reached out to push them down, back into their strappings. But the movement unbalanced him somewhat, and he ended up grabbing one of the massive mammaries through the gown that covered it and holding on as he swayed where he sat.

I'm drunk, he realized with dismay, then decided it didn't matter and raised the nearly empty pitcher in his other hand to his mouth and gulped the last of the liquid down.

"That's enough, that is." Grabbing the pitcher from him, Kelly set it on the small table next to the bed where Duncan sat. When he scowled at the loss, she laughed slightly and took his empty hand, placing it against her other breast. "Ye've been a naughty man, me laird, not comin' to see me fer so long. Kelly's missed ye."

"Aye, well, I've been busy." Duncan's head lolled forward, landing between her generous breasts.

"Aye, with yer English wife." The woman pouted, but when Duncan did not raise his head to see it, she frowned slightly and tugged his head back. Her lips tightened when she saw that his eyes were closed and he appeared on the verge of sleep. "Yer in yer cups, ye are."

His eyes opened at that and he grinned, one hand dropping from her breast to slip around and pinch her behind. "Aye, but not so far in it I cannot doin' me business."

"Aye, well, I've yet to see the day when yer that fou," she agreed with dry amusement, then gave him a gentle push that sent him dropping back onto the bed.

Smiling at the surprise on his face, she tugged the neckline of her gown down so that her breasts popped out, her smile deepening at the hunger that immediately lit his eyes. "Let us see if ye can still ride the night out, or if that English wife o' yers has ruined ye," she murmured, yanking the skirt of her plaid up to her thighs and crawling atop him on the bed.

Duncan had just opened his mouth to deride that possibility when the woman leaned forward and plopped her breast into it. Eyes widening, he began to suckle automatically, only to pause as the acrid scent of sweat intruded on his senses. Frowning, he caught the woman by the arms, ending her efforts at tugging up his own plaid, and pushed her away.

Sighing, Iliana rolled onto her back once more and glared into the darkened room. It was impossible for her to gain her sleep when her mind kept racing over the fact that Duncan was right this minute thrusting himself into another woman's body. The pig, she thought irritably. Was it so much to ask that he take a bath? Even if he would just wash himself down, she would be pleased to remove the belt.

Muttering under her breath, she shifted onto her side away from the door, then stiffened at the soft click of it opening. She heard it shut softly, then the rustle of rushes as he crossed the room, and anger immediately began to burn within her. So, he had pleasured himself elsewhere, then thought to join her in this bed? If that was the case, he had another think coming.

Rolling abruptly onto her back, Iliana opened her mouth to blister him with her tongue. The words that would have bubbled forward were replaced with a shriek of horror, however, when she saw the dark form poised over the bed, a knife upraised to plunge into her. If she was startled at the sight, her attacker was equally taken aback by the fact that she was obviously not asleep. A blessing that; it made him hesitate for a moment. Just long enough for Iliana to gather her senses and start to roll quickly away from him.

Her attacker regained himself at her movement and lunged forward, bringing the knife down as she moved. Iliana felt heat emanate suddenly from her side; then she crashed onto the floor with a thud. She screamed again as she found her legs tangled up in the bed linens, hampering her efforts to get as far from the bed and the attacker as possible.

The crash of the bedroom door brought an end to her shrieks and Iliana peered warily over the bed, relief making her sag when she saw that her attacker was gone.

"Iliana!"

Recognizing her mother's panicked voice coming down the hall, Iliana sighed wearily and began to push at the sheets tangled around her legs. Candlelight lit the room a moment later, and she glanced up to see her mother, Ebba, Gertie, and Lord Angus all rush into the chamber. They paused inside the door, peering around the seemingly empty room, until they spotted her on the floor on the other side of the bed. Then her mother handed her candle to her maid and rushed forward.

"What is it, dear?" Lady Wildwood hurried around the bed, seemingly oblivious to the fact that she was dressed only in her undertunic.

Laird Angus did not miss that fact, however; his eyes were glued to the older woman as she reached her daughter's side and bent to help her anxiously to her feet.

"Was it a nightmare? Did you fall out of bed?"

Angus drew his eyes reluctantly from the mother's scanty attire to peer at his daughter-in-law. His gaze was immediately drawn to the splotch of red blooming on her white gown. "Yer bleedin'!" He was across the room before he had finished making that observation.

Iliana glanced at her side with a frown. The heat she had felt as she had rolled off the bed had been the knife slicing through her side, it seemed. There was a tear in her tunic and blood soaking into it where she had been cut. " 'Tis not so bad," Iliana murmured. " 'Tis just a scratch, really."

Ignoring her words, Angus bent to pull the sides of the slit in her gown apart, and examined the cut beneath it. He was frowning when he straightened. "What happened?"

"Someone came into the room. I thought it was Duncan and rolled over to speak to him, but it was not him—"

"Who was it?" Lady Wildwood asked, wide-eyed.

"I do not know. It all happened so quickly. And it was dark. I saw a man, but his face was in shadow. Then I saw the knife." Shuddering, she pressed her hand to her side to ease the pain. "I screamed and rolled off the bed as he stabbed."

" 'Tis good ye did, else ye would not be alive to make these explanations," Angus muttered grimly, then glanced toward the door where a small crowd was gathering. When he did not see his son among them, he turned back to Iliana. "Where is my son?"

She hesitated briefly, then reached up on tiptoe to whisper in his ear.

Lady Wildwood raised her eyebrows at the action, her curiosity piqued. . . . Especially when thunderclouds began to gather on the man's face.

Cursing, he turned and stormed for the door. Spearing Gertie and Ebba with a look as he approached, he gestured over his shoulder. "See to her wound!" he ordered, then caught Allistair's gaze as he moved through the men. "Post someone to stand guard until I can fetch Duncan back."

He made such a commanding figure as he swept from the room, that one could almost overlook the fact that he wore only the shirt he slept in. A long shirt, thank goodness, that reached nearly to his knees, but only a shirt all the same.

"What is it?" Kelly asked, peering at Duncan with surprise as he eased her gently away from him.

Duncan hesitated briefly, unwilling to voice what had suddenly made him stop her actions. "I'm married now," he pointed out, sitting up on the edge of the bed.

"Aye, and so ye were when ye entered me cottage."

Duncan grimaced at the asperity of her words, then stiffened as she shifted to sit beside him and reached around to grasp him through his plaid.

"Why, yer as limp as wet flax!" she exclaimed with dismay, then stood quickly and shifted before him. "Ne'er mind. Old Kell'll take care o' that."

Dropping to her knees before him, she flipped his plaid out of the way and took him into her mouth. Duncan jerked in surprise at the summary action, then simply stared at the top of her head as she labored over him. Her hair was as red as fire. Or would be if she washed it more often, he thought, frowning at the dull, greasy look of her locks. In comparison, Iliana's hair shone like polished wood and smelled of lemons and honey. He had asked her about that the day in the woods. How did she make her hair smell so? He loved that smell. He had buried his face in it and breathed that scent the whole time he was loving her in the grass. God, just thinking of it made him hard.

Kelly gave a murmur of satisfaction as he grew within her mouth, shattering the image of Iliana in Duncan's mind. Opening his eyes, he peered down at her, stiffening when he thought he saw movement on her scalp. *Lice?* he wondered with dismay, unsure why he was so horrified. Lice were common enough, but . . . He would bet her entire dowry that Iliana had no lice.

"Ye've gone soft again!"

Duncan grimaced at that complaint, then pushed the woman's head away and stood. Stepping over her, he left the cottage without another word.

He was halfway back to the keep when he came across his father. Pausing on the path, Duncan took in the older man's grim expression and arched his eyebrows. "What is it ye've got in *yer* craw?"

"Finished lazin' about, are ye? Ready to return to yer wife? Ye do remember her, do ya not? Wee lass. Bonnie."

Duncan was a bit surprised at the apparent depth of his father's anger over the matter, but the fact that he *was* merely added to his own irritation. He was not at all pleased by the fact that he had walked away from a perfectly willing woman for the very reason that his wife claimed for denying him. "I don't ken what yer so bothered about. Yer the one who was sayin' I should let her get some rest."

The last word had barely left his mouth when his father's fist connected with his jaw. Not having seen the blow coming, and already unsteady on his feet from the whiskey he had been downing all night, Duncan went down like wheat under the blade of a sickle.

Sitting up slowly, he shook his head and raised a hand to rub at his jaw, his eyes moving warily to his father. "What'd ye do that fer?"

" 'Cause ye deserved it, ye great Gouk!" Angus roared as his son got cautiously back to his feet. "While ye were off tendin' those blasted baser needs of yers, an assassin

200

was up in yer room, *where ye should have been*, stabbing yer poor defenseless wife!''

"What?"

"Ye heard me. Someone crept into yer chamber while ye were out and knifed her. She—" Angus got no further. Duncan was no longer listening. He had whirled to race toward the keep.

Chapter Fifteen

"We shall have to tend to the wound," Lady Wildwood murmured once Lord Angus had gone. "Ebba, find my daughter a fresh tunic, please. Gertie—"

"I'll fetch my medicinals." Turning, the old woman hurried out of the room.

"You shall have to remove your tunic, dear," Lady Wildwood murmured, worry creasing her face as she took in the way Iliana was suddenly shivering. Shock was setting in, she realized grimly, and was only surprised that her daughter had remained so calm and matter-of-fact for so long.

Automatically doing as she was told, Iliana tugged her gown upward, lifting it over her head. It was not until she caught the shock on her mother's face that she recalled the belt of chastity. She nearly groaned aloud then.

"What are you wearing?"

Shoulders slumping in resignation, Iliana dropped the tunic and sat upon the bed. "You know what it is."

"Aye." Lady Wildwood nodded slowly. Her own had

spared her from Greenweld's advances, though it had cost her many beatings.

Seating herself on the bed next to her daughter, Lady Wildwood took one of Iliana's hands into her own. "I have suspected that all was not well in your marriage but hoped that with time . . . I had no idea things were so bad. Does he beat you?"

"Nay! Of course not!" Iliana exclaimed with dismay. "Why, he beat old Willie for daring to raise a fist to *his* wife. Duncan would never harm me physically."

"Then he is cruel to you mentally," she murmured unhappily.

"Nay. Even in anger he says naught that could be considered cruel. He is a most reasonable man."

Lady Wildwood's confusion was obvious. "Then he must be stupid. A buffoon?"

"Mother! How could you think that?" Iliana asked in horror, defending him at once. "You have met him. He is most intelligent. Why, just look at what he plans for this place. He is intelligent and ambitious and hard-working—"

"Then why do you wear the belt?" her mother interrupted with frustration, and Iliana fell silent, too embarrassed to answer.

"She does not wear it all the time, my lady," Ebba said helpfully. That information, however, only seemed to confuse the woman more.

"Does not wear it—Then the wedding *has* been consummated?" Her daughter's blush was answer enough, and Lady Wildwood's gaze became sharper. "Is he rough in bed?"

Flushing a deeper crimson, Iliana shook her head.

"Well, then, why?"

Iliana considered lying, but in the end just blurted, "He smells."

Lady Wildwood blinked at the blunt words, then disbelief began to fill her eyes.

"Truly he does, Mother. Surely you have noticed? You

sat right beside him at sup. He bathes only twice a year and—'' Iliana's voice died as she noted her mother's bewildered expression. Turning, she cast a pleading glance at Ebba.

Her maid was more than game to back her up on this. "She speaks the truth, my lady. This whole keep reeked when we first arrived. The rushes had not been changed in a year, and Lady Iliana ruined at least two dresses by merely sitting at table the first night. It took four women three whole days just to scrub the filth off the great hall floor." She hesitated, her gaze moving to the younger woman briefly before she finished. "Truly, the change Lady Iliana has wrought here is miraculous, but it gives a false impression."

"I see," her mother said solemnly, "And is this the only problem in your marriage?"

Iliana nodded.

"I see," she repeated, then rose as Gertie bustled back into the room. "You had best lay down on your side," she suggested as Gertie poked through her bag.

Giving up trying to read her mother's thoughts, Iliana shifted her legs onto the bed. Reclining, she rolled onto her side, facing away from the door so that the wound to her side was easily accessible. Then she raised her arm over her head and out of the way, wincing as the old woman began to clean the injury.

Duncan stormed up the stairs, guilt driving him as much as concern. Had he not strayed from his marital bed, this would not have happened.

Furious with himself, he snarled at the crowd outside his bedchamber, pushing through them and bursting into the room. The sight that met him was enough to bring him to a halt before he had even really managed to step through the doorframe. He was aware of his mother-in-law and his wife's maid's presence on the periphery of his consciousness. He even took brief note of the old hag now tending his wife's wound. But really, all of Duncan's attention was focused on the frail-looking woman on the bed.

Relief that she still lived was his first reaction. He closed his eyes briefly and gave up a silent prayer of thanks. His wife lived. And no matter what she did to provoke him, he would not neglect his duties again. He would see to her safety.

Whispers from the people behind him drew his attention to the fact that he had left the door wide open. Duncan immediately reached back to slam it closed, then strode to her bedside. He was sorry he had done so almost the very moment that he paused to peer down at her. She had on nothing but that damned belt of hers. The sight of her clad so was enough to set his blood pounding and frustrate him all at once.

Embarrassed by what he considered his own lack of control, Duncan dropped his gaze to the floor in an attempt to regain himself. Unfortunately, that merely replaced one blood-boiling emotion for another as he spotted the ripped and bloodied gown at his feet. Bending, he picked it up and looked it over carefully, taking in the size of the hole and the amount of blood soaking the cloth. He peered past Gertie at the wound. It was a relief to see that, while it had bled freely, it did not appear to be life-threatening. But that hardly cooled his temper. Her beautiful, flawless skin was now flawed. And by his failure. The scar she would bear would be the proof of his lack as a husband.

"What happened?" he asked, and she told him.

Silence descended once she had finished; then Duncan whirled on his heel and strode from the room. The door had barely crashed closed when he began bellowing orders and arranging guard duty; then he stomped below once more, trying desperately to ignore the pain he had seen in his wife's eyes.

* * *

"I don't think they meant to kill Iliana."

Duncan glanced toward his father in surprise.

Shaking away thoughts of his wife's near death, Duncan lifted the ale he had just poured for himself, grimacing over the way his hand shook as he brought the drink to his mouth. He was surprised by the depth of the emotion the attack had wrought in him.

"Nay," Duncan agreed at last, setting his mug back on the table and peering at his father. "Ye think 'twas one of Greenweld's men come fer her mother—to kill her before she can have their marriage annulled."

Angus nodded slowly. " 'Tis the only thing that makes sense. 'Twas common knowledge that Lady Wildwood has inhabited yer chamber since her arrival. 'Twas not common knowledge that she would not be there this eve. I did not even ken that."

The very same thought had occurred to Duncan. So far as he knew, only he, Iliana, and her mother had been aware of the change in sleeping arrangements. The assassination attempt must have been meant for her mother. "Think ye then that one of Greenweld's men managed to slip past the guard at the gate?"

"Aye. Hundreds of people enter and leave the bailey every day. The men would not be watching for a lone man on foot. 'Tis the only way he could have got in."

"I shall have to double the guards on the gate. Check all coming and going. I'll also arrange a search of the castle and bailey, then take a large party to search the woods, and the rest of Dunbar land as well. If he is still here, we shall catch him."

"Hmm," Angus murmured. "No doubt the cowardly bastard is gone by now, but better safe than sorry."

They were both silent for a moment, then glanced up as Lady Wildwood entered the room.

"Gertie is finished now," she announced. "Iliana is resting."

Nodding, Duncan shifted under his mother-in-law's gaze, then got uncomfortably to his feet. "I must speak with the men about what I wish done on the morrow," he muttered, easing his way around her, so eager to leave that he did not notice when she leaned toward him slightly and gave a gentle sniff.

Angus noticed, however. He also noticed the frown upon the woman's face. Curious, he raised his eyebrows at her as she stepped to the table and sank down next to him.

It was a moment before she acknowledged his questioning glance by murmuring, "Much to my distress, I have learned that all is not well with our children, my lord, and we must help them solve this trouble."

An hour later, she was smiling again as she rose to her feet. " 'Tis a sound plan, my lord. Mayhap we can yet salvage this muddled marriage."

"Indeed," Angus murmured, standing as well and taking her hand to kiss it with a gallantry that surprised her.

She was blushing brightly in reaction when footfalls announced Duncan's return. Flushing a deeper rose at his raised eyebrows, she muttered her excuses and fled.

Angus watched her go with a gleam in his eye, then smiled and shouted for Elgin as his son joined him at the table.

" 'Tis late. Elgin will have returned to his cottage."

"Oh, aye." Angus got to his feet again. "I shall have to see to it myself, then."

"What?"

"A bath."

"What?" Duncan could not have been more shocked had the man announced his intent to don a gown. "But 'tis not yet the end of July."

Shrugging, Angus moved toward the kitchen. "What matter is that? There are women present now. Attractive women, I might add." The grin he tossed over his shoulder was lecherous. "Lady Wildwood is a fine-looking female. She deserves a bit of effort. Certainly more than the wee bit of time and trouble that taking a bath will cause me. Women don't like a stinking man, son. Even a stinking man in fine clothes does not impress them. Unless they reek so bad themselves that they cannot smell them.''

Duncan glowered over his father's words, trying to take them in. His father had *never* taken more than two baths a year, and yet now he was willingly calling for one. It made no sense. In fact, the only thing that he seemed able to grasp was his father's last statement and that made him frown.

''Iliana smells like wildflowers,'' Duncan murmured, moving to stand by his father, who had paused at the kitchen door. His mouth worked briefly, then he admitted, ''She thinks I stink.''

''Ah.'' Angus nodded solemnly, already having been informed of this by the lady's mother.

'' 'Tis why she avoids me. She says my smell offends her.''

''Ah ha.'' Angus was silent for a moment, then leaned toward his son, sniffing curiously. Nose wrinkling as he caught whiff of him, he straightened and pursed his lips. ''Mayhap ye should take a bath, then.''

'' 'Tis not July yet.''

''So?''

''So, I bathe twice a year. In January and July. I willna change me habits to please her. 'Sides, *ye* only bathe twice a year.''

''Duncan, ye can't live yer life based on *me* habits,'' Angus interrupted impatiently. ''I have no wife so bathe when I wish.''

''And so shall I.''

''Then don't complain to me that yer wife avoids yer embrace, fer in truth ye *do* reek. 'Sides, I am bathing now,'' he added, storming into the kitchen and bending to shake the two young kitchen lads who slept on pallets before the fire.

''She is my wife!'' Duncan announced arrogantly, following on his heels. '' 'Tis her duty to—''

"Duty, me arse!" Angus roared, straightening from nudging the second of the boys. His prodding had barely roused the lads, but his bellow snapped them completely awake and brought them to their feet.

"What?" Duncan stared at his father's irritated face, wide-eyed.

" 'Tis not duty yer speakin' o' here, 'tis yer own blasted stubbornness."

When his son's jaw dropped at that, Angus nodded firmly.

"Ye think she should take ye as ye are. Well, me boy, I have news fer ye; the church can quack on all it wants about a woman's duty, but not a one o' these men are married or ken a damn thing about women. Women are not the simple creatures the church makes 'em out to be. In truth, I think they're about as unsimple as can be. And they can make yer life heaven on earth or eternal hell. If yer willin' to suffer the hell, then stand firm on this. But if ye wish yer wife to come to ye willingly, then take a damn bath!"

He paused to take a calming breath before resting his hand on his son's shoulder. "And if that doesn't help ye, I can tell ye this much. Yer mother was about as perfect a woman as ever walked this earth, but she would've booted me from her bed as soon as look at me, did I go to her smelling o' manure, sweat, and filth."

When Duncan's eyes widened incredulously at that, Angus nodded firmly. "A stickler was yer mother. Liked a clean home. Like yer wife. And liked a clean bed with a clean man in it. She made me bathe once a week. At least."

"Nay," Duncan denied at once. "Ye bathe twice a year—"

"I bathe twice a year *now*," Angus corrected grimly. "And I wouldn't even do that did I not start to smell so bad I offend even mesel'." Shaking his head sadly, he confessed, "I don't like to bathe. I used to, but no more. It reminds me o'yer mother. We use to bathe together.

209

Frolicking and teasing each other with the water and soap . . .'' His eyes clouded and drifted far away. Back to when his beloved Muireall had been alive. He stayed like that for a moment, memories playing out on his face; then his gaze cleared and he sighed. ''It breaks me heart to step into a bath kenning she'll never join me there again. Or anywhere else.''

''But no one here at Dunbar bathes more than twice a year.''

''Duncan,'' Angus interrupted, '' 'Tis fair unpleasant to bathe, then get back into a stinking plaid. No one has complained 'cause they knew ye wished to make a better life fer them. So they kenned they would have to give up some things 'til ye saved enough to do so.''

''But we have enough now, and the men don't bathe.''

''Because *ye* haven't bathed. They are following yer example.'' Suddenly impatient, he shook his head with disgust. ''Ye told me yersel' that yer wife smell of flowers, and judging by the way ye said it I would guess it pleases ye. How would ye like it did she smell as *ye* do?''

Duncan grimaced at that question, already knowing the answer. He had been repulsed by her the day she had fallen in the manure, and he had been even more repulsed by Kelly's stench and filth earlier that evening.

''There ye are, then.'' Angus nodded at his son's telling expression. ''Mayhap ye can then understand why yer wife reacts to you as she does.''

Duncan sighed his resignation at that but still complained, ''But she is changing everything, Da. Nothing seems the same since she arrived. The keep is clean, the women are clean and wear new plaids, the food is spiced, and my chamber is full of chests.''

''Aye.'' Angus nodded solemnly. ''Yer life has changed now that ye've taken a wife. But so has hers. 'Tis the way of things. Ye need to accept that and make the best of it.''

''Perhaps,'' Duncan muttered unhappily.

"There is no perhaps about it, boy. As far as I can see, Iliana has done all that is in her power to make our home more pleasant. Tell me, what have you done for her?"

"She's done it all fer hersel', not me," Duncan grumbled, not ready to concede yet.

"Has she? Well now, I did not notice that she instructed Elgin to cook fine fare only fer her but continue to offer slop to the rest of us. Neither did I notice that she had her room cleaned but left the common rooms to ruin. Nay. In fact, my room was cleaned and filled with fresh rushes just last week under yer lady wife's orders, and I ken that they cleaned Seonaid's room, too, and yet they have not got to clean the one she and her mother have been using. It seems to me she leaves the consideration of her own comfort last."

Duncan was silent, a startled look on his face. This was something he had to consider.

Iliana surveyed the room with displeasure. For two days she had lain in bed, staring at the filthy rushes and stained tapestries of her husband's room. And for two days the sight had stung her nerves like salt in a sore.

It was her own fault, she supposed. She had not really needed two days to recuperate from her wound but had allowed herself to be persuaded to rest by her mother. In truth, she supposed she had been hiding up here, just as she had been hiding up here while her mother was ill. It had been easy to do. Once again, Duncan had taken to sleeping in Seonaid's vacant room, leaving her to her own devices. But then, everyone had seemed to leave her to her own devices. Even her mother had not offered her company to pass the time and distract her. According to Ebba, the woman was spending her time regaling either Duncan, Angus, or both men with tales of Iliana's childhood. The very idea made her cringe.

This, the third morning after the attack, she had decided she'd had enough of lying about. There were things to do.

She had responsibilities. The first of which was to clean this room. She only hoped it would not be as large a task as the great hall had been.

With that question uppermost in her mind, Iliana cleared a small space on the floor with her foot to peer at the wood beneath the rushes. She nodded her satisfaction on seeing that, while it was dusty, there was no sign of the hardened spills that had filled the great hall.

"There is no need to scrub."

Iliana glanced up and smiled slightly at her maid's relieved words. "Nay," she agreed easily. "Merely a good sweeping once the rushes are removed."

Ebba sighed at that, and Iliana felt the chafe of guilt. The maid had been running up and down the castle stairs for the last two weeks, fetching this or that; first for her mother, then for Iliana herself.

"Laird Angus is arranging for men to fetch fresh rushes, but why do you not take the women and go out and collect heather to add to them?" she suggested impulsively. "I shall see to removing these and sweeping up."

When Ebba glanced at her doubtfully, Iliana felt herself flush with shame. Ere coming to Dunbar, the woman would never have been surprised at the idea that Iliana was willing to work. But she had done little real labor of late. Not for the last two weeks.

"Take your time," she added firmly now. "The fresh air will do you good."

"You are sure?"

When she nodded, the maid beamed at her and hurried off.

Iliana turned to survey the room again, sighing as she realized just how much work she had set herself up for. But she did not regret it. Her mother had taught her well the importance of treating one's servants with consideration.

"What has you looking so thoughtful, daughter?"

Iliana glanced up as her mother entered the room and

managed a smile. "Good morn, Mother. How do you to-day?"

"Very well." Pausing at Iliana's side, she kissed her cheek, then glanced about the room. "Ebba has gone to collect some heather."

"Aye. I sent her."

"So she said. I sent Gertie with her," Lady Wildwood murmured, then raised her eyebrows. "With your maid gone, who is it you plan to have empty and sweep the room?"

"I thought to borrow some of Duncan's men to move the chests but will remove the rushes myself."

"What of your side?"

"Gertie has put on a liniment to keep it from paining me. So long as I do not overdo—"

"You shall not overdo because ye shall not do it."

Iliana whirled toward the door at that announcement from her husband, and eyed him with displeasure as his words sank in. " 'Tis little enough effort to push a broom around, husband. Surely—"

"Then 'twill be easy work fer the men I send to do it."

Iliana blinked at that, positive she had misunderstood. Had her husband, the man who griped and complained about every spot of cleaning she instigated, just suggested he would send some of his precious men to do it for her?

" 'Tis most thoughtful of you, Duncan," Lady Wildwood claimed when Iliana remained silent. "But surely 'tis not necessary to waste the time of the men who work on the wall? Mayhap the guards you have posted to watch me could—"

"There is only one guard now," Duncan interrupted. "I sent one of the men to the kitchen to breakfast."

"Well, surely even one could—"

"His job is to guard ye, and he'll do so. I'll take two men off the wall to see to this."

Impossible! Iliana thought incredulously. She must have caught a fever. Her wound was infected; she had caught a fever and was now hallucinating, she decided.

"Well." Lady Wildwood frowned as her daughter remained mute, then sighed and offered thanks for her. " 'Tis obvious you have taken my daughter's breath away with your generosity. The offer is greatly appreciated."

Obviously disappointed by Iliana's silence, Duncan moved forward and stooped to pick up the only chest in the room that was his. Turning toward the door with it, he muttered, "I shall remove this to my room, then send some men up to help with the rest."

"Husband?"

Pausing in the doorway, he turned back, one eyebrow arching slightly.

Iliana hesitated, unsure what to say. He had yet to take a bath, and she did not wish to unintentionally make an offer that she was not willing to keep. In the end, she hesitated too long.

His mouth tightening, he shifted the chest impatiently in his arms. "If ye've naught to say, I've better things to do than stand about—"

Iliana caught a glimpse of motion over her husband's shoulder even as the words died on his mouth. The next moment, he stumbled forward, the chest slipping from his hands and falling open as it crashed to the ground. Its contents spilled across the floor, among them a bottle that slid across the rushes to shatter against the wall, filling the room with the biting scent of whiskey.

Iliana and her mother rushed forward as Duncan collapsed atop the now empty chest. Kneeling on either side of his prone form, they peered at the blood gushing from his head, then glanced to the door in unison as a lit torch flew into the room and the door slammed closed.

Neither woman moved for a moment, shock holding them still as the far end of the room exploded into flame. The fire spread swiftly, rushing toward where she and her mother knelt by her husband.

"Duncan?" Grabbing his arm, Iliana tried to turn him over but was unable to move his great bulk until her mother added her own efforts. Once he was on his back, Iliana felt terror well up within her as she saw the pallor of his complexion.

"He is alive, and we must get out of here."

Her mother's calm words broke through her panic, and Iliana glanced toward the flames licking their way toward them. Without discussing it, each of them got to their feet, took one of his large hands in their own and dragged him across the rushes, panic seeming to add strength to their efforts. At the door, Iliana reached out to press against the wooden surface. Frowning when it did not open, she released the hold she had on Duncan and pressed with both hands, but still the door stuck.

"What is it?" Her mother was at her side in an instant.

"It will not open."

Lady Wildwood pushed against the door, paling when her daughter's words proved true. "Someone has blocked it." Pounding on the door, she yelled for her guard, but Iliana stopped her with a hand to her shoulder.

"If he were out there, the room would not be afire."

"Well, surely he would not leave?"

"Nay," Iliana agreed, and her mother's eyes widened with understanding. The guard was either dead or unconscious.

Turning away from her stark expression, Iliana peered toward the fire devouring the room. Smoke was rolling across the ceiling above and she could see that her chests were already in flames. Soon the blaze would reach Duncan's feet. The heat almost unbearable, Iliana glanced frantically around the small section of room that was not yet on fire.

Lady Wildwood began to pound at the door again, screaming for assistance, but impatience covered her face when she saw that her daughter had moved to the bedside. "What do you? We must get some attention here."

"The castle is practically empty, Mama. The women are out fetching fresh rushes and the men are out practicing in the bailey. No one will hear us."

Already pale with fear, Lady Wildwood blanched further. Whipping the linen off the bed, Iliana hurried to drop it in the water she had used earlier for her ablutions, then just as swiftly pulled the soaking material out and moved toward the fire to beat at the flames with it. Her main concern was to keep the flames away from Duncan; they were far too close to his inert body for her liking.

Lady Wildwood quickly moved to collect the bottom linens from the bed. After dampening them with what little water was left in the bowl, she moved to her daughter's side, but Iliana shook her head and waved her away.

"Yell out the window," she ordered, coughing. "We must get someone's attention."

Wrapping herself in the wet sheet, Lady Wildwood hurried to the window and screamed at the men who worked below.

"They are coming," she gasped a moment later, returning to Iliana's side and adding her own efforts to battle the fire.

All of her concentration on the task she had set for herself, Iliana did not spare the energy needed to acknowledge her mother's words.

The heat was scorching. The smoke, thick and black, was stealing her breath away, hampering her efforts at fighting the flames. And hacking coughs were wracking her body as the acrid air burnt her lungs. Iliana had never experienced fire before in such a manner; it seemed almost to be alive. She would beat at one spot, damping the flames there, only to find them turning their attack and seeming almost to try to run past her. It was a war she could not win and had little hope of holding off for any length of time at all did help not come soon. Iliana had already been forced backward to stand directly before her husband as she fought the flames. She was managing to slow the spread somewhat, but not by much. In a moment she would be tripping over her husband's legs.

"Dun-can." The name came out on Iliana's cough, but her mother seemed to understand. Giving up her weak efforts to aid in combating the fire, Lady Wildwood began tugging his legs sideways, trying to shift them out of Iliana's path. She had managed to move them a bare few inches when they both heard shouts and feet pounding up the hallway. In the next second, the door crashed open and cool air rushed into the chamber. As if in response, the fire Iliana faced jumped up and forward with a roar of fury.

Crying out, she stumbled backward, tripping over her husband's legs and tumbling to the floor as her skirts went up in flames. She heard her mother's scream join her own; then something heavy crashed down upon her, knocking the air out of her lungs and sending her head bouncing back against the floor.

Chapter Sixteen

"She's awakening."

Iliana opened her eyes at those words, wincing at the pain reverberating within her head as she squinted against the light in the room.

"Thank God!"

Angus and her mother suddenly appeared above her from opposite sides, worry apparent on their faces as they peered down at her.

"Are ye a'right, lass? Ye took a fair knock."

Iliana blinked at those words from Angus, confusion her first reaction until she noticed the burning pain in her lungs and recalled the fire.

"Duncan?" The name came out on a croak, and Iliana winced as she became aware of the pain in her throat as well.

"He is fine." Tears of relief filling her eyes, Lady Wildwood patted her shoulder. "And you shall be too, now."

"Aye," Angus agreed, his own relief apparent. " 'Tis

lucky ye are. The room went up like a torch."

Iliana closed her eyes at that, frowning. "I have never seen a fire spread so quickly."

"Aye, well, it seems *uisgebeatha* is fair flammable."

Iliana's eyes opened at that. *"Uisgebeatha?"*

"The bottle that rolled out of Duncan's chest and smashed into the wall," her mother explained. " 'Twas *uisgebeatha*. Whiskey. Angus thinks 'tis why the fire spread so quickly. The liquid went everywhere when the bottle shattered."

"Aye, it did."

"Hmmm. Well, that bottle was his birth batch."

Her eyebrows rose at that. "Birth batch?"

"Aye. 'Tis a tradition me father's father started. A batch of *uisgebeatha* is made the day the heir to the chieftain is born and a bottle of it is given to 'em to save 'til the day he takes over. Then he mourns his father's passing and his own raise in position with it."

Iliana had already come to the conclusion that the Scots, or at least these particular Scots, used any excuse they could to drink. Still, the bottle had been saved since his birth, and he would most likely be furious at its loss. "Is Duncan very upset?"

"He doesn't even ken yet. He hasn't awoken." At Iliana's sudden alarm, he patted her arm reassuringly. "Don't fash yersel'. He took a mighty kosh on the head is all. He'll wake soon enough. In truth, he came through better than ye, I think."

Iliana blinked at that. "What mean you, my lord? I was not harmed, other than the knock on the head, and I am already awake."

"Aye. That's true enough. Ye took no other injury. . . . But ye do look kinda funny."

Eyes shooting anxiously to her mother, she caught her glaring at Lord Angus and felt her anxiety increase.

" 'Tis your hair, dear," Lady Wildwood murmured in resignation, catching Iliana's expression. "I fear 'tis a mite melted."

"Melted?" Iliana's eyes rounded at that.

"Aye, and ye've no eyebrows or lashes to speak of," Angus added for good measure, his smile becoming more sincere. Then, seeing her dismay, he cleared his throat. "Yer still bonnie to me, lass. 'Sides, the hair'll doubtless grow back."

"Where is she?"

They all stilled at that roar from the hallway. Then the door crashed open and both her mother and Angus straightened to turn toward the sound.

Recognizing her husband's voice, Iliana felt a rush of both relief and panic. Relief because it was obvious from the strength of his voice that Duncan was truly all right, and panic because she did not wish him to see her if what Lord Angus said was true. Her hair was melted and her eyebrows and eyelashes had been singed off by the fire? She could not even imagine the sight she must be.

Grabbing for the bed linens that had been drawn up to her chin, she jerked them childishly over her head and closed her eyes as she heard him stomp across the room.

Duncan's heart seemed to pause its pumping in his chest as his father stepped aside and he saw the linen drawn up over the form on the bed. He had awoken only moments before to find himself in his father's bed, his head pounding with a vicious beat that seemed to make his very teeth ache. Allistair and Ebba had been standing on either side of him. His cousin had managed a smile of relief when his eyes opened, then announced he would go inform Angus that he was awake. But Duncan had called him back as he moved away and questioned what had happened.

The explanations had stunned him mightily. He recalled standing in the doorway to his own chamber, about to leave, but that was all. Being told that someone had apparently struck him over the head and tossed a lit torch and bottle of *uisgebeatha* into the room, then blocked him, his mother-in-law, and his wife into the room to die a fiery death had been a shock. Learning that Iliana had tried to fend off the fire with wet linen while her mother shouted out the window for help had raised some pride in him for her ingenious thinking. But when Allistair had told him that Iliana had been engulfed by flames when they crashed into the room, nothing could have kept him in the bed. Not the throbbing in his head, not the dizziness that had assailed him as he rose, nor the way his vision had blurred frighteningly as he had stumbled out into the hall.

Only the sight of her shrouded body could bring him to a halt as the fact hit him that she was dead. He should not be so affected by her death, he knew. She had not been a good wife. She'd refused him his rights and done exactly as she'd pleased despite his orders to the contrary. And yet, his brain seemed suddenly full of her. He recalled with crystal clarity the day she had arrived. He remembered her false bravado as she had refused him his rights the morning after their wedding, saw her face alive with intelligence and good humor as she had spoken with Lady McInnes, smelled the flowery scent that clung to her and felt her in his arms, shivering with desire. He heard her passionate moans in his ears, followed by breathless laughter as he had . . . loved her? Aye, he'd loved her.

Swallowing thickly, he took the last step to the bed and tugged the linen slowly down to reveal her features now. He did not know what he expected. Charred flesh, he supposed. The rancid stench of death . . . He certainly did not expect to see her lying with her eyes clenched shut and her nostrils flaring as she breathed.

"Yer alive!"

Iliana's eyes blinked open in surprise. It had not occurred to her that her husband might assume she was dead. Now, however, the stunned little-lost-boy-quality to his voice drew her eyes to his face. Relief, joy, then con-

221

fusion flickered over his face before settling finally into a perplexed frown.

"What be the matter with ye? Ye look funny somehow." Tilting his head to the side, he narrowed his gaze, noting the hair that usually flowed sweet and fresh about her head appeared to have shrunk and melted somewhat. There were clumps of it laying about her pillow. From the fire, he realized, but could not pinpoint what else it was about her that looked so odd. Then it struck him. "Yer eyebrows and lashes are gone!"

Iliana groaned and tugged the linen back up over her head.

She heard Angus's voice chiding her husband, "What the devil be the matter with ye, lad? Guard yer tongue! Ye'll hurt her wee feelings." There was a pause, and then her father-in-law spoke again to Duncan. "Come along, you. Ye shouldna be up. We'd best git ye back to bed ere ye fall over." She heard them move toward the door. "How's yer head?"

"Achin'," she caught Duncan mutter, and she fought the urge to peer out at him.

"Aye, well. We'll pour some *uisgebeatha* into ye and fix ye up right fine."

Duncan's only response was a grunt.

Sighing with relief as she heard the door close behind the two men, Iliana lowered the linen. A touch on her hair brought her glance to her mother. Her expression as she caressed the damaged tresses was mournful.

"Is it very bad?"

Lady Wildwood smiled wryly at that, then nodded. "Aye, I fear so."

Iliana shifted in the bed, then asked, "What of my eyebrows?"

"Those will grow back. We must just be grateful that you were not burned. Your gown went up in flames. Had Angus not been a quick thinker and covered you with his own body to smother the flames . . ."

"Aye. We are fortunate to even be alive." She closed

her eyes wearily, then popped them back open. "What of the guard?"

"His throat was slit."

Iliana blanched and her mother nodded solemnly. "The worst of it is that Greenweld's man is still out there. Angus had the men search the keep again, then searched the inner and outer bailey, but they could not find him. Whoever he is, he is clever."

"You found nothing?"

Angus nodded unhappily at his son's question. "We even searched the keep again but found nothing that would hint that there was anyone here who should not be."

"Damn."

"He is clever, I shall give him that."

"Too damn clever," Duncan muttered bitterly. "He almost succeeded this time."

"Aye. Were it not for the fact that Iliana and her mother remained calm, I should have lost all o' ye." He shuddered even as he said the words, but Duncan did not notice. He was sunk in bitter reflection.

"Once again I failed to protect her. 'Twill not happen again. I shall not leave her side until the bastard is found."

Angus frowned as his son got to his feet. "But I thought we had agreed 'twas her mother the man is after."

Duncan nodded. "Unfortunately, me wife seems to be cursed with the dubious skill of getting in the bastard's way. Repeatedly. So, I will guard me wife. Her mother is yer problem."

"My problem?" he asked warily.

"Aye. As me wife, Iliana's safety is my problem. As laird here, her mother's safety is yours." He grinned suddenly. "Guard her well. Iliana would be mighty upset with ye did ye let her mother come to harm." Turning on that note, he headed up the stairs, leaving his father staring after him.

"My problem," Angus muttered again, then glanced up as Allistair entered the room.

"I have informed the men that we would be searching the woods on the morrow. Is there anything else ye wish from me ere I retire?"

"Aye. Fetch one o' the men to me. I would have a guard at Lady Wildwood's door this—" He paused, suddenly recalling the sweet smell of her as he had held her in his arms earlier that day, soothing her and reassuring her that her daughter would be well. Iliana had been covered with soot at the time, her gown in scorched tatters about her body as Gertie had worked over her. Despite his worry over his daughter-in-law, Angus had found it difficult not to notice the sweet scent of the woman in his arms, and how good she felt there.

"Ye wish a guard fer Lady Wildwood this night?" Allistair asked when Angus continued to sit, lost in thought.

Giving his head a shake, the older man blinked at his nephew, then stood. "Nay. Nay. I'll tend to it mesel'. There is naught else this evening. Ye may go to yer bed. Sleep well," he added as the younger man nodded and turned away.

Reaching for his tankard of whiskey, he downed a good deal of it, then set it aside and got to his feet. Straightening the English surcoat he wore, he headed up the stairs, planning what he would say as he walked. He would announce that he felt she needed a guard and as laird it was his duty. He would insist on having the maid dismissed and on himself sleeping on the servant's pallet in the room. 'Twould be an uncomfortable bed, but he could see to her safety. Besides, mayhap she would offer him a more comfortable alternative.

It seemed to Iliana that her mother had barely left the room when the door was opened again, this time for Duncan to enter. Iliana eyed him uncertainly as he crossed the room, trying to gauge the reason for his presence.

"Yer hair."

Iliana reached up to touch her shorn locks self-consciously. Her mother had cut most of it off, and her hair now reached no further than her chin and curled about her head in a most untame fashion. "It is very short," she murmured uncomfortably when he merely stared at her.

"Aye."

Iliana let her hands drop to her lap and stared at them unhappily. Perhaps it was the after-effects of the fire. Or perhaps it was the stress caused by the two attacks and her worry for her mother, but Iliana suddenly found her vision blurring with tears. They pooled at the corners of her eyes and began to leak down her cheeks.

Spotting the droplets of water slipping down her face, Duncan moved quickly forward. After a hesitation, he sat carefully on the side of the bed and reached out uncertainly to grasp her hands where they rested in her lap.

Iliana blinked her eyes, clearing her vision enough that she could see the large, clean hand holding hers, but that only made her cry harder. "You bathed," she sobbed.

Duncan's eyes widened in surprise at her wail, and he peered at himself curiously for a moment; then understanding covered his features. "I was most like covered with soot. They must have cleaned me up while I was unconscious."

The last word had barely left his lips when his wife suddenly slid a hand around his head, turned him toward her, and drew his face down to hers. Duncan was so stunned by the action and the passion of her kiss as her lips slid hotly across his, that he merely sat frozen, hardly breathing as she slid her tongue into his mouth. He was actually afraid to move, afraid that it would bring this stunningly sweet interlude to an end.

Misunderstanding his lack of reaction, Iliana tugged her mouth away and leaned her forehead on his chest, shuddering with silent sobs. It seemed she could do nothing right. Her marriage was in ruins as far as she could tell and 'twas all her fault. She'd been unreasonable. Most men did not bathe much. She'd been to court. She knew the nobility had a distrust of bathing.

In truth, while the others had stank to Iliana, she had always felt to be the one out of place. Seonaid had been right about Iliana's having had a lonely childhood. She had not had friends. Even at court she had not been allowed to play. She had only been able to stand and wistfully watch as the other children had raced about, muddying their good clothes and laughing. Now, as an adult, she seemed to be repeating that part of her life. Standing by and watching wistfully as her husband took on a mistress who had no problem with his smell and most likely stank herself. Why could she not be like others?

"I don't want ye to be like others."

Iliana blinked at that announcement and flushed as she realized that in her distress she had spoken her thoughts aloud. Shuddering around a sob, she raised her tear-stained face slowly to peer at him, positive she could not have heard him correctly.

"I like the way ye smell, and I don't mind the keep clean and the food tastier. I even like yer hair all short and curly like that. I wouldn't have ye change. And if this marriage is a mess, 'tis sure I am that I had more than a hand in making it one."

That was when Iliana realized that she must be dreaming. Surely no other explanation would do for what was going on here.

" 'Tis no dream, love," Duncan murmured, letting her know she had spoken aloud again. Standing now, he tugged at the shoulder of his plaid. It unraveled and slid to the ground. He then quickly shrugged out of the shirt he had worn beneath it. Dropping that to the floor, he faced her silently for a moment, letting her look her fill before reaching for the linen that was clutched to her chest.

"Or if 'tis a dream," he said now, tugging the material gently away, " 'tis a dream I don't want to end."

Iliana swallowed and glanced down at herself as the linen slid smoothly across her body. She was clad only in the chastity belt. Her gown and undertunic had both been ruined in the fire, as had all the chests bearing the rest of her clothes. It seemed that the belt was the only thing she had left in the world to wear. That was why, after bathing and before having her hair cut, she had re-donned the item. At that moment, however, she wished it too had burned.

Duncan paused when he saw what she wore, but before he could feel disappointment or upset at the sight of it, Iliana reached for the ring of keys on the rough wooden table beside the bed. When she singled out the odd-looking key he had noticed on a much earlier occasion and moved it toward the lock, Duncan caught her hands and relieved her of the ring. He would undo the lock himself. He had fantasized doing so for quite long enough.

Holding the keys in one hand, he offered her his other and urged her to sit on the side of the bed. Once she had shifted to sit as he wished, he knelt on the floor before her and set the keys on the bed.

"Do you not wish to—" Iliana began with bewilderment, then fell silent as his lips covered hers. This time, it was she who sat still and breathless as he kissed her, but not for long. Groaning as his tongue swept inside her mouth, she slid her arms around his neck and clutched him closer as he seemed almost to devour her. It was a sore disappointment when his lips left hers to wander across her cheek, but then they nibbled eagerly at her earlobe as he breathed into her ear, and Iliana shuddered, arching instinctively until her breasts brushed across his chest, the hair there teasing her nipples to small, pebble-like peaks that seemed to beg for his attention.

As if they begged out loud, Duncan suddenly kissed a trail down her neck and over her collarbone, dropping lower still until he found and laved one eager nipple.

Iliana knew she was moaning, and embarrassment made her pause briefly until she realized that her husband was not silent either. He was muttering words of appreciation and grunts of pleasure as he suckled at her. Those sounds only managed to enflame her more and she clutched her hands in his hair, tugging on the soft strands slightly until he released her nipple and peered at her. Iliana kissed him with all the pent-up passion within her.

This time their kiss was rough and hungry. They were both panting heavily when he suddenly tugged his lips away and knelt to attend to her breast again, nipping and biting gently at the tender flesh there. Crying out, Iliana tossed her head back and clutched him closer to her. When he pushed at her shoulders suddenly, she tumbled backward onto the bed. She lay with her legs hanging off of it, her belly rippling and quivering as his lips traveled across it. He licked her flesh along the top of the belt, his hands sliding down to grasp her hips and hold her still as she began to thrash slightly on the bed.

He continued that way for what seemed forever to Iliana, licking, nibbling, and kissing the flesh around the belt, her belly, the sensitive curve of her hips, her thighs. She was positive that he was trying to drive her mad and was thrashing violently on the bed when he finally reached for the key and unlocked the contraption.

Iliana had barely gasped her relief of being free of the obstruction when his head suddenly bowed between her legs once more, his kisses finding the very core of her. Startled and already almost mad with passion and need, Iliana cried out and began to buck beneath him, every muscle in her body seeming to convulse at once. When it ended and she was left with only the occasional small spasm, she lay limp on the bed, positive she would never be able to move again.

She was wrong. Duncan showed her that a short moment later as he began to caress her again.

The Key

Sunlight was pouring in through the window when Iliana awoke the next morning. Smiling, she sighed and stretched on the bed, then rolled onto her side, frowning when she saw that the spot beside her was empty. Duncan had already left the chamber.

Stifling the disappointment that that realization brought her, Iliana sat up on the bed and frowned. She was in Seonaid's room. It was where they had put her after the fire the day before. The fire that had devoured her room and every stitch of clothing she owned, she realized suddenly with dismay. But before she could get too worked up over that, Ebba rushed in carrying a collection of gowns.

"Lord Duncan sent me up with these for you," she explained excitedly, dumping the gowns on the bed, then picking them up one at a time and spreading them out. "Are they not lovely?"

Iliana reached out to brush a hand gently over the material of one of the gowns. "Aye. They are lovely," she said unhappily, bringing amazement to her maid's face.

"Are you not pleased at his thoughtfulness?"

"Oh, aye, 'twas thoughtful. I hope their owner does not mind," she added with a bit of asperity.

Understanding dawned. "Ah. You fear they were his mistress's castoffs," she guessed correctly, then shook her head. "Fie on you. Think you he would be so insensitive? These are his mother's gowns. Can you not tell by the quality? No village girl would have such finery."

"His mother's?" Iliana murmured faintly, noting now that while they were of good quality, they were somewhat old-fashioned.

"Aye. And that is not all. He has spent the morning talking with your mother while you slept and now has sent Allistair to seek out the material merchant."

Iliana's eyebrows rose at that. "He has?"

"Aye."

Iliana was out of bed in a trice and shifting through the gowns on the bed. After a moment, she paused, disappointment on her face. "But these are all undertunics, Ebba. I cannot go below in any of these."

"Oh, aye. I almost forgot." Rolling her eyes, the woman moved to the chest beside the door and quickly opened it to shift through its contents. A moment later she straightened, a neatly folded swath of material in hand.

"Your husband told me this was for you," she announced, returning to her side. " 'Twas to be a wedding gift, but he never got around to giving it to you."

The maid avoided meeting her gaze as she said the last part, and Iliana smiled wryly. No doubt the truth was, Duncan had not given her this "gift" ere now because she had not behaved as a true wife. It seemed last night had changed things. They were getting a new start on their marriage. Mayhap all would turn out well now. In fact, she was determined it would. She and her husband had straightened out quite a few things the night before . . . hadn't they?

Frowning suddenly, she considered that. The truth was, she had revealed her soul to her husband, and he had made love to her with a tenderness and passion that had been different than the first time they had consummated the marriage, or even the time he had loved her in the woods. It was the tenderness that had made it different, she supposed. Not that he had been rough those first two times. But this time there had been something different, something more than the passion that had flamed and consumed them both those other times. He had almost seemed to be paying homage to her.

That must mean something, mustn't it? She wondered over that worriedly, chewing on her lip. In truth, her husband had said very little that would make her think things would be different now. While he had said that he did not wish her to change, he had not said that he himself was willing to do so. He had made no promises to bathe more often or . . . Or anything, she realized, sinking to sit on the bed.

"Why do you not unfold it and take a look?" Ebba asked with a frown, bringing Iliana away from her glum thoughts.

Sighing, she unfolded the material, slightly surprised when she saw that it was a plaid she held.

"He told me how to help you don it," Ebba announced suddenly with a smile. "He even showed me. Was that not thoughtful?"

"Aye." Iliana forced a smile and stood. " 'Twas most thoughtful."

She would not despair. Despite the fact that her husband had made no promises and voiced no pledges, she would give him the benefit of the doubt. He had given her this plaid. It must mean something. Perhaps it was his way of saying what he could not say with words.

It was time for the noon meal when Iliana arrived below dressed in one of the undertunics and the plaid her husband had gifted her with. Everyone seemed to be at table but for Duncan and Allistair. Iliana took her seat beside her mother and glanced curiously around.

"You slept late, my dear. Are you quite recovered from our excitement yesterday?"

Iliana nodded at her mother's question. "Where is my husband?"

"He is meeting with the material merchant."

Iliana's gaze narrowed on the older woman's secret smile. "Why?"

"He has things he wished to purchase," was the obvious answer, and Iliana grimaced at it.

"What things?"

"Material, I suppose."

Before she could question her further, Iliana's attention was turned by Duncan's entering the room. She was aware of his presence the moment he stepped through the keep doors. It seemed to her that the very air itself in the hall was suddenly different, and she could not understand why no one else noticed. She seemed the only person who had sensed his entrance.

He caught her gaze then and grinned, making Iliana realize that she had been smiling widely at him. Flushing slightly, she lowered her gaze abruptly to her trencher, feeling suddenly shy.

Her self-consciousness was short-lived, however, for the keep door slammed open behind him, and Iliana peered around to eye it curiously. Allistair was coming through the door shouldering the weight of an unconscious man. It was an injured Englishman.

Chapter Seventeen

Duncan stood and scowled at the unconscious man Allistair was half-carrying into the keep.

"Who—" Duncan began, only to be cut off by his cousin.

"He is a messenger from Lord Rolfe."

Duncan cursed. He had hoped this was Greenweld's man. "How was he injured?"

"Saving my life."

Duncan stilled at that, and Allistair grimaced, his gaze sliding past him to Laird Angus, Lady Wildwood, and Iliana as they moved to join Duncan and hear the explanation. "I thought I spied someone duck behind a tree as I was riding back with the cloth merchant."

"Why did you not tell me?"

Allistair shrugged. "By the time I got to the tree there was no one there, and I thought mayhap I hadn't really seen anything at all."

"But you went back to check."

"Aye . . . Well, it was bothering me. I thought if there

233

truly had been someone there, he would have left some sign somewhere in the area.''

"And did you find any signs?" Angus asked, stepping forward now to lift and peer at the head of the man his nephew held upright.

"Aye. The remains of a small fire. I was about to head back to call out a search party when I was jumped from behind. When I awoke, this fellow was leaning over me, bandaging me hand.''

Duncan glanced at his cousin's sword hand as he held it up. It was wrapped tight with a strip of plaid.

"I must have broke it as I fell," Allistair admitted grimly.

Duncan frowned at that, then glanced down when his wife slid her hand onto the crook of his arm. She smiled at him gently and he raised a hand to cover her own where it now lay on his arm, then turned as Allistair continued.

"A second man was there as well, already dead. This fellow told me that he be a messenger from Lord Rolfe. He said he'd been sent with news of Seonaid, and that he had come along as Greenweld's man was about to cut me head off. He interfered, they fought, he was injured, and the other one died.''

Both Duncan and Angus were silent for a moment, exchanging a glance, then Angus asked, "You were not conscious when the two fought?''

"Nay."

"And you never saw who hit you over the head?''

Allistair shifted uncomfortably, his gaze sliding to the man he held upright. "Nay."

"Then you have no proof he is who he claims to be?'' Angus sounded more disappointed than anything as he murmured that. Allistair was looking pretty disappointed himself; then he suddenly brightened.

"He showed me the message.''

"The message?''

"Aye. He was afraid he would bleed on it, so he gave

it to me. 'Tis in my belt, I stuck it through there ere helping him onto me horse."

Angus moved forward to search for the message as Duncan asked, "Where was his horse?"

"I put the dead man on it."

"The message must have fallen out on the way back," Angus muttered, straightening. "Where was the dead man's horse?"

"I don't ken." He glanced at the man he held. "Mayhap he kens."

"Ye say ye brought the other man back, too?"

"Aye. He's hung over a horse outside."

Angus turned and gestured to one of the men in the room. The fellow immediately moved out of the great hall.

"Do you not think we should tend his wound?" Iliana asked at last when they all continued to stand around glaring at the unconscious man. Angus and Duncan peered at her as if she was quite mad.

Even Allistair looked taken aback at the suggestion as he asked, "Tend to the wound of an Englishman?"

Iliana frowned at their reaction. "He is injured."

"He is English."

"What has that to do with anything?"

"Scots don't heal an Englishman's wounds, wife," Duncan explained gently. "They cause them."

Iliana's mouth tightened and she tugged her hand off his arm. "Well, then your *English* wife will tend this Englishman's wounds," she snapped irritably, sure they were teasing her, but that this was really no time for it.

"Nay." He tugged her hand back over his arm. "Yer not English."

"I am so," she protested, tugging her hand loose again.

"Nay," he corrected, pulling her hand firmly over his arm once more. "Yer me wife. Ye wear the plaid. Yer Scot now."

As Iliana gaped at him, her mother spoke up. "Well, I am English, not married to a Scot or wearing a plaid, so

I will tend to him. Bring him to the table." She moved determinedly forward as she spoke, fully expecting Allistair to obey. And he did, but not until he received a nod from Angus.

Iliana paused long enough to glare at her husband for his behavior, then followed her mother.

Duncan arched an eyebrow at his father. "Now what have I done?"

Shaking his head, Angus slapped his son on the back, urging him to follow the women. "I believe yer wife would appreciate a bit more diplomacy." When Duncan stared at him blankly, Angus grinned and shrugged. " 'Tis something I've never bothered to teach ye. But don't fash yersel' about it over much. 'Tis something ye'll gain with age. Or not. 'Tis not really important anyway, but women seem to prefer it."

Iliana caught the dirty look her mother sent her father-in-law's way after that statement, but paid it little attention. The Scot Angus had gestured to had come back into the keep, the other man's body slung across his shoulders like a sack of vegetables. Carrying him to Angus, he pulled the man off his back, dropping him on the floor at his feet.

Wincing as his head struck the hard stone, Iliana left her mother and Gertie tending to the man on the table and moved forward to peer curiously at the dead man's face. He was a gruesome sight. His face was as pale as a sheet, most of his blood seeming to stain his surcoat. It looked as if he had suffered a rather large, gaping wound to the stomach and chest. Judging by the grimace of pain on his face, death had been slow and painful.

"Is he the one who attacked you in our bed?"

Iliana swallowed thickly. " 'Twas dark. I saw little but a silhouette. Still . . ." Peering down at him again, she frowned slightly. "He does look familiar to me."

"Ah."

Iliana peered at her father-in-law and raised her eyebrows at that.

The older man shrugged. "Ye were held at Greenweld, were ye not?"

"Aye."

"Then ye must have seen him there," he said simply, then turned to Allistair. "Did ye spy anyone else around?"

The younger man had just shaken his head when Iliana's mother glanced over and announced that their guest was awake. Iliana followed her husband and father-in-law back to the table, where the man was attempting to sit up, struggling against Gertie's equally determined efforts to keep him down.

"Let 'em up, wench, I would talk to him," Angus ordered, pausing beside the table.

Muttering that he would rip the stitches she had just put in his body, Lady Wildwood's maid stepped out of the way.

The man sat up at once and eyed them all rather warily, relaxing only when Allistair approached to stand beside Angus.

There was a tense silence for a moment; then Angus shifted impatiently. "My nephew tells me you saved his life."

The man's gaze skittered to Allistair then away and he nodded. "Aye."

"What happened?"

His gaze slid to Allistair and back again. "I was heading for the keep when I heard a shout. When I came upon your nephew he was unconscious on the ground and a man was standing over him about to cut off his head."

"A man?"

"An Englishman."

"Ye fought him?"

"Aye."

"He died slow," the older man commented, and the Englishman nodded solemnly.

"Slow enough to tell me he was from Greenweld, sent to kill Lady Wildwood."

Iliana glanced instinctively toward her mother, noting the way she paled as Angus asked, "Did he say if Greenweld had other men in the area?"

"He said not. He said Greenweld had expected to catch her fleeing to the king's court; however he'd overheard a rumor that she'd escaped to Scotland. He'd been dispatched to learn if it was true. If he found her, he was to kill her."

"Hmm." Angus eyed him narrowly. "And you are?"

"Hugh. Lord Rolfe sent me to bring a message to you."

"What is the message?"

He appeared confused for a moment. "I gave it to your man. Did he not—"

"I would have it from you," Angus interrupted. "Surely you know the contents?"

He nodded slowly. "Aye. We traveled to St. Simmian's, but Lady Seonaid was not there. She and her companion had not arrived. They have been taken by your enemies, the Colquhouns. Sherwell and Lord Rolfe were going to follow, and asked that you send men to assist them in gaining her freedom. It seems old Colquhoun is intent on shaming her by making her bear him a child so that he may kill it before her."

Iliana gasped in horror, then glanced worriedly toward Duncan as he whirled suddenly toward the doors, shouting instructions and orders as he went. His face was a mask of stone.

"Wait fer me!" Allistair hurried after him, only to have the other man turn on him.

"Nay. Ye'll stay here."

"The hell I will!"

"Yer injured; ye would be useless to me. Ye stay," he announced firmly.

Allistair appeared about to argue the matter, but Angus reached him then and stopped him with a hand on his shoulder. "He's right. Ye stay."

Expression stony, the younger man whirled away and

stormed out of the keep. Angus sighed, then nodded to Duncan. "Let's go."

Duncan frowned at that. "Nay, Da. I will lead this battle."

"She is my daughter."

"And my sister. But someone must stay to mind the castle."

"Allistair can—"

"Yer the one who is forever telling me that either ye or mesel' must always stay behind to mind the keep."

"Aye, but this is different. Seonaid needs us. 'Sides, there is no threat here now. The assassin has been killed."

"And what if the bastard lied as he died? What if there is another? We would be leaving the women untended but fer a handful o' old men and a lame soldier."

Angus glanced toward Iliana and her mother, taking in the concern on their faces. Sighing reluctantly, he nodded. "Go then. But bring her back to us safe."

Turning away, Duncan left the keep, every man in the great hall following. Iliana glanced from the departing men to her mother, then hurried after her husband, unwilling to let him leave without saying good-bye. It was silly, she supposed. Duncan was a great, strong man. But then, so had her father been, and the thought was nagging at her that she had not had the chance to say good-bye to him when he had left on his last trip.

He was halfway to the stables by the time Iliana hurried through the keep door. Grabbing at the skirt of her plaid, she hitched it up slightly and raced after him.

Duncan was stomping toward the stall holding his horse when he heard his wife call his name. Pausing, he turned impatiently toward her, his expression softening slightly as he took in her breathless appearance. She had obviously run to catch up to him, and her brows were drawn together in a worried frown that warmed his heart.

"What is it, wife?" he asked, trying to hide his impatience. His mind was focused on Seonaid and getting her back, and he knew he should not waste his time on marital matters.

Iliana paused a few feet away and grasped at the nearest post, leaning on it while she tried to catch her breath. "I— I—" Sighing impatiently, she let go of the post and rushed at him, throwing herself against his chest and hugging him tight.

Duncan gaped down at her, briefly stunned by her impulsive action. Then, realizing that Rabbie, the stablemaster, was standing not three feet away, grinning widely, he glowered and ordered him out of the stables. Once the man was gone, he raised his hands to pat her back gently.

"Why," he murmured uncomfortably. "What is all this in aid of?"

Embarrassed now, Iliana shook her head and closed her eyes, clutching him for a minute before pushing herself away. "Nothing," she mumbled, peering at the ground before her feet. "I just thought to see you off. Wish you godspeed, and luck, and—"

She paused when he placed a finger beneath her chin and raised her face to meet his gaze, unable to hide the expression in her eyes.

"Do you mean to tell me that me wee prissy wife is worried fer her great, smelly oaf o' a husband."

Iliana flushed at that, wondering when he had heard her refer to him as that, but nodded honestly. "You do not smell now, my lord. Mayhap if you did I would feel differently, but—"

This time he silenced her with his lips, drawing her into a kiss that took her breath away. She was quite dazed by the time he released her. Leaning her head against his chest, she closed her eyes. "I love you."

It was the way he stilled against her that made Iliana realize what she had said. Good God! Where had that come from? she wondered in horror, then tugged free of him and fled the stables, too confused and embarrassed to look him in the eye. Iliana heard him shout after her but did not slow her step. Unfortunately, she had much shorter legs and was hampered somewhat by her skirts. She nearly groaned aloud when she felt his hand clasp her arm before she had taken more than a dozen steps from the stables. When he tugged her around, she jerked into him with a gasp, and it was the last sound she made.

Duncan kissed her. He kissed her right there for all to see and with a passion that made her toes curl. When he finally set her away, her lips were swollen and red, her cheeks flushed, and she was swaying on her feet.

Duncan took in her condition with satisfaction, then turned her toward the keep before bending to whisper: "We'll discuss this further when I return. Now get ye back." He released her then with a light slap on the derriere, and Iliana stumbled toward the keep, embarrassment painting her cheeks as she noticed all the grinning people about her. The courtyard seemed filled with men preparing to leave for battle, and every one of them had witnessed the shameless display.

Shriveling inside, she forced her head up and continued on to the castle.

Iliana watched Janna work at weeding the garden. The other woman seemed to alternate between viciously ripping the weeds from the ground and pulling them out almost absently as her gaze gained a faraway look. It seemed to her that the young woman—and most of the women of the keep—were suffering the same lack of concentration and worry that she herself was. It was the men's fault, of course. It had been one day since Duncan and his men, including Janna's husband, Sean, had marched off after Seonaid.

Sighing, Iliana moved along the path toward Janna, her thoughts turning to her mother. Lady Wildwood seemed to be the only person within Dunbar who was unaffected by moodiness. She, Ebba, and Gertie had spent the re-

241

mainder of the day after the men had left performing some mysterious task in one of the newly built rooms. Whatever it was, they had finished shortly ere sup the eve before. Today, Lady Wildwood had split her time between trying to reassure Iliana that Duncan would be all right and telling Angus that his son would bring his daughter back well and unharmed.

Iliana was growing so sick of hearing her good-intentioned platitudes that she had abandoned Angus to the woman and spent as much time away from the two people as possible.

"Me lady!" Janna straightened to sit back on her haunches when her mistress blocked out the sunlight with her body, making her aware of her presence. "I did not hear you approach."

"You seemed lost in thought."

"Aye." The other woman sighed, her gaze moving absently to the wall around the garden, as if she could see beyond it. "Think you they will be a'right?"

"Of course," Iliana murmured, hoping her own worry was not obvious. "You do not have to do this today. Why not leave it for now?"

Janna shook her head sadly. "'Twould just give me more time to fret."

Understanding, Iliana nodded. "Well, I just thought to have a peek at the garden to see how it fares before joining Lord Angus and my mother to survey the wall."

"The wall?"

"Aye. Mother asked Lord Angus to show us the improvements Duncan has made. I believe 'tis another attempt of hers to distract us from worrying."

Janna grinned slightly. "I am sure she means well."

"Aye." Iliana smiled wryly. "'Tis the only reason I agreed to accompany them. Stop when you wish, Janna. It seems to be faring well enough on its own."

Nodding, the other woman went back to her work and Iliana turned away, moving slowly along the rows of growing plants, back toward the kitchen.

* * *

" 'Tis a fine sturdy wall. You must be proud of your son."

Angus's expression softened at Lady Wildwood's words. "Aye. Duncan is a good lad. A bit too stubborn for his own good at times and quick to anger, but he has a sharp mind and a good heart."

"My daughter was fortunate to—" She paused, frowning as she realized her companion was no longer listening. He had stiffened quite suddenly, his eyes narrowing on the trees beyond the wall. "What is it?" she asked, anxiety rippling down her back.

Angus was silent for a moment, then gave a slight shake of his head. "I thought I saw—" Cursing, he turned abruptly toward the gate. "Close the gate! Lift the bridge!" he roared. "Now! Now! Now!"

Lady Wildwood started to peer toward the gate, then whirled back toward the man at his gasp. Reaching out instinctively, she caught him as he stumbled forward, taking a great deal of his weight and crying out as she saw the arrow protruding from his back. A second arrow whizzed past them then, and she instantly dropped to her knees, taking Angus with her.

"Mother!" Iliana rushed forward at a crouch. She had just stepped onto the battlement when Angus had yelled for the bridge to be raised. His order had surprised and confused her until the man fell beneath an arrow a moment later. A glance over the wall had explained all. Mounted men were charging from the trees, archers following more slowly. The castle was under attack. One glimpse of the tabards of the men on horseback had been enough to tell her that their attackers were English.

For a second, Iliana was paralyzed with fear as she saw that the drawbridge was still in place. Then it slowly began to lift. Still, she feared that at least the first two of the horsemen charging toward it might manage to leap atop the rising bridge, but they were a cautious pair. Instead they slowed and drew in their mounts, watching it rise unhampered. Greenweld, Iliana saw with dismay.

Turning away grimly, she hurried along the wall at a crouch.

Reaching the spot where her mother now knelt worriedly over a prone Angus, she took in his injury and pale face at a glance. There was little blood just yet, but his pain was obvious. Sweat had already formed a film across his brow. His expression as he lay on his side on the stone surface was a grimace of agony.

A glance down into the bailey showed mass chaos reigned there. The cry of attack had rung out even as Angus had fallen beneath the arrow, and now the people, normally so stern and stoic, were rushing willy-nilly, looking for loved ones and children to be sure none had been caught outside of the walls. The noise was thunderous. No one would hear her call for help to move Angus. They were on their own.

Feeling a hand grab her own, Iliana glanced back at Angus to find his eyes open, if a bit glazed. "Can you move under your own power?"

He nodded grimly. "I'm a'right. 'Tis just a scratch."

Iliana's mouth tightened at that. He sounded weak and breathless, and she knew that his claim was just male pride speaking. She peered back the way she had come, then ducked instinctively lower as another rain of arrows flew overhead. There was no question but that they had to get him off the wall and tend to his injury. She would have preferred dealing with it there on the spot, but arrows were still flying overhead and it was possible another one might find a target.

"We cannot walk."

Iliana glanced back at her mother's worried words.

"I can so," Angus snapped, shifting as if to rise.

Iliana stopped him with a hand to his shoulder. "She said *we* cannot walk, not *you*," she explained quietly. "And she is right. We risk another arrow do we try. Even bent over, you are too tall to keep beneath the safety of the wall.''

"What do we do?"

Iliana hesitated for a moment, then began to remove the plaid she wore over her undertunic.

"What are you doing?" her mother asked with dismay.

"We shall use this to drag him to the steps."

"I can walk, I tell ye," Angus muttered faintly as she laid out her plaid flat on the stone parapet beside him, then shifted out of the way. "Think you you can roll onto your stomach on the plaid?"

"I'll not be carried off the wall like—"

"Stop being a stubborn old fool and roll onto the plaid. If my daughter is willing to run about half-naked in front of everyone, the least you can do is cooperate."

Angus flushed at Lady Wildwood's reprimand but did as instructed, though not without grumbling about what the world was coming to when women thought they could order their laird about. Ignoring him, Iliana and her mother moved to crouch at the top of the plaid. Each of them taking a corner, they straightened until they stood half-upright, bent at the waist; then they began to move forward, tugging the plaid behind as they went.

Chapter Eighteen

Angus grumbled all the way to the stairs leading down to the bailey. Once there, he insisted on moving under his own steam, and actually managed to do so with a bit of assistance. With one arm across Iliana's shoulders and one over her mother's, they managed to walk him sideways down the stairs, then half-walk, half-carry him to the steps of the keep, but that was as far as they got him.

Iliana and her mother wanted to take him inside to tend to his wound, but Angus would not hear of it. Not while his home was under attack. Giving in to his stubbornness, they sat him on the bottom step of the keep, so that he could shout orders at the few men who had been left behind while she and her mother worked on his injury.

The arrow had entered his right shoulder from the back, directly beneath his collar bone, and made it three quarters of the way through his body before stopping. Knowing what they would have to do, the two women exchanged a grim glance.

"Shall I fetch one of the men?" her mother asked.

Iliana peered hopefully around as Angus bellowed toward a passing man, asking where Allistair was. The response was most disheartening. He had ridden out an hour before the attack. Iliana felt her heart sink as the man rushed toward the stairs, bow in hand, obviously heading to the wall to return some of the arrows that had been sent over the wall.

The situation looked grim. There were very few men left behind to defend the keep, and most had been left because they were either too old or too young to be of much use in battle. Every single one of them was taken up with fending off their attackers at the moment, which left the women alone to deal with their laird's wound.

"My lady!" Ebba rushed down the stairs, Elgin and Janna on her heels. "Thank God you are all right. I was in the kitchen when Janna ran in shouting that we were under attack, and then when Elgin said that ye, yer mother, and Lord Angus were up on the wall I thought sure—Oh!" The last word was a gasp as she saw the arrow.

Pausing, she glanced over the two women once more to make sure that they, too, had not been injured, then whirled away, nearly running over Elgin and Janna as she charged back up the steps. "I shall fetch some linen to wrap the wound," she cried breathlessly before disappearing back inside the keep.

"Ye'll need fresh water," Elgin decided, whirling to follow.

"What would you have me do?" Janna asked anxiously.

"Fetch Gertie. Have her bring her medicinals. Especially her sleeping potion."

Nodding, the woman hurried to do her bidding, and Iliana glanced toward her father-in-law, slightly surprised to find him eyeing her suspiciously.

"What would ye be wantin' a sleeping potion fer?"

"I thought to give it to you ere removing the arrow."

"The hell ye will!"

247

"But we needs must push the arrow through the front to take it out."

"I've been a warrior fer longer than ye've been alive, lass. I ken what ye have to do, but ye'll do it with me awake. We are under attack. Me men need me."

Iliana glared at him briefly, then heaved a sigh and gestured for her mother to take position in front of the man to help brace him, even as she moved behind. Grasping the arrow carefully in her sweaty hands, she paused and glanced at his pale face. "Ready?"

Angus braced his hands on his knees and started to nod, then shook his head. "I need some *uisgebeatha* first."

"I shall fetch it." Lady Wildwood rushed after the servants.

Angus immediately turned his attention to barking orders at this person and that as they flew by. Iliana envied him his ability to turn his mind from what was coming. She herself felt positively ill at the prospect of what she must do. Moments later, her mother came flying back down the stairs, Ebba, Gertie, Giorsal, Janna, and Elgin on her heels.

Stopping in front of Angus, Lady Wildwood started to hand him the pitcher she had returned with, then paused to down some of the fiery liquid herself. The laird half-smiled and half-grimaced with pain as she began to splutter and cough.

Iliana noticed all of this rather distractedly. Most of her attention was on Gertie as the servant examined the arrow protruding from the Dunbar's back.

"He'll bleed," old woman announced.

"Bleed?" Iliana asked warily.

"Once the arrow is out of the way, he'll bleed."

Lady Wildwood had been about to hand the pitcher to Angus again, but paused at those words to gulp some more of the liquid. Giorsal and Ebba began shredding the linen they had both brought into long narrow strips.

"Do you have anything to slow the bleeding?" Iliana

asked, slapping her mother's back when she began hacking again as the whiskey burnt its way down her throat.

Gertie pursed her lips. "Pressure."

"Pressure?"

She nodded. "Hold the blood in."

Lady Wildwood groaned and tipped the pitcher to her lips again.

"Mother!" Iliana bit out impatiently, noting the wistful way Angus was watching her mother devour his liquor.

"Sorry, dear," she gasped, a chagrined look on her face as she handed the half-empty pitcher to Angus.

Grunting, he lifted the pitcher to his lips, downing a goodly portion in one chug before straightening and bracing his arms on his legs. "Do it."

Wishing she could have a swig of the liquid herself, Iliana gestured to her mother and Elgin. Both moved to press their hands to his shoulders to help hold him in place.

Assured that all was ready, she took a deep breath, brushed her suddenly damp hands down the skirt of her tunic, then grasped the arrow. Silently counting to three, she took another breath, then began to push with all her might, nearly groaning aloud when Angus stiffened and began to bellow.

His roar of pain ended when she stopped pressing on the arrow. One glance at her mother's tear-streaked face told her that she had not succeeded. While the tip of the arrow had pushed deeper, it had not yet pierced the other side. Eyes blurring with her own tears, Iliana readjusted her stance and immediately began to push again, this time putting all her weight behind it.

Angus cried out as the arrow finally tore through and out, his shout ending on a string of curses that were muttered in a much fainter voice.

Stepping to the side, Iliana grasped the arrow where it still protruded from his back. Hands shaking with the effort and eyes blurring with her own tears, she tried to snap

it in two. It took three tries for her to break the stem of
the arrow. Iliana was sobbing by then with each groan
from her father-in-law as the shaft shifted in his body.
When it finally broke in two, she dropped the end with
the flights on it, then stepped around to stand before him,
pausing there to brush her hand across her eyes so that
she could see.

"Whist, lass, I'm the one who should be crying," Angus chided gently.

Iliana glanced at his face then, frightened by the gray
tinge to it and amazed when he managed to offer her a
weak grin.

"Go ahead, finish it," he whispered.

Straightening her shoulders, she grasped the arrowhead
and pulled it out with one clean jerk, then stepped quickly
out of the way as Gertie and Elgin applied cloths and
pressure to the wound.

Iliana watched dully as the others worked over him,
applying pressure, then the salves; one to clean the
wound, and one to encourage healing. Then Gertie
quickly stitched and bandaged him front and back.

Once it was finished, the others stepped back to eye
him worriedly. Despite Gertie's quick work, he had lost
a good deal of bood. Even his lips seemed gray now.

"Are ye done?" he asked, grimacing.

Gertie nodded solemnly.

"Good. Then I'd best see to our visitors." He pushed
himself off the steps then, swaying but managing to gain
his feet, much to the amazement of the people surrounding
him. He even managed a shaky step forward. Then he
collapsed like a tree under the ax.

Crying out, Iliana and the others hurried to catch him
as he pitched forward, then gently eased his unconscious
form to the ground.

"Laird!" Willie, the stablemaster's son, came to a
shuddering halt before them, eyes wide in horror as he
saw that the man would be of little assistance.

"What is it?" Iliana asked impatiently.

The boy hesitated, then seemed to decide there was little harm in telling her. "My father sent me to tell the laird that the English are erecting a causeway. Once 'tis done, they will no doubt either ram the bridge or set it afire.

Iliana frowned and glanced toward her unconscious father-in-law.

"Go," her mother murmured. "See what you can do. You are in charge now."

Iliana stiffened in dismay, for her mother was right. With Angus out of action and her husband away, she was in charge. Even Allistair was not there to relieve her of the burden. 'Twas a frightening realization, made more so by the anxious expressions on the faces of those around her.

Realizing she had no choice, Iliana gathered her courage. "Where is your father?" she asked at last.

"On the wall."

"Go," her mother repeated when Iliana glanced toward her uncertainly. "We shall see Angus to his room."

Nodding unhappily, Iliana turned to walk toward the stairs she and her mother had helped Angus down not more than half an hour earlier. Aware that Willie was lagging behind, she glanced back at him sternly. "Pick up your feet, lad," she ordered with as much authority as she could muster. " 'Tis not a Sunday picnic we are heading to."

The boy's eyebrows rose at that and he did speed up to walk beside her. He even managed to look a little less positive that they were doomed.

One glance down the wall when she reached the stablemaster's side told Iliana that this was not a problem that could wait for her father-in-law to regain consciousness.

Greenweld was below. She recognized him in his armor. He was mounted and shouting orders at the men building the causeway across the moat.

"If they finish that, they'll be within the walls in no time," the stablemaster announced as she straightened. "They'll set fire to the bridge and gate."

"Aye." Iliana racked her brain for a solution.

"Our arrows are no good with that barricade over their heads," he informed her helpfully.

"I realize that." Iliana sighed, then glanced toward the mound of boulders in the inner bailey. The men had just managed to finish the wall ere leaving on the expedition to rescue Seonaid. That was a blessing. They would have been in quite a spot had they not. Still, there was stone left.

Iliana remained silent for a moment, her mind working over the problem that had been presented to her. Her gaze slid to the rocks again. Most of them were too large for the idea forming in her mind, but the smaller ones would do quite nicely.

"Collect as many men as you think you will need and fetch that rock up here."

"Rock?" He peered where she pointed dubiously.

"The smaller one on the edge of the pile," she explained.

"I don't think—"

"Do it."

"But 'twill take at least six men to get it up here."

"Then take six men," she responded promptly. "And send four more to the kitchens with two long posts to fetch Elgin's vat of stew up here as well."

"The cook's *stew?*" He goggled at her.

"You heard me."

"Aye, but—That will leave only two men up here to keep shooting arrows at—"

"There is nothing to shoot at, sir," she pointed out dryly. "As you have said, they cannot shoot through the barricade, and the others are out of range. Now, stop questioning me and do as I have ordered. I have a plan."

Rabbie opened his mouth to argue further with her, caught a glimpse of her stubborn expression, and thought better of it. Closing his mouth on a sigh of resignation, he turned and moved away, shaking his head.

Iliana watched him go, then peered down on the Englishmen again, watching them work until she heard a series of muttered curses coming from the steps.

"Be careful! Ye'll spill the—Damn ye fool men!"

Iliana whirled toward the stairs at those harassed words from Elgin, who had apparently accompanied the product of his labors.

"Me lady!" Elgin's florid face came into view as he mounted the last of the steps. Wringing the hem of his apron in his hands, he hurried toward her. "These buffoons came charging into the kitchens, slid those damn posts under the handle of my vat, and started to leave with it. When I asked what they were about, they claimed ye wanted it up here. I told them they must be mistaken—"

"They told you true," Iliana soothed, patting his shoulder gently. Stepping past him, she instructed the four men to set the vat of steaming liquid down as close to the wall as possible to make as much room as they could for the six men huffing and puffing along behind them, carrying the boulder she had requested.

"Where do ye want it?" the stablemaster gasped breathlessly as soon as he and the other men had maneuvered gingerly past the steaming vat.

"Set it on the wall, directly in the center," Iliana instructed, then turned to the four men still standing by the vat. "I would like that on the wall right next to it."

That they followed her instructions at once was good, but the exchanged looks made her grimace. She was not a stupid woman, nor was she mad, and the fact that they had not yet caught onto her plan was rather irritating.

"Me lady?" Elgin was glancing from her to the vat that was teetering dangerously on the edge of the wall, looking nearly ready to burst into tears. Iliana smiled at him gently and patted his shoulder once more.

"Do not fret, Elgin. All will be well."

"But me stew . . ."

Iliana's mouth thinned out into a straight line. "We have guests at the door. Would you turn them away without at least offering them some sustenance?"

His eyes widened in horror at that, but the other men suddenly began to grin as they understood her intentions. Iliana turned toward Rabbie.

"The rock first to smash the barricade and causeway. Count to three, then tip the vat after it."

"Me stew," Elgin whimpered, twisting his apron more frantically.

" 'Twill be put to good use, Elgin," Iliana murmured sympathetically.

"Aye." The stablemaster grinned at the cook as he and two of the other men shifted in preparation of pushing the boulder off the wall. " 'Twill be a meal those English dogs'll not soon forget." Pausing, he glanced toward the men now manning the vat. "Remember, on the count of three."

Iliana took a step to the side and leaned over to peer down the wall as they pushed the rock off. It plummeted downward so swiftly there was little chance for those watching to shout a warning. The crash as it smashed into the barricade was incredibly loud, the screams of the unfortunate men in its path louder still as the entire structure shuddered and collapsed beneath. Stew poured down over the now unprotected men.

"Me vat!" Elgin cried as it followed the stew, the men unable to hold the hot vessel. His voice was drowned out by their cheers, however, when the heavy metal vat crashed through the causeway, sending it shuddering and collapsing into the moat, taking a great many of the men below with it.

Iliana herself was silent as she stared at the devastation below. Dead or dying men were strewn about like fallen chess pieces, their moans rising to batter her ears. A few of the men who had waited in the cover of the woods charged forward to aid their fallen comrades, and Iliana's men immediately loosed arrows upon them. They would give no quarter.

Turning away, she muttered something about checking on Lord Angus and walked blindly back toward the stairs, nearly stumbling into her mother.

Lady Wildwood took one look at Iliana's stark face, then raised the pitcher she had brought with her. "Here. Have some of this." Unwilling to be denied, she lifted the pitcher to Iliana's lips herself, and tipped it up. The fiery liquid poured down her throat, burning a path into her belly. Iliana tugged her head away after a few swallows to splutter and cough.

Lady Wildwood thumped her back hearteningly, watching her face with concern and muttering, "Well, at least you have some color back in you."

The coughing fit slowing, Iliana raised a hand to ward off her mother and swallowed grimly. "Why would anyone drink that stuff? It tastes like liquid fire."

"Aye." Lady Wildwood smiled wryly and brought the pitcher to her own lips, then shook her head with satisfaction as she swallowed. "I fear I've found a taste for it."

Iliana snatched the pitcher from her with a scowl. "How is Angus?"

Lady Wildwood sighed glumly. "He has not regained himself yet. He is resting. I left Gertie with him and came to see what was about up here. Your plan was very clever. You have earned the men's respect."

Iliana waved the words away. She had no interest in discussing what she had just ordered to be done. She wanted no credit or praise for it. She opened her mouth to say as much, then whirled at a shout of pain from behind her. The stablemaster had fallen to the ground, clutching his arm. An arrow protruded from his shoulder.

"I shall fetch the women," her mother gasped, whirling to hurry down the stairs.

Mouth tightening, Iliana hurried to the man's side. Thankfully, this arrow had gone right through. This time there would be no having to push the arrow through. The end merely had to be broken off. Remembering the trouble she had had breaking the earlier arrow, Iliana glanced at Elgin as he knelt on the man's other side. "Are your hands strong, Elgin?"

"What?" He glanced at her in confusion and she shook her head.

"Never mind. Doubtless they are stronger than mine. Help me sit him up."

"I don't need help."

Iliana rolled her eyes as the stablemaster forced himself to a seated position. It seemed men's pride came before their good sense. Pressing her hands to either side of his shoulder, Iliana glanced at Elgin. "I need you to break the end off the arrow."

Elgin and the stablemaster both winced, and Iliana nearly sighed aloud.

"It must be broken to remove it, else we shall have to pull either the arrow or the flights through the wound. 'Twould cause more damage."

Rabbie began cursing and Elgin quickly joined in, even as he reached for the shaft of the arrow. Their cursing reached a crescendo as he snapped the arrow in two; then they both fell silent.

Casting a sympathetic glance at the stablemaster's pinched face, Iliana stood to replace Elgin as he got out of the way. Kneeling again, she glanced toward the stairs, relieved when she saw her mother hurrying toward her. Giorsal, Janna, and Gertie followed, bearing salves and bandages.

Casting a reassuring smile at the man, Iliana quickly removed the arrow and grabbed for the bandages Janna rushed forward to hand her. She was pressing the bandages against the wound to staunch the flow of blood when another shout drew her attention. Even as she saw that another man had been hit, a third stumbled backward from the wall, an arrow in his chest.

Crying out, Iliana jumped to her feet, hurrying forward

to stop his backward movement. But she was too late; he tipped off the wall, tumbling backward into the bailey far below. Cursing, Iliana left Rabbie to Gertie's tender mercies and rushed to the second man, relieved to see that he still lived. She knew that the third man had not been so fortunate.

She grimaced as Elgin knelt across the injured man from her, then glanced toward the stablemaster as he regained his feet. His injury had been tended and bound, and he was moving toward the wall again. "Nay, Rabbie! You should rest."

"Rest'll not keep these bastards from our gate. And what good will rest do if it sees me dead later?" And with that, the man moved back to his post.

Iliana sighed. It would be a long siege; she only hoped they could hold out.

Chapter Nineteen

"Iliana?"

She raised her head slowly from where she was resting, her eyes slightly bleary as she peered at her mother.

Lady Wildwood's gaze slid from her daughter's morose expression to Elgin and Rabbie, both of whom sat swaying on either side of her. The table before them was littered with empty pitchers that had once held whiskey. "Angus is awake."

Rabbie straightened abruptly at that, as did Elgin.

"Awake?" the cook murmured, his eyes suddenly bright. "He'll be wantin' to eat then. I'd best fetch something." Stumbling to his feet, he hurried toward the kitchen.

Lady Wildwood frowned at Iliana's complete lack of reaction to the news, then moved forward, holding a hand out. "Come. Angus may not be able to stay awake long, and he seems to have something to tell you. You, too, Rabbie."

The stablemaster was on his feet at once and following them toward the stairs.

Angus was awake, but terribly pale and frail-looking when Iliana's mother led her into the room. He took one look at Iliana's glum expression and struggled to sit up. "What is it? Has the wall fallen?"

"Nay, all is well," Lady Wildwood soothed, urging him to lay back on the bed.

"All is better than well, me laird." Rabbie grinned as he hurried to the bedside to tell of what had been done. He waxed enthusiastic about Iliana's clever use of the rock to crush the barricade and her substitution of stew for the boiling pitch.

Angus listened calmly, his gaze never leaving Iliana's face. When the man had finished, he asked, "Then what happened?"

Rabbie glanced uncomfortably away. He was not eager to give the bad news and she could not blame him. The responsibility was hers anyway.

Straightening her shoulders, she moved to the side of the bed. "They responded with volleys of arrows. Four of our men were killed, and three injured before I told them to withdraw from the wall."

"You left the wall unguarded?" Angus looked horrified at the possibility and Iliana quickly shook her head.

"Nay, I stayed to watch their activities." If he had looked horrified that the wall might have been left unmanned at all, he looked even more so that Iliana herself had insisted on staying there to watch alone. "The men were busy helping to move the dead and injured," she added quickly as he started to turn a furious gaze on the stablemaster. It was not Rabbie's fault. He had tried to argue with her, as had everyone else, but she had been stubborn and taken full advantage of the fact that she was now in charge by ordering them off the wall. " 'Sides," she added now, "once I saw what they were up to, I called the men back."

"Saw? Ye *saw?* Ye had the stupidity to look over the wall when they were shooting arrows?!"

"Well, someone had to do it. Would you have me stand

259

safely back and order another to risk his hide? You would not do that.'' Iliana grimaced at the cursing that followed her words.

When Angus finally fell silent, Iliana thought it prudent to continue quickly. ''They had been busy while they kept us pinned down with their arrows. The wounded and dead had all been removed, a second shield was already in place, they had repaired the damage to the causeway and were attempting to finish it.''

''Aye,'' Rabbie piped up now. ''She ordered two more boulders brought up. Big ones this time. 'Twas a nasty business getting them up there, but once we had, we pushed one off the top again and put paid to the causeway—and a good many of their men as well. She had us leave the second one sitting on the wall as a warning. They gave up the causeway and have done naught since then.''

Angus glanced briefly at Iliana's unhappy expression before turning back to Rabbie. ''Go back to the wall and keep an eye on things. *But know this*: Lady Iliana is in charge until I am recovered enough to take over. Report to her.''

''I do not think I should be in charge, my lord. I do not have the experience,'' Iliana said as Rabbie left the room and Elgin entered, a bowl of broth in hand.

'' 'Tis not experience that will save us here. 'Tis intelligence, and you have that.''

''Nay, I am not nearly smart enough to manage Greenweld. I tried three times to escape him in England and failed all three times. I would not wish to fail you here.''

''Ye will not fail,'' Angus announced calmly.

''Aye,'' Elgin agreed, moving to her side. ''Yer very clever, me lady. Why, your plan with the rock and the stew were most clever. . . . Except for losing my vat,'' he added with a frown. ''S'truth, that part could have been planned better, as I've naught to cook in now, but—''

''Elgin!'' Angus snapped, managing some strength behind his words. ''Leave us.''

The cook hesitated, then handed the broth to Iliana and hurried out. Angus then turned a frown on the female servants. They immediately moved toward the door. Within moments he, Iliana, and her mother were alone in the room.

"I could tell by yer expression that ye feel responsible fer the deaths of Greenweld's men on the bridge," Angus commented as soon as the door closed.

Iliana nodded her head silently.

"Well, ye are. Yer as responsible as if ye had taken a sword to each of them yersel'," he announced firmly, nodding solemnly when she winced. "And ye'd do it again to save the people within these walls, so don't fret over it. 'Twas their choice to attack. Yer choice is whether to fight or surrender and walk out like lambs to a slaughter. Yer not a lamb, lass. Accept the guilt as the part of ye that makes ye human, but don't let it rule ye. Ye did right. I'm proud to call ye a Dunbar."

"'Tis not just Greenweld's men who died this day," she pointed out miserably. "We lost four of our own."

"They gave their lives for their loved ones. There are two hundred women and children within these walls. Any one of my men would give their life to keep them safe."

"Men? Two of the dead were but boys!" Iliana protested with disgust.

"Even boys have honor. Do not take it from them to salve your own conscience."

Iliana stiffened at that, and Angus smiled gently, holding a trembling hand out to her.

"There." He sighed when she slid her small smooth hand into his large, scarred one. "'Tis obvious ye don't understand our ways, but this is what 'tis all about. Meself and any one of my people would give our lives for ye. Me, because I am yer laird. Our people, because they swore an oath to protect ye with their lives on the day ye wed me son. 'Tis not so different from what ye did today, risking yer bonnie neck with that foolishness on the wall rather than ordering another to do it," he added with a glare. "There is nothing more honorable to a man than to die in defense of those he loves. As for those two ye claim were just boys, they were not. They were men. Leave them their honor and let go yer guilt. They will be remembered for their bravery this day."

Iliana felt some of the tension in her ease and nodded solemnly.

"Good." Angus managed a smile, then let his head drop wearily back on the bed. His eyes closed for a minute, then opened again. "We are in a spot of trouble."

"Aye," Iliana agreed quietly. "It would seem either Greenweld's man lied when he claimed to be alone, or Greenweld changed his mind and was on his way here and the fellow did not know."

" 'Tis more like he lied. 'Twas just damn lucky for Greenweld that Duncan was called away. Too damned lucky."

Iliana stilled at that. "Think you the message was a ruse to lure Duncan away?"

"I do not know. From what he said, Allistair ne'er saw the message. He merely saw a rolled-up scroll, and that was gone by the time he arrived back."

"The Englishman could have removed it on the ride back without his noticing. They were both on the same horse."

"Where is the messenger now?"

Her eyes widened. "I had forgotten all about him."

"So had I. Check on him when ye leave me, and send someone back to tell me what is about. Ye might set a guard on him as well." Catching the worried frown on her face, he reached out to pat her hand reassuringly. " 'Tis a spot o' trouble to be sure, but just a spot. So long as we keep them outside the wall, all will be well. Duncan will roust them when he returns."

"How long do you think 'twill be ere he returns?" Lady Wildwood asked, speaking up for the first time.

The way Angus hesitated over answering made Iliana

a bit nervous. She understood why when he spoke. " 'Tis four days' travel to reach Colquhoun."

"Four days?" Her mother was openly horrified at that news.

"Four days there, four days back, and however long his battle lasts," Iliana said morosely. "We have lost many of our men on the first day, my lord. I do not think—" She paused when she saw the exhaustion on the man's pale face. She could not burden him with her fears. Instead, she forced a smile and reassured him. "I do not think 'twill be a problem to fend them off for that long."

"Yer a braugh lass. I like that," Angus muttered, then closed his eyes.

Iliana peered at him silently for a moment, then glanced toward her mother when the woman murmured, "He'll rest now for a while."

"Aye." She frowned at the dark smudges under her eyes. "You should do so as well. You have been up here the whole day helping Gertie with him."

Lady Wildwood shrugged her worry away. "He would not have been harmed were it not for me."

Iliana had been about to walk past her to go check on the messenger when those words stopped her. " 'Tis not your fault, Mother."

"Aye. 'Tis. Greenweld would not be here were it not for me."

"Greenweld is a selfish, greedy bastard. If you wish to blame him, then do. But do not be so foolish as to blame yourself along with him."

"We cannot withstand him for two weeks. We do not have enough men."

"We will do well enough."

An expression of despair crossed her mother's features. "I should never have come here. I knew he would follow. I came here and put my child and all of her people at risk," she muttered with self-disgust, then, "He would leave you in peace, did I but surrender to him."

Iliana felt a chill run up her spine at those words and her eyes widened in horror.

"You must see the truth of that, child?" she said pleadingly. "It is all he wants."

"Do not talk like that. You are here now and we shall find a way out of this."

"Even does it cause the death of every man, woman, and child within these walls?" she asked gently.

"It will not come to that," Iliana said firmly. "Now go get some rest. You will be of little to use to anyone without it."

Shaking her head unhappily, Lady Wildwood turned and left the room.

"Ye must watch her," Angus said, drawing Iliana's gaze. "Despite the time she suffered under him, I don't believe yer mother kens the kind of man Greenweld is."

"What kind of man do you think he is?" she asked curiously.

"Greedy," he said simply. "Very, very greedy. Even were she to surrender, he would not stop."

Iliana's shoulders sagged at that. "I hoped I was wrong in thinking that myself," she murmured on a sigh.

"You will have to post a guard on her."

"The men are too busy—"

"Then use the women."

Iliana nodded.

"Arrange that, then check on the messenger."

"Aye." When he closed his eyes again, Iliana left the room. She found Gertie, Ebba, Giorsal, and Janna in the hallway, trying to decide who should sit with Angus to watch for fever. When Iliana asked where her mother had gone, she was told she had retired to her room.

"Good. While you are trying to decide your schedule for sitting with Angus, you might as well decide who will stay with my mother as well. I would ask at least two of you to sit with her at all times. I fear, if left alone, she will convince herself to flee and perform the supremely foolish and misguided act of surrendering for our sakes."

While the other women looked stunned, Gertie nodded unhappily. "Aye. I feared she was thinking of something of the like."

"She is. And because of that, she is never to be alone. Even when she sleeps at least two of you shall be in her presence. Set a guard on her, or tie her up if you must, but see that she does nothing foolish."

She waited just long enough to see their nods of assent, then turned her attention to the matter of the messenger, asking where he had been put. She was told he was in one of the new rooms that had been built, and went to check on him. It was not a great surprise when she found the room empty, but it gave her something to think about. She returned to Angus to report the news but found him fast asleep. Leaving the message with Gertie, who sat with him, she returned to the wall to check on the activities of Greenweld's men.

She could hear the banging and crashing going on outside the wall as she ascended the stairs. Anxiety flooding her, she rushed to Rabbie's side. "What is it? What are they doing?"

"Cutting down trees to build something," he announced as another crash filled the air.

"What could it be?"

Rabbie shrugged at that. "A mangonel, perhaps. Who can say? Ye should rest," Rabbie suggested. "If 'tis a mangonel they build, we'll need our wits about us on the morrow to deal with the blighters."

Sighing, Iliana nodded. A mangonel; tomorrow they'd be able to hurl missiles over the wall. "Call me if anything happens," she murmured and turned to leave.

Iliana was not sure at first what had awoken her. She opened her eyes to see the first faint streaks of dawn as they crossed the sky, glowing orange and yellow. . . . Those streaks were moving much too swiftly. 'Twas not dawn streaking the sky, she realized with sudden horror.

"Fire!"

That panicked shout brought her rolling onto her back to see a man standing over her. For a moment, in the half light, she thought her attacker had returned to finish the job he had started the night she was stabbed. But then she recognized the voice shouting at her as Elgin's.

"Rabbie sent me to fetch ye, me lady! That English bastard is shooting fire over the wall!"

Grateful that she had decided to remain fully clothed when she had retired, Iliana leapt from the bed and hurried toward the door. She had it open and was moving through it when she suddenly whirled toward the man following her.

"A plaid!"

Confusion covered Elgin's cherubic face. "Me lady?"

"My attacker. The man who stabbed me," she explained. "I just realized that he wore a plaid."

Elgin's eyebrows rose. "There was no plaid among his things, me lady. I was there when Laird Angus searched the body. He had naught but a few coins."

Iliana frowned; then her gaze moved to the window as another fireball flew over the wall and a wave of screams rose from the bailey. "Damn!" she murmured, hurrying from the room.

"What is it? What is about?" Drawn by the shouts and screams below, Lady Wildwood came rushing into the hall, Ebba and Janna on her heels. At the same moment, Gertie and Giorsal appeared in the door to Angus's room.

Shouting an explanation, Iliana hurried down the stairs with Elgin on her heels. Reaching the front doors of the keep, she pushed through them, then froze. Burning debris was strewn about the bailey, threatening to set fire to the many cottages within the wall. Women and children of all ages were running this way and that, attempting to douse the fire with whatever they could find.

"My God."

Glancing over her shoulder at her mother's whisper, Iliana saw that all of the women had followed, and were now crowded behind her and Elgin on the top step. She was about to order them back into the keep when the cook pointed past her.

"The stables!"

Even as she turned back, Iliana could hear the frightened whinnies of the animals within the stables. It was aflame. Cursing, she started down the steps, intent on rescuing the few animals that had remained behind when Duncan had marched out. There had only been a dozen or so left behind, but most of those were ponies and pregnant mares who were near their foaling.

She was barely halfway to the building when the next fireball came over the wall. Staggering to a halt, she shouted a warning and waited to see which way the missile would go. It seemed to be one large ball of flames at first; then she realized that it was actually a collection of debris that had been set alight and shot over as one. As it came down the pieces separated, spanning a large section of the bailey as it flew in every direction.

Iliana's shout was taken up by the others, becoming one panicked cry as the women and children began to scatter, fleeing the fiery rain of debris. Iliana herself leapt to the side to avoid one falling shard, only to step into the path of another. She stumbled when it struck her shoulder but kept her feet. Brushing at her arm to be sure that her gown had not caught flame, she glanced behind her, relieved to see that, while Elgin had followed her, he was unharmed.

"Tend to the horses!" she yelled above the shrieks filling the bailey, then hurried to the nearest victim of the flaming debris. Helping the woman to her feet, Iliana glanced at her mother with surprise when she was suddenly there, tending to the woman's burns.

"Take her into the keep and stay there," Iliana ordered, pushing them in that general direction. "We must get them all to the keep," she shouted to the others, who were trying to douse the flames.

267

"They will not go." Janna approached her. "These are their homes they try to save."

"Their homes will do them little good if they are not alive to enjoy them," Iliana snapped impatiently.

"Then you'd best get up on the wall and see what you can do."

"Do?" Iliana peered at her as if she thought her mad, and Janna nodded.

"They tried this same tactic in Lady Agnes's day."

"Lady Agnes," Iliana sighed the name. Giorsal had used the woman often against her when she had first arrived here. Black Agnes had been able to hold the keep against the English for six months in her husband's absence. "What did she do?"

"Giorsal told us that, after each volley, she distracted them with insults and curses while the women rushed about, dusting up the fire."

"Insults?" She looked doubtful, but Janna nodded.

"And curses, me lady."

"I see." She peered at the flames the women were hurriedly trying to put out, then whirled away, hurrying to the wall.

"Me lady!" Rabbie's relief at seeing her would have been gratifying if Iliana had not felt so incapable of managing this mess. 'Twas obvious she was the only one who seemed to realize how inadequate she was to the task.

Forcing a somewhat stiff smile for the man, Iliana took in the fact that he and the other remaining men were all busily shooting arrows down at the men on the other side of the wall. For all the good it appeared to be doing. Moving to the wall as he turned back to continue shooting his arrows, she leaned through an opening and peered down at the men below. The mangonel was positioned at the base of the causeway, directly across the moat. She supposed Greenweld had positioned it close by so that he could get maximum range into the keep. It might as well have been on the other side of the forest, for it was surrounded by men bearing shields. Even now they were preparing another ball of fire.

Iliana took in the collection of debris they were preparing to light. A glance back at the bailey showed women hurrying this way and that. Turning back, she shouted for Greenweld.

One of the figures disengaged himself from the crowd of men about the catapult and moved to stand behind the barrier of shields to peer up. "Would that be my sniveling brat of a daughter?" he bellowed.

"I'm no daughter of the devil!" she snapped. "But you, sir, are a coward."

"Coward, is it?"

"Aye! Only a coward would force a woman to marry him, then beat her near to death! And only a coward would sneak up on his adversary as you have done!"

" 'Tis not my fault your husband left you unprotected." His words made Iliana's gaze narrow, but before she could ponder them he roared, "Give her to me, brat!"

"Lady Dunbar to you . . . you pig!" Not very impressive, she decided glumly.

"Send her out! She is my wife by law. You cannot refuse me!"

"She is my mother. I cannot agree. Besides, I do not know that she is your wife any longer. The annulment may already be complete."

Furious, Greenweld turned to yell at one of the men beside him, and an arrow came shooting toward her. Iliana instinctively thrust herself to the side, heart pounding as she heard the missile hiss by.

"You bastard!"

Iliana whirled back to the wall at that, gaping at her mother as she bellowed down at the men below. She had not even heard her join them on the wall. Neither had she ever heard her speak so.

"Turning your weapons on a female! Fie! Have you no shame at all?"

"Ah, my stubborn, shrewish wife."

"Not for long! Mayhap not even now!"

Since it was the same taunt Iliana had cast and earned an arrow for, she knew instinctively that he would take it no better from her mother. Muttering under her breath, Iliana tugged her to the side just in time. A second arrow whizzed past them both.

"Mother, *I* am supposed to be taunting him."

Lady Wildwood gave a breathless laugh and brushed the hair back from her face. "That was close, was it not? My, I must say it feels good to speak my mind to the beast."

Rolling her eyes, Iliana turned back to the wall and chanced a quick peek down. Greenweld was gesturing at the man with the torch. Even as she watched, the soldier set the debris ablaze. Cursing, she straightened and turned back toward the bailey, shouting a warning to the other women. When they immediately began fleeing for cover, her gaze slid to the stables. It was engulfed in flames. "Did Elgin get the horses out?"

"Aye. He took them around behind the kitchen. They should be safe there."

"Behind the kitchen? Not through my garden!" The words had barely left her mouth when she heard the catapult being released. Grabbing her mother, she jerked her back against the outer wall. A split second later another fireball passed overhead.

Iliana hurried to look down at the bailey the moment the danger had passed. Assured that no one had been harmed by the latest missile, she moved back to peer at the army outside. The arm of the catapult was back in place and already half-loaded in preparation for another shot, she saw with dismay.

"He will continue to pummel us with fire until Dunbar is a pile of ashes," her mother predicted grimly, balancing herself on Iliana's back with one hand as she leaned up to peer over her.

"Then we shall have to destroy the catapult," Iliana

decided, straightening now and moving out of harm's way behind the wall.

"And how will we manage that?" Lady Wildwood asked dubiously.

"I ordered the women not to leave you alone. How is it you come to be up here without at least two of them trailing you?"

"They were busy. And you still have not said how you plan to destroy the catapult."

Grimacing, Iliana glanced down at the bailey again. The stables were merely a pile of glowing embers now. They would never house horses again. She supposed the building had been rather old. That was the only reason she could think of for it to burn so quickly. It was not as if it had been doused with whiskey first, as the bedchamber had been ere it was set alight.

"Rabbie." She straightened abruptly.

"Aye, me lady?"

"I need some *uisgebeatha*."

His eyebrows rose at that, but he moved past her and bent to retrieve a pitcher that she had not noticed sitting next to the wall. "It kept the nip off during the night," he explained when she raised her eyebrows.

Lifting it to her nose, Iliana sniffed the contents, then glanced at him. "Do you suppose Laird Angus has a lot of this?"

He pursed his lips. "Well, that would depend on how much ye thought was a lot."

Iliana turned to peer down at the catapult again before answering, "As much as you can bring me. All of it."

"All of it?" He goggled at her, then narrowed his eyes unhappily. "This wouldn't have something to do with another one of theose plans of yours, would it?"

"Buck up, sir," Lady Wildwood said cheerfully. "My daughter's last plan worked."

"Oh, aye I worked a'right. But it cost us our supper . . . Now she's wantin' the *uisgebeatha*."

Chapter Twenty

"Do you understand what I want you to do?"

Rabbie nodded morosely. "Aye. But 'tis a fair waste o' good whiskey if it doesn't work."

"Then we must pray that it works," Iliana commented dryly, peering at the people lined up before her. Eight women and eight men. The women had resented being pulled away from the task of dousing fires below, until she had explained that she hoped that her plan would put an end to the volley of fireballs that continued to whiz over the wall. They had settled in to help with a small measure of contentment then. Ripping the linen Iliana had sent for into strips, they had wrapped them around the tips of arrows, then set them to soak in the half-empty barrel of whiskey she had had Rabbie split open for them.

Now the women waited by the barrel of soaking arrows, lit torches in hand, while the men stood by the eight barrels of whiskey that Rabbie had found.

"All right. Remember, you must try to get them as far as possible as quickly as possible," she reminded them once again, then leaned to the wall to see what Green-weld's men were doing. Seeing that they were about to light yet another fireball, she told the people on the wall to get ready, then shouted a warning to those below.

The people on the battlement pressed themselves close to the wall just as the fireball flew over, then hurried back to their places. The men rushed to the barrels. Working in twos, the four pairs picked up a barrel each and hurled them over in unison before rushing back to get their second. The women moved to the arrows then, each of them grabbing up a whiskey soaked weapon in their free hand and moving to the men's sides as they hurled the last barrels over.

Assured that they were doing exactly as she had instructed, Iliana moved to the wall to peer down at the Englishmen. They seemed quite confused by this turn of events. Four barrels of Scottish liquor had just flown off the wall and crashed on the half-built causeway, splashing every which way, and soaking a lot of the men as well as the catapult. Even now, another four were tumbling through the air. It was obvious that her fellow countrymen did not know what to make of it. But then, doubtless they did not know what she had learned by accident. *Uisge-beatha* was like food for a fire.

Glancing over her shoulder at her own people again, she saw that the men had split up to their individual slots and were even now loading their bows with the arrows the women handed them. Once that was done, the women each used the torches they held to spark the whiskey-soaked cloth tips to life. The men turned, aimed, and fired.

Iliana turned to peer below again. She had been very specific about where to aim the arrows. Four of the men were to shoot at the catapult, two at the causeway, and two at the barricade of shields, which she had hoped might get splashed. Her men were right on target. The first arrow hit the causeway, and even she was startled at the way it burst into flames, the fire splashing outward just as the whiskey had done before it, following its trail.

The other arrows seemed to hit all at once, sparking the catapult and the men's shields at the same time. The whole area burst into flames with a whoosh.

Swallowing, Iliana peered at the catapult again, sighing when she saw that it was now gloriously ablaze. Hearing the people along the wall begin to cheer, she straightened and turned toward the stairs wearily.

"Watch them, Rabbie. Do they do anything else, fetch me. The rest of you get below and help put out the fires," she ordered without looking back. The Scots all fell silent at that, peering worriedly at her slumped shoulders before moving to follow her instructions.

When she reached Angus's room, Iliana found her mother and Janna already there, doing their best to hold the old warrior down in his bed.

"Nay. You will not get up," her mother was arguing as Iliana entered.

"Aye," Janna panted, pressing down hard on his un-injured shoulder in an attempt to keep him down. "Ye've been sore injured."

" 'Tis naught but a scratch, woman. Let me up." When that had no effect on Iliana's mother, he turned to glare at Janna. "I am yer laird!" he pointed out on an outraged roar.

The maid hesitated at that, then shook her head. "Nay. Ye said Lady Iliana was in charge until ye recovered. Yer not recovered."

He opened his mouth to blast the poor woman for that, then spied Iliana. "Lass! There ye are. Tell these harpies to let me up."

Iliana smiled slightly at his pleading expression and moved to the bedside to peer down at him, taking in the angry red in his cheeks. "You are feeling better then?"

"Aye."

Reaching out, she felt his forehead, relieved to find that fever was not the reason behind his new color.

"Good," she announced abruptly, gesturing to Janna and her mother to leave him be. Janna moved away from the bed at once, but Lady Wildwood hesitated.

"He should not be up yet. He needs rest to heal properly."

"He will rest. We will not let him do anything strenuous, but he can sit below and give orders now."

Her mother relaxed at that while Angus stiffened.

"I am laird here, lass. I'll decide what I can or cannot do." He shifted his legs over the side of the bed and stood abruptly, then paled and swayed sickly on his feet.

Iliana reached out to steady him at once.

Grabbing her hand gratefully, he sank back onto the side of the bed again. "Well, mayhap I shall take it a bit easy." Even saying that made him grimace with distaste. Frowning, he speared Iliana with a look. "Yer mother told me o' yer plan with the *uisgebeatha*. Did it work?"

She nodded solemnly. "The causeway and catapult are ablaze. Rabbie is watching to see what they try next. I told him to call me if they did anything."

"Good." He nodded solemnly. "And the messenger?"

"You were asleep when I returned. Gertie was to tell you that he was missing."

"Missing?" Janna asked with obvious surprise.

"Aye. He must have slipped out ere the gate was closed."

"Nay." She shook her head firmly. "He was abed after we brought the laird up here. I checked on him myself."

"He was not there yester eve when I looked."

Janna frowned at that, as did Angus.

"Go check on him again. If he is not there, post guards and start a search," he ordered.

Nodding, Iliana turned toward the door. Janna started to follow her, then hesitated and glanced toward Lady Wildwood, then Angus.

"Go with her," Angus waved her away. "I'll keep an eye on Lady Wildwood."

Iliana's mother scowled at that, then smiled sweetly. "Aye, and I shall be sure he does not overdo."

Shaking her head at the war of wills that was about to play out between the older couple, Iliana led the servant out of the chamber and down the hall to the room the messenger had been given. She truly did not expect him to be there, so when she opened the door and stepped inside to see him lying in the bed, apparently sound asleep, she stopped abruptly and frowned.

"See," Janna whispered. "Mayhap in all the excitement ye peered into the wrong chamber."

"Nay. 'Twas this chamber." Shifting her feet, she glanced around the room, looking for any sign that might prove he had not been here the last time she had looked, but there was nothing. Peering at his face again, she shook her head and stepped back out of the room, pulling the door quietly closed.

"Mayhap he went in search of the privy," Janna suggested.

"Aye, mayhap, but . . ."

The woman raised her eyebrows at Iliana's hesitation. "But?"

"There are a couple of things bothering me just now." Iliana sighed. "It probably means nothing . . . but I shall tell you anyway. This morn, when the attack started, Elgin came to fetch me."

"Aye?"

"Well . . . you remember the night I was attacked?"

The woman nodded, shuddering. "Laird Angus said 'twas a mighty close call."

"Aye, well, when I rolled over this morn and found Elgin looming over me, I thought the attacker had returned."

Her eyes rounded at that. "That must have been distressin'."

"Aye, but it was then that I realized that he wore a plaid."

Janna frowned. "Elgin?"

"Nay. Well, aye. But I meant that the attacker did as well."

She considered that briefly. "Maybe he stole it and—" She paused when Iliana began to shake her head.

"The dead Englishman had no plaid in his belongings. Besides, there is something else. When I spoke to Green-weld, he said something that bothered me as well."

"What was that?"

"He said 'twas not his fault that Duncan had left us unprotected. How did he know Duncan had left?"

"Mayhap he and his men were already here when Duncan and the others rode out."

"Mayhap," Iliana agreed. "But he knows not what Duncan looks like. How did he know it was my husband leading the men, and not Angus? 'Sides, if he was nearby when Duncan left, why did he not attack right away?"

Janna frowned. "You are thinking that the reason the messenger was not here was that he was somehow sneaking about, giving Greenweld information? But why would he do that? If he works for Lord Rolfe—"

"*If* he works for Lord Rolfe."

The servant gasped. "You think—"

" 'Twas most convenient for Greenweld that Duncan was called away when he was, do you not think?"

Her face darkened. "No one saw the message," she whispered.

"Aye. What if the dead man was the messenger? What if the live one was Greenweld's man? What if the reason the message went missing was that it did not say what they wanted it to?"

"Gor," she breathed, her expression frightened. Then she frowned. "But how could they have been nearby all this time? Laird Angus had the woods searched twice. He even led the first search. And how could the fellow have gotten information to them? The gate is closed tight."

Iliana sighed and shook her head. "I do not know. I have not pieced it all together yet," she admitted, then stiffened at a muffled sound from the door they stood in front of. Exchanging a glance with the servant, she quickly pushed the door open and stepped inside, Janna directly on her heels. Iliana had taken several steps before she realized that, not only was the bed empty, but the messenger was nowhere in sight. Just as she realized that, the door slammed closed behind them.

Whirling, she stared at the messenger. He had been behind the door. Now he stood before it, sword in hand. Raising her chin, she eyed him coldly. "You appear to be well healed, sir."

"'Twas a paltry wound at best," he said with a shrug. "Most of the blood on me came from Lord Rolfe's man when I killed him."

Janna gasped at that, but Iliana merely let her shoulders sag slightly. "You are Greenweld's man."

"Aye, but then, you had all but figured that out, had you not?"

Iliana shrugged. "I presume that Lady Seonaid is all right, then?"

"Aye. Lord Rolfe's message merely explained that they would be delayed. He did not wish her father to worry. Most considerate of him, would you not say?"

Iliana ignored his sarcasm. "So, what do you plan to do next? 'Tis clear that now that you have been discovered, you shall not leave this keep alive."

"'Tis not so clear to me," he disagreed easily. "All I need do is kill you and your companion and my secret is safe."

Iliana ignored Janna's gasp of horror and forced her own expression to remain calm as she murmured, "I fear not. Laird Angus is aware that you were absent earlier. He also knows we came to check on you. Should we go missing you would be his first suspect."

"Then 'tis good that that was not the plan."

Iliana's gaze narrowed on him grimly. "And what exactly is your plan?"

"Well, it *was* to take Lady Wildwood, and deliver her to my lord."

"Take my mother to Greenweld? How the devil did you plan to accomplish that? The gate is down and the bridge up. There are guards posted."

"I have it on good authority that there is another way out, Lady Wildwood."

"Lady Dunbar," Iliana spat. "And there is no other way out."

"I fear you are wrong. I've already seen it. It is a very narrow, presumably secret passage and opens only one way, from the inside out. 'Tis why I had to be inside, to allow the others in. They cannot open it from the outside."

Iliana glanced sharply toward Janna. 'Twas obvious from her expression that if such a passage existed, the woman had no knowledge of it. She looked as uncertain as Iliana felt.

"I was originally to take Lady Wildwood out. Holding her, it was expected that you would be forced to surrender the keep."

"It would seem then that I have ruined your plans. You shall never get your hands on my mother now."

"Nay, but I am sure you will do just as well. Unfortunately, I see no need to drag your maid along."

Both women blanched at that announcement, but when the man stepped toward Janna, raising his sword, Iliana stepped before her. "I think not. Do you try, I shall surely shriek the stone walls of this castle down. How far do you think you would get then?"

"Most like as far as I would did you not," he answered with vague amusement. " 'Tis only women, children, and old men within the walls. Hardly a threat to me."

"Then there is surely no need to kill Janna. We are but two women. What harm could we do?" she argued. " 'Sides, should someone find her, they may be alerted to your plans. Angus may figure out where we disappeared to when we are not found in the keep. He could block the passage."

He hesitated at that, then shrugged and lowered his

sword slightly. "It matters little, I suppose." Reaching out then, he grabbed Janna and dragged her up to his side, then glanced at Iliana. "We are going to the burned-out room. You shall lead the way. Move quickly and quietly. Do you cry out or attempt to flee, I shall kill your maid. Understand?"

Iliana took in the woman's frightened expression and tried to offer a reassuring smile even as she nodded at the man. She moved abruptly to the door when he gestured with his sword toward it.

She had hoped that someone might find reason to be in, or enter, the hallway as they moved through it. However, they reached the room without incident.

The bedroom she had slept in on first arriving at Dunbar was now mostly empty, and a sooty mess. Her chests were a charred mass at one end of the room, the floorboards around and beneath them half-eaten through by fire. The other end of the room was empty but powdered with soot everywhere except for a large square where the bed had been, and four small squares where the legs of the bedside table had been.

Pausing, Iliana turned to face the Englishman as he pushed Janna in behind her and slammed the door.

"Over there. Beside the fireplace." He gestured with his sword, and the two women moved dutifully toward the wall. Following them, Greenweld's man kept his sword slightly up and pointed toward them as he felt along the wall. It was only then that Iliana noticed that some of the soot had been brushed away, obviously during an earlier search he had made, and she wondered briefly why he had not simply made his escape then.

"He said 'twas to the left of the fireplace. A stone would move under pressure and the wall would open."

"Who said?"

He opened his mouth as if to answer, then caught himself and turned on her sharply. "Very clever, my lady, but I think I shall keep that information to myself."

He continued his search then, and Iliana glanced at

Janna. She wanted somehow to prepare her for an escape attempt, but the other woman was staring wide-eyed at their captor. Before she could get his attention, he gave a cry of triumph that drew her gaze back to him as the stone his hand pressed on began to slide backward with a heavy, low, grinding sound. The wall followed suit a moment later, opening into what looked to be a black hole. Greenweld's man frowned into the darkness unhappily, and Iliana could almost read his thoughts. He had not thought to bring a torch.

Taking the opportunity while he was distracted, Iliana leapt forward and gave him a shove that sent him stumbling into the darkness with a shout. Whirling, she gave a stunned Janna a push as well, this one sending her stumbling toward the doorway leading to the hall.

"Go!" she cried, harrying her forward. Janna regained herself enough to obey. Leaping at the door, she dragged it open and flew through it. Iliana was directly behind her when Janna crashed into her mother and Angus. It appeared Angus was prepared to return to the wall, for he was armed. Despite his weakness and having the woman slam into him, the man managed to keep his feet, and Iliana began to relax, thinking she was safe, but even as they all turned to look at her, she felt a hand catch in the short curls on the back of her head. When that hand yanked viciously, wrenching her head backward, she came to an abrupt halt, wincing as the icy edge of a blade was raised to her throat.

For a moment there was silence. Iliana could hear her captor panting by her ear. She herself was breathing heavily as well but tried to control it, for each time she sucked in air her throat rose slightly with the action, pressing the sharp blade farther into her neck. Angus was the first to regain himself.

"Let her go," he ordered grimly, pulling free of Lady Wildwood's panicked grasp and taking a step toward Iliana and her captor.

Greenweld's man stepped back at once, dragging Iliana

with him, and she winced as the sword edge pressed tighter to her throat.

Angus stopped at once. "There is no where fer ye to run. Let her go unharmed and I'll make yer death quick."

Iliana closed her eyes at that. Had Greenweld's man not known of the passage, Angus's offer might have held sway, but he did. Death was not his only option. She was not surprised when he gave a dry, breathless laugh and merely pulled her back into the room, cautiously backing toward the passage. Angus followed. Both he and her mother noticed the passage a moment later.

"Nay!" she cried, hurrying into the room. "Take me. It is me Greenweld wants. Take me."

Her captor stopped at once and Iliana felt his indecision. "Get her out of here!" she yelled at Janna. "Tie her up if you have to, but do not let her go."

Janna's eyes widened; then she nodded with determination. She and Lady Wildwood were of a size, but the Scot was stronger from years of heavy work. She had no problem removing Iliana's struggling mother.

Once they were out of the room, Angus closed the door. "Let her go and fight like a man," he demanded grimly, pulling his own sword from its sheath.

"Another time, old man," Greenweld's man muttered, backing toward the passage again. "Stay where you are or I'll kill her."

Expression grim, Angus stopped, turning his hard gaze to Iliana. "Don't fret, lass. We'll get ye back."

Iliana just managed a nod before she was dragged into the dark passage and the stone door slammed closed.

They were entombed in cool, black silence. Iliana stood completely still, waiting for her eyes to adjust, even as her captor did. It took a few minutes before she realized that there was nothing to adjust to. There was no light anywhere. They must make this trip sightless or return. Her captor cursed quietly and relaxed his hold on her neck to drop his hand to her arm. When she heard the scrape of metal on stone, she guessed he was using his sword to measure the width of the passage in which they stood, and testing to see if the path held anything that they might stumble on. Apparently assured that the way was clear, he began to move, dragging Iliana behind him.

Rabbie burst into the room, Janna directly on his heels. Pausing to catch his breath now, he took in the grim expression on his laird's face and the way he glared at the wall beside the fireplace and frowned.

"I was told ye wished to see me, me laird?" he said at last, when Angus did not acknowledge their presence.

The Dunbar turned sharply at his words. He had been deep in thought and had not even heard them enter. "What are they doing?"

Rabbie's eyebrows rose at the abrupt question. "Building another mangonel, I think, me laird. They are cutting trees and pounding away at something."

Angus turned back to the wall. "They must still be in the tunnel then."

Rabbie blinked in confusion at that. "The tunnel, me laird?"

"Aye. A secret passage. The entrance is right there." He gestured at a section of wall that looked the same as the rest, then confirmed what Janna had said. "The messenger has taken me daughter-in-law through it and is headed out to Greenweld's men with her. I want this passage blocked. Set Ebba and Giorsal on the wall to watch the Sassenach, then fetch all the men who are left and begin bringing boulders from the bailey up here."

"Boulders?"

"Aye. I would have this entrance and the one in me own room blocked. The English'll not use it to sneak up on us."

Nodding, Rabbie moved past Janna toward the door as the woman asked, "What of Lady Iliana? Greenweld'll use her to try to force us to surrender."

Angus was grim-faced. "We shall stall fer as long as we can."

"And when we can no longer stall?" Rabbie asked from the door.

"Then we shall pray. Do as I ordered."

Nodding, the stablemaster left the room.

Her captor's curse was the only warning she got before Iliana found herself stumbling into his back as he stopped. It seemed to her that they had been inching their way through this hellish passage for hours. Completely sightless, she had stumbled along, dragged behind the man by a hand on her arm. She had tried to come up with a plan of escape as they had traveled. Unfortunately, nothing brilliant had come to mind. The floor, as far as she could tell, was smooth, uncluttered by rocks or boulders that she might have used to club him over the head. Not that he really gave her any opportunity anyway, not even when they had traversed the set of slippery steps hewn into the rock near the beginning of this journey. That had been a terrifying ordeal in itself.

Sighing, she straightened from his back and waited. They were near the end of the passage; her nose told her that. The smell when they had first entered the tunnel had been stale and dusty. But for the past several minutes that smell had given way to the rich, dank scent of earth. She was positive that they were near the end of the passage, and she felt a mixture of relief and anxiety.

She sensed her captor feeling around on the wall for something, and realized he must have set his sword aside to do so. Before she could take advantage of that fact, a portion of the darkness around them moved and light surrounded them. The light was like two arrows to her eyes after the darkness they had endured for so long.

Squeezing her eyes tightly closed, she nearly groaned aloud at the pain shooting through her head. Then she felt the hand on her arm tighten and was dragged, stumbling out into fresh air. Unfortunately, she had not been prepared for the abrupt jerk forward, nor the uneven ground that was suddenly beneath her feet. Crying out, Iliana stumbled and lost her balance, instinctively throwing her hands out to cushion her fall.

Wincing at her stinging palms, Iliana blinked frantically, trying to get her sight back as she glanced about. They were in a small cave that opened out into bright daylight.

A muttered curse drew her head around. The Englishman was trying to hold the passage door open, while stretching to retrieve a boulder a few feet away. But he could not reach. Cursing again, he raised his head to glare at her. "Fetch me that damn rock," he ordered grimly.

Eyes widening, Iliana got carefully to her feet, hesitated, then turned and made a mad dash for the entrance to the cave and the sunlight beyond.

Her captor began shouting at once, the sound bouncing off the walls and vibrating so that it almost deafened her before she made the mouth of the cave and started blindly across the clearing outside it. She had no idea where she was going. Truly, she had no idea even where she *was*, but fleeing seemed in her best interests. A plan started to form as she ran. She would run all the way to McInnes keep and fetch help back. She would be able to find her way; all she needed to do was stop and look for the towers of Dunbar to get her bearings. Which she would do just as soon as she felt she had gotten a safe distance away from Greenweld and his men.

Her heart was already pounding fit to burst, but when her captor's shouts were finally answered by others ahead of her and she realized she was charging straight toward the enemy, her heart nearly jumped right out of her chest. Changing direction at once, she veered to the left just as a man broke from the trees ahead of her. Iliana managed a desperate burst of speed, but it did little good. Even as she sprinted toward the cover of the woods, she was tackled from behind and sent crashing to her stomach on the forest floor.

She started struggling at once. Bucking off her attacker,

she tried to lurch to her knees, but he had a hold on her skirt. Whirling, she turned onto her back to kick the man, and that was her mistake. The sight of Allistair clutching at the plaid she wore made her hesitate. Only a moment, but even that moment was too long, she realized, as he released her skirt in favor of the ankle of her half-bent leg, preventing her from either kicking him or fleeing.

Chapter Twenty-one

"Ye don't look overly surprised to see me, m'lady." Allistair was grinning as he eased to his feet. Reaching down, he pulled her up to stand as well.

"Mayhap that is because I am not terribly surprised."

His smiled slipped slightly, but he got no chance to question her, for Greenweld stormed into the clearing just then, his bald head shining in the sunlight and his florid face eager. That eagerness fled, replaced by fury, when he recognized Iliana.

Her captor came charging out of the cave just then and ran straight into the path of his lord's rage. Catching the man by the back of the neck, he dug his fingers into the tender flesh there and shook him violently. "What is this? I told you to bring Lady Wildwood, not her whelp!"

"Mother was not available," Iliana said with feigned sweetness when the man's mouth opened and closed several times, but nothing came out. "He had to make do with me."

She had expected her words to anger Greenweld; 'twas

why she said them. Still, it took her by surprise when he suddenly released his man and swiftly closed the distance between them. Iliana took an instinctive step backward as he approached, but she was not quick enough to avoid the blow he gave her. He used enough force to send her stumbling backward to the ground again.

"I shall take no sass off of you, brat! Do not make the mistake of thinking I will."

Iliana drew a hand across her mouth, grimacing at the blood staining her fingers when she took it away, then got slowly to her feet once more. Facing him again, she shrugged with false bravado. "And you shall have neither Dunbar nor my mother. Do not *you* make the mistake of thinking you will."

He drew his fist back again and Iliana prepared to dodge the blow this time, but Allistair tugged her roughly to his side and out of reach before either could finish their action. "Let her be. She is my problem. Treat Lady Wildwood as you will, but Lady Dunbar is mine."

Greenweld glared at the Scot for his interference, then wheeled away and applied his fist to his man instead, slamming it into his jaw and sending him stumbling backwards to the ground. Bending down, he grabbed him by the collar of his tunic and jerked him back to his feet, giving him a shake as he roared, "You were to open the passage yesterday."

"I tried," the man blurted quickly, forestalling the fist that was rushing toward his face again. "Really, I did, my lord. It was his directions." He pointed a shaking finger accusingly at Allistair.

"I told ye 'twas the darkest stone to the left of the fireplace, Hugh," Duncan's cousin muttered with open disgust.

"They are *all* dark. They are soot-stained."

Greenweld raised an eyebrow at Allistair. The Scot frowned slightly, then understanding came to his face and he sighed. "The fire. I have not seen the room since the fire. He may be right."

Grunting his disgust at that, Greenweld set the man reluctantly down, propping his clenched fists on his hips as he questioned him. "He claimed the passage is straight with no side trails to confuse a body; is that true?"

"Aye. 'Tis good it is, too, for things happened so quick, I did not manage to collect a torch on the way. 'Twas black as pitch in there. I had to feel my way out."

Greenweld frowned at that. "We shall need torches then. I shall take half my men and go in through the passage. The rest will continue to work on the new mangonel so that those inside do not suspect anything."

Iliana glanced toward the man named Hugh, fully expecting him to inform Greenweld that their leave-taking had been witnessed, and that the passage was most likely blocked by now. It seemed he was not eager to pass on that news, however, for he stood, pale, trembling, and as silent as stone, his eyes locked warily on Greenweld's fists as he eased carefully step after step away from him. Her gaze slid to Allistair as he nodded in agreement with Greenweld's plans.

"You'd best move quickly. 'Twill not take long fer them to notice Iliana missing."

"Aye. Take her to my tent and keep her out of sight. I shall order the men to make up torches."

Turning away, he left the clearing, and Iliana felt herself relax somewhat. While Allistair was a traitor to his own blood kin, at least he seemed unwilling to beat her. He had stopped the man from hitting her. That gave her some hope that there was a drop or two of humanity left in him. Mayhap she could persuade him to switch sides again.

"Come." Taking her arm, Allistair urged her from the small clearing, leading her through thick woods to the temporary camp they had set up. There were three tents huddled close together beneath the trees. Allistair ushered her inside the largest one.

Pushing her in the general direction of a pallet set up along one side of the tent, he moved to a small table against the opposite wall and grabbed a dented and tarnished mug from the tabletop. Dipping it into the open barrel of ale beside it, he raised the mug to his lips and turned to eye her over the top of it as he drank.

After glancing with disgust at the rumpled pallet, Iliana had decided she would prefer to stand. She faced him, waiting warily for what came next. At first, nothing happened. Allistair leaned against the wobbly table and continued to drink, eyeing her thoughtfully as he did, but after several moments he spoke.

"What meant you when you said mayhap you were not surprised?" The very casualness of his tone told her that her answer was important to him.

"Just what I said. *I was not surprised.*"

His mouth tightened and he straightened impatiently. "Why?"

"Because it was you who tried to kill me that night in the bedchamber."

He paled at her words, and Iliana nearly sighed her disappointment aloud. She had been hoping she was wrong, that selling out to Greenweld was his only sin. But from the moment when Elgin had awoken her that morning, she had been fretting over the fact that her attacker had worn a plaid. And when she had found herself confronted by Allistair in the clearing, she had feared that he was the answer to everything that had been happening of late. She had not wanted to believe it. He was Duncan's cousin. He'd shown his affection for Seonaid openly. How could he betray them like this? Why?

"Ye kenned it was me that night?" The horror on his face gave way to sudden suspicion. "Nay. Had ye kenned that, ye would have tol' Duncan and he would have killed me."

"I did not at first recognize that it was you. It was not until this morning that I recalled that my attacker that night had worn a plaid," she explained grimly, her anger finally coming to life. "Now, will you tell me why you would join with Greenweld to see my mother dead? She has done naught to you."

He waved her words away. "She was never really my target at all. Duncan was."

Iliana peered at him blankly. "But the night I was attacked—"

"I meant to kill Duncan."

"But how did you know my mother—?"

"Was no longer sleeping there?" He smiled slightly. "I sat next to you at dinner. Don't ye recall? I was on yer left, yer mother on yer right. I heard every word she said to ye that night. And one of the last things she said was that she was vacating yer room so that ye and yer husband could get to ken each other better. It was too perfect. No one else would ken that. They would all assume that the attack had been meant for Lady Wildwood." When Iliana merely continued to stare at him blankly, he shook his head with mild disgust.

"Ye still don't understand, do ye? Ye disappoint me. I had not thought ye just another stupid Sassenach female. Think. Had I merely set out to kill Duncan . . . well, and sure enough it wouldn't have been hard to deduce who the culprit was. After all, why would anyone kill Duncan? The only reason to do that was to—"

"Take his place as heir," Iliana realized suddenly as the answer clicked into place in her head.

"There ye are! Now yer thinkin'," he applauded.

"But you are his cousin," she protested at once. "His blood kin."

"Aye." He nodded calmly. "His father and mine were brothers, but mine was the younger. That small fact cut me out from inheriting. So long as Duncan lived."

Iliana shook her head at his deliberate misunderstanding of her meaning. "His father took you in. He raised you alongside his own children. He—"

"Tossed us crumbs from his table," Allistair inserted coldly. "It was charity and we were never allowed to ferget that."

"Surely Duncan and his father would never—"

"Oh, they never said as much. But others did, and the great Dunbars let us ken in other ways. Fer instance, Duncan and Seonaid, as children of their father, had rooms o' their own in the castle. Do ye ken where we slept?"

Iliana blinked at that. "Nay."

"In Giorsal's cottage. She was our mother's sister and we lived with her. Oh aye, we took all our meals with the great laird and his wondrous children, but we were not good enough to sleep under his roof with them."

Iliana blanched and shook her head in confusion. That did not sound like the Angus Dunbar she knew.

"Ye don't believe me." He smiled slightly. "Well, ye can be askin' yer wondrous husband about it when he gets here."

"Gets here?" Iliana's eyes widened in alarm.

"Aye. I told ye ye weren't the target and yer not, not fer me and not fer Greenweld. 'Tis yer mother and Duncan who are really the ones we would see dead. 'Tis just unfortunate ye got in the way. And that ye ken too much."

Unwilling to consider the meaning behind his words, Iliana ignored them and muttered, "Duncan will not come."

"Aye. He will. When he gets to Colquhoun he will find out the message was a fake. If he doesn't get hisself killed by attacking the Colquhouns without reason, he shall return. When he does, it'll be to find ye've been taken. He'll come fer ye."

"Nay." Iliana shook her head.

"Aye. I ken me cousin. He'll come fer ye."

"If ye heard so much that night at the table, then you also heard that all is not well between my husband and myself. The reason he was not in our room the night you came for him was because he was with his mistress—"

"Aye. Kelly's also my mistress," he told her with amusement, giving a name to the faceless woman her husband had gone to that night. "Another one o' the great Dunbar crumbs that I'm allowed to feed on. I ken he was with her that night. She told me all about it. It seems ye've ruined him. He couldn't mount her no matter her tricks."

Iliana was not sure whether she should be grateful at this news or not. On the one hand, her heart nearly soared at the knowledge that Duncan had not been unfaithful to her. On the other, it made convincing Allistair that Duncan would not come for her that much harder. Especially since she herself very much feared he might do just that. She had learned a great many things about her husband in the time they had been together. Not least of which was the fact that he took his duty to his people very seriously. He would indeed come for her. And when he did, they would both be dead, for he had no idea of his cousin's treachery.

"Once Duncan is dead, I shall be clan chief."

Iliana stiffened at those satisfied words. "You are forgetting Angus."

"I forget nothing. Angus is old. Once he acknowledges me as his heir, 'twill be little enough trouble to see he has an accident."

"What of Seonaid?"

A slow smile spread across his lips at the question. "Ah, sweet Seonaid. She will be my wife and rule beside me. She's a good woman, my Seonaid. I've loved her all me life. Never met another woman like her. Strong. Fast. Cunning—"

"And she loves her brother," Iliana pointed out dryly. "I am sure she will not be pleased to learn who his killer is."

"She will never ken. No one will but ye and Duncan, and neither of ye shall be alive to tell. I will comfort her in her sorrow and arrange the wedding as quickly as possible."

Iliana gave a disgusted snort that brought Allistair's irritated eyes to her at once. "Have you forgotten Sherwell? It seems to me you have gotten things in rather a muddle. With Duncan dead, Seonaid shall be heir to Dunbar, and when she marries Sherwell, he will be laird here."

"That wedding shall never take place," Allistair snapped. "Greenweld will see to that."

Iliana felt a chill go up her back at that news. "And what must you do to earn that favor from Greenweld?"

"What do you think?"

"My mother?" she asked faintly.

"Aye. Unfortunately, she'll not live to see me acknowledged as heir, but so be it."

"So be it?" Iliana echoed faintly. "Are you mad? Your plan cannot possibly work. Angus will not name his son's killer his heir."

"He will not ken—"

"So you keep saying," she snapped impatiently. "Seonaid will not ken, Angus will not ken, and Duncan will not ken 'til 'tis too late. Yet if I, a stupid Sassenach female," she threw the words back at him sarcastically, "if I can figure it out, they will also."

When Allistair stilled at that, Iliana nodded with satisfaction. "You left many clues. All it needs is piecing together."

"I left no clues," he denied with a frown.

"Nay? What of the message?"

"What of it?"

" 'Twas just too convenient that Duncan should be called away the day before Greenweld laid siege to the castle. And then there is also the question of how he and his men managed to get all the way to the castle without news of his approach reaching us. Lady McInnes told me that there is little if anything that the laird of a clan does not know or learn about right quickly. Yet Greenweld marched across not only the better part of Scotland, but the entire stretch of Dunbar land without anyone noticing. He must have had help."

Allistair smiled his relief at that. "He did. The messenger."

"The messenger?"

"Aye." His smiled turned wry. "Greenweld is as clever as he is greedy. He came across the messenger while still in the lowlands. Recognizing the king's standard and suspecting the message the man carried might have something to do with his wife—''

"My mother is not his wife!" Iliana snapped irritably.

Allistair gave a half-apologetic shrug. "I fear she is."

"Not for long."

"Whatever the case, thinkin' the man might have news he could make use of, Greenweld gave a false name and invited him to join his camp fer the night. Around the fire, he learned he was headed fer Dunbar. He offered his escort. The messenger thought 'twould be safer to travel in a group and agreed. Little did he ken that he actually offered safety to Greenweld."

Iliana frowned over that and Allistair explained, "He held the king's banner. We Scots learned long ago not to make trouble with the king's men; it tends to bring his wrath down on us."

"So, because Greenweld traveled with the king's messenger, he traveled safe?"

"Aye. No one even approached to ask what his business was. Most like they just assumed it had something to do with the business Lord Rolfe has been tending to."

"But once they arrived at Dunbar there was no more need for the man," Iliana concluded grimly.

"Not once I met with them."

"That was the day Duncan left?"

"Aye. I truly did notice something amiss when I went to fetch the merchant back. 'Tis hard to hide signs of so many men."

"So, you returned to seek them out."

He nodded.

"They could have killed you," she commented solemnly.

He shrugged. " 'Twas a chance, but not much o' one. In truth, Greenweld needed me as much as I needed him." Moving back to the barrel, he dipped his tankard in again.

"That explains how he got here unfettered, but there are other things people will question."

"Such as?"

Iliana moved to sit on the pallet and peered at him calmly. "The message."

He arched an eyebrow. "What of it?"

"Greenweld could not have known that Seonaid had gone to St. Simmian's. I did not even know that until after Lord Rolfe returned with Sherwell. As far as I know, he probably did not even know that my husband had a sister. Nor could he know that the Colquhouns were enemies of the Dunbar and might seek revenge such a way."

"Everyone in Scotland kens the Dunbars and Colquhouns are at war," Allistair argued with amusement. "As for St. Simmian's, the real message Lord Rolfe sent spoke of it. It said that Lord Rolfe and Sherwell had collected Seonaid from St. Simmian's, but that she had escaped. Several times." The words brought an affectionate smile to his face. "They've been chasing her all over Scotland. Lord Rolfe was writing so that Angus didn't fret." He shook his head again. "Nay, the fact that they kenned about Seonaid wouldn't give me away."

"Mayhap not," Iliana murmured, then peered at him silently for a moment before asking, "Why did you leave the keep the morning of the siege?"

"I couldn't be present once the siege began."

Iliana's eyebrows rose. "Why?"

"Well, how could I do that? I would have been forced to tend to Greenweld then. No one would want me for laird did I allow the castle to fall to an English."

"Ahh," Iliana muttered dryly.

"It was for the best anyhow. Greenweld needed to ken how many men were left and the like."

"Knowing how few men there were, why did he not attack the day Duncan left?"

Allistair shrugged. "They had only arrived that morning and had been traveling hard for days. The men needed the rest, and then there were a few things I had to ready first."

"Such as?"

"The boiling pitch."

Iliana's mouth tightened as she recalled Angus's irritation on hearing that the fire had gone out below the pitch and 'twas cold. Then she realized that Allistair was smiling at her crookedly and she arched an eyebrow questioningly. "What?"

"Nothing." He shrugged, then asked, "What was it you substituted for pitch? The men said it tasted good but burned like the devil."

"Elgin's stew. I shall pass along your compliments. Mayhap it will help him forgive the loss of his vat."

"You shall not see him again," he reminded softly.

Iliana managed a shrug. "Mayhap not. We shall see."

His expression tightened in displeasure at her seeming lack of concern and he started toward her.

She spoke quickly to distract him. "So, Greenweld avoided attacking the first day Duncan left, out of care and concern for his men? I find that difficult to believe. I have yet to see him show concern for anyone."

Allistair paused, hesitated, then relaxed and shrugged. " 'Twas more like because he himself was tired. 'Sides, there was the slight possibility that Duncan might turn back for some reason. It seemed better to wait until the next day."

"And what if he still returns early?"

Allistair smiled slightly. "Unless he returns within the next hour or so, it will not matter. Once Greenweld takes the men in through the passage, we shall have succeeded."

"Ah, yes. The passage."

Allistair frowned at her sudden smile. "What amuses ye so about the passage?"

"Naught, my lord. Except that if nothing else does, it shall surely see you hanged."

Allistair stilled at that.

"I presume the passage is a secret? Known only among close family?" she queried gently and smiled at his expression. Janna's not knowing about the tunnel leading out of the castle had made her wonder. That and the fact that no one had mentioned it to her. The dismay on his face confirmed her belief that only close, trusted members of the family knew of the passage, and she nodded. "I realized that on the way through the tunnel. And that is why I was not surprised to see you in the clearing. Duncan is away, as are Seonaid and your sister, and Angus is within the walls, doing his best to defend it. None of them could have revealed the presence of the passage. If close family are all who know of it—"

"Then the only suspect left would be ye."

Both of them whirled toward the tent entrance at those hollow words. Iliana was as stunned as Allistair to see Duncan standing there flanked by two men. One of them was Ian McInnes, Iliana did not recognize the other man, but he wore English clothes.

"Surprised to see me?" he asked dryly when both of them continued to stare at him as if he was a ghost.

Allistair's expression tightened. "Greenweld's men?"

"Gave up without a battle once surrounded by McInnes men, ours, and those of their own king."

"The king?"

Duncan nodded. "He had men watching Greenweld from the moment he received Lady Wildwood's message. When news reached him that Greenweld had headed north in pursuit of Lady Wildwood, he sent a regiment after him. They arrived on the border of Dunbar land just as we returned from that wild goose chase ye would have sent us on."

"How did ye ken—"

"That 'twas a ruse? We came across the Campbells on our way north. They had just come from a rather entertaining evening sharing a fire with my wayward sister, Lord Rolfe, and Sherwell. On hearing the tale, I realized the message had been a ruse and we had left Dunbar unmanned. We returned at once, collected the Inneses on the way, and met up with the king's men, who affirmed my worries. As I said, Greenweld's men have surrendered. Only Greenweld remains to be found.''

''He is attempting to enter the castle through the secret passage,'' Iliana blurted at once. The sudden anxiety on her husband's face, made her hurry to add, ''He will not succeed. Your father was there when I was forced into it by Greenweld's man. He could not stop my being taken, but no doubt he has the passage blocked by now.''

Relaxing somewhat, Duncan glanced over his shoulder at the two men who stood silent and stern behind him. ''Take the men to the clearing outside the cave my mother favored, Ian. The entrance to the passage my wife speaks of is in it. They shouldn't give ye much more o' a fight than the others, but call me if there is any trouble.''

Nodding, the men turned and exited the tent, leaving the three of them alone. Duncan was the first to speak. Sounding weary, he murmured, ''So, my own blood has betrayed me.''

Allistair cast a glance toward Iliana. Apparently deciding she was too far away to use as a hostage, he gave a resigned sigh and set his tankard down, then slowly, calmly drew his sword.

''Put yer weapon down,'' Duncan barked.

''Nay. I think not,'' he murmured with an almost sad smile, raising the sword to confront him.

''Ye canna win, Allie. Ye ken that. Even if your hand isn't broken. We have battled many a time and ye have never won. Put the weapon down.''

''Then what? Ye banish me? Send me far and away from me people? From the only home I have ever known? From the woman I love?'' His voice cracked slightly then, and his face suffused with sudden rage. ''Seonaid would have been mine.'' With that, he raised his sword and lunged at his cousin.

Iliana cried out and jumped back as Allistair's sword met Duncan's in midair. Her heart thumping violently in her chest, she clenched her hands and watched helplessly as the men stood, swords locked, glaring at each other.

"I don't want to kill ye, Allie. Yer me own blood."

Allistair laughed slightly and shrugged. "That didn't stop me from tryin' to kill you to get what I wanted. Not the night I stabbed yer wife, nor the day I knocked ye out and locked ye all in a burnin' room."

While Duncan absorbed that, Allistair pulled away and swung his sword again. Stunned as he was, her husband managed to fend off the blow.

Allistair gave a breathless laugh as they stared at each other across locked swords again. "It wouldn't have stopped me from having yer wee wife either. While I love Seonaid, yer wife is a tasty bundle. I hoped to get the chance to have her ere killing her." Pulling away again, he grinned. "Mayhap I still will."

Iliana saw the change that came over her husband then and knew that his cousin did not have long for this world. She offered up a quick prayer for his soul even as Allistair raised his sword and charged Duncan. This time, Duncan did not meet the blow; instead he stood perfectly still until the man was nearly upon him, then stepped to the side and thrust his sword straight for his heart. Allistair let out a small grunt as he was impaled, peered into his cousin's face, opened his mouth as if to say something, then dropped to his knees. He swayed there briefly, then collapsed to the ground, his sword crashing to the dirt beside him.

Iliana turned away from the dead man and glanced at her husband. His face was a mask of anguish. Her mind turned to all the others who had loved the man; Angus, Seonaid, Aelfread. "What will you tell them?"

"Nothing," Duncan murmured grimly. " 'Twould just sadden them to learn of his perfidy. They loved him dearly. I shall merely tell them that he died in battle."

Iliana nodded solemnly at that, then moved to step out of the tent, breathing deep the fresh air.

As she glanced back, she saw Duncan take one last look at the face of his cousin. Then he took a blanket from the cot in the corner of the tent and covered him gently with it before stepping out to join his wife.

Chapter Twenty-two

"Oh, my lady! Yer safe! How did you escape?"

Letting the keep door close behind her, Iliana smiled wearily at Ebba, as she, Gertie, Janna, and Elgin all crowded around her. "Duncan," she answered. "He and the men returned with the Innes and the king's men. Greenweld's men gave up quickly."

"And Greenweld himself?" Gertie asked anxiously.

Iliana grimaced at the memory of her last sight of the man. He had been lying dead in the clearing.

She and Duncan had joined the party outside the cave just moments before a furious Greenweld led his men out into the clearing. The frustration of finding the passage firmly sealed and returning to the clearing only to discover himself surrounded had seemed to push the man over the edge. With an enraged roar, he had raised his sword and charged forth. His men had not followed. Dropping their weapons, they had stood calmly by and watched as their leader singlehandedly tried to take on three armies. He died quickly.

"There will be no need for an annulment. Mother is a widow once again," Iliana assured the old servant solemnly. Her brows drew down on her forehead, her gaze sweeping the great hall as she suddenly realized that the one person who was most affected by her news was not present to hear it. "Where is my mother?"

"Oh."

"Well."

Iliana's eyes narrowed on Ebba and Janna as the two women exchanged glances of mingled guilt and alarm.

"What have the two of you done?"

"Tied her up and locked her in her room," Gertie announced with amusement.

"What?" Iliana gaped at her with patent disbelief, but the maid merely grinned and shrugged.

"She was wantin' to surrender hersel' fer ye. And ye did tell them that, above all—no matter what occurred— they were to keep her safe."

"Actually, ye even told me to tie her up did I need to," Janna reminded her quietly.

"Oh, my Lord," Iliana breathed, then whirled and hurried toward the stairs.

Iliana was breathless by the time she reached the door to the bedchamber. That was the only reason she did not screech in amazement when she opened the door to find her mother, not bound and gagged in a chair, but lying on the bed . . . with Angus. She was caught up against the Dunbar laird's chest, his strapping arms wrapped tightly around her as he gave her what appeared to be a most passionate kiss.

Iliana was still standing there gaping at the entwined pair when Duncan caught up with her. Pausing at her side, he peered curiously into the room, his own mouth dropping.

"Da!"

"Mother!"

The two of them cried those words at once, bringing an abrupt end to the interlude the older couple had been enjoying and drawing them guiltily to their feet.

" 'Tis not how it looks," Lady Wildwood murmured in a strained voice, her hands moving to straighten her hair and brush at her mussed gown at the same time. "I was tied up, you see, and—and . . ."

"Aye, and I was passing the room," Angus continued when she peered up at him helplessly. "I thought I heard something in here and looked in to see her tied up."

"Aye. And he very kindly untied me."

"Aye." They both nodded, looking for all the world like a pair of children caught stealing sweets.

Iliana and Duncan merely gaped at them blankly for a moment; then Duncan suddenly burst out in peals of laughter. When everyone else in the room merely peered at him uncertainly, he shook his head. "Now who be the randy bastard?"

Lady Wildwood blushed and Angus flushed purple as he drew himself up to snap back at his son, but it was Iliana who reprimanded him. "Duncan! How could you even think such a thing? My mother is not some—some common camp follower. If they say 'twas innocent, then 'twas."

"Oh, aye," Duncan agreed, amusement still tugging at his lips as he murmured, " 'Twas plain to see me father was busy untying yer dear mother when we entered. 'Tis just a shame he didn't try usin' his hands to accomplish the task rather than his tongue. It may have made the deed easier." He then let loose a loud guffaw at his own wit, oblivious of Iliana's dismay.

"Enough!" Angus roared. "Yer not so big I cannot still whup ye, lad. And do you not shut yer mouth, I'm like to prove it."

There was a brief silence and they all stood uncomfortably around, no one seeming to want to leave. Then Iliana stepped forward, her gaze focusing on her mother. "Your gown is fair wrinkled. No doubt you would like to change ere the sup,'' she suggested stiffly.

Lady Wildwood glanced down at herself and nodded with a sigh. Not only was her gown wrinkled, it was also filthy. In the excitement of the last two days, none of them had bathed or changed.

Smiling with feigned pleasantness at the two Dunbar men, Iliana moved again until she stood between her mother and Angus. ''Perhaps you gentlemen would be good enough to arrange for a bath to be brought up? My mother and I would like to refresh ourselves.''

Angus looked about to argue, but a glance at Lady Wildwood's expression made him sigh resignedly. Nodding, he moved to the door. ''Come along, lad. Let's leave the ladies be.''

''Are you very angry?''

Iliana turned from closing the door behind the two men to peer at her mother uncertainly. ''Angry?'' she queried evasively, unsure herself of how she felt. She supposed part of her felt a touch of hurt and betrayal on behalf of her father; part of her was just plain shocked, and another part . . . Well, she simply wasn't sure how she felt.

''Nay, of course I am not angry,'' she chided gently, moving abruptly toward the chests lining the wall. Throwing the nearest one open, she began to search through it, only to have her hands clasped by her mother's and herself drawn around to face the woman.

''I loved your father very, *very* much.''

Iliana nodded silently, unable to meet her gaze.

''For a long time after Greenweld arrived with the news of his death, there was not a moment that went by that I did not think of your father. The pain of losing him was horrible.'' Sighing when Iliana's head remained bowed, she released her hands and sat back on her haunches before confessing, ''Between that loss and the abuse I suffered at the hands of Greenweld, there were many days I thought of taking my own life.''

Iliana did glance up at that, but Lady Wildwood went on. ''You were all that kept me alive, child. Worry for you, your future, and even your inheritance. My love for you would not see me end my life before assuring your own.''

''Oh, Mother,'' Iliana cried, throwing herself into the older woman's arms and hugging her close.

''I love you dearly, child. Just as I loved your father. But he is gone now. I did not think I would ever feel about another in the same way I did him.''

Iliana pulled back slightly to meet her gaze, and her mother smiled slightly as she continued, ''And I was right.''

Iliana blinked in surprise at that. ''But you and Lord Angus were—''

''I find myself attracted to him, 'tis true.'' She smiled gently, her gaze drifting as if she saw him in her mind's eye. ''He is handsome and strong. A bit rough around the edges, mayhap, but I think I can help him to soften those.''

Now Iliana was completely confused. ''But you just said—'' she broke off when her mother gave a laugh and a self-deprecating wave of one hand.

''I am not saying this well. 'Tis true that I will never love again as I loved your father. He was my first love, a good and strong yet gentle man who treated me with more care and respect than I could ever have hoped. And for quite awhile after he died I thought he had taken my heart with him. But that just is not so. I am still alive. I still have feelings. Angus made me realize that.''

Iliana sighed and sat back, contemplating her hands briefly before glancing up to ask, ''You love him?''

Her gaze drifted off again as she considered the question, then she shrugged. ''I do not know. I am not yet sure. But I do believe I shall greatly enjoy finding out.''

Iliana blinked at that, then slowly relaxed. ''I love you, Mother,'' she murmured, leaning forward to hug her. Her father was beyond her now, and the most important thing for Iliana was that her mother should not suffer.

A knock at the door drew mother and daughter apart.

"Enter!" They called in unison, then shared a smile as Gertie entered, leading a small army of servants. The first two struggled under the weight of a tub. Those who followed bore pail after pail of water, some steaming hot, some not.

Reaching out to clasp her mother's hand and give it a quick squeeze, Iliana smiled and moved toward the door. "I shall leave you to your bath and see you at dinner. I needs must arrange for my own bath to be brought up."

"'Tis already done," Gertie murmured, making Iliana slow and glance back as she reached the door.

"What?"

"A bath awaits you in the new room at the end of the hall," she was informed.

"Oh." Her surprise faded slowly and she smiled and shrugged, "Laird Angus must have ordered it. How thoughtful." She glanced at her mother teasingly as she opened the door. "It would seem he has fewer rough edges than you thought, Mother."

Iliana caught only a glimpse of the smile that accompanied the woman's answering blush as she closed the door behind her. She was still smiling when she turned to walk down the hall and found herself facing an oddly nervous Laird Angus.

Eyebrows rising slightly, she nodded at the older man. "My lord."

Angus cleared his throat uncomfortably. "I thought to have a word with ye ere ye sought yer bath, lass. About yer mother—"

"There is no need, my lord," Iliana assured him gently, reaching to clasp one of his nervously fidgeting hands. "My mother and I have spoken and she is . . . well, I am happy so long as she is happy."

He relaxed slightly at that, but still looked wary. "Then 'twould not bother ye to have me fer stepfather as well as father-in-law?"

Iliana blinked, her mind slowly absorbing his words; then she glanced sharply back toward the door.

"I haven't asked her yet," he announced, drawing her gaze back to him. "In truth, I will not ask her fer a while yet most like, and I would be glad if ye could keep this talk to yersel'. But I just wanted to be sure ye would not be troubled by our marryin' when it happens."

"Nay, my lord. It would not bother me," she assured him gently. "But what if she does not wish—" Iliana began, only to be waved to silence.

"She'll marry me. She doesn't love me yet, but she will, and once she does, we'll be married," he announced confidently, then patted her shoulder and walked on down the hall, leaving her alone.

Iliana stared after him for a moment, then smiled wryly and shook her head as she continued down the hallway, to the new room Duncan had had built. Truthfully, she hadn't even seen the new chamber he had worked so hard to build for them, and she was curious to do so. The men had made quite a racket building it. She hoped the results were worth it.

The shock that met her when she opened the door to the new room was almost as great as the shock of coming across her mother in the arms of her father-in-law. It was a near replica of her room at Wildwood.

Closing the door slowly, she moved farther into the chamber, her gaze moving to the bed. It was the bed from Duncan's room, the only item that was not an exact replica of her room at home. His bed was much larger than hers had been. It had been cleaned since the fire. The wood frame shone in the sunlight pouring through the window. The faded and smoke-stained material that had previously draped it had been removed, replaced with fabric that was very similar to the one that had draped her bed in her childhood home.

Marveling, she turned to peer around the rest of the furnishings, taking in the tables at either side of the bed and the two large chairs set before the fireplace. That was another difference. In her room at home there had only been one chair before the fire.

The sound of splashing water reminded her of the bath that Gertie had said awaited her here, and Iliana's forehead puckered with confusion. There was no bath to be found. It was the second splash that drew her eyes to the door beside the bed. She had not noticed it at first but now did so with surprise. There was no such door in her room at home, but it seemed here, a second room was attached to the bedchamber, and that seemed to be where the bath was.

Thinking the servant must still be filling the tub for her, she moved slowly to the door and peered curiously into the room. Inside was a tub: quite the largest Iliana had ever seen. But the sound of splashing was not from servants filling it with water. It was the sound her husband made as he shifted about inside it, washing himself.

"I could use some help with me back."

Iliana started at those words. Duncan had not even glanced up, yet he was aware of her presence. "How did you know I was here?" The question slipped from her lips in surprise and Duncan raised his head slowly to meet her gaze, his own serious.

"I always ken when yer near. Were I blind I would ken," he repeated her words from the other day, but added gently, "Ye bring the scent o' wildflowers with ye."

Iliana swallowed, her gaze sliding over his broad, bare chest as he rinsed it. "The room . . ." Her voice faded away into uncertainty and he paused in his actions to lean back in the tub and smile at her gently.

"I thought ye might be more comfortable were ye to have a more familiar room. Yer mother and Ebba helped me."

"That was not necessary."

"Nay, I ken. I was wrong that day. Yer not afraid o' change as I accused. At least, if ye are, 'tis no more so than anyone else. Me, for instance." He gazed briefly down into the water surrounding him, then smiled crookedly and confessed, "I suppose I had not fully realized what taking a wife would mean when we married. I thought ye would just be another mouth to feed, and a body to warm me bed of a night."

Iliana's eyebrows rose at that and he shrugged.

"I am an ignorant man at times, wife. 'Tis not that I am stupid, but sometimes I seem to get all wrapped up in concerns about safety and such and forget such gentle concerns as comfort and carin'. I suspect that may be a problem with most men. Mayhap 'tis why God made women. To supply the softer needs." Sighing impatiently, he shook his head. "I am not saying this well. I had it all planned out and—"

"You are saying it well enough," Iliana corrected gently, taking a step farther onto the room, a smile trembling on her lips. "You have said it with both your words and deeds."

He tilted his head slightly, expression solemn. "And what is it I be saying?"

Iliana hesitated, head turning so that she could take in the room he had made for her, then back to the tub he sat in, in this, the second room. She smiled uncertainly. "That you would wish me happy because you care for me?"

"Care?" He said the word with some disgust. "Nay, wife. 'Tis not carin' I feel fer ye. Ye've flouted me authority on countless occasions. Refused me me rights on others. Ye are disobedient, contrary, and stubborn. And yet," he added gently when Iliana started to protest, "yet I was never so scared in me life as I was when I realized I had left ye here with but a handful o' men to protect ye and Greenweld battering at the castle. And I was never so proud o' anyone in me life as I was o' ye when Rabbie told me all ye had done to defend yersel' and our home. Ye fire me blood. Ye awaken all me passions. I feel alive when I am with ye."

"Husband," Iliana took a step toward the tub, only to pause when he stood suddenly, holding out his hand as if warning her away. The water cascaded off him, splashing down into the tub and onto the floor around it, leaving his body gleaming wet where he stood.

"Nay, there is something I would tell ye first," he said solemnly, drawing her heated gaze reluctantly back to his face. "I love ye. I kenned it when I thought ye dead from the fire and I realized that I might have to spend the rest o' me life without ye. I love ye, Iliana. 'Tis only sorry I am that I didn't tell ye when ye blurted yer feelings out to me. I thought to save it fer when I returned. I wanted it to be a special moment. I didn't ken I might have lost ye ere I could tell ye. But I'm tellin' ye now, I love ye, Iliana Dunbar . . . and I need ye."

Nothing could have held her back then. A small murmur of joy slipping from her lips, Iliana rushed forward, meeting him at the edge of the tub and throwing herself against his upper chest.

Shifting to maintain his balance, Duncan caught her there and kissed her with a gentleness far different than the passion he normally poured over her.

Her eyes opening slowly, Iliana smiled at him. "Husband?"

"Aye?" he murmured, pressing her head to his damp chest and cradling her there.

"You are bathing," she pointed out, using one finger to trail a drop of moisture down his bare chest.

"Aye. 'Tis not so much o' a chore to please me wife. Once I put aside me own stubbornness I find I can even admit to likin' it."

Iliana pulled back to eye him doubtfully. "You are claiming to like bathing?"

"Well . . ." He grinned slightly. "When the conditions are right."

"Conditions?" Her eyebrows arched slightly.

"Aye. Fer instance . . ." Putting her a little away from him, he began to work at the stays of her gown. "When yer naked and in it with me, I find I rather like it."

Iliana chuckled softly at that, her hands trailing down

over his body. "It must be because I can help to scrub your back, my lord," she murmured teasingly, and he considered it briefly, then nodded.

"Aye. Though in truth I prefer it when ye scrub me front with yer own sweet soapy body."

"Oh, my," Iliana breathed huskily as a memory of their soapy bodies sliding slickly together came back to her from the first time they had consummated their marriage.

Duncan had just managed to undo the last of her stays when the faint sound of knocking came to them from the bedroom.

"Ignore it," he ordered firmly, pushing her gown off her shoulders so that it slithered to the floor.

"What if 'tis important?" Iliana asked as the knock sounded again. "After all, they know we are in the bath; surely they would not interrupt unless it was important?"

Releasing the undertunic he had been about to divest her of, Duncan sighed and stepped out of the tub. Trailing water, he crossed to the doorway between the two inner chambers and bellowed, "What is it?"

"Lady Seonaid has returned." Ebba's voice came muffled through the outer door as Iliana stepped up behind her husband. "She rode into the bailey just moments ago followed by Lord Rolfe, the bishop, and Lord Sherwell."

"Good," Duncan said firmly, turning to smile at Iliana and wrap her in his arms. "Now go away!"

"I . . . but . . . she has locked herself in her room and will not come out."

Duncan rolled his eyes at this news. "Tell me father. 'Tis his problem."

"I tried, but he . . . er . . . was preoccupied."

"Preoccupied how?" Duncan asked suspiciously.

There was a pause, then Ebba half-whispered her answer, obviously not eager to say it loud enough for all the keep to hear. "He is . . . er . . . assisting Lady Wildwood."

"My mother?" Iliana frowned. "But my mother is taking a—"

"Bath?" Duncan asked with a smile when she hesitated.

Iliana's eyebrows rose. "How did you know?"

"Father was telling me that he used to enjoy 'assisting' my mother in her bath," he answered with a devilish grin. "Just as I enjoy assisting you."

"My lord?" Ebba's uncertain voice queried. "Did you hear me?"

"Aye! And I am likewise engaged. The English will have to cool their heels!" he bellowed back, then swept Iliana up in his arms.

"Duncan! What are you doing?" she asked in dismay as he kicked the door closed and carried her toward the tub.

"Following my father's example and assisting me wife in her bath."

"But my mother, and your father—"

"Are full-grown adults. They neither need, nor would appreciate, our interference."

Iliana frowned at that, but let it lie. "Well, what of Seonaid, then?"

"Seonaid can take care o' herself."

"But she is locked in her room. Obviously Lord Sherwell wishes you to get her out."

"That is Sherwell's problem. Every man must prove his worth." He gave a slight laugh then.

"What?"

"I do not envy him. Seonaid is a handful, and I ken how difficult it can be to train a wife."

"Train a wife?" she echoed slowly, beginning to glower at him as he set her on her feet before the tub.

"Aye. There are many lessons a man must teach his wife when they marry," he assured her solemnly as he tugged her undertunic off and let it slip to the floor.

"Oh? And what, pray tell, would they be, my lord?" she asked grimly.

"Many things," Duncan murmured, lifting her up and over the lip of the tub to set her down in the knee-high water before stepping in himself. "For instance, the value of silence."

Iliana blinked, then closed her eyes as he bent to kiss her, his mouth caressing her own. When his lips finally lifted from hers, a small smile was tugging at the corners of her mouth. She opened her eyes slowly, understanding in their depths taking the place of her earlier indignation. "That would not be anything like teaching me to scream, would it, my lord?"

"Aye." Nodding with satisfaction, he bent to pick up the soap, dipping it and his hands in the water they stood in, and beginning to work up a lather. "Ye're a fast study, lass. Ye should have a full grasp o' this subject quickly enough."

"Not too quickly, I hope." Iliana sighed as he began to rub the lather he had made across her chest, concentrating most of his efforts on her breasts.

"Nay," he assured her huskily and kissed the tip of her nose, then her lips, before murmuring, "But I give ye me oath 'tis a lesson ye'll never forget."

"I think I begin to like yer lessons, my lord," Iliana murmured as his soapy hands slid around to her buttocks and he pulled her tight against him. "Aye," she gasped as she felt his manhood press against her belly. " 'Tis certain I am that I do."

CONQUER THE MIST

Susan Kearney

Promised in marriage to Britain's foremost Norman knight, Irish Princess Dara O'Dwyre vows that neither the power of his sword nor the lure of his body will sway her proud spirit and her untamed heart. But as enemy troops draw close, Dara realizes that only when she learns to trust this handsome outsider can they save her homeland and unite in rapturous bliss.

___4437-4 $5.50 US/$6.50 CAN

Dorchester Publishing Co., Inc.
P.O. Box 6640
Wayne, PA 19087-8640

Please add $1.75 for shipping and handling for the first book and $.50 for each book thereafter. NY, NYC, and PA residents, please add appropriate sales tax. No cash, stamps, or C.O.D.s. All orders shipped within 6 weeks via postal service book rate. Canadian orders require $2.00 extra postage and must be paid in U.S. dollars through a U.S. banking facility.

Name_____
Address_____
City_____ State_____ Zip_____
I have enclosed $_____ in payment for the checked book(s).
Payment <u>must</u> accompany all orders. ❑ Please send a free catalog.
          CHECK OUT OUR WEBSITE! www.dorchesterpub.com

SEDUCED

CATHERINE LANIGAN

"Catherine Lanigan is in a class by herself: unequaled and simply fabulous!"

—*Affaire de Coeur*

Even amid the spectacle and splendor of the carnival in Venice, the masked rogue is brazen, reckless, and dangerously risqué. As he steals Valentine St. James away from the costume ball at which her betrothal to a complete stranger is to be announced, the exquisite beauty revels in the illicit thrill of his touch, the tender passion in his kiss. But Valentine learns that illusion rules the festival when, at the stroke of midnight, her mysterious suitor reveals he is Lord Hawkeston, the very man she is to wed. Convinced her intended is an unrepentant scoundrel, Valentine wants to deny her maddening attraction for him, only to keep finding herself in his heated embrace. Yet is she truly losing her heart to the dashing peer—or is she being ruthlessly seduced?

_3942-7   **$5.50 US/$7.50 CAN**

THE LION'S BRIDE — CONNIE MASON

Winner of the *Romantic Times* Storyteller Of The Year Award!

Lord Lyon of Normandy has saved William the Conqueror from certain death on the battlefield, yet neither his strength nor his skill can defend him against the defiant beauty the king chooses for his wife.

Ariana of Cragmere has lost her lands and her virtue to the mighty warrior, but the willful beauty swears never to surrender her heart.

Saxon countess and Norman knight, Ariana and Lyon are born enemies. And in a land rent asunder by bloody wars and shifting loyalties, they are doomed to misery unless they can vanquish the hatred that divides them—and unite in glorious love.

_3884-6 $5.99 US/$7.99 CAN

Catherine Archibald — HAWK'S LADY

Haughty young Lady Kayln D'Arcy only wants what is best for her little sister, Celia, when she travels to the imposing fortress of Hawkhurst. For the brother of Hawkhurst's dark lord has wooed Celia, and Kayln is determined to make him do the honorable thing. Tall, arrogant and imperious, Hawk has the burning eyes of a bird of prey and a gentle touch that can make Kayln nearly forget why she is there. As for Hawk, never before has he encountered a woman like the proud, fiery Kayln. But can Hawk catch his prey? Can he make her...Hawk's lady?

___4312-2 $4.99 US/$5.99 CAN

Dorchester Publishing Co., Inc.
P.O. Box 6640
Wayne, PA 19087-8640

Please add $1.75 for shipping and handling for the first book and $.50 for each book thereafter. NY, NYC, and PA residents, please add appropriate sales tax. No cash, stamps, or C.O.D.s. All orders shipped within 6 weeks via postal service book rate. Canadian orders require $2.00 extra postage and must be paid in U.S. dollars through a U.S. banking facility.

Name_____
Address_____
City_____State_____Zip_____
I have enclosed $_____ in payment for the checked book(s).
Payment <u>must</u> accompany all orders. ❏ Please send a free catalog.

THE MASK

DONNA LEE POFF

Sitting in the moonlight at the edge of the forest, she appears to him as a delicate wood elf, but Anne of Thornbury is no spritely illusion. A fresh-faced village girl, Anne has no experience with love, until she meets the brave yet reclusive lord with the hidden face and mysterious history. She soon realizes that only with her love can Galen finally overcome the past and release his heart from the shadow of the mask.

___4416-1 $4.99 US/$5.99 CAN

Dorchester Publishing Co., Inc.
P.O. Box 6640
Wayne, PA 19087-8640

Please add $1.75 for shipping and handling for the first book and $.50 for each book thereafter. NY, NYC, and PA residents, please add appropriate sales tax. No cash, stamps, or C.O.D.s. All orders shipped within 6 weeks via postal service book rate. Canadian orders require $2.00 extra postage and must be paid in U.S. dollars through a U.S. banking facility.

Name_____
Address_____
City_____State_____Zip_____
I have enclosed $_____ in payment for the checked book(s).
Payment <u>must</u> accompany all orders. ❏ Please send a free catalog.
CHECK OUT OUR WEBSITE! www.dorchesterpub.com

The first time he sees her she is clad in nothing but moonlight and mist, and from that moment, Thorne the Relentless knows he is bewitched by the maiden bathing in the forest pool. How else to explain the torrid dreams, the fierce longing that keeps his warrior's body in a constant state of arousal? Perhaps Fiona is speaking the truth when she claims it is not sorcery that binds him to her, but the powerful yearning of his viking heart.

___4402-1 $5.99 US/$6.99 CAN